This book should be returned to any branch of the
Lancashire County Library on or before the date shown

11/14   CSH

− 4 JAN 2016

2 1 NOV 2017

03 APR 2019

0 3 APR 2019

Lancashire County Library
Bowran Street
Preston PR1 2UX

Lancashire
County Council

www.lancashire.gov.uk/libraries

LL1(A)

HER VAMPYRRHIC HEART

Tom Westonby may have lost his wife to a powerful curse, but the war against the ancient evil has barely begun...

She will come back to me, Tom Westonby tells himself. *We'll be reunited.* It has been five years since he's seen his beloved wife, Nicola Bekk. Five years since their wedding day – when he won her hand, but in doing so triggered the curse that has blighted the Bekk family for centuries. Nicola became a vampire, and fled, lest she harm the one she loves the most. Since then, Tom has lived a remote life in Nicola's ancestral home in the woods, patiently awaiting the return of his vampire bride. But little does he know that someone else is returning to the village – someone who holds great power over the supernatural forces that dwell within it, waiting for revenge. Soon, Tom will be forced to risk his life – and the lives of those he loves – in the fight against an ancient evil that cannot possibly be beaten...

HER VAMPYRRHIC HEART

Simon Clark

Severn House Large Print
London & New York

This first large print edition published 2014
in Great Britain and the USA by
SEVERN HOUSE PUBLISHERS LTD of
19 Cedar Road, Sutton, Surrey, England, SM2 5DA.
First world regular print edition published 2013 by
Severn House Publishers Ltd., London and New York.

British Library Cataloguing in Publication Data

Clark, Simon, 1958- author.
  Her vampyrrhic heart.
  1. Vampires--Fiction. 2. Horror tales. 3. Large type
  books.
  I. Title
  823.9'2-dc23

  ISBN-13: 9780727897176

Severn House Publishers support the Forest Stewardship Council™
[FSC™], the leading international forest certification organisation. All
our titles that are printed on FSC certified paper carry the FSC logo.

MIX
Paper from
responsible sources
FSC® C013056

Printed and bound in Great Britain by
T J International, Padstow, Cornwall.

NICOLA AND TOM:
THE STORY SO FAR

A NOTE FROM THE AUTHOR

Her Vampyrrhic Heart is a direct sequel to *His Vampyrrhic Bride*. It's not essential to have read *His Vampyrrhic Bride* in order to understand and enjoy the novel that you now hold in your hand. Having said that, it might help if I give you an idea of the story so far.

In *His Vampyrrhic Bride*, twenty-three-year-old Tom Westonby falls in love with Nicola Bekk. Nicola lives a solitary life with her mother in a remote cottage in the woods. Nicola's mother tells them both that the relationship is doomed from the start, and if they continue to see one another an ancient curse will be triggered. This will lead to Nicola being transformed into an inhuman, vampire-like creature. Of course, when two young people are in love that's a powerful magic in its own right. They'll move heaven and earth to be together. If they're told they must not continue the relationship they will steadfastly ignore such warnings. Love conquers all, or so they believe.

However, the curse is a powerful one. To Tom Westonby's horror Nicola is transformed into a vampire and vanishes from his life. Tom refuses

5

to believe that the woman he loves has gone for ever. He moves into Nicola's family home in the forest. *She will come back to me*, he tells himself. *We'll be reunited*. Living alone in the cottage, Tom patiently waits for the return of his vampire bride. And, five years later, this is where we pick up Tom's story in *Her Vampyrrhic Heart*.

So, my friends, it's time to invite you warmly into the pages of this novel where there'll be plenty of surprises and excitement – not to mention cold, shivery touches of fear and 'Vampyrrhic' horror. Get ready. We're just about to enter the loneliest and darkest part of the forest.

Simon Clark,
Yorkshire, England

PART ONE

'The human heart is like Indian rubber.'
From *Agnes Grey* by Anne Brontë

PART ONE

ONE

DARKNESS ... The word *darkness* didn't adequately describe that absolute absence of light in the forest. *This is the darkness of the grave.*

The man turned the key in the ignition. Nothing happened.

'Don't worry,' said the woman sitting beside him in the passenger seat. 'The car's electrics are just a bit temperamental, that's all. Come on, sweetheart, I know you won't let us down.'

Even though the darkness meant he couldn't see his girlfriend, he knew she'd gently patted the dashboard when she'd coaxed the car. After all, Rose had done this plenty of times before, because the fact of the matter was the car had clocked up a hundred thousand miles over the last ten years, and however much they did love every inch of the old girl's dented body that didn't guarantee that the dicky electrics and worn-out motor wouldn't let them down one day. Or, rather, one night – when the darkness inside the car seamlessly merged with the darkness outside.

He found her hand and gave it a loving squeeze. 'I'm going to have to call out someone to help us.'

'The old girl's had a rest. Try again.'

Without so much as a shred of optimism he turned the key.

'There is a God!' He laughed with relief as the engine started.

Straight away, the headlights came on, too, lighting up the track through the trees. The man could now clearly see his girlfriend's sparkling eyes and smiling face in the dashboard lights. He also glimpsed the cast on her right leg. A nasty slip when she was rock climbing had left her with a cracked bone. The cast had scraped his back when they made love tonight. Although he wished they were doing exactly that back in their apartment. It had required real willpower to climb out of their warm bed for the twenty-mile drive across the moors to this remote valley – all in order to replace a battery in a camera that was fixed to a tree. But this was part of the job. One of their many duties as park rangers required them to try and capture footage of woodland animals. Motion sensors attached to the cameras would trigger them when a creature had been detected.

However, driving into this wilderness in a car that creaked and clattered towards the end of its mechanical life hadn't been at all straight-forward. But at least they were now making progress again.

He glanced at Rose. 'When we get there, I'll leave the engine running, dash down to the river, swap the battery, then get back as fast as I can. With luck, the engine won't die on us if I don't switch it off.'

Rose smiled. 'I thought we could continue

what we had to interrupt earlier.'

'You mean engage in wild, outrageous sex out here?'

Her eyes held a mischievous twinkle. 'Why not? Sex in wilderness places is invigorating.'

'Says the voice of experience?'

'Oh, I'm experienced, John. I can show you not only paradise, but what lies beyond paradise.'

She stroked his leg as he drove between lines of massive tree trunks.

'If we do erotic stuff in this car,' he told her, 'it will kill off the old girl once and for all.'

Rose laughed. 'You switch that battery in record time, and when you get back to the car I'll show you something that you'll remember for the rest of your life.' She ran her fingers up his thigh.

'OK. I'm going to break records. I'll be back in five minutes.'

John stopped the car, kissed her on the mouth and opened the door.

'Make it four minutes.' Teasingly, she pulled the fleece zip down as far as her full breasts. 'Do you hear? Four minutes max.'

After kissing her again he stepped out of the car and closed the door. Quickly, he checked that the replacement battery was in his pocket. *Good, all present and correct.* That done, he switched on the flashlight. The distinctive musty, damp smell of a forest in winter struck him – the aroma of fallen leaves, wet bark and earth. He smiled at Rose as she switched on the interior light. Pursing her full, red lips, she blew him a

11

kiss. *Damn it, she's hot. Sex on legs.*

John Cantley hurried along the woodland path, the light from the torch glaring against trees. His breath came in billowing, white gusts. Already he could hear the River Lepping as it flowed down the valley towards the nearest village five miles away. Apart from a cottage and a few farms nothing much in the way of human life existed between here and Danby-Mask.

Eager for his erotic surprise, just minutes from now, he moved quickly. Within seconds he'd reached the river. The specialized camera, inside its protective box, had been fixed to a tree trunk at head height. Earlier in the week he'd angled the camera to film whatever scuttled down the river bank to take a drink. In a few days he'd collect the camera and review the footage.

Gripping one end of the flashlight in his teeth, he slipped the device out of its waterproof casing in order to switch the dead battery with a fresh one. He focused on the fiddly job – especially fiddly when his fingers were as cold as this.

So when he heard the enormous splash from behind him he nearly leapt out of his skin. The sound shocked him so much that he spun round fast enough to send the flashlight spinning from his mouth. Now he could see nothing. Once more the absolute blackness of the night-time forest filled his eyes. As he dropped on all fours to scrabble for the light he heard more splashes. It sounded as if some large animal churned the river. A deer? Maybe. Possibly even a wild boar. Those could be violent brutes if riled.

A second later, he had the flashlight again.

Fortunately it hadn't broken, and when he thumbed the switch the light instantly returned. Quickly, he snapped the new battery into place before pushing the camera back into its housing. He realized his heart was pounding. *Stupid idiot*, he thought, *you're not scared of a hairy pig, are you?* Although he had to admit that huge splashing sound had startled him. What's more, his hands shook so much he found it difficult to slide the camera back into its protective case. At last, however, he'd done the job. *Good! Now get back to the car.*

Sounds of a heavy animal lumbering through the bushes reached him. Whatever the beast might be it was close. Maybe several wild boar? Meeting a pack of those vicious porkers didn't appeal. Time to go.

He checked his watch. One minute remained of the four teasingly allocated by Rose. Maybe she'd slipped off her fleece jacket? Or was she in the back seat? Totally naked? With the light splashing against the trees, he ran along the path. Behind him, he heard the crunch of branches. Maybe a stag? Or a wild pony? A big brute whatever it was.

Now he could see the car. Its windows had misted up, yet he heard music. Rose must have turned on the radio. He saw her silhouette through the fogged glass. That sexy outline made him eager to find out what erotic treat awaited him.

Only John Cantley never made it to the car. For a moment he thought that a gigantic oak tree had fallen on him. The concussion was fantastic. The

13

flashlight went flying from his hand. Even though it remained lit, darkness swept over him. Although this was very much a different kind of darkness: this would be a darkness that could never ever be banished by anything so mundane as an electric light. This darkness claimed his soul.

Rose sat in the car. The engine idled just as her boyfriend had left it. Neither wanted to be stranded in the forest if the faulty electrics died on them again, so best keep the old girl ticking over. Her leg began to itch in its cast. She wished they were back in bed again. Making love is the perfect distraction from the realities of life – including being forced to endure six weeks with her leg encased in this itchy shell.

As Rose waited for John to return, she listened to the radio. Meanwhile, the car's windows had misted over. When she was a little girl she liked to wipe away just a tiny bit of condensation so she could peep out as if looking through a key-hole. Peeking through an area of clean glass the size of a penny felt like having a secret view into another world.

Rose did this now. With her finger squeaking on the glass, she cleaned a coin-sized area of white condensation from the passenger window. Beyond the glass, the blackness of the forest. Night times in the wilderness are incredibly dark compared to those in town. Here, not a single glimmer of light showed amongst the trees – those silent giants had stood there for centuries. World wars, revolutions and the deaths of kings and presidents left them untouched. Those oaks seemed eternal – unaffected by either the triumphs or tragedies of the human race.

She glanced at the dashboard clock. Smiling, she realized John would be back any moment now. The side window had fogged over again. Quickly, she wiped a small area clean to create another of her peepholes. That done, she put her eye to the glass.

John was there ... her boyfriend's face was just inches away at the other side of the glass.

And he's dead. The moment Rose saw his face – swollen and grazed and smeared with blood – she knew he'd been killed. And now his murderer held the dead face to the window, showing her.

Fear exploded inside of her. With an utter sense of dread, she thought: *I'm next ... they'll kill me.* That's what she expected ... but what happened next took her by surprise.

Because her boyfriend's eyes snapped open. His eyes locked on to hers, and he began to shout: 'Rose! Help me! Please, help me!'

Those words were shocking enough, yet other voices began to shout, too – they shouted in the same desperate, agonized way at exactly the same time:

'ROSE! HELP US! PLEASE HELP US!'

With a frantic swipe of her hand, she cleaned away the condensation. Now she saw the monstrosity, which was out there just beyond the glass. And that's when Rose began to scream.

15

TWO

June Valko packed in a hurry. The doctor had told June that her mother had deteriorated overnight. Into the holdall went clothes, a toilet bag, together with a document holder bulging with newspaper clippings, copies of witness statements and disks containing TV news reports that she'd harvested from the Internet. Snow had been forecast, which was unusual for November, even here in the North of England. So, along with a keen sense of urgency, she could now add the worry that trains to Whitby might be cancelled.

However, June Valko absolutely needed to make this journey. She had to talk to a man she'd never met before, but whom her mother had once mentioned several years ago. The name of the stranger she needed to find was written in large letters across the document file: TOM WESTONBY.

THREE

That November night the forest had been silent. Flakes of snow drifted down through the branches. A fox padded beneath the trees. The animal paused as its sensitive ears picked up a sound that suddenly grew louder and louder until it turned into a vicious bellow as a monster with a pair of blazing eyes appeared.

The fox fled before the rampaging beast. This roaring, snorting thing lurched along the track at whirlwind speed. Riding on its back were two figures. One crouched down, scared half to death, and holding on for dear life. The other whooped. This exhilarating ride excited him so much that he beat the cab roof with his fist and yelled at the top of his voice.

'FASTER! FASTER!'

The other youth, a green cap scrunched down on his head, forced himself so tightly against the bodywork he seemed to be trying to weld himself there, so he became one with the vehicle – and could therefore avoid the very real danger of being hurled from its back as they hurtled through the forest.

Sixteen-year-old Owen Westonby grinned down at his friend who clung there in terror. 'Isn't this brilliant? Isn't this the way to feel

17

totally alive?'

'Shit! We're going to be *totally* dead if he crashes.'

'Come on, Kit! Live dangerously! *Whoooo!*'

The *Whoooo* came about because the driver had just hit a bump in the road that sent the truck flying into the air.

Kit screwed his eyes shut. 'Oh, God. Oh, God. I'll never do anything bad again!'

The motor roared. Owen gripped the steel bar that ran along the top of the cab. He faced forward, feeling the blast of cold air in his face, and loving it – dear God, loving every moment of this amazing ride. A ton of steel lurched under him. He bruised his knees every time another lurch sent him crashing forward. *Who cares? This is Fan Tastic! This is the best antidote in the world to boring school.*

Owen Westonby and Kit Bolter had called on their pal, Jez Pollock; he lived on a farm a couple of miles from the village. Jez's parents had gone out for the evening, so they took their chance for some fun. Jez had fired up the big old beast of a pickup: then they went for a little drive in the countryside.

With the Pollock farm sprawling between moorland and the river, they'd been able to stick to private roads without using a public highway, where there was a danger they'd be spotted by cops. Here the dirt tracks ran through dense woodland. This is where the excitement lay. This is where they got their hard-earned teenage kicks.

Owen diced with death. Standing in the back

18

of the truck meant that his head was eight feet above ground level. All of which put him nicely at decapitation height. Branches scythed out of the darkness in front of him. He liked to play chicken, ducking at the last second. More than one strand of his blond hair remained sticking to a tree limb as they hurtled by.

Feeling a tug on his leg, he glanced down to see Kit Bolter's terrified eyes. 'THIS HAS GOT TO STOP!' yelled Kit. 'We're gonna be killed!'

Owen glanced forward to see a huge branch emerge from the blackness. He ducked just in time. From the cab Jez signalled his glee by sounding the horn.

Then two things happened at once.

First: Kit screamed. 'I've lost my cap!' The green headgear fluttered away.

Second: the truck swerved. The sheer violence of the manoeuvre flung Owen from its back. The next moment he lay on the ground. Snowflakes drifted down to land on his face. The bellowing truck vanished. Silence returned to the forest – the kind of silence that had haunted this mass of ancient trees at night for the last ten thousand years.

Then the sound of running feet and voices.

'Look at what's happened to Owen.'

Kit Bolter's voice rose to a squeal. 'You've killed him, you idiot. Look at his eyes. He's stone dead!'

Branches rustled as a breeze sighed through this frozen world.

That's when Owen sat up, threw back his head and laughed so much his ribs hurt.

19

Kit yelled, 'Jesus, Owen! That's not funny. I thought you were dead!' He stomped off to retrieve his green cap.

Jez held out his hand. Owen grabbed it and hauled himself up to his feet.

'You pulled a massive swerve there, Jez. It was fantastic!'

'I didn't do it deliberately,' said the towering youth. 'Something crawled out in front of me.'

'Crawled?'

'Yeah, kind of crawling.'

'You mean, like a hedgehog or something?'

'Nah, it was huge. Big as an elephant.'

Owen stared at the youth's serious expression. However, Jez couldn't hold it in any longer; laughter blurted through his lips.

Owen laughed, too. 'You had me believing you then. I thought you were going to say you'd nearly hit our famous dragon.'

'Right ... the dragon.' Jez grinned. 'You know, when I was a little kid, my mother used to tell me stories about a dragon living in the forest – the woman gave me nightmares.'

Kit returned with the cap back on his head again. 'Did anyone mention our neighbourhood dragon?'

'Jez nearly smacked into it, that's why he swerved.'

'Really?'

'Yeah, really, Kit.' Jez pinched the green cap and put it on his own head. 'You can't drive down a road here without smacking into 'em, and getting dragon blood and giblets all over your car.'

20

The three friends spluttered with laughter.

As suddenly as they started laughing they stopped.

'What was that?' Kit asked.

'Dunno.' Jez tilted his head, listening. 'I heard it, though.'

There was another crash.

'Something's out there,' said Owen. 'It's smashing up the forest.'

Kit stared anxiously into the gloom. 'This is actual wilderness out here. The forest has existed since the last Ice Age.'

'You astound me, Holmes.' Jez adopted a loud, theatrical voice. 'Do you declare that to be a mammoth of woolly appearance out there?'

'Animals that were thought to be extinct are being found all the time.'

'Did they pipe Wikipedia directly through your arse into your brain?' Jez climbed into the driver's seat. 'A cow'll be wandering about in there or something.'

Owen took the green cap from Jez's head and put it on his own. 'Kit. This has stretched out of shape, because your brains have grown too big.'

Jez started the engine. 'Hop in the back. My dad'll be back in twenty minutes. If he finds out I've been driving this he'll kill me.'

As the truck headed back to the farm, this time at a slower speed, Owen Westonby kept his eyes fixed on the trees behind them. For a moment, he thought he saw a shadow moving through the gloom. A tree swayed as if some massive body had pushed against it.

'When I fell back there, I think I took a knock

21

on the head,' he called to Kit over the engine noise. 'I'm sure it's making me see things.' He grinned at his pal, who still held on tight despite the slow speed. 'OK. Use this to keep your brains warm.' Owen plonked the green cap on to Kit's head, and then settled down to enjoy what remained of the ride.

FOUR

On a cold November morning Tom Westonby stepped into the river despite there being snow on the ground. Here the river ran through a ravine. Winter had robbed the trees of their leaves so branches formed a mass of black spikes against the sky.

Tom wore a thick-skinned 'dry suit', which differed from the traditional diver's wetsuit. As the name suggested, the suit kept his body dry; what was more, he'd donned layers of thermal underwear – although deeply unattractive to behold, they did keep him warm. The river's temperature stood just a few degrees above freezing. Without the dry suit the cold would kill him.

After twisting the aqualung valve to start the flow of air, he pulled down his face mask before moving deeper into the river. Within seconds, the black water had risen over his head, and he swam from a world of light and sound into another world entirely – this was a silent, alien place. Strands of weed floating by. Fish ghosting from the darkness to stare at the intruder. He switched on the helmet light. A cone of yellow illuminated rocks carved by the current. These natural sculptures resembled strange creatures. More than once Tom Westonby found himself half-believing that they were the remains of ancient statues. They even seemed to possess faces with deep-set eyes.

Tom allowed the current to carry him downstream. If he remained in the water for long enough, the flow would eventually take him to Whitby and the open ocean. As he drifted, he took photographs of different species of fish, or interesting features such as unusually deep chasms. An electronic instrument package attached to his belt automatically recorded his route, depth and speed. Tom had been hired by Yorkshire Woodland Heritage to survey the river that ran through the forest. They needed an accurate chart of the riverbed in order to assess if the channel was changing its course, or if there were archaeological remains, sunken boats, the bones of prehistoric animals or anything that might be of scientific importance.

What especially interested Tom Westonby were the underwater caves. He'd found ten so far. To explore these tunnels running away into submerged cliffs was incredibly dangerous. Even so, he had ventured inside to shine his flashlight into these tomb-like caverns. Anyone seeing him would probably surmise that his scientific curiosity had been aroused by what he might find. But Tom Westonby knew exactly what he searched for when he swam through that liquid darkness. The man looked for his long-lost bride.

FIVE

The River Lepping carried Tom Westonby half a mile downstream. Six feet above him, the surface resembled crinkled silver foil. Ten feet beneath him, the riverbed consisted of pale sand and dark boulders that had been deposited here long ago when the Ice Age glaciers had finally melted. There were rumours that gold coins lay scattered at the bottom of the channel. When he saw a gold disc beneath him he swam down to retrieve it. Instead of being precious metal, the disc turned out to be nothing more than the metal cap from a shotgun cartridge. Not that finding gold would mean much to Tom Westonby – no, he searched for an infinitely more valuable treasure.

His underwater survey had been straightforward this morning. During the forty minute journey the Diver's Instrument Package, known simply as DIP, automatically collected GPS information and other readings much in the way an aircraft's Black Box operated. On his return home, he'd connect the DIP to the computer by USB cable, and upload the data to the Yorkshire

Woodland Heritage computer in Bradford.

When he'd won the contract to do this work it meant he'd be his own boss. He liked it that way, because he needed to remain living here in the forest. With every day that passed his determination to bring Nicola Bekk home grew stronger and stronger. Some might call it obsession. He called it LOVE.

A *ping* in his earpiece warned that he'd ten minutes of air left in the tank. Slowly, he ascended to the surface, hearing the rush of bubbles past his helmet. The PIP GPS would tell him where to restart the survey tomorrow; however, he liked to get a fix on his location with his own eyes. When he broke free of the water he saw trees overhanging the river. The bank to his right consisted of heaped-up boulders, so he chose the one to his left, which would allow him exit across a gentle slope of sand. A tree, with two upright branches forming a Y shape, grew at the water's edge. That would provide a good marker for when he started the next leg of his survey.

Tom waded through the shallows. As he did so, he pulled his face mask away, together with his helmet. He glimpsed his reflection in the shallows: a rubber-suited man, loaded with heavy air tanks and a weight belt. Now a twenty-minute walk faced him. Not that he minded. He loved the forest. What was more he sensed Nicola's presence here. Often he'd get such a strong feeling that his lost bride could see him somehow.

Once more he noticed his reflection. This time he focused on the face: a twenty-eight-year-old man with dark hair. Nicola had vanished from his life five years ago, and sorrow and grief had aged him. His eyes were dark and melancholy, and haunted by those memories from half a decade ago that began so happily when Nicola danced into his life. That precious time with Nicola had ended the night the village had been flooded, and tragedy and horror had changed his life for ever. Tom saw shadows gathering behind his eyes. Darkness was coming. He could feel it. As if storm clouds approached. He could almost smell terror in the air. The signs were present. Bad dreams every night. Perhaps some primeval instinct warned of danger. Whispers of death. Predictions of disaster.

'Hey. Are you ever going to get those stinking bones of yours out of the river?'

The voice wrenched him away from those morbid thoughts.

He saw a figure on the river bank. 'Owen? Are you allergic to school?'

'I hoped for a "Great to see you, bro".'

Tom smiled. 'Great to see you, bro.' He stepped clear of the water.

'You're right, school is pissing me off.'

'They'll suspend you if you keep skipping days.'

'I'm in the clear today,' said the sixteen-year-old. 'The heating's busted so they sent us home.' He flicked snow from a branch. 'Isn't winter wonderful? It frees us from the tyranny of school and mind-shagging boredom.'

'So you came and found me.' Tom unbuckled the aqualung. 'I'm touched.'

26

'Nah. I'm meeting Kit and Jez. I saw you floating face down in the river, so I thought I'd check if you were dead.'

'I'm touched again.'

'Touched in the head, more like. Who'd go scuba diving here in winter?'

'It's work, Owen. There's bills to pay.'

'Aye, and beer to be bought.'

'You're sounding more like Jez every day.'

Owen held out his hand. Tom took it and allowed his younger brother to help him to a rock where he could sit down and prise off his flippers. Tom liked Owen. They got on well together, and Owen was one of the few people who could make Tom laugh again.

Tom noticed a mark on the teenager's face. 'Someone took a swing at you?'

'Uh, the bruise? You should see my back. It's every shade of purple, and then some.'

'Someone has attacked you?' The thought of his brother being beaten up immediately fired up Tom's anger.

'No, I fell off the back of Jez's truck.'

'Damn it, Owen. Have you been riding with that idiot again?'

'Hey, Jez is OK.'

'No, he's an IDIOT. Everyone knows he takes off in his dad's truck and drives like a maniac. He's going to get the attention of either the cops or a coffin-maker.' He stood up. 'Now you're making me sound like Dad, but I don't want you getting hurt.'

'I'm fine. Westonbys are made out of iron and steel.'

Tom pointed at Owen's bruised face. 'But we still break if we take a hard enough knock.'

Tom wore thick rubber bootees so the woodland paths wouldn't be a problem. Owen walked with him. He didn't seem annoyed that Tom played the caring big brother role. He took Tom's concern in his stride, just as he'd taken falling off the truck in his stride. Owen was easy-going ... sometimes too much so. Tom didn't want him drifting into a lifestyle of heavy drinking and drugs, which could become the fate of teenagers in rural villages. Often, the biggest danger in isolated communities is boredom.

Owen suddenly paused. 'I've got something to show you.' He swung his rucksack from his shoulder. 'It's interesting, but I haven't a clue what it is.' He pulled out a steel canister about the size of a Thermos flask and handed it to Tom. The thing had been crushed almost flat.

'Where did you get it from?'

'I found it upstream.'

Tom peered through a split in the casing. 'There are wires and circuits inside.'

'Do you think it fell off a plane?'

'Could have done. It's hit the ground hard ... or something crushed it.' Tom handed the canister back.

'What do you think it's for?'

Tom shrugged. 'Could be from a weather balloon. Are you going to hand it in?'

'To the police? Nah. Kit's good with this kind of thing.'

'Kit Bolter?'

'Yeah. Kit'll find out what it's for.' Owen

28

grinned. 'Don't you love a mystery?'

'I used to.'

Owen shook the device.

'Make sure that thing doesn't blow up in your face,' Tom told him. 'RAF jets practise bombing runs over the moor.'

'A bomb? You really think so?' Owen smartly tapped the canister against a tree. 'Shit, it's a dud.'

'Very funny.'

'Are you having dinner with us on Sunday?'

Tom shook his head. 'I've got a job checking a wharf downriver.'

'You never come across to see Mum and Dad these days.'

'Maybe next week.' Tom continued walking as Owen pushed the canister back into the rucksack. 'Let me know when you find out what your gizmo is.' Although he didn't really believe that the object contained explosive. If anything, it probably came from an old television or microwave oven. Some people aren't ashamed at dumping crap in a national park.

Owen laughed. 'If you hear a loud bang a couple of hours from now you'll know exactly what it is.'

Before going their separate ways Owen looked Tom up and down and shook his head. 'You know, anyone bumping into you out here is going to be scared witless. When they see you dressed in a black rubber suit they'll think you're either some kind of monster or nuts.'

Tom tried to sound light-hearted. 'There are more frightening things than me out here,

Owen.'

Owen laughed, taking the comment as a joke. 'Yeah, monsters galore. See you later, Tom.'

'See you later, Owen.'

Tom Westonby headed in the direction of home. As he walked he wondered what on earth he could do next in his search for Nicola Bekk.

SIX

Tom Westonby switched on the TV as he warmed up some chicken soup for lunch.

Local news covered a major fraud case in Sheffield. A moment later, the scene changed to one of Whitby harbour. The newsreader spoke over stock footage of boats and a view of the famous swing bridge: *'In Whitby, the mystery of the woman who lost her memory, and whose boyfriend is currently missing, has yet to be solved. Local police found Rose Dawson wandering near the harbour in the early hours of Friday morning last week. Despite the cold weather, Miss Dawson was dressed only in a T-shirt and jeans. She had a cast on one leg as a result of breaking a bone in a recent accident. Miss Dawson is unable to remember how she came to be in Whitby or tell the police anything about the whereabouts of her boyfriend, Mr John Cantley. Anyone having information about the couple is asked to contact Whitby police.'*

Tom Westonby turned off the TV and carried his soup into the lounge. He saw that a piece of paper had been pushed under the front door. Since he'd only used the back door after returning from the river, he hadn't noticed it before now. He picked up the paper. Written there in forceful handwriting were the words:

Mr Westonby. My name is June Valko. I need to speak to you urgently regarding events five years ago. I think we have many important issues in common that have impacted on our lives. Please call me as soon as you can. Believe me, this is important.

A telephone number had been added to the bottom of the letter.

Tom murmured, 'Thanks, but no thanks.' Crunching the paper into a ball, he threw it into the fireplace. A month didn't go by when he wasn't visited by self-appointed ghost hunters, vampire slayers and monster hunters. Tom would have nothing to do with them. Wouldn't even listen to what they had to say. What engulfed his life five years ago was hugely important to him – and hugely personal. He wasn't going to be portrayed as some lunatic on television so someone could earn a fistful of cash.

Tom had no appetite for the soup now. He hated it when his privacy wasn't just invaded but trampled on like this. He closed his eyes and listened to the angry beat of his heart. *Why don't they leave me alone? What do I have to do to escape the gossip and the finger-pointing?*

SEVEN

Owen Westonby and Kit Bolter sat on bales of straw. The pair were in a barn that belonged to Jez's family. Jez had been called away to help his father with a recalcitrant computer.

Kit examined the metal cylinder. 'Let me get this straight. You found the pod by the river?'

'Pod? It's a cylinder.'

Kit shook his head. 'It's a pod in the sense that it contains an object or objects.'

Owen grinned. 'So you're going to get all scientific on me?'

'You asked me to find out what this does.'

'OK, pod it is.' Jokingly he made the introductions. 'Mr Pod, meet Kit Bolter. Kit Bolter, meet Mr Pod.'

'Just plain "pod" will do.' He poked a pencil through a split in the casing. 'Interesting. Very interesting.'

'Any ideas?'

'Some. Where did you find it exactly?'

'Oh, up the valley near the old footbridge.'

'How was it lying?'

'Lying? Is that important?'

'Might be.'

Owen thought for a moment. 'Sort of pushed into the soil. Like it had fallen from a plane and the impact had embedded Mr Pod in the muck.'

'Or a heavy weight had crushed it into the earth?'

'Yeah, s'pose so.'

'The pod's been crushed.' Kit indicated the mangled casing. 'Whatever did that was well heavy, mega-heavy.'

'If you say so.'

'Did you see any tyre tracks?'

'You mean, if it had been run over?'

Kit nodded.

Owen laughed. 'You're really taking this seriously, aren't you?'

'I'd like to get into forensics. This is good practice.'

'Really? You in the police?'

'Why not?'

'Yeah, OK, why not?' Owen nodded. 'So what have you deduced, Sherlock?'

'If you're going to take the piss ... you find out what this is.' He dropped the pod on to Owen's lap before walking out of the barn.

Owen sighed. Kit Bolter must have been fathered by an alien or something. His family were notorious for getting into all kinds of trouble, which usually led to visits from the police. Kit Bolter, on the other hand, had a sensitive, thoughtful nature. That sixteen-year-old with the pale blue eyes and gentle manner must be a foundling.

Owen went to find Kit. When he caught up with him in the farmyard he apologized, insisting he'd been joking. 'I'm a thoughtless goon,' Owen confessed.

'You are,' Kit agreed.

33

'I'm sorry. I shouldn't have made fun of you.'

'Apology accepted. Where's the pod?'

The cylinder that Owen had found that morning fascinated Kit. He'd seen a mystery there and wanted to find some answers. They returned to the barn. This time Owen sat quietly while Kit took the floor.

'This is an instrument pod,' he told Owen. 'There's electronics inside, and the pod must have been contained in a housing of some kind. See? There's no sign of weathering even though it looks as if it was designed for outside use.'

'Could it be part of a missile from a military aircraft?'

'Doubtful. If you hold it up to the light you can see a USB plug, so it's meant to feed data into a computer.'

'Any idea what the pod is?'

'Could be a roadside speed camera. Maybe someone tried to destroy the evidence to avoid being fined for speeding.'

'So it's just a load of busted crap now.'

'The pod's in a bad state, but there's hope.'

'How come?'

'If I get the electronics out, and replace the USB plug, I can probably transfer the data stored here on to my computer.'

'Then we'll find out what it's been filming?'

'With luck, yes.'

'Great. How long until we see what's stored in there?'

'A day or so.'

Jez suddenly bounded through the door. 'Surf's up!'

'What do you mean, surf's up?'

'That's what surfers yell when there are waves to go surfing, don't they?'

Kit shook his head. 'He's crazy.'

Jez grinned. 'My Dad's going to the village. We've got time to grab the truck and drive up the valley and back.'

Kit shuddered. 'No way. We'll get ourselves killed.'

Jez brandished the truck's keys. 'Come on, no time to waste.'

Owen followed, shouting with excitement. At the barn door he paused. 'What are you waiting for, Kit?'

'I'll sit this one out, thank you very much. I'm going to take Mr Pod apart.' As an afterthought he shouted, 'And when you get yourselves killed I'm not going to your funerals!'

EIGHT

Confession, they say, is good for the soul. Tom Westonby couldn't say whether the statement held a profound truth or not. However, the words ran through his head as he sat on the sofa with a tablet computer in his hands. He began to read what he'd written there. His confession. His *De Profundis*. Tom didn't know the exact meaning of *De Profundis*, other than it suggested a comprehensive outpouring of the heart. A baring of the soul.

Tom Westonby spent many a night tapping words into the tablet. He'd recorded as accurately as he possibly could what happened to him five years ago, and the loss of his bride, Nicola Bekk. Those were dark chapters in his life. What he wrote here was for his own eyes only. He certainly didn't want anyone to see this particular document.

The corner of the screen showed the time as four p.m. Outside, the forest lay in darkness. Through the window he glimpsed more snowflakes drifting past. A fire blazed in the hearth of the ancient cottage. Something told him that this winter would be a harsh one, so he'd made sure he'd gathered plenty of logs for the fire. If the blizzards came down with a vengeance, he could be trapped here for days.

Tom switched his attention back to the tablet. The lines written there detailed his first meeting with Nicola Bekk, when he'd seen her in the garden at midnight. That was the time she dipped her bare feet into the pond, while smiling with the sheer bliss of it all.

He read and reread his *De Profundis* as if it had become part of a sacred ritual. Was this akin to gazing at a photograph of a dead loved one in the hope that if you looked long enough and hard enough you could conjure them back to you? Perhaps so. Whatever the motivation, he knew he'd keep adding to his confession. He'd keep re-reading it, too, while wishing with all his heart that one day he'd open the door to find Nicola Bekk standing there.

NINE

Owen Westonby and Jez Pollock walked through Danby-Mask. This small, far-from-anywhere village had already gone to sleep for the night, even though it was just a shade past six o'clock. At least that's how it seemed to two bored teenagers. The pair were getting philosophical.

Owen declared, 'Being sixteen is like getting stuck in a waiting room.'

'Yeah.' Jez nodded. 'I know what you mean.'

'It's like being stuck in a waiting room right next to another room where there's an amazing party going on, only you're still too young to go through the door and join in.'

'Sixteen is a shit age. I hate it.'

'Me, too.'

They glared their disapproval at the street, which enjoyed Danby-Mask's habitual peace and quiet.

'What a place.' Owen shook his head. 'Even the God of Boredom would die of boredom here.'

Jez laughed. 'Hey, that's funny. God of Boredom. Ha-ha!'

A car with a throaty motor snarled along the street.

'If only we were old enough to get some wheels.' With envy in his eyes, Jez watched the

37

car go by. 'We could get right away from here.'

'As soon as we're seventeen, that's what we're going to do.'

They high-fived to seal the deal. Even so, Owen knew the truth. Yes, boredom killed the soul here. Kids talked about nothing else other than buying cars. They promised themselves they'd roar out of this dull, brain-deadening village without looking back. But what did teenagers *really* do as soon as they bought a car? They drove up and down Main Street like this idiot. They never would point their cars towards brave horizons. No, they revved their engines, spun their wheels to impress the girls, and they followed the same boring route from the war memorial at one end of the village to the farm store at the other. Then back again. And so on ... and so on.

Jez's expression changed to one that meant business. He jabbed his elbow into Owen's ribs. 'Girls ... *Girls.*'

Four girls walked along the street. Owen had seen them before, though he'd never spoken to them. They went to some posh school near Whitby. They had straight backs, carried themselves well, glowed with confidence and vitality and... 'Oh, God, they are beee-utiful,' breathed Owen.

'There's four of 'em,' whispered Jez. 'Two for you, two for me.'

'In your dreams.'

Owen and Jez waited for them to get nearer. However, they took an interest in an area outside the grocery store. They were pointing at the ground while looking quickly at one another, as if they'd seen something that shocked them.

'A faint heart never won two birds in a bush,' murmured Jez, 'or whatever that saying is.'

'They're too posh for us,' warned Owen.

'Are you saying I'm a farm boy, or something?'

'You *are* a farm boy, Jez. We're a pair of sixteen-year-olds. We still ride mountain bikes and muck about in the woods.'

Jez cracked his knuckles. 'The time's come for you to grow from a boy to a man. Follow me.'

They had to wait as cars passed by, sounding their horns, while high-spirited guys inside shouted insulting comments at Jez and Owen, and then whistled and made suggestive comments to the four teen beauties. The cars would follow the usual route. Down to the war memorial before turning back up Main Street. Owen remembered an old man telling him that Main Street used to be known locally as 'Monkey Walk'. In the evening, young single people would turn out in their best clothes and walk up and down Main Street from the war memorial to the farm stores, then back again. Boys would remain in male-only groups; girls would parade by in strictly female groups. They'd appraise one another, make comments, sometimes the men would whistle. At that moment, Owen suspected an important and profound truth: every generation of the village repeated the courting rituals of the previous generation. OK, cars had mainly replaced the evening strolls, but the spirit of Monkey Walk hadn't died – in fact, it was stronger than ever.

At last, Owen and Jez reached the open area outside the grocery store where the girls stared at the pavement. To Owen's surprise he saw that part of the area had been cordoned off with bright yellow police incident tape. The girls stared in shock at the chalked outline of a man on the ground.

One of the sixteen-year-old girls, with long blond hair and the bluest of eyes, turned to Owen. 'We haven't heard about anyone being killed, have you?'

'Not us.' Owen shook his head.

A girl with dark hair shivered. 'This is just frightening. Really frightening. Look at me, I'm shaking.'

Both Owen and Jez were happy to look at the girl as she stood shivering with fear.

Another girl had a suggestion. 'Maybe it's something to do with the woman that was found wandering in Whitby? She'd lost her memory and her boyfriend is missing.'

'Maybe they found the boyfriend.' Owen nodded at the chalked outline. 'Murdered.'

The girls did some more shuddering and moved closer to Owen and Jez. Owen stood taller, trying to resemble the kind of strong, heroic guy to have close, if trouble broke out.

'Has anyone seen any blood?' Jez asked with a deliberate expression of innocence.

'Oh God, is there any?' The blonde stood even closer to Owen.

Owen glanced sideways at Jez; both knew they'd broken the ice with the girls. This could be the start of something extremely exciting. *I could end the day with a new girlfriend*, thought Owen, pleased. *I'll invite the blonde girl to the cinema.* Then a worrying thought struck him. *I hope Jez doesn't make a move on the blonde.*

Jez studied the ground by the light of the street lamps. 'My God ... there is something. I think I can see blood.'

The girls dropped silent. Owen could sense their tension. All four leaned over the police tape to see a dark smear on the pavement. Next to the chalked outline of the victim stood a large bin made from yellow plastic. Printed on its front was the word GRIT. The bin contained a mixture of sand and salt, which could be shovelled out on to paths if there was ice or snow.

By this time, the four girls had bent right over to examine what appeared to be blood. The tension was electric.

Then – BANG! A figure lunged from the plastic bin that contained the grit – a human jack-in-the-box. The man yelled. Blood covered his face and he clawed his hands in the air as if trying to reach the girls.

Screaming, they fled. Owen caught one last glimpse of the blonde vanishing into an alleyway. His romantic trip to the cinema vanished with her.

Jez recognized the man who'd been captive in the yellow bin. 'Shaun!'

The kid grinned. 'Did you see their faces? They were bogging terrified!'

'*Shaun!*' Owen and Jez shouted the name together.

'What did you do that for?' Owen couldn't believe his bad luck. 'We were getting somewhere.'

'That was fantastic.' Shaun laughed. 'See this?' He touched his cheek. 'Fake blood left over from Hallowe'en. I found the police tape on the beach at Whitby months ago. I've been waiting for just the right moment to use it. I drew the chalk outline, too,' he added proudly.

Jez sounded murderous. 'You scared 'em away. The most beautiful girls we've ever seen ... and you scared 'em away!'

'It was funny.' Shaun seemed offended that no one else was laughing. 'I've been planning this all week. Pretend there's been a murder, chalk the outline, then burst out of here with blood on my face. Hey, there's no need for that. No ... let go ... keep your frigging hands off me.'

Jez pushed the youth back into the yellow bin, slammed down the lid, then sat on it. Owen sat beside him. Shaun had ruined their evening, but at least he was now their prisoner.

Shaun pounded on the inside of the bin. 'A joke ... that's all ... just a joke.'

'Rot in jail, you idiot.'

'Can't breathe ... let me out.'

'You breathed OK when you hid in there earlier.'

Jez turned to Owen. 'At least we spoke to them now. Next time they'll know us.'

'Which one would you ask out?'

'The blonde,' Jez said.

'Me, too.'

'We can't let a girl stop us being friends,

42

though, can we?'

'No, we'll never do that. Never.'

Shaun coughed inside the yellow box. 'I'm really, really suffocating. You're going to have a corpse on your hands, if you don't let me out.'

'That's alright,' Owen told him. 'We'll leave your dead body inside the chalk outline.'

Jez and Owen high-fived and laughed. Meanwhile, guys of seventeen and eighteen drove their cars up and down Main Street – just as their fathers did – and as their yet-to-be-born sons would do in the future.

TEN

At the same time that Owen and Jez sat on the grit bin to keep the prankster in captivity, Kit Bolter worked on the canister. He'd taken the mystery artefact up to his 'lab' in the attic. He never mentioned the lab to his friends; they'd only tease him, and make endless jokes about Doctor Frankenstein and Mad Scientists. Kit often felt as if he had no control over his life. Up here, however, in the attic of his mother's house, he had his comfort bubble. Here he had his space. Here he was surrounded with computer parts, monitors, cables hung like black snakes from hooks that he'd screwed into the rafters – all neatly ordered for his work. Shelves contained lines of tools, neat as surgical instruments laid out in an operating theatre. Here he tinkered with pieces of electronic equipment. OK, he enjoyed repairing toasters, vacuum cleaners and so on for family members, but what he enjoyed most of all was composing pieces of music by modifying sounds made by ordinary things. He could record the sound his finger made rubbing the top of a wine glass, then multi-track it, and vary the speed until that humming sound of a wet finger on glass sounded as magnificent as a choir of angels.

Kit didn't think that there'd be any commercial application for his Noise Music – a homely name for something that was really quite special in his eyes – and ears. Maybe it was psychological. His parents tended to run wild. They took drugs, drank enough to knock a bull off its feet and got into fights. His father now lived in Leppington (after a stay in prison); nevertheless he still lived a wild life, just as he'd always done. So Kit Bolter had his Noise Music. He knew this had become a psychological compensation for growing up with unstable parents. His music granted him emotional stability. He controlled the sounds. Controlled what he heard. Made the music fast or loud, soft or harsh, or pleasantly melodic, or just downright doom-laden, if that was where his mood took him. Above all, however, he exercised control over his compositions.

Tonight would be different. He had the pod to examine. Owen Westonby had told him he'd found the pod in the forest. It was a metal cylinder that had been crushed. Perhaps by a heavy weight, such as a tractor driving over the thing. So far, he'd managed to open up one end of the cylinder. Carefully, he'd extracted the electronics. They seemed in reasonable condition. The worst damage had been to what appeared to be a camera lens. So, a camera?

At that moment, a text came through from Owen. *So what's pod for?* His friend was keen to unravel the mystery, too. Kit texted back: *Should have answer soon. But not a bomb. Danby-Mask and your ugly face are safe from destruction.*

As he eased away the USB cable that had become detached from the electronics he murmured to himself, 'I know, I'll let you tell me what you are ... all I have to do is replace the USB. After that, I'll link you up to my computer; then you can show me what's stored inside of you.' He enjoyed this mystery ... he loved the idea of activating the device so it would reveal its secret. He had control of this machine; therefore, he had control of his life. Even if only for a short time.

He selected a USB cable from a hook above his head. 'Now, speak to me, sweet pea.'

'Who ya got up here with you? A girl?'

He turned to see that his mother had climbed the ladder, so her top half poked up through the loft hatch. She wore a yellow cardigan buttoned up to her throat. As always, she had that bewildered expression, as if something had gone badly wrong with her life but she couldn't figure out exactly what.

'I've got nobody up here with me, mother.'

'Everyone else in the village calls their mothers "Mam". But I'm "Muth-haaa".'

He could smell whisky on her breath from here. She'd been locked into a passionate embrace with the bottle since breakfast time.

Her voice grew louder, 'I asked who you've got up here.'

'No one.'

'Oh, talking to your electrical *bibs and bobs* again, eh?'

'Just passing the time.'

'You're a strange boy, you know? You're not like the other Bolter men. I can't even believe I gave birth to you.'

'Because I keep myself to myself?'

'Because you're weird. Really, really weird.' Her voice slurred away into a grunt.

'It's not a good idea standing on the ladder, mother. I'll help you back down.'

'What you got there?'

'What?'

'There ... right in front of you. The silver thing?'

'It's nothing.'

'If it's nothing then I won't be disturbing you, will I? I won't be taking you away from your work?'

'Did you want to tell me something?' He made a point of being patient with his mother. He'd seen enough of his father's fiery impatience to last a lifetime. Genuinely, he felt sorry for the horrible way her life had turned out. 'I could make you some supper?'

'I've just decided...' She took a deep breath. 'There is something important you should know.

And now you're sixteen you're old enough to know the truth.'

'Yes?' He had chills as he looked at his mother. She'd never spoken like this before.

'Do you remember your uncle who died when the village was flooded?'

'Yes.'

'Well, listen to this: that friend of yours, Owen Westonby... his brother was responsible. That's right, lad. Tom Westonby murdered your uncle.'

ELEVEN

Everything began that night with a knock on the door. When Tom Westonby crossed the lounge to the door his heart began to pound. For some reason he believed he'd find Nicola there. His Nicola, with the pale, blonde hair and blue eyes. An impossible notion, yet it suddenly blazed into life inside his head. *This is Nicola ... somehow she's found a way back to me.*

His heart raced so fast that he felt light-headed. Quickly, he wrenched open the door, expecting to see the girl that he loved. Light from the room spilled out on to the pathway. When he saw the stranger standing there he froze as disappointment came crashing down on him like a deluge of cold water.

The young woman seemed tense, incredibly tense, yet she asked politely, 'Excuse me, is this

Skanderberg?'

Tom stared at her. At that moment, he couldn't move, never mind speak. His optimism had cruelly persuaded him that Nicola had come back. Now this stranger? What on earth was she doing here?

The woman asked again, 'Is this cottage called Skanderberg?'

Stiffly, he gave a curt nod. He found himself unable to take his eyes from the stranger's face. Somehow she seemed familiar. He judged her to be around the same age as him – twenty-eightish. Small, slightly built, wearing a pink leather jacket, she had short, black hair and coffee-coloured skin. Yet despite her dark colouring she had blue eyes. They were striking. In fact, the blueness of the eyes seemed to glow as she stood there. The woman carried an electric lantern – a ridiculous, ineffectual one that cast hardly any light.

What the hell is she thinking? Walking through the forest at night? That's an incredibly stupid thing to do.

The woman grew increasingly nervous at being stared at. She must have been asking herself: *Is this a madman? Will he attack me?*

Once more, she spoke to Tom. 'If this is Skanderberg, then you must be Mr Westonby. My name is June Valko.'

He still stared at her in disbelief. 'Have you walked through the wood by yourself?'

'Yes.'

'What the hell for?'

'To see you, Mr Westonby. There wasn't a

driveway that led up to the cottage, so I had to leave my car back on the main road and walk here.' She tried to sound light hearted, though she now trembled with fright. 'I didn't realize it would be so far. I must have taken some wrong turnings, because I've been walking for almost an hour.'

'June Valko? You left me a note earlier?'

'Yes.'

'I threw it away. I don't talk to monster hunters.'

'Pardon? Monster hunters?'

'That's what you are, aren't you? A dragon spotter? Let me tell you, Miss Valko, there are no such things as dragons. You won't find any monsters roaming through this forest.' He'd not looked her in the eye when he told her that dragons didn't exist, and he wondered if she realized he wasn't telling the truth. Because five years ago something had roamed these woods. And it had claimed lives.

He stepped backwards. Not to invite her in, but to grab his coat and boots. She took a step over the threshold.

'Stay there, please, Miss Valko.'

'You can't turn me away.'

'I'll walk you back to your car.'

'But you haven't let me tell you why I'm here.'

'I'm not interested.'

'But—'

'No more interviews. I just want to be left alone.'

Despite his telling her not to come into the house she did exactly that. Those blue eyes

49

became piercing – the woman was getting angry. Now that he saw her clearly in the light of the room he could tell she was beautiful. Many men would have been asking her to stay, but not him, not Tom Westonby ... *I want her out ... I want her gone.*

'Mr Westonby, you must listen to me. I've got something important to tell you.'

'Every reporter, cryptozoologist, ghost hunter and nut-job that comes to that door has something important to tell me. If it's not promising me worldwide fame, it's some lunatic telling me the secret to immortality can be found in this forest, or a way to travel through time, or speak to the dead, and I'm sick of it – and I'm sick of people like you.'

'Just listen to me!'

'No way.' Tom pulled on his boots. 'I'll walk you back to the car, because you might get lost again – or simply end up dead out there.'

'Listen.'

'This isn't a safe place to be, Miss Valko. In fact, it's incredibly dangerous.'

'I won't leave until you hear me out.'

'Then I'll drag you all the way back to the car.' He turned on her now, feeling all the pent-up fury roaring out. 'I don't want to hear your crap! I don't want anything to do with you! You're nothing better than a grave robber!'

'Wait.'

'Start walking, or I'll carry you out.'

'We belong to the same family. I'm Nicola Bekk's niece.'

Tom stared at her in shock. Those blue eyes ...

he realized now why this woman had seemed so familiar. She had Nicola's beautiful eyes.

In a calm voice she asked, 'So will you listen to me now?'

TWELVE

Tom Westonby murdered my uncle? After hearing the revelation from his mother, Kit Bolter sat inside his attic lab in something close to shock. He'd met Tom plenty of times before. He was a great guy – OK, a bit preoccupied and distant-looking, like he'd got stuff on his mind. He was Owen's brother, of course, and Owen was Kit's best friend. Kit knew that Owen and Tom weren't biological brothers. Owen's mother had died a long time ago, and the Westonbys had adopted the boy.

This statement of Kit's mother had blasted him like a bomb: *'That's right, lad. Tom Westonby murdered your uncle.'* Just like the echoes of a bomb exploding, the sentence kept reverberating inside his head. *'That's right, lad. Tom Westonby murdered your uncle.'*

Jesus ... that can't be right, can it? What his mother had told him made him feel like puking all over the floor. *The whisky must be making her imagine things, surely? My uncle died in an accident.* When Kit heard his mother climbing the ladder to his lab he managed to pull himself

51

out of his trance.

Puffing, while muttering about the steep ladder, she held up an envelope. 'It's all in here. Read it for yourself.' Climbing into the attic was beyond her, so she stood there with her head above the hatchway. 'Well, come and get it, or do you want me to lose my grip and fall?'

He took the envelope from her.

'Read every bit of it,' she told him before climbing back down to the landing.

The whisky fumes made his eyes water. His mother depended on the spirit of Scotland to keep life's woes at bay. Kit placed the envelope on his workbench where the light shone brightest. For now the pod would have to wait.

The large gold envelope had once contained a birthday card that he'd sent to his mother. MOTHER covered the front in black felt-tip. This gold material was hardly an appropriate receptacle for what must be grim contents, but then that was the kind of thing his mother did. No doubt there'd be a bottle of whisky in the laundry basket, and a jar of marijuana in the larder next to the sugar and flour. Yes, his mother got stranger, making Kit worry about her more and more.

Carefully, he laid out the contents of the envelope on the workbench. Straight away he saw a document headed CERTIFICATE OF DEATH. That lettering jumped right off the page at him. The death certificate listed medical terms that identified the cause of his uncle's death. They stated that the man's fatal injuries were consistent with falling from a considerable height.

After that, Kit read newspaper cuttings about the 'tragic night a Yorkshire village was hit by the worst flood in a hundred years' and the accidental death of one Todd Bolter. Kit knew that his uncle had got mixed up with drugs. Another case of a bored individual growing up in a little village with a hunger for excitement and nothing to do. Newspaper stories also referred to the deceased Todd Bolter's trouble-strewn past; that is to say, numerous convictions for drug offences. However, every single cutting confirmed what Kit already knew: for some reason, his uncle fell from the top of the church tower. *So why is my mother adamant that Tom Westonby committed murder?*

Kit worked his way through the crumpled mass of newspaper clippings. As incongruous as the gold envelope, there was another document that declared that Todd Bolter had succeeded in swimming a length of the pool. He turned the swimming certificate over. On the back he found a handwritten statement. Typically, a member of the Bolter family had simply used whatever came to hand. Ice-cold shivers ran down his back when he saw that this was his grandmother's handwriting. The shakiness of the script suggested she wrote this towards the end of her life, which would be around eighteen months ago. His grandmother could barely read or write, so this statement, ungrammatical though it was, must have been a considerable achievement for her.

To who it might concern. My name is Maureen Bolter. I am dying. I want to get this off my chest about Thomas Westonby. Westonby is a murderer. I heard the truth with my own ears from people in the church when the village got flooded. Thomas Westonby hit my grandson, Todd Bolter. Later that night, him and my beloved grandson got into a fight again on top of the church tower. I've been told that Westonby and Nicola Bekk pushed my grandson off the roof so that he'd be killed. As God is my witness, I am writing these words to inform you that Westonby is a murderer and should be in prison.

Kit had difficulty in deciphering some of the sprawling scribble. He doubted that the police would investigate, given the poor mental state of his grandmother when she scrawled this down before she died. What troubled Kit was that he couldn't dismiss what he'd read about Tom Westonby murdering his uncle. Just because the Bolter family were cynically dismissed as thieves, drug sellers and liars didn't mean that they, themselves, weren't sometimes victims of crime. There were times when Bolter folk told the truth, too.

Kit Bolter wondered how he'd react the next time he met Owen Westonby. Should he tell Owen that the Bolter family believed that Tom had murdered one of their own? Even just a mention of an accusation like this could explode a friendship to nothing. Kit closed his eyes and thought hard about what he should do next. Because all of a sudden, the immediate future looked darker – storm clouds were gathering over Kit and the best friend he'd ever had.

THIRTEEN

She wanted to talk. Tom, however, knew she must get away from the cottage and back to the car as soon as possible. He finished tying his bootlaces, fastening his coat, and retrieving a powerful flashlight from the kitchen.

The beautiful woman with the coffee-coloured skin and those amazing blue eyes watched him with an expression that blended sorrow with desperation. 'Mr Westonby. Now that I've told you that I'm Nicola Bekk's niece, won't you listen to me?'

'How do I know that you really are related to Nicola? Journalists have tried all kinds of tricks to get information out of me.'

'My eyes don't lie. These blue eyes are pure Bekk, aren't they?' June Valko thrust a phone towards him. 'This is a photograph of my father. See his eyes? They're the same blue.'

Tom sighed when he saw the photograph. A man stood with a dark-skinned woman. His eyes were blue, and his hair possessed that same shade of blond as Nicola's – an extremely fair blond that wasn't far away from being an ethereal white. He sighed again, because he couldn't avoid the truth any more. This indeed was a blood relative of Nicola's.

'So you do believe me, Mr Westonby?'

He nodded. 'Call me Tom.' This time he held out his hand.

Shaking it, she smiled, though her eyes remained deadly serious. 'Please call me June.'

'OK, June. The bottom line is you must get back to your car as soon as possible.'

'You believe I'm Nicola's niece, so why do you want me to leave?'

'This forest is dangerous after dark.'

She laughed as if he'd made a joke. 'Dangerous? It's just a forest.'

'If I trust that you're a blood relative of the Bekk family, then you must trust me when I say it's not safe out there.'

June's blue eyes strayed to the sofa. 'Can't I stay? I thought we could talk?'

'We can meet up again. But not here – and certainly not at night.'

Her eyes narrowed as she looked at him.

Tom had seen that look before. 'Yes, I know, you think I'm insane. But it's not safe out there. I only go into the forest after dark if there's an emergency, and lives depend on it. Do you follow what I'm saying?'

'Perhaps we could just talk for a couple of minutes?'

'No can do.' He checked the flashlight. 'You have to get back to your car. Give me your phone number.'

'I already did. It's on the note I left you.'

'I burned it.'

She didn't ask why. Instead, she pulled a card from her purse. 'My name and number's on there. I'm stopping at the Station Hotel in Leppington. Do you know it?'

He nodded. 'I'll give you a call. We'll meet up at the hotel.' The look she gave him prompted him to add, 'In the bar.'

Even though June began to fasten her jacket she moved slowly so she could talk. Clearly she needed to reveal information that was important to her. 'I came here by train from Manchester. When I reached Leppington I hired a car so I could find you.'

Despite a sense of urgency to get her away from here, he had to ask the question: 'Why?'

Those astonishing blue eyes locked on to his. 'Twenty-nine years ago my mother met a man called Jacob Bekk. My mother's the lady you saw in the photo. They fell in love. Before I came along, however, my father returned to this cottage. My mother never saw him again.'

'So they split up?'

'No. They loved one another. My mother said Jacob began to change. He seemed to be haunted by something – and she did use the word "haunted". Also, he became physically different. His skin grew paler; she could see veins through the flesh. His eyes changed, too.'

'As if the colour had begun to leach away?'

June's eyes flashed with surprise. 'Hey, how did you know that?'

'How did you know how to find me?'

'My mother collected news reports of a flood that happened five years ago in this valley. Your name cropped up a lot, and as the name Tom Westonby was linked to Nicola Bekk, my

57

mother drew plenty of conclusions.'

'We should be going.' He opened the door.

'Aren't you curious about why I'm here?'

'This isn't the time to talk. Already I might have left it too late to go through the wood.'

'I'm here to save my mother's life.'

The sentence stopped Tom dead. 'Save her life? How can coming here save anyone's life?' He paused. 'Sorry, that sounded brutal. You just took me by surprise.'

'My mother's name is April. She married Jacob Bekk. He left her soon after she found out she was pregnant with me. She was so angry she changed her name back to Valko. But the absolute truth is that she loves Jacob. She can't accept that he stopped loving her. For years now she's been slipping deeper and deeper into clinical depression. Two weeks ago she was hospitalized. This might sound over the top, but she's literally dying of a broken heart. If she meets Jacob again, she might find some peace ... she might even get well again.'

'I don't see what I can do.'

'Help me find Jacob Bekk.'

'I don't think I can do that.'

'I found you.'

'All you need do is type "Tom Westonby" into a search engine; you'll be taken to all kinds of websites about the paranormal and monster hunting.'

'Other missing people can be found, if you try hard enough.'

'June, I've been searching for Nicola Bekk for five years.'

'Then we'll find them both together. Nicola and Jacob.' Her blue eyes held a fierce determination. 'We can help each other, Tom.'

'Even if I could take you to Jacob, I wouldn't.'

'Why?'

'Because I would not inflict such a thing on my worst enemy.'

'Do you always talk in mysterious riddles?'

'It's better than you hearing the truth.'

'You've just answered me with another riddle. So why is it better than hearing the truth?'

Tom held open the door. 'We have to go now. I mean this very second.'

She hesitated.

He said, 'I promise to phone you tomorrow.'

'Alright, but please, *please* come and see me as soon as you possibly can. OK?'

'OK.' He looked her in the eye. 'What I'm going to say next will seem strange ... it'll even sound worrying ... but when we walk through the wood stick close to me. You might see things that seem odd, but don't stop. Keep walking. Don't look at them. Don't look back. Just keep moving forward, and I'll get you back to your car.'

'What kind of things?'

'I'll explain when I see you again. Now, are you ready?'

When she nodded, Tom Westonby led the way. He hoped that the path ahead would be clear.

FOURTEEN

They walked away from the cottage. Out here in the remote part of the forest an absolute darkness engulfed them. June Valko stuck close by Tom's side as he'd asked. That distinctive forest-in-winter aroma filled his nostrils – the scent of damp earth, the mustiness of vegetation and sharper tang of dead leaves. Their breath billowed from their mouths. The brilliant light from Tom's torch made those bursts of breath look like clouds of white steam.

June Valko scanned her surroundings. 'I passed through an impressive stone arch when I came into the garden. The arch looks a lot older than the cottage.'

'It is.'

'Something had been carved on it. Is it an animal?'

'I'll explain when we meet up.' He walked faster, intending to get her back to the car as soon as possible. 'You say you parked near a large house on the main road?'

'Yes.'

'That's Mull-Rigg Hall. My parents live there.'

'Oh.' June's expression became thoughtful, as if she'd picked up some inflection in his voice when he'd mentioned his parents. June carried the little electric lantern. 'I tried to buy a flash-light,' she explained, 'but this is all they had at the village store. I think it's just a toy lamp they had left over from Hallowe'en.'

'Watch where you put your feet. It'll get slippery down by the river.'

June Valko continued to talk. He guessed she'd picked up on his tension, and talking was a way to try and disguise her nervousness. 'I wouldn't have thought a forest in England would be dangerous. But then what do I know? I'm a city girl. I work for a freight company. So, why is it dangerous out here? They don't have bears and wolves in Yorkshire, do they?'

'There are wild boar. They were reintroduced ten years ago.'

'They're just fluffy pigs, aren't they?'

'You wouldn't want to bump into one. They're big animals, and they've got tusks. They can also be vicious.'

'Oh. I hadn't realized that it could be so risky coming to see you.'

He glanced at her. Even though this pretty woman was slightly built – she could even be described as dainty – there was real strength there. What's more, he sensed that June Valko possessed intelligence and determination. *This woman's smart – and she's a fighter.*

The nerves kept her talking. She would be used to the constant background noise of the city. She must find this kind of silence unset-tling, even frightening. 'So my mother married Nicola's brother,' she said. 'All I know of my grandmother is that she lived at Skanderberg,

61

and had of lots of children. The first came along when she was seventeen, and the last when she was in her late forties, which is why my father is so much older than Nicola.'

'She was reclusive. And even though I might be speaking ill of the dead – she died last year – your grandmother was downright strange.'

'I don't even know her name, other than it's Mrs Bekk. She disowned her son when he moved away. Something to do with betraying family heritage.'

'I heard plenty about family heritage from Mrs Bekk. She'd got totally obsessive about tracing the Bekk bloodline back to Viking settlers over a thousand years ago.'

A dead sheep lay at the side of the path. An open eye glinted in the light of the torch. Tom caught sight of teeth marks on its throat. No blood, though. He knew that not a drop of blood would be found on the animal. A hungry tongue would have licked the wound clean.

June followed him along the path, which hugged the course of the river. Down here the rapids sounded loud. Light from the torch splashed against the water, revealing a spot where it foamed round boulders.

'Tom? How did you come to live in Skanderberg?'

'I rebuilt it after the fire.'

'What fire?'

'It might seem like bad manners, but I don't really want to talk. What's important right now is getting you back to your car.'

'Wild boar might eat us?'

'Yeah, something like that.'

'I was joking, Tom.'

'Stick to the right of the path. It gets swampy on the other side.'

June Valko fell silent. He took this to mean she'd got the hint about closing her mouth and carrying on walking. However, just the tone of her voice when she spoke a moment later sent shivers down his spine.

'Tom ... I've just seen a man.'

'Keep walking.'

'He's over there by the big rock.'

'Don't look at him.'

'But he's looking at me.'

'He won't hurt you, June. But whatever you do, don't stop.'

'Tom, you're frightening me.'

'Hold my hand.'

He gripped her hand fiercely enough to make her gasp. Tom Westonby didn't do this to reassure her; he'd seized her hand so he could keep her moving forward.

'Why is he staring at us?' she whispered. 'Look at him. He's just standing there like a statue. But ... oh my God ... can you see his eyes? His eyes are like—'

'I told you not to look at him.'

'Tom.' She sounded alarmed. 'There's something wrong with his face.'

He tugged her by the hand as if she was a child who dragged its feet. 'Come on, walk faster.'

'Why's he out here at night?'

'June, he won't hurt you. Not if you keep walking and don't look back.'

She hissed, 'But his face is so strange ... my God, it's scaring me just to look at it.'

'I told you not to look back.'

June Valko did more than just look back. She raised the electric lantern she carried. The light fell on the strange figure that stood, as still as a statue, perhaps thirty paces away.

'His feet?' she gasped. 'It's winter ... he hasn't got any shoes on his feet. They're bare.'

She tilted the lamp so its rays would illuminate the stranger's face. Before she could get a clear look at that face, with its staring eyes, Tom knocked the lantern from her hand.

'Ow!'

'Come on.' He hauled her so forcefully that she cried out again in pain.

'I'm not afraid of him,' she cried. 'Give me the flashlight. I want to see his face.'

'This might seem brutal, but the last thing you'd want to see is that thing's face.'

'Thing? It's a man, not a thing.'

'Hurry up.'

'Stop! You're hurting me!'

That's when the silent figure moved. And, dear God, it moved so fast. Tom didn't even have time to react before the figure slammed into him. He tumbled down the river bank. Seconds later, a hand grabbed his hair. An enormous force pressed his face down into the water at the river's edge. Brilliant lights exploded inside his head. He couldn't breathe. His attacker was hell-bent on drowning him.

Though he struggled, he couldn't lift his face clear. Bubbles spurted from his lips. Cold water jetted up his nose. Then the lights inside his head grew dim. They became clots of purple. Then the purple became darker ... blacker ... he stopped moving. Terrifying thoughts flowed through his head: *I can't breathe. I'm going to die.* Everything after that: darkness. Just darkness.

FIFTEEN

At nine o'clock Owen Westonby and Jez Pollock dropped by Kit's house to find out if he'd uncovered the pod's secret. Kit lived here with his mother at the end of a dirt track on the edge of the village. Owen always felt a twinge of sadness when he visited Kit. The house, which had once been part of a farm, had seen better days. Its wooden window frames had rotted. The garage roof had collapsed. Owen knew that Kit made running repairs, but Mrs Bolter often complained of the noise if he used a hammer or power drill, and she made him stop work.

Kit's mother was antisocial, and that was putting it mildly. When she'd too much booze inside of her she'd subject visitors to vicious rants about whatever happened to be preoccupying her at the time. Normally, Kit's friends avoided the Bolter house. However, Kit had sent Owen a text: *Pod progress:-) Call in. Mother asleep.*

Jez spoke in a low voice as they picked their

65

way through the gloom. 'I bet Kit's counting the days until he goes to university, then he'll be able to get away from this dump.'

'I don't suppose Mrs Bolter likes living in squalor, either.'

'You always see the best in people, don't you?' Jez had to lift the broken garden gate in order to open it. 'Mrs Bolter likes living inside a whisky bottle. Get my meaning? She chose to wind up like this.'

Owen opened his mouth to disagree; however, he saw Kit at the door, so he kept silent. He didn't want Kit to know that they'd been discussing his mother.

Instead, Owen hooted, 'The mad scientist. Found out what Mr Pod is yet?'

'Shush. My mother's in bed.'

'Are you sure you want us here?'

Kit stood back to let them in. 'Usually a bomb wouldn't wake her, but best not make too much noise. I'll only get an earful if she knows you've been round.'

Both Owen and Jez pretended to zip their mouths shut. Kit smiled, though Owen noticed his manner seemed odd, as if his friend had something on his mind.

'Go through to the back room.' Kit pointed to a door along the passageway.

Soon they found themselves in a parlour that had been crowded with mismatched furniture. Again, Owen felt that keen twinge of sadness. The hand-me-down sofa, chairs and table signalled that not everyone led a problem-free life. He didn't believe for one moment that Mrs Bolter was a bad person – even at sixteen he realized that given enough personal setbacks and broken dreams anyone could find themselves down on their luck like this.

Kit indicated the sofa. 'Grab a seat.'

Owen and Jez sat down.

'So, what you got for us, Kit?' Jez nodded at the metal pod that sat on the floor beneath the TV.

'It's a camera,' Kit announced.

'Is that all?' Owen felt disappointed.

'Not just any camera.' Kit knelt down beside the pod. 'I've dismantled it and found a movement sensor; you know the sort, you get them in security lights. They trigger the light when something moves in front of them.'

'So, a security camera?'

'Nope. A wildlife camera. That's why you found this baby out in the forest. The pod got smashed up, the housing's vanished completely, but this was designed to film whatever triggered the sensor.'

'I really expected it to be a missile that'd dropped off a fighter.' Jez groaned with disappointment. 'Something interesting.'

'This is interesting ... very interesting.' Kit smiled as if ready to spring an exciting surprise. 'You should see what's been filmed by the camera.'

'A manky squirrel?' suggested Jez.

'A one-legged dormouse,' added Owen.

'Better than that. In fact, something you'd never guess in a million years.'

Jez became interested again. 'Naked people

67

getting rumpy-pumpy in the woods?'

'Just you wait and see. All I have to do is connect the cable to the television; then I use this chopstick to press a tiny play-button inside the pod.'

Owen and Jez stared hopefully at the blank television screen.

Jez grinned. 'I bet it's people. Stark naked.'

'You've got a dirty mind,' Kit told him. 'In fact, it's a lot more interesting than bare flesh.'

Kit poked the chopstick into the pod's casing. He poked again.

Jez slapped the arm of the sofa. 'C'mon, Kit. This suspense is killing me.'

Kit grunted. 'Battery's flat.'

'What?'

'No power.'

'You mean, you can't show us what's been recorded by the camera?'

'I'm going home.' Jez stood up.

Kit disconnected the lead from the pod. 'The battery's been damaged. For some reason it discharges even when the camera's switched off. It'll only take me twenty minutes to put some juice back into it.'

'This secret film better be worth the wait,' grumbled Jez.

'It is, guys. Believe me: it most definitely is. You're not going to believe your eyes.'

SIXTEEN

'Tom, you said it couldn't hurt me ... well, it went and hurt you.'

Tom Westonby looked up at the beautiful woman who spoke to him. The dark skin contrasted so strikingly with the blue eyes.

'Tom, can you understand what I'm telling you?'

He nodded. A ferocious ache in his neck made him flinch.

'Do you remember? You said the man wouldn't do anything to us if we kept walking. You were so wrong. He knocked you clean across the path. After that, he pushed your face into the river and half-drowned you. If I hadn't been there you'd be dead now.'

Tom rubbed his aching head. His hair was damp. A towel lay on the arm of the chair. Had she dried his hair? Evidently so. He saw half a cup of coffee on the table beside him, and though he could taste coffee on his lips he didn't remember drinking any.

'Nearly drowned?' he echoed as her words sank in. 'Were you hurt?'

'I'm fine. But I had to yell and fight the guy who tried to murder you. Finally, I got him to scoot.'

'Bravo.' OK, maybe not the perfect response. This groggy feeling made thinking difficult. He tried again. 'Thanks. You saved my life.'

'The cottage was closer than my car, so I decided to get you back here.'

He groaned as he sat up straight in the armchair. This felt like the meanest of hangovers.

'Try not to move. You've been unconscious for the last ten minutes.'

'Did you get a clear look at who attacked me?'

June Valko shook her head. 'When he pounced, the torch went flying away into the bushes. I decided to fight the monster off before getting the light back, so I'm afraid I won't be able to give the police a description. It was too dark to see much.'

'Monster? You said monster?'

'Figure of speech. Monster, psycho, weirdo, nut-job. He must be one of those to just dive on you like that. He didn't say anything, but I could tell he'd gone totally berserk.'

'He didn't try and attack you?'

She gave a grim smile. 'No, it was your blood he wanted.'

'Thank God you know how to fight.'

'Or shout. It was only when I yelled that he stopped trying to drown you and ... *ffft*. He vanished back into the trees.'

When he coughed he could taste the river. He must have swallowed a bellyful. June watched his face closely. He could tell that she was worried about him.

'Don't worry. I'll live,' he told her. 'What time is it?'

'Half past nine.'

Tom noticed that she'd piled logs into the huge fireplace. They blazed up the throat of the chimney so powerfully that they filled the room with a golden light as well as warmth.

'Here.' She handed him the coffee. 'I found some brandy; that's gone in with three spoons of sugar.'

The coffee tasted syrupy sweet. Immediately, the brandy shot fire through his veins. 'Phew. Now that's what I call medicine.'

Just as he finished speaking there was a tremendous crash of breaking glass.

'Damn,' she hissed, 'he's come back again.'

'*Again?*' Tom lurched to his feet. 'You mean that guy's tried breaking in here?'

'When you were passed out in the chair he was doing his best to smash down the front door. Now he's gone round the back.'

June sped towards the kitchen, Tom followed. Even before they made it through the kitchen door the lights suddenly died. Some of the firelight filtered through the doorway, however. In the gloom, he made out the back door. Set in the door itself were glass panels. One had been smashed. A pale hand reached through the broken pane, trying to reach the key in the lock. Whipping the key out, she threw it to Tom. She began dragging a stout timber dresser towards the door. Plates trembled on the shelves of the dresser, and then one after another they began to topple. To the sound of smashing crocks, Tom helped June shove the dresser against the door to act as a barricade.

On the other side of the kitchen window a face loomed from the darkness. Soon that pale oval was just inches from the glass. Tom quickly dragged down the blind.

She spun round to Tom. 'Who's out there?'

Instead of answering, he shoved the heavy kitchen table across the floor, adding its weight to the dresser.

'Why are they trying to kill you?' she demanded

'They never tried this before. It's got to be something to do with you.'

'ME!' Her reaction was one of total shock. 'What has you being attacked got to do with me?'

'I wish I knew.'

'Tom, who's out there?'

Once again he didn't answer. This time because the sound of pounding came from the other room. Tom ran back into the lounge. The timber door shook as fists pounded on it from the other side. Thankfully, June had remembered to turn the key in the lock. Even so, he didn't waste any time sliding across a pair of thick iron bolts.

'Keep an eye on the door in the kitchen,' he told her. 'There's a chance he might be able to break through.'

'What about the windows?'

'They've all got bars over them.'

'Even upstairs?'

'This place is built like a fortress.'

Once more he went from window to window, pulling down blinds and drawing curtains, sealing them from prying eyes.

Meanwhile, June's eyes flashed with fear. 'Why don't you want them looking in?'

'It's not just that. I don't want you seeing them.'

'Why?'

'Because I want to keep your reason intact. We're going to have to rely on our wits tonight if we're going to survive.'

'Riddles ... riddles! Why don't you give me plain, straightforward answers?'

'Because there are no plain, straightforward answers. You've landed in the middle of the mother and father of all mysteries.' He added more wood to the fire in order to provide light rather than heat. 'You've stepped across a threshold where the real world can be turned upside down and inside out. A place where death doesn't mean the dead stop moving.'

'Now you really are starting to frighten me.' She backed off until she reached the wall. 'Are you insane?'

'I wouldn't be as terrified as I am now if I was.'

Another crash filled the lounge as a heavy object struck the door. A second crash came from the kitchen.

'Now there are two of them,' he told her. 'More will be here soon.'

'What should we do?'

'Prepare for a siege. Whatever happens we can't let them get in.'

June swallowed. 'Did I tell you that I'm too young to die?'

He admired her ability to make a joke in the face of being surrounded by ... OK, use her word: MONSTERS. The house had been surrounded by monsters, they were under siege, and he didn't know whether they'd make it until morning. Within a few hours, they might be dead ... or worse than dead. Much, *much* worse than dead.

SEVENTEEN

Tom Westonby had almost been drowned an hour ago. He'd been attacked as he'd walked June Valko back to the car. Right now, he assessed the situation – and the danger they faced.

As he lit candles dotted about the room, he ran through the facts. 'So we're under siege here.'

June shuddered. 'At least this place has got thick walls and bars over the windows.'

'The downside is they seem to have cut the power. We'll keep a big fire going – it kicks out plenty of light. We've food and drink, of course. And as soon as it's daylight I'll get you out of here.'

June sounded puzzled, 'How can you be sure that these siege guys will leave when it's light?'

'At least I do know that much.'

'So you know who they are?'

'Yes.'

Once more she appeared baffled. 'Then why

74

won't you tell me who's out there?'

'I was going to explain when we met up again.'

'Tell me now.'

'OK. They're vampires.'

'Pardon?'

'There's no subtle way to tell you. All I can do is hit you with the brutal truth. The man that attacked me is a vampire. The people who have put us under siege are vampires.'

Those blue eyes of hers gave the front door a sideways glance. He knew she was calculating her chances of making a dash for the door in order to escape from Tom – a man she clearly had decided was a lunatic.

'Don't even consider trying to escape,' he told her bluntly. 'You wouldn't last two minutes out there.'

'Vampires ... you said vampires. That's...' her voice dried for a moment. 'Unusual.'

'You don't believe in vampires?'

'Does anyone outside a psychiatric ward?'

'I didn't believe in vampires once. I do now.'

'Tom. I'd like to phone the police. Will you let me do that?' She eased the phone from her jacket pocket.

'My plan was to explain everything methodically.' Something rustled against the other side of the front door. 'But as you know only too well circumstances have changed. You need to hear the truth, and quickly, because the truth might save you.'

'OK.' Her finger got ready to hit some phone numbers.

'Don't do that.'

'The police will put an end to this. They'll arrest those guys out there.'

'No, *those guys out there* will attack the police. You'll have the blood of innocent police officers on your hands.'

'I'm sure they can handle all kinds of trouble, Tom.'

'Even the police can't defeat vampires.'

'There's no such thing as vampires, Tom.'

A thud against the door made her flinch.

He said, 'Now's not the time to give you the full Bekk family history, or how and why the family is cursed. But this is the condensed version: the ancestors of the Bekks were Viking invaders. They came to England from Denmark over a thousand years ago.'

'Is that so?' She was clearly humouring him.

He added wood to the fire, which blazed in that vast cavern of a fireplace. 'The Bekk ancestors made a pact with the Viking gods. The gods would protect them, providing they stayed loyal to the pagan faith. Consequently, the Bekks were protected from hostile Englishmen by a monster that the Viking gods made out of dead bodies.'

'Why are you trying to frighten me?'

'I'm not trying to scare you. I'm giving you information that will improve your chances of survival. Forewarned is forearmed. Do you understand?'

'I really am scared now.'

'Listen. Although the Bekks were protected, they were also cursed. If one of them moved away from the valley for long enough, or married someone who didn't worship Viking gods, then that person gradually turned into a vampire.'

She shot Tom a startled glance.

'That's right,' he told her. 'If any Bekk man or woman shunned their family heritage they were transformed into something that wasn't human.'

'No.'

'So can you work out what I'm suggesting?'

'No. Stop it.'

'Your father moved away from this valley and married your mother. Then he went missing after coming back here.'

'You're insane.'

'That means he's probably outside right now. He's one of those things laying siege to the house. Your father is a vampire.'

June began punching numbers into the phone at frantic speed. Tom launched himself at her and snatched away the phone. She fought back, her eyes blazing with sheer ferocity. With all her strength she tried to throw him off balance.

'You liar!' she screamed. 'I should have let him kill you!'

Although he didn't want to hurt her, he gripped her wrists tightly to prevent her from attacking him.

Both suddenly froze. They'd heard the sound of something sliding over a hard surface followed by a crash. Straight away, the sound was repeated.

'Those are tiles being broken,' he hissed. 'They're on the roof.'

'Whoever they are, they aren't vampires ...

they're not ... they can't be.'

'They are vampires. One of them is likely to be your father. What's more, it was almost certainly your father who attacked me by the river. Until tonight the vampires never even approached me. You see, June, your father misunderstood when I grabbed hold of your hand. He thought I was attacking you.'

Her eyes fixed on his face. Yes, there was horror there. He saw hope, too. The woman had begun to believe that she might have found her missing father.

Before he could speak again, he heard another sliding sound. Only this time it seemed to come from inside the house. He turned round just in time to see something plunge down the throat of the chimney and into the fire. A pair of bare feet crashed into the burning logs, sending up a shower of sparks. Both he and June stared in shock. For there, in that pyramid of flame, crouched a figure.

The man remained crouching there, staring out of that vast hearth at them. His eyes were completely white ... no sign whatsoever of a coloured iris ... instead a fierce black pupil in each eye fixed on them. Oblivious to the searing heat, he stayed there, bathed in flame.

She gasped. 'Tom? Is that my father? Jacob Bekk? Is that him?'

'I don't know.'

'Why doesn't he come out of the fire? It must be killing him.' She held out her hands, ready to help him step out of the murderous heat.

'June! Stay back!'

'He's burning!' she cried. 'My God! He's burning!'

The ragged clothes the creature wore ignited. Even his skin seemed to catch light. Yet still he crouched there. Not moving. Not making a sound. All he did was stare into her face.

Then he moved. For a terrifying moment Tom thought he'd attack them. But with the speed of a cat, the vampire climbed back up the chimney, his hands and feet scratching and scraping the stonework as he went.

Tom opened the window blind. The vampire hit the dirt outside the house with a thud. Sparks flew. The vampire burned brightly. Even so, he didn't give any sign of being in pain. Instead, he raced away into the night. As he ran, he resembled a fiery comet that flew just above the ground. June stood beside Tom, watching the fireball race through the trees until it dwindled to a spark of light that grew smaller and smaller before vanishing completely.

'Was that my father?' June's eyes swam with tears. 'Was it him?' Trembling, she sat down on the sofa – there she spoke the words that shocked Tom to the core: 'If it is him, how do I find him again? *And how can I take him back to my mother?*'

EIGHTEEN

At the same moment that Tom Westonby and June Valko watched the fireball dwindle as it raced away into the darkness, Owen Westonby had to remind himself why he sat there in Kit's house. Kit had told Owen and Jez that the mysterious pod was an automatic camera. But waiting for the battery to be charged so they could find out what the device had filmed had become a kind of torture. As Jez neatly put it, 'This waiting around is boring the bones out of my arse.' For a while, they'd amused themselves by throwing to one another a dried-up orange that Owen had found on the floor behind the sofa. But that soon lost its entertainment value.

'That's it.' Jez headed for the door. 'I'm not waiting for Kit any longer. I'm going home.'

Before he reached the door, however, Kit appeared. 'I need to be quick. The battery's been damaged; keeps losing its juice.'

'It better be worth it,' Jez grunted. 'The last bus goes in twenty minutes.'

'This'll only take two...' Kit plugged the lead from the pod into the TV. 'Trust me, what you'll see is worth it.' As he'd done before he used a chopstick to activate the mechanism inside the damaged cylinder. 'Here goes.' Kit sounded excited. 'We have lift-off.'

The TV screen flashed from black to blue. Following that, an image of trees appeared with the river flowing in the background. At the bottom of the screen a clock recorded the time and date.

'Why's the picture weird?' Jez wasn't convinced that this would be worth his time.

'The camera had been set up to operate automatically at night when an animal triggered the sensor. The image looks odd, because the camera's on a night setting. It's using infrared as a light source, so it's basically a flat, black and white image. If there's any light at all, it's exaggerated to the point where it becomes a brilliant glare.' Kit talked like an enthusiastic teacher presenting a fascinating science experiment. 'See the flashes on the river? That's moonlight being reflected in the water.'

Owen studied the TV screen. 'So every time an animal comes in range it sets the camera running?'

'Yup.' Kit pointed at the bottom right-hand corner of the screen. 'You can just make out a fox there. Notice the high angle. Someone must have fixed the camera to a tree trunk at about head height.'

The fox glanced in the direction of the camera. Infrared mode made it look as if electric lights had replaced its natural eyes. An effect of the moonlight being reflected from the animal's eyes, of course. The fox paused to scratch its ear with a back leg then scuttled off. More shots followed. They captured glimpses of creatures that made the forest their home. A pair of badgers rooted through fallen leaves. A boar trundled past, snorting loudly. After that, shots of roe deer, a water vole, more foxes, and a stag heading down the river bank to take a drink. Each creature possessed those unnaturally bright electric light bulb eyes as a result of the night setting on the camera exaggerating the natural moonlight.

'Maa ... annn...' groaned Jez. 'I live in the countryside. I see animals like this every day.'

'Wait.'

'I've had enough, I'm going home.'

'Any second now.' Kit's eyes fixed on the television, completely absorbed by the images.

The screen blinked as the camera cycled through to the next shot. At first nothing appeared other than the black and white view of trees and the river. Owen heard something, however. Crunching. Rustling. The sound of a large animal shouldering its way through the trees. The sound grew louder, then a loud crunch: wood snapping. After that, an altogether more mysterious sound came from the TV.

'Is that whispering?' Jez took a close interest now. 'Can you hear whispering?'

Kit nodded. 'Lots of people whispering, that's what I thought, too.'

The sounds grew even louder. A tree creaked as some hugely powerful force pushed it aside. And yet Owen still didn't see what caused the sounds. Not for another five seconds, that is. Suddenly the camera shook. The tree to which it was fixed must have been subjected to a violent shaking.

After that, it arrived. A huge, humpbacked silhouette. If the camera had been placed at head height then this creature, whatever it was, must stand higher than a human being. The whispering intensified. As if a dozen people whispered furiously amongst themselves. Apart from the black silhouette, the body that passed in front of the camera was featureless. That is until pairs of bright lights sprang from it. For all the world, it looked as if bright light bulbs had been embedded in the beast.

'Tell me if I'm wrong,' Kit said quite calmly and slowly, 'but am I right in thinking those are eyes? Lots and lots of eyes.'

NINETEEN

Calm after the storm...

That's how this time felt to Tom Westonby. Earlier that night a figure had climbed down the chimney and had remained in the fireplace as if the flames were no more harmful than warm bathwater. After staring into the face of June Valko the creature had scrambled up the chimney again. Now here they were, in the calm after that extraordinary event – that is to say, an extraordinarily disturbing and frightening event.

The fire still burned brightly, filling the living room with light. June sat on the sofa, a mug of coffee in her hands. The woman gazed thought-fully at the burning logs in the fireplace, no doubt still haunted by what she'd experienced tonight. Tom occupied an old leather armchair. An outsider might have thought Tom and June were relaxing there – a contented couple, sleepy and ready for bed. Tom knew they were anything but sleepy. Yes, they were emotionally and physically exhausted. However, neither would allow themselves to fall asleep tonight. Too much had happened. June must be in turmoil – her world had been turned upside down.

In a low whisper she asked, 'Will he be dead? Because he was there in the fire, wasn't he? The man ... the thing ... that you said was my father.' Her expression suggested she was mentally replaying what she'd witnessed earlier. 'A man wouldn't be able to stand in all those flames and not be hurt, would he?'

'The heat wouldn't have caused much damage. After all, he's no longer human.'

'You used the word "vampire".'

'To be more accurate, vampire-like. Those things out there don't run away from crucifixes or garlic, their reflections can be seen in mirrors. But they do avoid daylight, and they do use blood. I say "use", because I don't believe they ingest food like any other—'

'Of God's creatures?'

He nodded.

June gazed at where those bare feet had slammed down into the fire. 'What if he comes back? What then?'

'My feeling is that your father ... if that was

your father ... needed confirmation of what he saw out there in the forest before he tried to drown me.'

'You mean he wanted to take a second look? To make sure it was me?'

Tom nodded again. 'Did you recognize him?'

'Not with all those flames rushing up over his face. Besides, I've never actually met him. He'd gone before I was even born. All I've got are photographs.'

'Did you have at least an impression that it might be your father?'

June gave a shudder that went down to the roots of her bones. 'His eyes ... my God ... I might have recognized those, because they're as blue as mine in the photos. But his eyes were white, completely white, apart from the pupil.' Her chest heaved as if she were close to having a panic attack. 'I've never seen anything as terrifying.'

In an attempt to appear reassuring, he said, 'I'll check the windows are secure. We don't want any more of those things trying to get in.'

'Vampires,' she said with feeling. 'Don't be shy about calling them vampires. We need certainty about what we're dealing with here.'

'So you believe what I told you?'

'Yes, I do.' She gave a faint smile. 'Now go and check the windows. I'll feel better if I know that those *vampires* aren't creeping into the bedrooms.'

Tom Westonby soon confirmed that everything was secure. He took a peek out through the blinds – all he could see were trees.

When he returned to the lounge June Valko asked bluntly, 'How long have you known that there are vampires in this forest?'

'Five years.'

'You said they've never bothered you before?'

'Frankly, they always struck me as being ineffectual ... in fact, completely harmless. If I caught a glimpse of them they simply stood there without moving. Like bizarre statues.'

'If they never attacked you before, what's changed?'

'As I said, the answer is simple. It's because of you.'

'Why?'

'Those things out there were once members of the Bekk family. As far as I know, you're now the only person alive ... genuinely alive, that is, not a vampire ... who is a living descendent of the Bekk bloodline.'

'I live over a hundred miles away in Manchester. You said that any Bekk who left this valley would become a vampire. Why am I not a vampire?'

'You were born in a different part of the country. Maybe that changed your biology to prevent the transformation.'

'But I have Bekk blood in my veins. Viking blood?'

He shrugged. 'To be honest, I don't know what rules apply to the transformation. What governs those vampires out in the forest aren't natural laws. As far as I'm concerned, they're walking mysteries, wrapped up in even more mysteries.'

'Is this what happened to your wife? Did

Nicola Bekk change?'

He couldn't even bring himself to say 'yes', the memory of seeing the blue fade out of her eyes still hurt with such a furious intensity. A lump formed in his throat. After a moment he managed to nod. 'Then she was taken away.' He took a deep breath. 'It was the night the village was flooded. He took her.' He nodded at a slab of rock set into the wall.

'He?'

'Helsvir.'

She followed the direction of his gaze. When she saw the slab with its carving of a strange creature she looked dumbfounded. 'How could that take your wife?'

'That's Helsvir, guardian of the Bekk family.'

She went to examine the image, and ran her finger over the legs etched into the stone. 'You're telling me this monster is real?'

'Monster? The Bekk family referred to it as a dragon.'

'Dragons *and* vampires.'

'Fortunately, there's only one Helsvir.'

'Being attacked by vampires is bad enough. Being attacked by a dragon might be more than I can handle in one night.' She tried to smile but she was clearly afraid.

'I'm sure Helsvir is never coming back.'

'Then I only have to be terrified of vampires.'

'Something tells me you don't have to be worried about being attacked. The vampires will protect you. You've Bekk blood in your veins. I'm sure that was your father in the forest. Like I said, he probably thought I was hurting you;

that's why he attacked me. And earlier, when he climbed down the chimney, he wanted to check that I hadn't imprisoned you here. Even though he might not be human, he's still a Dad hell-bent on protecting his daughter.'

'You can't really be sure about that. How does he know I'm his daughter?'

'The vampires will know alright.' Tom spoke with conviction. 'Imagine these stone walls are as transparent as glass. Now imagine that you are a brilliant, blazing light. Picture your body firing off enormous flashes that can be seen for miles around.' He looked her in the eye. 'That's how the vampires see you. Especially your father. I'm certain of it. You, June, are a huge, brilliant light shining in the darkness. That's why the vampires came rushing to the house. Your presence here is a siren and beacon rolled into one. The vampires now know that the last living Bekk has come back to them.'

'But I haven't come back to them, have I? I came to find my father.'

'And now they've found you.'

'Don't, that's scary.'

'What's more, you've changed the dynamic. By coming here you've made them behave differently. For the first time they've become aggressive...' He rubbed his aching neck. 'Violent.'

'The change might be temporary?'

Tom shook his head. 'Your arrival here is as dramatic as this house being struck by lightning. Things are going to happen. And we're going to have to be ready when they do.'

TWENTY

While Tom and June talked through the night in the depths of the forest, Kit Bolter lay in bed four miles away, staring up into the darkness. Earlier, Jez and Owen had watched the footage captured by the automatic camera. The device must belong to a wildlife enthusiast, he decided, or one of the countryside rangers. Both Jez and Owen had left to catch the bus, talking about what the footage had revealed.

Kit lay there, turning those images over in his mind. The automatic camera had been triggered by the arrival of a huge creature. Surely it had been bigger than a horse. Much bulkier, too. Almost a whale-shaped thing that bulldozed through the forest, shoving aside trees, snapping branches. Probably the creature had dislodged the camera, and that's how it came to be damaged. After all, there'd been no more footage of other animals after the arrival of the behemoth. But what was that thing? All they'd been able to make out was the hulking great silhouette. The infrared shooting mode of the camera had picked out glistening spots of light on its flanks. They had resembled eyes – though that had to be some optical illusion, surely?

Kit decided to visit the place where Owen had

found the camera. This warranted closer investigation; perhaps take casts of footprints, and check for animal fur caught in branches. Heck, even search for its droppings. He grinned. 'They will be the size of elephant poo.'

This would be terrific practice for a career in forensics. If he found some unknown animal roaming the woods it would look great on job applications. *Kit Bolter, the amazing monster finder.* He chuckled.

'What's so funny?'

The voice startled him so much he nearly jumped clean out of bed. 'How long have you been there?'

His mother switched on the light. One eye was so bloodshot it had turned crimson. 'I needed the bathroom. I noticed you were lying there awake.'

'I'm just thinking about things.'

'Were you thinking about what I told you earlier? That Tom Westonby murdered your uncle?'

He remembered only too clearly what she'd told him. 'There's no proof Tom did anything.'

'Oh? Proof? Is it that you're needing? You want to be one of those forensic scientists, don't you? So why don't you find proof that Westonby is a murderer?'

'His brother's my best friend.'

'Then you best be careful, son. Watch out that Tom Westonby doesn't try and do away with you.'

He sat up in bed, his scalp prickling as he shivered. 'Why did you say that?'

'Because he's got a taste for killing. He didn't just kill your uncle. There are rumours he murdered his girlfriend, too. It all happened when the village got flooded way-back-when ... He was with Nicola Bekk when she vanished. Nobody's ever seen her since.' She fixed that crimson eye on him. 'People who are near Tom Westonby wind up either dead or missing. That's why you've got to watch out that he doesn't do the same to you.'

With that, his mother switched off the light, leaving him alone in the dark.

TWENTY-ONE

The night seemed endless. Every so often Tom left his armchair to patrol the house, just to make sure that the vampire siege had been lifted. The sure way to find out would be to unlock the door and step outside. That would be reckless beyond belief, of course. If they were still out there, he'd either be killed, or he'd become a vampire himself. Doomed to haunt the forest for ever.

With the power out and no electric light, he lit his way using a candle, feeling like a character out of a Charles Dickens novel. *Tom Westonby: the Hermit of Skanderberg House' – now there's a title for a twisted little horror story*, he thought with a splash of tomb-dark humour. *If I'm the hero of the story, then June Valko must be the heroine. She has the right characteristics – a beautiful, exotic woman in search of her father, because she hopes to cure her mother's broken heart. All it takes to do that is for June to reunite her mother with her father. The problem is that her father has been transformed into a vampire. Bundling a bloodsucking monster into a car and driving him to visit June's mother is going to be a humdinger of a job.* He laughed softly as he headed towards the kitchen.

'Are you going to share the joke?'

He glanced back at June on the sofa.

'I'm sorry.' He smiled. 'Maybe a mixture of sleep deprivation and shock.'

'Could be low blood sugar. I'll make you something to eat.'

Although he wasn't hungry he thanked her, and said something about finding cold roast chicken and salad in the fridge. June followed him into the kitchen to conjure up a tasty snack out of leftovers. With it being quiet outside he sensed that the danger had passed for now. Taking a brush from the larder, he swept up the glass from the broken door pane.

June buttered the bread. 'You've told me about vampires and the other creature.'

'Helsvir.'

'But there must be more I need to know.'

'Lots more.'

'Then you'll come to the hotel in Leppington, so we can talk?'

'You plan on sticking round? After all this? Seeing me almost get drowned? A vampire coming down the chimney?'

'What do you think?'

'I thought you'd get out of this valley and never come back.'

'If you think I'm quitting now...' she ripped the chicken apart with her bare hands '...then you don't know me.'

'I'm starting to. After all, most people would have run like hell when that thing attacked me in the wood. You stayed and fought.'

'And I plan to stay here and keep fighting until I get what I need.'

'And what's that?'

She looked him in the eye. 'You must have guessed.'

'You actually want to meet up face-to-face with your father?'

'Yes. I'm going to talk to him.'

'You don't know what kind of monster he's become. He might not want to attack you, but his instincts might override what's left of his human mind. That thing could rip you apart, just like you've done with that chicken.'

'That *thing* is my father.'

'For the want of a better description that *thing* is a *vampire*. And as such will be unpredictable and therefore dangerous.' Tom did not raise his voice: he simply wanted her to understand.

June spoke with calm certainty. 'For the sake of my mother, I'm staying. I'm going to learn whatever I can about my father and what he's become. Then I will do whatever it takes. After all, although this might sound melodramatic, it is a matter of life and death.'

'But I don't understand how you can use your

father to ... what? Snap your mother out of her depression? How will you bring them together?'

'I don't know.' Her eyes glittered with tears. 'But I'm going to find a way. I have to. I won't stand by and do nothing while she fades away. I won't let her die without a fight, Tom, I won't.'

Three o'clock in the morning came and went. They ate the chicken salad in silence. Tom realized that this petite woman had a backbone of steel. When the vampire had tried to drown him she'd fought it off and saved his life. Though in truth, her fists would not have driven the creature away – it could easily have killed them both – rather the vampire had somehow understood that the woman was its child, and had simply left to avoid harming her, either accidentally, or if its monstrous nature took over and it couldn't stop itself seeing her as prey.

Later, the clock chimed four. Everything appeared quiet outside. Tom kept the fire blazing. Although whether the flames would deter another visitor using that particular mode of entrance had to be doubtful.

Five o'clock. He showed June photographs of Nicola Bekk, told her that they'd married in an unconventional ceremony. Then he sat alone for a while in the kitchen, wondering if Nicola would ever return to him as June's father had returned to her.

Six o'clock. 'Light in just over an hour,' he told June as he handed her another mug of coffee.

To be certain of their safety, he waited until it

94

was fully daylight. Red sunlight glowed against the treetops when he finally unlocked the front door. After that, they walked quickly along the woodland path. Even though they hurried, it took fifteen minutes to reach the main road where June had parked the hire car. Tom had often wondered whether he could create a track through the forest that would allow him to drive a car right up to his house. After what happened last night the benefits of getting vehicles to and from Skanderberg were screamingly obvious. However, that wilderness would be difficult to tame. He'd be forced to cut down dozens of trees and dynamite outcrops of rock.

When they reached the car June said, 'That was quite some night, wasn't it?'

'Memorable.' He shot her a tired smile. 'Definitely memorable.'

'So we're going to meet up at the Station Hotel in Leppington?'

'Sure.'

'This afternoon?'

'I've got a diving job this afternoon.'

'A diving job?'

'I make my living as a diver.'

'Oh.'

'I can make it over to Leppington tomorrow.'

'Shall we say three o'clock, then? In the hotel bar?'

'Three it is,' he said.

'After what happened, will you leave the house and find somewhere else?'

'No. I have to stay there.' He shrugged. 'Call it my destiny.'

June seemed to understand that he had important reasons to remain at Skanderberg, because she nodded. 'Tom, keep safe. Goodbye.'

A moment later, the car headed away along the narrow road.

For five years Tom had lived the solitary existence of a hermit. Life had been passing him by. Now he felt he'd finally woken up after all these years. He'd rejoined the flow of life.

'And this is the start of something big,' he murmured to himself. 'Lives are going to change for ever.' Then he shivered, as if he'd just caught a glimpse of a gravestone with his own name written on it.

TWENTY-TWO

Saturday morning began bright and cold. Kit Bolter made his mother's breakfast and took it up to her on a tray. He noticed she'd worn the yellow cardigan for bed.

'Don't look at my hair.' She sounded drowsy. ''S a mess. I'm going to get it cut off.'

'I've opened the marmalade that Mrs Kenyon made. You said it was your favourite.'

'You treat women well. Which means you're nothing like your father. Uh, my head.'

'Do you want me to get you a painkiller?'

She waved his offer away. 'It'll pass. What're your plans today?'

'I need to buy some food for the weekend. This afternoon I thought I'd go for a walk up the valley.'

'I don't see any harm in that. Thanks for the breakfast, son.'

Kit returned to his bedroom where he ran the footage that had been recorded on the automatic camera. He'd watched it for the first time yesterday evening, then saw it again in the company of Owen and Jez. Once more he watched the bulky creature with what appeared to be dozens of eyes studding its body. Now that was one weird animal. Fascinating, too. He longed to find out what it was. Although logic suggested that he must be seeing a stag, perhaps, or an escaped cow, and the odd sparkling points of light on its flanks were just an effect of the camera's infrared setting. Kit also wondered when he should hand the camera over to the police. Perhaps give it until after the weekend? That way he'd have more time to search the area where the camera had been discovered.

Owen Westonby had been interested in finding out about the animal, too, so Kit decided to ask Owen to come along. He'd have liked Jez to join them, but at weekends Jez worked on his parents' farm. Somehow Kit always felt more at ease when the three amigos were together – him, Owen and Jez. They'd been friends since they were tiny kids at school. Even now they were sixteen they still stuck together, which brought comments from people like, 'Here they come, the Three Musketeers.' Or 'I've heard of Siamese twins, never Siamese triplets. These three must be joined at the hip. You never see them apart.' Yeah, exaggerations of course, all for the benefit of a joke. Because as they grew older they did spend more time leading their own lives. In a year or so, the three amigos would go their separate ways. He knew they'd email, text and talk to one another via webcams from whatever part of the country they found themselves in. But eventually they'd lose touch. The old friendship would inevitably fade.

Sadness crept over him. He hated the idea of no longer being friends with Owen and Jez, so he decided to make the most of their time together now.

He grabbed his phone and called Owen. 'You out of bed yet? No? My mother always told me I'd get brain worms if I stayed in bed too long. She said the worms lived in pillows and they'd migrate through my ear if I slept for too long.' After Owen had finished laughing Kit said, 'Hey, listen. Are you doing anything this afternoon? No? Great.' Kit grinned. 'I thought the two of us could go on a monster hunt!'

TWENTY-THREE

'A monster hunt?' Owen smiled. 'Yeah, why not? Anything to kill the boredom.' He recalled what he'd seen last night over at Kit's. The automatic camera had caught shots of wildlife found in a typical Yorkshire forest: deer, foxes, unremarkable stuff like that. Then they'd seen the big bugger. The elephant-sized beast. Then again, he knew full well that it might have been a much smaller animal that had got in close to the camera, making it *seem* gigantic.

Owen decided to browse some websites. No harm in finding out what kind of animals did hang out in the woods. Besides, if he appeared to be busy with homework, his parents wouldn't ask him to join them on the supermarket trip. He switched on the tablet, checked his emails (nothing but junk, damn it), and then he typed 'Danby-Mask wildlife' into a search engine. The word *wildlife* brought up some sex websites. Tempting, but he decided to focus on four-legged wild animals.

What struck him straight away was that his search took him to crypto-zoology websites that were devoted to mythical creatures, such as the Loch Ness Monster, Knuckers, Yeti and Bigfoot. Owen knew that paranormal enthusiasts regu-

99

larly tried to get in touch with his brother. Owen had grown up hearing about reporters, TV crews, ghost hunters and the like turning up at Tom's door. But Owen had been just a kid then, so the appearance of inquisitive strangers had largely gone over his head.

Now here were websites with names like Swabs Always Taken that obsessively recorded sightings of strange creatures. Owen immediately began to wonder about the footage he'd seen last night of the big, if indistinct, animal. He went through website after website. When his father tapped on the door he was so deeply immersed that Dad just held up a finger, mouthed 'Going shopping', then left again.

What struck Owen so powerfully was that his brother Tom was at the centre of so many rumours. Even though he never talked to investigators, all the stories returned to him. Tom was like a suspect caught with the smoking gun, but there was no body. In this case, no monster. There were photographs of Tom in his diving gear as he undertook salvage work in Whitby harbour, or buying potatoes at the village farm store. *Hell, it's like they kept Tom under surveillance. Did these people think that they'd catch Tom talking to monsters?* The thought had been a flippant one, yet Owen became angry. Strangers had hounded Tom. They'd followed him, stared at him, photographed him, speculated about him on websites and repeated stupid rumours. *That can't be right*, thought Owen. *There should be laws against that kind of harassment. No wonder Tom looks so haunted.*

Owen clicked on to another site called Hidden Realms, Secret Beasts. This time he saw that one of the monster hunters had made a video. He touched the 'play' icon.

He saw footage of St George's Church in Danby-Mask. A title appeared on-screen: SEARCH FOR THE DRAGON. Straight after that a confident female voice began speaking: *'Rumours have circulated for centuries in this remote valley that something lurks in its forest and its river. In a letter dated the tenth of September, 1654, Bishop Leonard of Sheffield writes: "Hereabouts in the parish of St George there are tales of a dragon. The creature prowls forest lands by night. Its hide is so thick that it is impervious to sword and musket shot. People are forewarned of its approach by the sound of its whispering. Old men and women have revealed under sacred oath that the dragon has troubled this valley for a score of centuries, and that it is born of pagan magic. Moreover, the creature does not consist of a single physical body, but is a mingling of much flesh from different sources." Sightings of the so-called dragon have been recorded in almost every century since the Dark Ages, which reinforces the belief among crypto-zoologists that here, in this remote Yorkshire valley, is a monstrous survivor from a prehistoric age.'* Owen's scalp prickled as general views of the valley were replaced by a sneak shot of his brother walking alongside the river. *'And those who devote their lives to searching for hitherto undiscovered species are all asking the same question: "What does this man know about the mysterious creature that so many reliable witnesses have encountered?" If you are watching this, Mr Tom Westonby, confess to what you have seen. Tell us about the dragon that walks where you walk. You owe it not just to us seekers of truth, but to science and the world at large.'*

TWENTY-FOUR

That Saturday afternoon Kit Bolter sat on a wall that overlooked the forest. For mile after mile, trees stretched into the distance. With it being winter, and with all their leaves stripped away, the trees had turned this wild landscape completely black. The sky darkened, too, as clouds streamed from the north. This was the kind of sky that promised snow. There were no houses nearby. The country road snaked towards Danby-Mask in the distance, the only vehicle in sight a green bus. From a text he'd received Kit knew that Owen would be on board, no doubt grinning from ear to ear at the prospect of their monster hunt. *Crikey, this is like being ten years old again.*

The bus would take at least five minutes to reach this isolated stop, so Owen decided to read a couple more pages from *The Mystery of Danby-Mask*, which he'd borrowed from the library this morning.

The flood that struck Danby-Mask was the greatest disaster in the village's history. Raging waters destroyed dozens of homes, swept away cars and buses, and resulted directly and in-directly in the deaths of at least a dozen people. Todd Bolter, who was under the influence of illegal drugs, died after falling from the church tower. Several men and women are missing, presumed drowned. So what did really happen in Danby-Mask? When the flood was at its height, a strange night-time marriage took place in St. George's Church between Thomas Westonby and Nicola Bekk. The ceremony was presided over by the local priest, the Reverend Joshua Squires. No full explanation has been given for this bizarre and unorthodox wedding. The Reverend Squires said later, 'When peoples' lives and souls are in mortal danger then God himself will not quibble over whether the rites of marriage are technically correct. What matters is that those two people, who loved one another, were joined together in matrimony.' Since then the priest has remained silent about the incident.

After the flood, many of those who were present at the wedding ceremony moved out of the area; some even left the country. Joshua Squires, for example, joined an Anglican mission in Africa. What is most extraordinary is that the bride vanished just hours after her marriage. The authorities believe Nicola Bekk drowned in circumstances that remain unexplained. The woman's body has never been found. Adding to the strangeness of it all is that men and women who were there at the wedding ceremony refuse

103

to discuss what happened. None more so than the bride's husband, Thomas Westonby. Everyone, it seems, took a vow of secrecy never to reveal the truth about why Westonby and Bekk married in such haste the night the floodwaters lapped at the church door. Or exactly what led to Todd Bolter's fatal accident. The floodwaters have long since vanished, yet the mystery that originated on the night of the flood endures.

The green bus arrived. Kit slipped the book into his rucksack and stood up as the door opened. Owen Westonby stepped out. As soon as Kit saw the expression on his friend's face he knew something was wrong.

A second person alighted from the bus, too. For a moment, Kit didn't realize the significance of the stranger. It was only when the girl remained standing there instead of walking away that Kit realized that Owen hadn't come alone.

'Kit. This is Eden Taylor.' Owen wore an expression that combined blushing shyness with absolute delight. 'Eden, this is Kit Bolter.'

The beautiful, fair-haired stranger gave him a warm smile that must have melted many a heart. 'Hello, Kit. Owen said it was alright if I tagged along, too. You don't mind, do you?'

Recovering from his surprise Kit smiled, then told his first lie of the day. 'No, I don't mind you coming along.'

'Thank you, Kit, nice to meet you.' Eden's voice radiated 'posh'; she politely held out her hand for Kit to shake. 'I'm rather looking forward to this. I must say I've never explored this part of the valley before.' Her smile was perfectly complemented by twinkling blue eyes. 'After you, Kit.'

Kit led the way. Neither Eden nor Owen could see his expression of sheer, thunderous anger. Fortunately, they couldn't read his mind, either, as these thoughts stormed through his head: *What's Owen playing at? Why did he bring that girl with him? A stranger, for God's sake! She'll ruin everything!*

TWENTY-FIVE

Eden is paradise. Owen Westonby smiled as the words entered his head. *Eden is paradise. Not just the Biblical garden but the girl ... because here she is: a beautiful girl called Eden.* Today was the kind of day when he wanted to start a diary. Mainly to write all kinds of things about Eden Taylor. As he walked beside her, with Kit marching away in front of them across the field, Owen found himself writing the diary entry inside his head. *Saturday, 18 November: the strangest and most amazing thing happened today. As I waited for the bus a girl walked up and started to talk. She'd been with the group of girls yesterday when Shaun played the prank with the chalk outline of a body and the police crime scene tape. Today, she just came right out with: 'Hello, I saw you yesterday, didn't I? When*

*that idiot jumped out of that big salt tub thing?
I'm Eden Taylor. I've seen you around the
village.'*

They'd quickly hit it off. She told him she was
sixteen, went to a school near Whitby, had a
black and white mongrel called Prince and hated
the boring winters in Danby-Mask. Her mother
owned an exclusive hotel in London, and had
begun renovating a newly acquired one in Scarborough. 'That's why we're living here,' she'd
said as she regarded Danby-Mask with those
vast, blue eyes. 'Don't get me wrong. It's such a
pretty village. But what does one actually do to
avoid dying of boredom?'

Without really intending to tell her what he'd
planned for that afternoon it had spilled from his
lips anyway.

'A monster hunt? Gosh! That sounds exciting.'

For a moment he thought she was being
sarcastic, but she genuinely appeared thrilled. Of
course, he immediately invited her along. *And
why the hell not?* he thought. *Nearly every other
guy who's sixteen has a girlfriend – so why not
me?* When she'd stood chatting happily at the
bus stop his heart had begun to beat louder and
louder until it seemed he'd got a machine gun
blazing away inside his ribcage. He thought
she'd put her hands over her ears and cry out,
'What on earth is that noise? It's deafening.'

Of course, only he could hear his own heart. It
was sheer excitement at being with this pretty
girl that made it beat so thunderously.

Now, as they headed along the path towards
the forest, she touched his arm to draw his

attention to a view of Danby-Mask in the distance. A picturesque cluster of red-roofed houses by the river. Although, in truth, his attention never really strayed from her face. That pretty face, framed by blonde hair and set with sparkling, blue eyes. Somewhere in the back of his mind it occurred to him that he'd planned to talk to Kit about those websites, which were devoted to a legendary creature that supposedly roamed this valley. Only that intention stayed in the back of his mind, because now he'd met Eden Taylor she'd become the focus of his attention. Everything else seemed strangely unimportant. *What's that perfume she's wearing? I need to find out its name. How would she react if I gave her some as a present? Grateful? Or wary? Maybe she'd think I was moving in on her too fast?*

Kit paused. 'Owen, show me where you found the pod.'

Eden said, 'Owen told me about what he found. An automatic camera, isn't it?'

Kit nodded.

By now, the Monster Hunt, which had been a fun idea earlier, seemed excruciatingly childish so Owen tried to make light of it; he dreaded Eden thinking he was some kind of idiot. 'Kit asked me to show him where I found the pod thing. If you ask me, it filmed a stag or a wild pony.'

'Isn't there a local legend about a dragon?' Eden seemed genuinely interested, rather than mocking.

Kit wore a stony expression. 'There have been sightings of an unidentified animal for centuries.

The first one was in the Domesday Book, compiled after the invasion of Britain by the Normans in 1066. A water mill got smashed. The king sent knights to find the dragon. If you read the medieval chronicles of—'

'Just a myth,' Owen said quickly. 'You know, a stupid story like Nessie and Bigfoot?'

'There are eyewitness accounts.' Kit sounded annoyed. 'Sworn testimonies.'

'And your camera filmed it.' Eden smiled. 'Will you let me see the film, Kit?'

To Kit's irritation Owen answered on his behalf, 'Of course he will. But my mother said the dragon myth was used by locals to frighten their children.'

'Charming.' Eden's tone hinted that she thought local parenting skills might be suspect, to say the least.

Owen continued, 'People use the story to discourage children from playing in the forest.'

'Is it dangerous?'

'There are ravines, caves, cliffs. The river's pretty wicked, too. If it rains, it can become a raging torrent, just like that.' He clicked his fingers.

'Goodness.' She took a step closer to Owen as if the forest had begun to frighten her.

'It'll be getting dark in an hour.' Kit sounded grumpy. 'You best show us where you found the camera pod.'

Owen grinned. 'Why? Are you scared of being here after dark, in case the monster rips your head off?' He couldn't resist letting out a monster roar. Realizing that didn't come across as at all mature, he laughed it off. 'Just kidding. Come on. We're only a couple of hundred yards away from the spot.'

Eden, meanwhile, did her best to shine a little sunshine on their expedition. 'I'm enjoying this. I've found two new friends. And I'm actually doing something interesting on a Saturday afternoon instead of homework or chores. So, yes, this is fun. Lots of fun.'

She smiled brightly. He smiled back. Kit Bolter, however, had decided to be sullen. *The killjoy.*

Owen explained how he'd walked along the river bank, looking for his brother. Eden expressed a keen interest when he told her that Tom was a professional diver, and that he'd been hired to make an underwater survey of the river.

'This is where I found the pod.' He pointed under a tree. For Eden's benefit he added, 'It was a metal cylinder about this big.' He held his hands about eighteen inches apart. 'The metal casing had been crushed. Look, you can still see the hole where it had been squashed into the ground.'

Kit pulled a camera out of his rucksack and began taking photographs of the hole, and of scuffs and gouges in the dirt where something looked to have been dragged. Eden appeared surprised that Kit took this seriously enough to photograph the area. Owen smiled and gave a little shake of his head as if to say, *It's OK, humour the kid.*

Kit noticed the gesture and reacted defensively. 'I'm planning to study forensic science at university. This is a useful exercise. I'm assessing what would be normal in a forest – things like the state of tree bark, branches, undergrowth and the condition of the ground, then I look for anomalies.' He pointed at a tree. 'See there? An area of bark the size of my hand has been scraped off. Where you're standing the soil has been disturbed as if large animals have been tearing at it with their paws or hooves.'

Eden politely examined the scuffed-up earth.

Owen called across to Kit, 'You might want to photograph these.'

'What are they?'

'Huge paw prints, about a foot across.'

Kit's eyes burned with excitement. *'Where?'*

'All around here. Look.'

Then Kit noticed the expression on Owen's face. 'Yeah, very funny, Owen. One day I'm going to split my sides laughing at one of your jokes, and you'll get blood all over your shoes.'

Kit resumed his investigation, going from tree to tree. Meanwhile, Owen and Eden casually mooched along the path; soon they stood on the river bank watching the water dash by.

'When I was a boy,' Owen said, 'I wanted to ride a canoe from here all the way down to Whitby.'

'That's too adventurous for me,' she laughed. 'I can get panicky in a swimming pool.' The force of the river sent droplets of water soaring into the air. Soon her nose and forehead twinkled with silvery specks. More glinted in her hair.

'Instead of a canoe, we could ride down to Whitby on the bus?'

'That sounds a lot safer than shooting the rapids.' Her eyes twinkled. 'I've just been thinking it would be nice to spend more time together.'

Kit shouted, 'Hey...'

'By ourselves,' she added.

'Hey,' Kit shouted from amongst some bushes. 'I've found where the camera pod had been fixed to the tree. Something ripped the bolts right out of the trunk.'

Owen wasn't listening to Kit. No, he heard his heart again, pounding away. This time he was certain Eden would hear it.

'How about tomorrow?' He spoke in what he hoped was a laid-back way, but was absolutely terrified she'd say 'No'. 'There's a bus at twelve. We could get something to eat down by the harbour.'

'Yes ... that sounds nice.'

His heart whooshed into overdrive. Those blue eyes of hers seemed to light up the whole forest ... no ... the whole world.

'Hey, guys, did you hear me?' Kit's voice was getting lost in the forest, receding, becoming less important – that's what it seemed like to Owen Westonby. Because right at that special moment Owen stood there with the amazing Eden Taylor, and she'd just said 'Yes' to a date. Kit tried shouting even louder to get himself noticed: 'The camera pod was torn off its mounting. Something big came through here. Something huge!'

TWENTY-SIX

Tom Westonby peeled himself out of the diver's suit in a bathroom at the angler's clubhouse. He'd finished the inspection dive at the jetty and had been able to report to the guy who'd hired him that the structure was basically sound. After showering, he changed his clothes and packed his aqualung, mask, rubber suit and assorted diving equipment into his van. The representative of the angler's club that owned the jetty paid him his fee in cash.

Tom waved his farewell as he drove away in the direction of Leppington where he'd arranged to meet up with June Valko. After her experience with the vampires last night, he knew that the time had come to tell her the whole story regarding the flood five years ago, and about the vampire-like creatures that haunted the wood, and the truth about Helsvir – this was the monster guardian of the Bekk family that had been stitched together from corpses by the Viking god Thor. If it hadn't been for the fact that June Valko had seen a vampire with her own eyes (and possibly her own father at that) climb down the chimney to stand there in the blazing fire, Tom knew he wouldn't have been able to convince her that he spoke the truth.

A sign up ahead read LEPPINGTON. He drove into the market town determined to explain to June as clearly as possible his mission in life – *and that mission is to find Nicola Bekk, and to bring her back home.* However, he needed to overcome two major obstacles. One: he didn't know where to find Nicola. Two: Nicola was a vampire.

TWENTY-SEVEN

Tom Westonby parked in the yard behind the Station Hotel in Leppington. When he stepped out of the van he shivered. A cold north-easterly carried flakes of snow, but it was more than the icy breeze making him shiver. He realized that when he saw June Valko today they wouldn't just discuss the past. They'd plan what they were going to do in the future. The main part of that plan for June would be somehow finding and communicating with her father. Considering that the man had become an inhuman creature, a vampire, that was nigh on impossible.

Just as impossible as me being reunited with Nicola Bekk, he thought grimly as he walked towards the hotel.

Leppington was bigger that Danby-Mask. Whereas his home village consisted of quaint cottages built from yellow stone, Leppington consisted mainly of red-brick buildings. The place had a tougher, industrial feel. Across the road stood the huge slaughterhouse. Next to that, the formidable railway station, while facing the railway station stood the equally imposing Station Hotel. Over a hundred years ago whoever had built this hotel clearly wanted to dominate the town. It was as if they were bluntly stating: 'I'm staying here for ever, so get used to it.' The streets were busy with pedestrians, rushing to do their Christmas shopping before the snow really started to fall. In this part of England, a blizzard would lead to the moorland roads being closed, leaving travellers stranded.

Tom passed through the big entrance doors and headed across plush carpet towards the lounge bar. It was ten minutes to three; already daylight was fading. The main bar at the front of the hotel buzzed with people. However, the residents' lounge was deserted. Good; he could talk to June without anyone overhearing. After all, he had a shocking story to tell.

Tom headed for the counter with its long line of beer taps. Nobody appeared to be serving. He could use a large mugful of hot coffee right now. Even though he'd worn the dry suit for the dive, the sheer coldness of the River Lepping had seeped into his veins. He glanced up at a small TV screen fixed to the wall and saw his own image there as he stood at the counter. There must have been another screen showing the identical image elsewhere in the hotel, because a woman breezed through a door. She appeared to be in her thirties and had thick, wavy red hair tied back with a green ribbon.

'Good afternoon,' she said cheerfully. 'What can I get for you?'

He realized he was hungry, too. 'Good afternoon. I'd like a large coffee, please.'

'Milk or cream?'

'No, thanks, just as it comes. Are you serving meals today?'

'Right up until five o'clock. Bar menus are on the tables.'

'Thanks.'

'You'll have to excuse me if I'm slow at this.' She gazed at the elaborate coffee machine for a moment. 'We've only just taken over this week.'

'Has Electra sold the hotel?'

'You know Electra Charnwood?'

'I've met her a few times when I've had meals here.'

'Electra's taken a year off to go travelling. So this is a baptism of fire for me and my husband. We've never run a hotel before.' She grinned back over her shoulder. 'But don't let that put you off eating here. We haven't poisoned anyone yet.' She turned her attention back to the coffee machine's controls. 'I think it's this one ... wait ... ah, yes, that's it, we have lift-off.' The machine began to gurgle.

'I'm meeting one of your guests at three. I'll see if she wants to eat, too.'

'A guest, you say? That must be Miss Valko. We only have one person staying with us at the moment.'

'That's her. June Valko.'

'She's beautiful. Such amazing blue eyes.'

'Oh, we're not meeting on a date.' He realized

the woman wasn't being nosy. In fact he found himself liking her. Being so reclusive meant that he didn't see many smiling faces. 'She's interested in local history.' That seemed an understatement – of course, he wasn't going to come right out and tell the manageress of the Station Hotel that he and June Valko intended to track down June's inhuman father and Tom's vampire bride. The truth would lead to all kinds of complications.

The manageress chatted pleasantly. 'See the poster on the wall?'

'The movie poster?'

'That's the one. My grandmother starred in the film. It was shot in Whitby during the Second World War.'

The framed poster showed a beautiful woman and a handsome, strong-jawed man standing face-to-face with the silhouette of Whitby's ruined abbey behind them. Searchlights picked out planes in the sky. Bold letters proclaimed:

THE MIDNIGHT REALM
Starring Beth Layne, George Crofton
& Sally Wainwright
~ Written & Directed by Alec Reed ~
'They defied terror from the skies!!!'

'Is that your grandmother on the poster?' Tom asked.

'Beth Layne.' The woman nodded. 'She moved to Hollywood in the 1950s to appear in a television crime series. It ran for over ten years. Ah ... there she blows.' Freshly brewed coffee

116

trickled from a chrome sprout. 'It always work-ed faster when Electra was in charge. But we finally got there.'

'Thank you.' Tom handed over the money. He knew he hadn't thanked her for the coffee alone; he'd been grateful to occupy this bright, normal world for a while with a friendly human being. Five years of living a solitary life as a recluse isn't healthy. He realized that fact, just as he realized that as a twenty-eight-year-old he should be living life to the full. But he felt to the depths of his heart that somewhere out there was Nicola. One day he'd find her. He'd bring her back home. That was a certainty.

The manageress said she'd take the food order in a few minutes, and vanished back through the door. Tom stood at the counter, sipped his coffee and relished the normality of it all: being in this warm room with its seats upholstered in red velvet made such a pleasant change from the rustic stonework of the cottage. The sounds of people laughing and enjoying one another's company drifted from the main bar. He savoured the conviviality of the place. The friendly atmos-phere. The air of genteel comfort. This world was far away from his world of vampires and a savage monster created by embittered and vengeful gods.

Tom Westonby glanced out of the window. Dark clouds gathered there. They were ominous, somehow dangerous-looking. Already the forces of nature were getting ready to inflict a wither-ing storm. Tom sensed that there were other forces at work, too. These were definitely *not* natural. They were the supernatural entities that occupied their own realm parallel to this one. The gut feeling that dangerous times lay ahead filled him with a sense of foreboding. In his mind's eye, he could see Death getting ready to step into his world once more. But who would Death claim this time? June Valko? His brother, Owen? Or would he, Tom Westonby, feel its icy hand upon his heart?

At three o'clock June Valko walked into the room. He nodded and she nodded back. They had no need for small-talk. The time had come to plan what they'd do next.

Hail struck the windows. The falling ice sounded as if Death itself tapped on the glass pane with fingers of bone. The breeze blew harder, drawing a long, sobbing cry from the chimney pots. Tom Westonby shivered. The real horror was just about to begin...

TWENTY-EIGHT

June Valko sat facing him across the table. The pair were alone in the hotel lounge bar. Despite it only being only a shade after three o'clock on that Saturday afternoon, darkness had already engulfed the town.

Tom asked, 'Would you like a drink?'

'I ordered in the other bar, but thanks anyway.' She leaned forward, plaiting her fingers together

118

on the table as if about to say a prayer. 'Tom, I've been thinking. You shouldn't go back home. That house in the woods is too isolated.'

'I have to be there.'

'Why?'

That's when he told her in more detail about Nicola, and about what happened five years ago. How he'd first met Nicola after seeing her barefoot in the garden pond at his parents' house. Following that there had been a hurricane of a relationship. June listened carefully when he explained that Nicola's mother had revealed the history of the Bekk family, and the fact that any Bekk moving out of the area or marrying a partner who didn't worship the pagan Viking gods would trigger an ancient curse. Then had come the most horrific part: Tom described Nicola's transformation from a beautiful, healthy woman into a vampire after their wedding on the night of the flood.

He said, 'Nicola's skin turned unnaturally white, the veins on her neck stood out in dark lines, like roads on a map. The colour bleached out of her eyes, so they were just plain white. The pupils remained, but they became these strange, fierce black dots that were so alien-looking.' He shivered. 'Nicola said she must leave me, because she was frightened of losing self-control. You see, what scared her most was realizing that she'd eventually see me as prey, and that she'd attack me.'

'What happened next?'

'The flood water had surrounded the church where we'd been stranded all night. Meanwhile,

Nicola's transformation was accelerating. At any moment she might have attacked me.' He gazed through the window without even seeing the street outside. Instead, memory pulled him down into that terrible graveyard of the mind, where horrific memories lie buried – but they're never buried quite deep enough. All too easily they can rise up to cause torment and pain. In his mind's eye, he saw his bride waiting anxiously at the edge of the floodwaters as she desperately called out to Helsvir. 'Do you remember the carving in my house? The one of the creature called Helsvir? According to legend he was created by the Viking gods to protect the Bekk family. Nicola wanted the creature to take her away. She realized she had to travel to some place from which she couldn't easily return. Because if she did come back she might not be able to stop herself from hurting me ... or even turning me into one of those creatures you saw last night.' He gave a melancholy smile. 'I wouldn't mind becoming one of those things. At least I'd be with Nicola. In fact, we could be together for ever. We'd be immortal.' His mouth went dry. 'That's what I need, June. To be with Nicola. I don't want to be alone any more. Being there in the cottage by myself is a living death.'

June reached across the table, took his hands in hers, and squeezed them – a gesture of absolute compassion. He felt her sympathy and the warmth of her humanity. And after not holding hands with another human being for so long he thought the emotion would shatter him.

'I'm sorry for taking so long.' A young waitress hurried in with a glass of orange juice. 'It's the Christmas shoppers. We're rushed off our feet. Would you like to order your meal?'

'Hungry?' he handed June a menu.

'Food's fuel,' she replied. 'Something tells me we'll need to keep our strength up.'

The waitress suspected that they had erotic activity in mind, because her cheeks went pink. 'Today's special is a casserole made with black pudding.'

'Black pudding?' June echoed.

'Black pudding is a kind of thick sausage,' explained the waitress. 'It's made from blood – pig's blood, I think.'

'Blood pudding.' Tom shuddered as the notion of blood cuisine sank in. 'No thanks. I'm not a vampire yet.'

The waitress chuckled politely at the joke. He found himself laughing as well. Such a strange laugh, too. It had its origins so deep inside him that his stomach muscles seemed to be shaking the laughter free. Soon he laughed so hard that tears rolled down his face, and then he realized he wasn't laughing at all. He wept for the girl he loved. He wept at the frustration of not being able to find Nicola again – even though he suspected that sometimes she was near to him. Sometimes hidden in a shadow of a tree, perhaps, or the inky darkness of the river, or even the night time cry of a fox.

Before the waitress realized that his laughter had turned to grief he wiped his eyes, and said, 'June, what would you like?'

June met his gaze and understood what he was

really feeling. 'I'll steer clear of the vampire special, although I'm sure it's delicious. Uhm ... mushroom pizza, please.'

Tom brought his voice under control. 'The Leppington Premier Burger. Thanks.'

The waitress tapped the order on to a tablet. 'Do you want slaw, fries and extra bacon?'

Tom smiled. 'Why not?' Outside, clouds of hail swept by the window – a parade of deathly, white ghosts. 'I'll have a pint of Black Dog ale, too. And would you let them know at reception that I'll be booking a room for tonight?'

The waitress left them alone again. June's electric-blue eyes were bright as she stared at him, as if wondering what this brooding man with all that volcanic, pent-up emotion was planning.

'You're going to stay the night?' she asked. 'Here, at the hotel?'

He nodded. 'We've lots to talk about. Besides, I was going to ask you to do me a favour.'

'Oh?' Her eyes widened. 'Oh, I see ... at least I think I do...'

TWENTY-NINE

Kit Bolter returned to the house he shared with his mother. Hailstones stung his face, which made him even angrier. Why had Owen brought that girl? Kit had been unable to concentrate on his forensic examination of the area where Owen had found the camera pod. Kit had played gooseberry to Owen and Eden Taylor: the bottom line was he felt so uncomfortable with the girl making goo-goo eyes at Owen.

When hailstones slammed into his eyes they made them water.

'Damn it, Owen, you went and ruined the afternoon.' He hunched his shoulders against the cold. 'She'll be telling her friends about us ... they'll be laughing.'

Kit had found some interesting clues. But Owen hadn't given a crap. All he'd wanted to do was talk to Eden. Kit shook his head. This afternoon should have been great. The two of them exploring and finding those fascinating marks on the trees where something huge had scraped away the bark. Angrily, he kicked open the gate. His mother stared out of the window at him; her eyes were vacant, and he wasn't even sure if she realized that her son was there.

Normally, Kit Bolter would do anything to

protect his friendship with Owen, but bringing that smirking girl on their own private adventure had been a stab in the back. So he made a decision. *I'm going to confront Owen. I wasn't going to do this, but he's forced my hand. I'll tell him that there are rumours that Tom Westonby killed my uncle. What's more, some people are saying he murdered Nicola Bekk and hid her body. Let's see what Owen Westonby has to say about that.*

Kit pushed aside any suspicion that he was becoming overwrought, or even irrational. *No, Owen's brought this on himself.* Kit couldn't wait to see the expression on Owen's face when he said, *Hey. Didn't your brother kill my uncle?* Or would it have a more devastating impact if he said: *Owen, I heard your brother murdered his girlfriend?*

Whichever accusation he went with first would be fantastic. Owen would be so shocked that he wouldn't give Eden Taylor a second thought. SHOW TIME!!!

THIRTY

In the Station Hotel, Tom and June ate their meal in the lounge bar. After that they talked. They discussed the attack on Tom again, and how he'd nearly been drowned by the menacing figure. Tom also explained that he'd discovered how the vampires had cut the electricity to the cottage. Not that there was much of a mystery attached to that particular incident – the electric meter was fixed to a wall outside the property. There was also a mains power switch. The vampire had simply flipped the switch and plunged the cottage into darkness. Tom had rectified the situation by flicking it back into the 'on' position again.

June had brought a hefty file stuffed with documents and photographs. Those electric blue eyes of hers earnestly studied pictures of her father. These were taken in happier times – in some of them he stood alongside a dark-skinned woman who was pregnant with June.

June scrutinized a photograph. 'I'm trying to find a resemblance to the man who attacked you and who climbed down the chimney.'

'Do you see any resemblance?'

'Just when I think I do...' she sighed. 'That's when I tell myself I can because I want to believe it was my father.'

'The first time it was dark when we were on the river bank, the second time he was surrounded by fire. It'd be a tough call to identify anyone in circumstances like those.'

June went to the bar and came back with another beer for him and a large white wine for herself. 'What's been really worrying me, Tom, is what if you're attacked again? You're alone out there in the forest.'

'Your being there was the trigger.'

'They ... those vampires ... let's not be shy about using the word. Those vampires have never done anything like this before?'

'Not to me. They're elusive. I don't think anyone's seen them apart from me in recent years. They tend to haunt the wood, for the want of a better word. They don't move, don't say anything, and I keep well away from them.'

'You see other members of the Bekk family, but never Nicola?'

'I've glimpsed her once or twice, or believed I have, which might not be the same thing.'

'So you really believe I triggered the attack?'

He sipped the beer. 'I'm certain you're the trigger. Your father believed I was attacking you in the forest, some residual instinct to protect his daughter kicked in, and *wham*! I ended up face down in the water.'

'Even if he was my father, he couldn't know what I look like.'

'He'd have sensed you. Maybe he knew you share the same blood as him, or at least a percentage of it. They might not be the usual kind of vampires you see in films but, believe me, those guys have powers we can only dream about.'

'So, will you stay away from the house? At least for the time being?'

'If you're not there, those vampires will return to normal – or what's normal for them. Inert. Harmless.'

She looked him in the eye. 'But what if you're wrong?'

They talked through into the evening. June Valko had shown Tom newspaper clippings that featured her father. Thousands of people go missing each year, so the major newspapers hadn't even covered the case. However, the local press had reported what appeared to be a standard missing person story. After all, no evidence of murder or kidnap could be uncovered. If anything, it appeared to be a situation where a young man had decided he didn't want to be tied down with a wife and child, and simply scooted off elsewhere. Charities that attempt to find people who've vanished couldn't help, either. Tom studied the photographs of Jacob – a good-looking young man who appeared completely happy with his new wife. What was more, he resembled Tom's Nicola so closely. They had the same fair hair that looked almost white in bright sunlight.

Of course, they both knew what had happened to Jacob. The old pagan magic that had both protected and cursed the Bekk clan had struck again. Jacob had rejected the old way of life.

Tom could imagine Jacob scoffing at the idea that Viking gods not only existed, but they had power over him. So, almost thirty years ago, he'd left Skanderberg cottage in the forest and headed west to Manchester, looking forward to an exciting life in the city. He'd met June's mother, fallen in love and married her.

But then the curse had struck. Before Jacob could hurt his wife, who was expecting his child, he'd fled back to his old family home in the forest. There the transformation to vampire had run its course. Now the man, who would no longer age, wandered the forest at night – something he would do until the end of time. A kind of lost soul in physical form.

Tom and June drank more beer and wine. By ten o'clock Tom felt decidedly mellow. June smiled woozily.

'Ready for bed?' he asked.

Nodding, she replied in a small voice, 'OK.'

Tom had already checked in and had the key to his room. They climbed the stairs together, pausing only to look out of a window as the hail rattled down. The roads of Leppington were white all over.

When he stopped to say good night, she stood on tiptoe and kissed him. 'Do you prefer your room or mine?' she asked.

'My room ... I mean, I'm going to my room. You're going to yours.'

'I thought we were going to...' her blue eyes searched his face. 'You know?'

'That's flattering, I'm flattered.' He realized both were more than a little tipsy. 'But while there's a small, tiny ... infinitesimal chance I'll find Nicola ... then no. Thanks, but no way.'

'Oh?'

'Sorry. I've embarrassed you.'

She shook her head, confused. 'Earlier, you said you'd ask a favour of me tonight?'

'And you thought I meant...? Oh.'

'Yes.'

'You thought I'd ask you to sleep with me as a favour? Sex?'

'Yes. I decided to agree ... I thought you needed to – I don't know how to say it – to release emotion. A way to relax.'

'Safety valve sex.'

'I guess that's one way of describing it.' She smiled. 'I must say I'm relieved about our misunderstanding. It would have been strange ending up naked together, and touching each other's bodies, and ... well, you know.'

'Thanks for being prepared to...' he swayed a little '...to be so generous.'

'No problem. Well ... I'll say good night.'

'Good night, June, and thanks again for ... well...'

'Good night, Tom.'

Tom headed towards his room. June opened her door. Then he heard her call in a soft voice.

'Tom?'

He turned round. 'Yes?'

'You said you were going to ask a favour? What was it?'

He came straight out with what had been on his mind. 'Bait.'

'Pardon?'

'I want you to become bait. I want you to come back home with me tomorrow, and draw the vampires out.'

Her eyes widened in shock. Then she thought about what he'd said and slowly nodded. 'OK. I'll do that. I'll be the bait.' With that, she went into her room and quietly closed the door behind her.

THIRTY-ONE

I'm playing a dangerous game, Tom thought as he sat on the bed in his hotel room. *I'm playing with fire.* Just a moment ago he'd said to June Valko: *I want you to become bait. I want you to come back home with me tomorrow, and draw the vampires out.*

June longed to have contact with her father – even if the man was no longer human but a vampire. Tom had formed a plan as he talked to her and drank glass after glass of potent Yorkshire ale down in the bar. Perhaps the intoxicating power of the beer had taken away his scruples, along with realizing that what he planned would be extremely dangerous for both of them. Because he really did intend to use June Valko as bait. Her presence last night in the forest had provoked at least one vampire into radically changing its behaviour.

Tom had suspected for years that Nicola could see him, even if he couldn't see her. *So this is the dangerous part*, he told himself. *If I assume Nicola can see me, and there is part of her original personality still intact, then what will happen when she sees me with a woman? What if she watches me walk into the cottage with June Valko?* There was a distinct chance Nicola would go berserk with jealousy, just as June's father had flown into a violent rage when he thought that Tom was attacking his daughter.

Tom Westonby understood his plan would be especially dangerous. Also, there would be so many unpredictable elements. The psychology of the vampire-like creatures was unknown territory. How much of the human personality remained? Might residual human feelings of jealousy, protectiveness and perhaps even love be amplified to an explosive degree? Even so, he still intended to provoke Nicola, his vampire bride of five years ago, to show herself. And damn the consequence.

He went to the window and looked out over the rooftops. Hailstones had cast a deathly white shroud over the town. The winter had come early this year. Soon blizzards would cut off the little communities scattered across the North Yorkshire moors and valleys. Already the physical appearance of the landscape had changed. Tom shivered. It was growing colder by the hour out there, and already it felt as if this isolated region had begun to drift away from the natural world. He sensed he approached a time when the impossible would become possible ... and that soon he would encounter a force that was as ancient as it was evil.

Winds ghosted down from the bleak moorland hills. Their mournful drone evoked an impression that a massive door had swung open on to some desolate, lost realm where monstrous things prepared to wage war on the world of the living.

THIRTY-TWO

The minibus roared along the valley road. The time approached midnight.

'This way's quicker!' the driver shouted over the shouts and laughter of his six passengers.

'As long as you don't drive us into a ditch.'

'Don't be a scaredy-cat, Ruth. I've got the hang of driving this now.'

Ruth gripped hold of her seatbelt. The minibus swayed as it accelerated downhill. She could barely see anything through the side window. Out here in the forest, nights were the ultimate in blackness.

'You'll end up killing us, if you don't slow down.' Ruth didn't intend paying for a trip to the cinema in Scarborough with her own life. 'These roads are lethal.'

'We'll be fine.'

Ruth tried a different argument. 'Put a dent in this thing, and the rental place will make you pay for repairs.'

Ruth's statement put its own dent in Luke's reckless attitude. He eased down the speed. The Saturday night out in the biggest town on this part of the East Coast had been fun. Ruth had enjoyed the meal followed by the film – but this was the curse of living in a place like Danby-Mask that was miles from anywhere. A trip to the cinema required planning, renting the mini-bus for her friends and then entrusting the vehicle to Luke's driving. The guy always drove as if he'd gambled his life savings on making the trip in record time.

Although she knew why he wanted to get home as quickly as possible. Luke would be sleeping with her tonight. It was a stupidly casual relationship, because she wanted commit-ment. Invariably, they never saw each other or phoned one another during the week – yet in-variably they'd still have sex on a Saturday night. *So is driving too fast his idea of foreplay to arouse me?* She pondered this as his speed began to increase again. *Or is he just wanting to rush home so he can get my clothes off?* At this rate he'd be kissing her breasts in twenty min-utes. *And I'll let him. That's the annoying part. Either Luke should be a proper boyfriend, or I should be finding someone new.*

The others on the bus were teasing Paul about the way he'd bleached his hair a bright, fluffy blond. Luke kept twisting round in the driving seat so he could see them ruffling Paul's yellow mop.

'Shave it off!' shouted a girl.

'Dye it black,' laughed another. 'Make him

133

look like Elvis!'

The passengers scrambled over the seats so they could ruffle Paul's hair. Paul enjoyed being the centre of attention. He laughed as he fended them off.

Ruth wiped away condensation from the glass. Trees, bushes, fences rushed by. The darkness resembled a thick, black fog. Apart from guessing they were heading down into the valley she hadn't a clue where they were.

Just then, a sign flashed by and now she knew exactly where they were. 'Hey! Hey, Luke.' She reached forward to pound the back of the driver's seat. 'Hey. I've just seen the sign for the ford.'

'So?'

'Cars aren't supposed to use the ford after all the rain we've had. The stream will be too high.'

'This isn't a car, Ruth, it's a bus.' Luke was damned eager for sex. He wanted to get her home as quickly as possible so he could wrestle her naked body into bed. Sometimes Luke got over-excited. He got rough.

She protested again, 'The water will be too deep.'

'It'll be fine. Besides, it's a lot quicker this way.'

Ruth pictured the way ahead. The narrow road cut through the forest where it eventually ran through a stream. This was usual for roads out here in the countryside. Bridge building was expensive. So, if the stream wasn't too deep, highway engineers simply ran the road across the stream to the other side. Usually the water

134

would only be three or four inches deep. However, Ruth knew that ford crossings shouldn't be used after heavy rain. And last week it had been HEAVY.

'Luke.' She tried again. 'Turn round, use the Whitby road.'

'That's the long way round, it'll take ages.'

'Luke—'

'It'll be fine.'

That *it'll be fine* phrase again. She took a deep breath ready to yell at this pig-headed guy. But the breath that would propel those angry words got knocked clean out of her lungs.

Deciding to use the ford crossing turned out to be a bad decision. In fact, a disastrous decision. A total catastrophe.

When the bus hit the stream, white spray exploded into the air. Luke yelled as he fought to regain control. The vehicle's wheels lifted clear of the road surface. Tons of steel were actually surfing across the water. Then another colossal jolt. Paul had been rolling about on the back seat as they'd ruffled his hair. Now he shot down the aisle. He landed head first in the little stairwell that led to the side door.

The bus came to a dead stop. The engine clattered, wheezed and then died. Silence. Darkness, too, because the headlights failed.

Luke swore at the top of his voice. 'Shit!'

Somehow, Luke found a switch that turned on the interior lights. At least they worked.

After that, he called down to where Paul lay in the stairwell. 'Paul? Are you hurt?'

Paul managed to shuffle his way backwards

before kneeling up. 'My hair ... my beautiful hair.' He grinned. 'Look, it's dripping.'

'Oh, shit,' Luke groaned. 'The water's coming in.'

'Are we going to drown?' a girl asked, clearly scared.

'No, but we're stuck,' snapped Luke. 'The water's killed the bloody engine.'

He glared at Ruth, daring her to make a comment. Ruth shot him a ferocious glance. However, instead of accusing him of idiocy and arrogance (*which is the damn well truth*) she wiped the condensation from the side window. Yup. Stuck in the middle of the stream. The interior lights shone through the glass, revealing that they were surrounded by water. She checked the stairwell to the side door. There were three steps into the bus. The first had been covered by water. She judged, therefore, the stream would have risen from its usual six inches deep to around two feet deep. Enough water must have splashed up into the engine to drown the electrics.

'What now?' asked one of the girls.

Luke gave a bad-tempered sigh. 'Push it back out again.'

'I'm not wading in that,' said the girl. 'It'll be freezing.'

'And I'm not ruining my shoes.' Paul shook his head. 'These cost me a fortune.'

'Take them off, then,' Luke snarled. 'Do you want to be stuck here all night?'

Ruth felt the bus shudder as the current tugged it. 'The water's rising. It won't be safe to stay

136

here. The Lepping's just a hundred yards down-stream. If the bus is swept into that we wouldn't stand a chance.'

'I'm getting out.' Paul tugged off his shoes and, holding them in one hand, hurried down the three steps to the door. 'Open up, Luke, we're abandoning ship.'

Luke stood up from the driving seat.

'Isn't the captain supposed to go down with his vessel?' Ruth asked tartly.

Luke grunted. 'There are three girls and four guys. We can carry the girls to dry land; then the guys *will* help me push this thing out.' He press-ed a button that operated the side door. Nothing happened.

'We're trapped.' Paul's eyes widened. 'We can't get out.'

Luke shook his head. 'The water's got into the wiring, that's all. We'll use the doors at the back.' He called to a guy at the other end of the bus. 'Tony. Open the back doors. There should be a lever, then it's just a case of pushing them open.'

Tony easily swung the twin doors open. In-stantly, cold air came rushing in. Ruth could see the black stream sweeping by. Now she could smell the water – the peaty, earthy aromas from springs that fed the stream. The seven occupants of the bus moved along the aisle between the seats. Paul and Tony stood in the gaping door-way. Both seemed reluctant to commit them-selves to climbing down into the ice cold water.

'I can hardly see the far bank,' shouted Paul.

'There all kinds of crap floating by,' Tony

137

added. 'Branches and stuff.'

'Are you sure we can walk through that?' asked a girl, whose name was Anita. 'We're not going to get swept away, are we?'

Luke called out, 'Paul, Tony, start carrying the girls across.'

'*Shit.*'

'What's wrong?'

Tony pointed into the gloom. 'There's something big floating towards us.'

Paul stared into the darkness. 'It looks like a whole tree's been washed away. It's enormous.'

A cascade of ice poured down Ruth's spine. 'That can't be right,' she shouted. 'That's downstream. A tree won't float *upstream* towards us. That means it would be moving against the current.'

'Well, that's where it's coming from.'

'Whatever it is,' called Paul. 'It's getting closer.'

Ruth leaned towards a side window, trying to see what approached them.

Tony gave a deafening yell. 'CLOSE THE DOORS! GET THEM CLOSED!'

Both he and Paul leaned outwards to grab the doors. The speed they moved at told Ruth they were panicky and scared. Before they could swing the doors shut a huge eruption of white foam flew upwards. Water splashed into the bus.

Then everyone was yelling at once. Paul turned to them, his eyes bulging with terror, as if they were going to explode from his head. A second later, his entire body jerked upwards. His

138

shoulder caught the edge of the door frame, shearing his arm away. The severed arm fell into one of the seats, its fingers clutching at the fabric; blood gushed from the mass of torn meat and skin at the other end.

Ruth's world descended into a vortex of screaming and violent movement. One after another, passengers were plucked from the bus. Through the open doors at the back was an explosive churning of water, foam and glistening, white spray. Ruth glimpsed a dark shape beyond the spray. Something enormous. Something that moved with brutal purpose.

Anita clung, screaming, to a seat. Until, that is, a tremendous force dragged her away. Ruth saw the girl's false red nails still embedded in the upholstery even though she was gone.

The bus lurched as a massive object slammed into the back. Luke ran to the end of the bus to find out what was happening. By the time he reached the doorway he was the only person left on board with the exception of Ruth. All the others had been dragged away. Luke abruptly turned and ran towards her. His eyes were like blazing lamps, fear distorted his face – he'd bitten his own tongue, so it now resembled a bloody red stick that protruded from his lips.

'RUTH! HELP ME!'

White spray jetted into the bus. This was like trying to see through a fog. And at that moment she could smell body heat ... feel body heat – that didn't make sense – only she was sure that an animal was near; one that radiated pungent warmth.

Luke had almost reached her when he stopped suddenly – just stopped, as if he'd slammed into a glass wall. Something had hold of him. She was sure she glimpsed hands gripping his body. Then he receded from her quickly, as if being yanked back by a rope. His body whipped from side to side. First his head cracked against the roof. Blood sprayed outwards, transforming the white mist into a crimson fog. Then his face slammed into a side window, shattering the glass – the force of the blow sliced away his face. It left a raw skull bone from which a pair of eyes bulged – like two white eggs that had been embedded in a slab of raw beef.

Ruth scrambled through the broken window. Shreds of Luke's facial skin clung to the edges of the glass. Those shreds of flesh were sticky and wet.

Then she was running through the stream. Although she didn't look back, she knew some *thing* followed. This was like running in a nightmare. The water came above her knees. It slowed her movements. More than once she fell. Behind her, a massive object moved faster. Gaining on her. When she broke free of the stream she ran as fast as she could.

But she knew she couldn't outrun it. She heard its feet slap wetly against the road. She tried as hard as she could to run faster, but her feet slipped from under her. She went crashing down into the roadway. Ruth lay there, panting and helpless, as she waited for the horror to take her, too.

THIRTY-THREE

Jez Pollock came upon the scene of the attack late. Midnight had been approaching on that Saturday night when his conscience got the better of him. Earlier, he'd argued with his father because he wanted to join Owen and Kit on a trip into the woods. Jez's father had insisted that he repair a stock fence. Cows had been escaping and wandering out on to a road. In a fit of temper, Jez had rushed work on the fence, simply bashing a few nails into the rails to hold them in place.

His parents had gone to stay with friends for the weekend, leaving him in charge of the farm. The farm itself had been suffering financial difficulties lately. If cows were lost then his parents would struggle to make ends meet.

So, after being nagged by his conscience, Jez had driven the truck up the valley to check on the fence and the cows. Since he was too young to own a driver's licence, he stuck to the private farm tracks. It was only for the last couple of hundred yards of his journey that he'd have to join the public highway. He gambled there'd be no police patrolling that remote neck of the woods at this time.

Jez had just passed a sign for the ford crossing

when he saw a remarkable sight. A young woman ran barefoot along the road. She ran with a wild kind of desperation ... as if her life depended on it.

Before the truck's lights fully lit up the scene, she'd fallen. Behind her, a vehicle seemed to be closing in. But this one had no lights ... in fact, it was no vehicle at all. He had an impression of a dark object moving smoothly forward. Although he couldn't identify what it was, instinct told him it would attack the woman. She'd balled herself up on the ground, trying to protect her head with her hands.

Jez slammed his foot down on the accelerator pedal. The engine roared, and the truck sped along the road like a missile. What he saw in the lights knocked the air out of him. Yet he kept his foot down hard on the pedal, the truck aimed squarely at the creature. The headlights blazed on the monstrous thing. He saw eyes ... rows of diamond-bright eyes.

The truck slammed into the creature at fifty miles an hour. Jez whipped forward, snapping the bone of his right arm in two against the steering wheel. Then his forehead impacted on the same part of the wheel. Jez blacked out. The sixteen-year-old never felt the final impact when the truck rolled sideways over the stock fence he'd repaired earlier, and came to rest wheels-up in the meadow.

THIRTY-FOUR

Eighteen-year-old Clarissa Prior waited for the minibus to return from the cinema. She'd met Paul last week. After teasing him about his mousy hair, he'd turned up at her house with his hair bleached a funny shade of yellow. Well, she'd found the sight of that yellow mop hilarious. Over the last few days they'd talked a lot as they'd hung out in Danby-Mask, watching the guys showing off in their cars as they drove up and down Main Street. Over the last couple of days talking turned to kissing.

Paul had told her about the trip to the cinema, and that a group of friends had hired a minibus. He wanted her to come, too. Clarissa would have done, but she'd already been committed, by her mother, to go to an aunt's seventieth birthday party. So she'd done the dutiful thing and gone to the party for sandwiches, sherry and cake.

Clarissa knew that the minibus would drop Paul off at St George's Church – right opposite where Clarissa lived with her parents. She made up her mind to surprise Paul when he arrived.

So, with her parents asleep, she tiptoed out of the house. The village seemed to be asleep, too. There'd have been complete silence if it hadn't been for the steady click of hailstones hitting the roofs. Clarissa grinned. She'd have a story to tell Eden Taylor when they caught the school bus on Monday morning. 'I've got a new boyfriend,' she'd say. 'He's twenty and he's called Paul.' *Don't know about telling Ruth that he's got funny yellow hair, though.*

Paul had sent her texts throughout the evening. The last one said that he'd be arriving about twelve thirty. She checked her watch. Twelve thirty-nine. OK, a little late. Though Paul wouldn't be driving, so she could hardly blame him. Well, OK, she'd blame him just a tad. She wanted to keep him keen. If she seemed the kind of girl who'd show up whenever he zipped off a quick text he'd take her for granted. She walked a few yards down the village street so she'd be in the right place when the bus arrived. 'Surprise!' she'd shout when she saw his sunburst hairstyle. Smiling, she pictured his expression of surprise turning to one of delight when she struck her casual, yet very sexy, pose under the streetlight.

Between two rows of cottages an alleyway ran back into the shadows.

'Help me.'

The whisper startled her.

'Help me.'

'Who's there?' She heard a tremble in her voice. 'What's the matter?'

Shadows were thick and dark in the alleyway. Almost a fog of blackness. Hail fell, *clitter-clatter* – this could almost have been the tap of fingernails on wood.

'Help me, my love...'

A figure stepped from the gloom. Clarissa gawped in horror. She felt her blood drain from her skull and down through her neck – even the crimson gore inside of her retreated from the awful sight. The man, the spectre, the demon ... whatever he was, moved closer. Her eyes flashed from his bare feet to his white face. His eyes had fixed on her. She wanted to scream at the sight of those eyes – only she'd frozen there, unable to move, unable to cry out.

'Help me live again.'

The man's eyes were white – absolutely white. They bulged from his head. Each eye possessed a fierce black pupil. The eyes appeared to swell from their sockets as he stared at her, while the pupils shrank into concentrated points of cruelty.

She managed to turn in the direction of home. Too late. A pair of arms encircled her from behind. In less than a moment, eighteen-year-old Clarissa Prior had been dragged away into the darkness. After that, she felt a mouth press against her bare throat – a mouth that was large, and round, and wet. The last thing she felt was the agonizing stab of his teeth.

No ... not the very last thing. The last sensation: the trickle of a single tear down her cheek.

PART TWO

(Doctor Edward Walton's letter to his brother, 16 November, 1844)

Dear Jack,
Don't believe the lies. I swear I am not to blame for that blasted monster breaking loose. Nor am I to be blamed for the creature's attack on the congregation at Mottworth church. These are the plain facts: a man by the name of Olaf Bekk was delivered to the asylum by a group of gentlemen from the village of Danby-Mask. They had bound this blond giant in chains, and brutally – and even blasphemously! – secured him to the cart by hammering iron nails through his hands into the wooden boards.
One of Olaf Bekk's captors made an extra-ordinary statement. As principal of the asylum I recorded what he told me in the admissions book. Mr Erasmus Bolter claimed that Olaf Bekk worshipped pagan gods, and had been struck down by lunacy. Moreover, Mr Bolter insisted that the Bekk family was subject to a curse, and if any of them left the valley of their birth they would undergo a bodily transformation and

147

become a vampire creature.

I observed Bekk to be unconscious; his skin had become uncannily white, probably on account of blood loss due to his hands being nailed to the cart. It was as my attendants prepared to transfer the patient to the asylum that he awoke, and behaved in such a furious manner that his captors and my staff fled. I noted that he possessed no irises; indeed, his eyes were pure white with the exception of the pupils. Quickly, the man broke free of his chains. To him, they seemed no more of a restraint than if a spider had spun its web over his body. He then used his teeth to draw the iron nails from the cart's woodwork. I tell you, my brother, what had arrived at the asylum as a man now departed as a monster.

Within a short space of time, he had run into town where he attacked the Christian congregation of the church. Many gentlemen and ladies of our noble borough were slaughtered by the monster.

Only after many hours of struggle, and many more casualties, did the bravest men overwhelm the monster. A strong fellow succeeded in removing Bekk's head with an axe. Nevertheless, the headless body writhed for two days. The jaws still attempted to bite anyone who strayed too close, while those dreadful, white eyes burned with great fury. And I knew that Evil and Satan's powers of darkness still haunt our God-fearing nation.

THIRTY-FIVE

Five hours ago Clarissa Prior had stood waiting for Paul to arrive. At that time she had no way of knowing that the minibus that carried Paul to Danby-Mask had broken down as it forded the stream. What Clarissa did know was that she had been attacked. She'd felt that wet mouth on her throat.

Now Clarissa Prior stood on the hillside. Even though the sun wouldn't rise for another three hours she could see clearly. Bare winter trees stretched out before her. Threading its way through the black mass of the forest was the River Lepping. Hailstones glinted in the grass – pearls of ice scattered over the hillside. When she exhaled there were no longer any plumes of white vapour, even though a cold wind blew. She slipped off her coat and let it fall. It was no longer of any use to her.

At either side of her, silent figures gazed over the forest. They seemed to be waiting for some-one, or something.

'I'm Clarissa Prior,' she whispered. 'I'm eighteen. I go to Ravendale School. Next year I begin studying for my degree. I'm eighteen, I'm Clarissa ... I'm alive.'

The man who'd attacked Clarissa stood next to

her. Those egg-like eyes of his gazed across the valley. His lips were bloody.

Slowly, and with an utter sense of dread, she lifted her fingers to her neck. Her fingertips slipped inside the wound in her throat. She pushed her fingers in as far as the knuckles. The wound gaped open – a yawning mouth with sticky, wet lips.

'I'm Clarissa...' She paused. 'What's my second name? I'm sixteen ... no, I'm eighteen. I'm alive ... I am alive.'

The people standing at either side of her continued to gaze out across the valley. Just like her, they didn't feel the cold. Her companions were young men and women. They resembled one another. Possibly from the same family? Each had white skin which revealed black veins. And each man and woman had identical eyes. There was no colour in them, just the fierce black dot.

She asked herself, 'Why don't I just walk away from them?' However, she had no inclination to leave. This was where she needed to be. Was this her destiny? To stand here in the dark with these strangers?

'I'm called...' She'd forgotten her name. 'I'm not old.' She'd forgotten her age. 'I'm not dead ... please, God ... tell me I'm not dead.'

The word VAMPIRE never entered her head. It would soon, though.

She examined the beautiful face of a blonde-haired woman standing nearby. The stranger had not shown any sign that she realized that Clarissa was even there. None of them had. So none had reacted to what must be a shocking

150

wound in her throat.

'I'm not badly hurt,' Clarissa murmured to herself. 'I'm not like them.'

Slowly, almost as if she were in a trance, she raised her hand level with her eyes. Veins bulged underneath the bone-white skin. The veins were black.

'I'm not like them.' Although by now she understood these profoundly grim facts: *she was exactly like them. And she wouldn't be going home ever again.*

'Goodbye, Mum. Goodbye, Dad. Goodbye, Robbie. I love you...'

THIRTY-SIX

Tony opened his eyes. People carried him through the forest. Tree trunks drifted by. Nettles brushed his face. For some reason they didn't sting. When he tried to lift his hands to push the nettles back nothing happened.

'Put me down,' Tony said. 'I can walk.'

Nobody replied. Yet he heard whispering. A dozen people or more appeared to be having a furtive conversation.

'Where are you taking me?'

Another voice abruptly asked the same question: 'Where are you taking me?'

A second voice on the other side of him uttered

151

the same words: 'Where are you taking me?'

Tony recognized the voices. One was Luke. He was the guy who'd been driving them back home from Scarborough when—

BANG! The bus had been attacked. Something enormous had carved through the water. All that spray and: POW! People had been torn out of the bus. Screaming and blood and violence – he'd felt terrible pain. Powerful hands had grabbed hold of him ... they'd torn him apart. That's how that agonizing ripping of muscle had felt. He'd heard his joints come out of their sockets with a loud POP! After that, a crackle as his bones snapped. But that was a nightmare, wasn't it? He'd lost consciousness and had a bad dream, surely? He was OK now. He was being carried, though he knew he was capable of walking.

Tony looked to his right. Luke's head was in profile, and maybe just a foot from his own. It swayed slightly due to the motion of being carried.

'Where are you taking me?' This was Luke's voice.

Tony asked, 'Luke? What happened?'

Luke turned to look at Tony as if he'd been startled by the voice. Tony would have flinched back in shock. Only he couldn't move away more than a couple of inches from that disgusting thing in front of him. That disgusting *thing* was Luke. The skin of his face had been torn away. A pair of bulging eyes stared at Tony. The eyes resembled glass balls that had been embedded in raw beef. Tony knew that blood-red *thing* was comprised of the muscles, ten-

152

dons, veins and bloody bones that lay beneath a human being's skin. An accident, or deliberate mutilation, had robbed Luke of his face. If it hadn't been for the familiar voice, Tony wouldn't have been able to identify his friend.

But he's still alive? Tony thought as waves of horror crashed through him. *Why isn't he screaming in pain? Doesn't he know that his face has been torn off?* Tony turned his head to the left. Anita, one of the girls from the bus, stared at the forest in a daze. All he could see of her was her face in profile, which was perhaps a foot away.

'Anita, are you OK?'

She turned to him. Her eyes were fixed into the characteristic 'thousand-yard stare' of someone suffering from shock. The poor girl had been traumatized.

'Anita?'

'I was still awake when it happened to me. I saw everything ... *I felt everything.*' Her eyes locked on to his. 'It got hold of my arms and tore them off. It broke me into pieces. I was still awake and I felt everything ... every awful thing...' Her voice trailed off to be replaced by broken-hearted sobbing.

At that moment, Tony noticed the sound of a fast-flowing river. What was more, it now seemed to him that he, Anita and Luke were somehow tied together. And still he couldn't tell who carried them. Then the strangeness of the situation grew much stranger. He glimpsed bare feet beneath him to his left and right. The feet splashed down into water.

'Don't take us into the river!' Tony shouted. 'It's deeper than you think. We'll be drowned!'

Tony thought that he, Anita and Luke, poor mutilated Luke, were going to be carried across the Lepping.

Then he knew that wouldn't be the case. Because he now saw his mirror image in the water. In fact, he saw dozens of faces there. The sight was so extreme, so astonishing and so terrifying that he was too shocked to close his eyes.

Tony stared at the monstrous body reflected there. *Picture a whale that walks on human legs. Lots of bare human legs.* He described the creature to himself in a cold way that lacked emotion. Shock had, for now, separated him from reality, so he could view this vile thing dispassionately. *The whale-creature is over thirty feet long. Protruding from its body are arms. These are in motion, almost like the tentacles of an octopus. Most striking of all: the heads. The heads are connected by human necks to the whale (or whale-like) body.*

'And I'm part of it,' he said aloud. 'I've become part of the monster.'

The other heads near him began to scream. He glanced from left to right at the heads of the men and women who'd been with him on the minibus. Luke screamed the loudest of all when he saw his reflection in the water. He'd realized, at last, that his head now lacked a face.

Tony wanted to scream. In fact, it would have been utterly appropriate in the circumstances. Yet he simply gazed at his reflection when the creature lowered its massive body into the water.

Moments later, it glided downwards into the deepest part of the river. It would rest there, as its harvest of new heads and limbs knitted themselves into its unnatural flesh.

THIRTY-SEVEN

Tom Westonby slept soundly until ten. As he climbed out of bed in his hotel room he couldn't remember when he'd last slept for so long. He realized he'd be too late to catch up with June in the dining room for breakfast. Never mind, he'd phone her if he didn't see her downstairs.

Since he'd never intended to book into the hotel for the night, and had brought nothing other than the clothes he was wearing, the manageress had provided a toiletry pack, containing toothpaste, a toothbrush and comb for only a nominal cost, along with a T-shirt that bore the words STATION HOTEL – A PROUD HISTORY OF COMFORT & ELEGANCE.

Outside, the hail had turned to grey slush in the streets. With it being Sunday, the bells were pealing from one of Leppington's churches. Tom switched on the television and had almost finished getting dressed when the local news bulletin came on-screen. Pictures showed the mangled remains of a minibus in fast-flowing water. If anything, the vehicle had the appearance of being disembowelled. Its seats were on

155

the outside of the wreckage.

A female voice related what had happened last night: *'A minibus returning from Scarborough, with seven young people on board, appears to have crashed before coming to rest in a stream. With the exception of one woman, all the passengers are missing. Police say that the search for survivors is continuing. Meanwhile, officers are waiting to question a youth who was driving a truck, which was found in a nearby field. Both the woman and the youth are receiving treatment at Whitby hospital.'*

Tom knew exactly where the crash had taken place. It was where the road forded a stream just a couple of miles from his house. Suspecting this was no accident, he quickly finished getting dressed. He needed to find June Valko. Circumstances were changing. The danger was no longer confined to the pair of them. The threat was spilling out like an epidemic to claim other victims. But what could he do to stop it? For now, that was a question he could not answer.

THIRTY-EIGHT

The hospital visit started badly. Kit Bolter and Owen Westonby stood outside the room where Jez had been put by the doctors. Kit had been given a lift by Jez's parents to the new hospital near Whitby's Pannett Park. Owen had turned down the offer of the ride, because he intended taking the bus to Whitby with Eden Taylor.

Owen grimaced. 'I hate that hospital smell, don't you? Makes you think of viral oozings and puke.'

Kit didn't attempt to conceal his irritation and asked, 'Where's Eden?'

'She's taking a walk round town while I see Jez.'

'What's your priority here, Owen? Coming to see your friend after an accident, which nearly killed him? Or going on a date with that girl?'

'Are you jealous, Kit?'

'Are you friggin' insensitive?'

Owen glared as if he'd no right to make comments like that.

The door opened and Jez's father stepped out. 'You can both see him now. I thought you'd like to have some time alone together, seeing as you're such old friends. I remember when you all got bikes that Christmas, and you'd ride up

157

and down the village street for hours. The Three Musketeers, that's what everyone called you.' Mr Pollock's eyes had tears in them.

'Thanks, Mr Pollock,' Owen said.

Mr Pollock held a cap in his big, powerful hands, which he anxiously turned round and round. 'You know what the police are thinking, don't you? They know my lad was driving illegally. They found the truck upside down in a field not far from that smashed-up minibus. They've already made up their minds that he caused that accident. But it's not true. A nurse told me that my lad saved a woman's life. Jez isn't a criminal ... he's a hero.' A tear rolled down the big man's cheek. 'Sorry, lads. You'll be wanting to see Jez. Thanks for coming. You're good boys. Jez couldn't have a better pair of friends.' With that, Mr Pollock walked away.

Jez lay propped up in bed. A bright orange cast encased one arm. Both of them stared at the teenager in shock. Kit even thought they'd entered the wrong room.

'Hey ... you've got to write on my cast. That's the rule.' Jez's voice came from a mass of purple and green bumps. 'Write what you want. Make it bloody rude.'

'Jez ... Shit.' Owen stared at the bruised face. 'You look like the Elephant Man.'

'Or an alien from outer space.' Kit decided to be cheerful and jokey for Jez's sake. 'Man, your face is puke-tastic.'

Jez seemed half asleep, his movements were sluggish. He raised the arm that was in the cast. 'The bone snapped. They had to fix it with steel

158

bolts. Doctors are turning me into a cyborg ... that means I'm now part man, part machine. I'm going to live for ever.' He grinned. 'I'm going to be the first immortal guy from Danby-Mask. Half man. Half robot.'

Kit and Owen exchanged glances. Jez's odd manner disturbed them both.

'Are you in pain?' Kit asked.

'Nopey nope. They're giving me pills ... they make me feel sooooo good.'

'The painkillers are making him...' Owen made a circular motion with his finger. 'Cuckoo.'

'I heard that, guys.'

'The main thing,' Kit said, 'is that you're not in any pain.'

'Broke my arm ... bashed my head on the steering wheel ... knocked cold. But I still got him.' Jez grinned.

'Got who?'

'The monster. The one that your mojo pod filmed. I got the monster. I hit the gas and *wham!* Drove the truck into him.'

Owen smiled. 'Great, you got him.'

'You're the number one monster killer,' said Kit.

'Nobody believes me.' Jez sighed. 'You don't either, do you?'

'Of course we do.' Owen's tone clearly revealed that he was humouring his friend. 'Human race one. Monster kingdom zero.'

'The monster would have got the girl. But I got him. Rammed him with the truck. He must have run off. Slithered off perhaps ... or whatever monsters do. They gave me prunes for breakfast. I hate prunes.'

'Maybe we should leave you to get some rest?' Kit suggested.

Owen tapped his friend's foot where it was covered by the sheet. 'You're looking groggy, pal.'

'Nobody believes me,' Jez repeated. 'I banged my head. They're keeping me in for observation. That's standard procedure. Just in case I go: *aaargh*.' He pretended to go into convulsions.

'Did the woman tell the police what happened?' asked Kit.

'Yep. Said I saved her life. Said the monster got everyone in the bus. It was going to get her, too, but I arrived and, *POW!* Smacked the truck into it.'

'What did the police say about this woman's story?'

'They don't believe her, either. They say she's confused. Out of her head ... gaga.' He sighed. 'Prunes. Who feeds a sixteen-year-old prunes?'

'We should be going,' Owen said. 'We'll come and visit you tomorrow.'

'Tomorrow might be too late. I might be gone...' He chuckled. 'I'm going home tomorrow morning.'

Kit patted his friend's uninjured arm. 'Take care, mate.'

'Kiss some nurses for us.' Owen saluted. 'That's an order.'

Jez laughed then winced. 'Ouch. Forgot about my arm. They had to pin the bone. Snappy-doo.' With his good hand he waved at the bedside table. 'There's a pen. Write stuff on my cast.'

Five minutes later Kit and Owen stood outside the hospital.

Kit said, 'Will you come with me to see Jez when he's back home tomorrow, or will you be fondling Eden Taylor?'

'What's eating you, Kit?'

'Because you only came to see Jez as an afterthought. I could tell that you didn't want to be there.'

'That's not true.'

Kit's voice rose, 'OK, you were in the room with us, but you were thinking about that girl.'

'You piece of shit.'

'I'm not the shit! You are!' Kit shoved Owen.

Owen, the bigger of the two, pushed back, slamming Kit against the wall.

Kit's face burned. 'Is that the Westonby way, huh? If you get into an argument, you start pushing people around and causing some pain!'

'Why are you behaving like this, Kit? What have I done to you?'

'That girl's got into your brain. I can see what's happening: you're turning your back on Jez and me.'

'I know your problem. You can't get a girlfriend – that's why you're behaving like a cockhead!'

Kit stormed off. After ten yards he stopped, turned on his friend and yelled, 'I know what your brother did! He killed my uncle! *Tom Westonby is a murderer!*'

THIRTY-NINE

Tom Westonby and June Valko checked out of the hotel. Tom suggested she leave her hire car here in Leppington. They could return to the cottage in his van. At this time on a Sunday the streets of Leppington were quiet. A man, carrying a newspaper, walked with a black dog at his side. A mechanized street cleaner ambled along, sucking up rubbish left by Saturday's shoppers. Meanwhile, a pair of crows picked at a beef burger that lay on the pavement.

Tom and June had decided to eat lunch in the hotel. That way they could talk about their plans for this evening. Although the plan lacked finesse, Tom knew that June would be powerful bait. There would be a result tonight. He was certain one or more of the vampires would come to the house again. What happened next was anyone's guess. He knew June was hopeful she could communicate with her father – or rather communicate with the creature he'd become. Meanwhile, Tom gambled that Nicola would appear: the woman he'd loved, and who he'd seen transform into one of those vampire-like creatures.

Tom had also been thinking hard about the news report he'd seen on television. A minibus carrying seven people had been found torn apart in a stream not far from where he lived. After he and June climbed into the van, he sat staring into space, the ignition key still in his hand.

'What's the matter?' June asked.

He glanced across at her. The woman's electric blue eyes were sparks of fire.

'I keep thinking about the accident last night.'

'The one involving the bus?'

They'd spoken about that, too, and he'd explained how he believed that the tragedy was no road traffic accident. What was more, he believed it tied into what had been happening in the Lepping valley for centuries: specifically, that there were supernatural creatures in the valley, which were capable of causing harm.

He said, 'The more I think about the accident, along with the fact that most of the passengers are missing, the more I'm convinced that those *things* are responsible.'

'Vampires.' She spoke with conviction. 'We said we wouldn't be shy about using the name to describe them.'

'OK, vampires. I think either they attacked the bus, or it was Helsvir.'

'If they're killing innocent people then we must do something.'

'No. They're not killing – they're recruiting.'

Those blue eyes widened. 'What do you mean?'

'Until you arrived, those creatures – the vampires and Helsvir – had done nothing for years. Like I said, they haunted the forest like ghosts. They were harmless. They weren't seen by

163

anyone. They didn't interfere in human lives. All that's changed now.'

'You said that my arrival triggered the change.'

He nodded. 'I'm sure that's the case.'

'Then I should leave.'

'But once a finger pulls a trigger and the bullet leaves the gun it doesn't matter about the trigger. It's been pulled, the bullet's on its way. There's no stopping it.' He sighed. 'Sorry. I've lived alone for so long that sometimes when I talk it sounds peculiar even to me.'

'No, I understand. You're saying that when I arrived at your house I set some change in motion.'

'I believe so. It's like the vampires and Helsvir were harmless germs. For some reason, however, those harmless bugs have mutated into a killer disease.'

He watched two crows sweep down on their black wings. They'd seen a dead rat on the ground. One bird snipped off its tail. The other went for the eyes.

June paid no attention to the feasting birds. Instead, she rested her hand on his arm. 'You still haven't explained what you mean by *recruiting*.'

'For years the vampires have been harmless. Now they've become active. In fact, they're downright aggressive. On Friday night one tried to drown me in the river. After that, they laid siege to the house, and even tried to break in. When that failed, one climbed down the chimney so it could get a good look at you. But...' He took a deep breath as the realization grew teeth, so it could gnaw at his peace of mind. 'But they've decided they need to be stronger. So they've started to increase their numbers. Although I'm not sure yet if it's the vampires doing it, or whether it's Helsvir.' He gave a grim smile. 'You'll need a strong stomach when I describe Helsvir in detail.'

'Helsvir is this dragon creature? The one created by the Viking god?'

Tom nodded. 'He's an ally of the vampires. And he's powerful, vicious and extremely dangerous. He makes himself bigger and even more powerful by attacking people and incorporating their bodies into his own body. Somehow he can glue limbs and heads to himself. I told you that you'd need a strong stomach. He makes those birds cute and cuddly in comparison.' Tom nodded in the direction of the crows that were now using their beaks to tug out the rat's wormy intestine.

'So, why do they want to become more powerful?'

'They've got big plans. They're building up their army.'

'Why?'

He started the engine. 'Are you sure you're not a reporter, June? You can't stop yourself asking questions.'

'I'm asking them,' she said firmly, 'because I believe you know more than you're telling me.'

'I've had a long time to speculate, and guess, that's all. The vampires and Helsvir are mysteries bundled up in yet more mystery. No living person knows exactly what they are or how they think.'

'But you suspect they're building an army. So why are they doing that?'

'Armies exist to protect a country's citizens.'

'So, who will this vampire army protect?'

'You, Miss Valko. They will protect you, because you are the last of the Bekk bloodline. Your DNA is valuable to them, and must be preserved.'

'Then they only want to safeguard my blood, not me?'

'Of course, armies exist for reasons other than protecting national borders and people.'

She nodded. 'Sometimes they're used for invasion, too.' She bit her lip as the realization sank in. 'So will I be responsible for starting a war?'

'For all our sakes, June, I hope it won't come to that. Because I don't know if it's a war that the human race can win.' With that, he drove away from the hotel, and joined the road that would take him home.

FORTY

Her eyes were open. There appeared to be no light entering the cave. She could still see, though. To her, darkness wasn't darkness any more. How she got inside the cave she didn't know. Tree roots had burst through the rock above her – a deadly tangle of witch hair.

'I'm...' she whispered. 'I'm ... my name is...' For a long time she lay on the floor, gazing up at the witch hair ... that's how that tangle looked to her. At last she remembered. 'My name is Clarissa Prior. I'm not dead ... am I?'

There were others in the cave, too. Gleaming white bodies, dressed in faded clothes. They lay on the slab of rock that formed the floor. They didn't move. They lay there as if dead. Not a trace of colour appeared in those wide eyes. In each eye was a pupil – a fierce black spot. Those eyes stared into infinity.

Clarissa didn't move ... couldn't move ... yet somehow she managed to whisper. 'Why am I in a cave? How can I see when there's no light?' But see she did. She no longer had need for light.

Something like a stone altar stood at one end of the cave. Animal skulls covered a block of stone. There were swords, too, leaning against the block; they were all rusted. Above the altar, a figure of a powerful, bearded man had been carved into the rock. *A sacred place*, she thought. *Sacred to pagans.*

Slowly, she managed to tilt her head sideways. In that silent tomb there were perhaps ten men and women. She was struck by their similarity; they could be members of the same family. Nearest to her lay the man who'd attacked her in the village. *And made me one of them* ... Her blood had left brown smears around his mouth.

'You all look like vampires,' she whispered softly. 'You look just like vampires waiting for the night to come.' Her eyes returned to the cave's ceiling. At that instant, Clarissa seemed to look through the very atoms of the rock into a face that gazed down at her from above. In the face, a pair of eyes that burned with the fires of hell. They gloated over Clarissa.

She murmured: 'And I'm lying here in the dark ... just like a vampire, too.'

FORTY-ONE

Tony floated over boulders. A light came from above; he knew that the sun shone down through the surface of the river. The boulders were the size of beach balls. Fish darted away in terror from what swam through the depths. He glimpsed the bones of a stag on the riverbed. Green weed flowed from its antlers, rippling in the current. The coldness of the water had no effect on him. Even though logic dictated he could not breathe and must drown he did not. He lived. Sort of.

What he did feel, and what filled him with total dread, was a pressure inside his skull. How could he describe the sensation? *This feels like a metal skewer being inserted through my neck, before being pushed deeper and deeper into my head.* How he could describe the frightening sensation in such a calm way, he just didn't know. Nor did he know how he understood what was happening to him. But he did. He knew that something extraordinary happened to the flesh at the bottom of his neck – the flesh that was left all ragged and torn after his head had been wrenched off. That flesh gradually fused with the body of the creature that had dragged him from the minibus. The stubby remains of his spinal column that jutted down from the back of his skull had become embedded in the monstrous carcass. He knew the arteries inside his neck were being fused with those of the monster.

But that sense of a cold skewer being inserted into my brain? That's the worst sensation of all. Somehow he realized that the 'skewer' was, in fact, a tough, worm-like nerve invading his skull. The creature's nervous system gradually merged with his brain tissue. Slowly, relentlessly, he was becoming part of this monster.

The *thing*'s nerves would also be invading the brains of Luke, Anita and the others.

With that cold, probing root came new emotions and thoughts. Sometimes he thought like Tony had always thought. The next moment, a flood of alien ideas roared through his head. They were so violent that his jaw opened and snapped shut with a savage ferocity.

He glanced at Luke. His friend turned to him. Luke's eyes stared out from a mess of raw meat that was his face now that the actual face had gone. The eyes glittered with excitement.

Tony turned his head the other way. Heads budded all along the flanks of the creature. Mouths twisted into savage grins as the personalities of his friends were transformed by the beast. New thoughts cascaded into their minds. When Tony recalled his neighbours in Danby-Mask a brutal anger erupted. Those men and women were vile, hateful creatures. They were the enemy. They had no right to be here in the valley. They were dangerous. Better to destroy them than run the risk of them destroying him.

The cold nerve that penetrated the core of his brain suddenly burned with a great heat. It became a living cable down which a single word rushed to inflame his mind. His lips mouthed the word. All the other heads furiously mouthed the same word, too. And though they were underwater, and though he could not hear the word, it seemed to pulse through his very flesh with such enormous power it made the rocks in the river tremble.

KILL! KILL! KILL! KILL!

Soon Danby-Mask, along with its population of loathsome men, women and children, would be destroyed.

KILL! KILL! KILL! KILL!

Tony had never felt joy like this before. His joy would be even greater when he saw his own family being torn to bloody pieces by this mighty beast of which he was just a humble part.

FORTY-TWO

His blood boiled with fury. Even so, Owen concealed his anger from Eden Taylor that Sunday afternoon when they walked through Whitby. He clowned around for her on the harbour wall, adroitly concealing his absolute rage.

But why oh why had Kit been a total bastard? Why did he stand there outside the hospital and tell me that my own brother murdered his uncle?

171

Why? Owen wanted to punch Kit. He wanted to inflict real hurt. Had Kit gone crazy? What drove him to make such an insane accusation? Tom would never hurt anybody.

Later, he and Eden ate Thai food in a little restaurant (normally, he'd have chosen burgers over Thai, but he wanted to impress Eden, and appear sophisticated and worldly). The food was delicious. He'd never tasted prawns like these. Then again, Eden might have been that extra ingredient that made everything taste so wonderful.

When they left the restaurant Eden said, 'Penny for them.'

'Pardon.'

'Penny for your thoughts.'

'Oh. It shows.'

Her smile was a sweet one. 'You're worried about Jez. That's only understandable. It proves you're a nice person, too.'

Then she kissed him.

FORTY-THREE

At the same time that Owen and Eden kissed in Whitby, and Tom and June travelled in the direction of Danby-Mask, the crow flew high above the River Lepping. The river – a glistening, black vein – threaded itself through the forest. Some legends say that crows are the eyes of the gods. Through a crow's eyes the gods could watch human beings as they worked, laughed, sang songs, fought their battles, or walked with the ones they loved. As the crow glided above the forest its sharp eyes glimpsed the secret entrance to the cave where the vampires slept by day. The bird glided low over the river as mighty Helsvir broke its surface. Spray flew into the air as the creature, studded with dozens of human heads, lunged out on to the shore where the poacher was setting snares for roe deer.

Soon, the screaming man had been dragged into the water. Helsvir, the creature made from the bodies of the dead, would dismember the poacher and weave parts of the corpse into its own flesh. The beast was a living mosaic – if this protector of the Bekk family line could ever be described as living.

FORTY-FOUR

The winter gloom was closing in by the time Tom parked the van in the garage at his parents' house. Neither his mother nor his father was home, which suited him fine – and saved on explanations why this dark-skinned, blue-eyed woman was with him.

He and June followed a footpath that took them through trees that had been turned into dark, looming sentinels now that winter had stripped them of their leaves. Roots burst out of

173

the ground. They'd trip anyone not taking care. If someone did fall, there were plenty of jagged rocks. Easy to shatter a kneecap if you fell on those. This part of the forest had taken a violent dislike to human beings, or so it seemed to Tom. The place was anything but people-friendly.

He said, 'June, take care when you walk by the river. Keep as far away from the water as possible.'

Helsvir ... am I warning her about that creature? After all, I know it spends time in the river. Swimming there like a killer shark. But there are other dangers, too. Tom explained as they walked: 'The banks crumble under your feet sometimes. It's happened to me before. One second I was walking on what seemed like a solid footpath, the next it broke away and I ended up tumbling head over backside into the water.'

She laughed, then her face became serious. 'Sorry. I'm sure that isn't as comical as it sounds.'

'The River Lepping can be a real psychopath.'

'How can a river be psychopath?'

'Because sometimes it pretends to be a pleasant stretch of water, but it's trying to lull people into a false sense of security. So they'll get too close then ... wham!' He clapped his hands together like a trap springing shut.

June shot the river wary glances, perhaps wondering if it might find a devious way of dragging her in. 'Come to think of it, there is something menacing about the Lepping. Have you seen how black the water is?'

174

'Liquid darkness.' He shivered, as if cold, dead fingers stroked his neck. 'That's what I always think when I see it. Liquid darkness. The river hides all kinds of unpleasant surprises. You might walk through what looks like shallow water, no more than ankle deep. The next step could drop you into an underwater ravine that's ten feet deep.'

'It's claimed lots of lives?'

He nodded. 'Sometimes I'm asked to search the riverbed for bodies.'

They walked in silence after that. Already, dusk had invaded this murderous terrain. Shadows grew darker. Sometimes the gloom required them to reach out their hands to make sure they didn't walk into a tree trunk. The pungent scent of the forest grew stronger.

All of a sudden, June spoke the words that stopped Tom dead. He stared at her in shock.

June repeated her remarkable statement: 'I've decided to bring my mother here.'

'That's impossible.'

'I've made up my mind, Tom.'

'You told me she's a sick woman.'

'My mother's not sick.' June spoke softly. 'She's dying.'

'I'm sorry to hear that, but—'

'Over the last few hours I've been thinking about her.' June had clearly made a decision. 'There's no other alternative. I'll bring my mother here. She can see her husband.'

'Husband? June, the man's a vampire. A monster. He's—'

'He's also my father, Tom.'

175

'Dear God. You can't be serious!'

'There's no need to shout.'

'Just look at this!' He spun round, flinging out his arms, gesturing at the forest and the forbidding river – that liquid darkness that had claimed so many lives. 'I can't even bring a vehicle to the cottage. Can your mother walk through this kind of terrain? If she can't, what do you propose then?'

'I'll carry her by myself if I must.'

With a determined expression, she continued walking. Tom followed. *Damn it, she's crazy.* Before he could stop himself he started to yell.

'June, listen! You can't bring an invalid into a place like this! Feel how damp and how cold it is – that alone could finish anyone who's seriously ill to begin with.'

'I've made my mind up, Tom.'

'What the hell do think your mother will do, if we could even bring her to the cottage? Do you really think she's going to have some kind of touching reunion with her husband?'

'She could see him from a bedroom window.'

'Like Juliet cooing to Romeo from the balcony?'

'If you're not going to take this seriously...'

'I am taking this seriously.'

'This is the last chance I have to save my mother's life.'

'Save her life? You'll kill her!'

June lashed out. The slap stung his cheek. Tom furiously grabbed her by the arms. Her blue eyes flashed as she glared up at him. The sound of the river seemed to grow louder, almost becoming a roar, and Tom realized that was actually the sound of his blood thundering through the arteries in his neck.

'I'm not allowing you to turn your mother into a corpse,' he thundered. 'It's enough for my conscience that I'm letting you risk your life. Don't you get it? Our lives are in danger! We might not survive until morning! Or we might end up becoming vampires, too!'

'Tonight, I plan telling my mother the truth about my father – and yes, he might be some kind of bloodsucking monster, but if she sees him that might heal her broken heart. I know it sounds crazy. But if she knows that Jacob Bekk was forced to return here because of a curse, then she'll know that he didn't dump her.'

'It's impossible. I won't let you bring her here.'

'Please, Tom. Please...'

The bushes parted as a figure loped through on to the path. June reacted with shock. Instinctively, she pressed her body to Tom's as if seeking his protection.

'Hey, Tom. I've been looking for you ... uh...'

Tom recognized the figure in front of him. 'Owen.' Releasing his grip on June's arms he took a step back. Too late, already Owen Westonby had seen him with June, and already the sixteen-year-old had misconstrued what they were doing. No doubt he interpreted their closeness as a romantic cuddle by the water's edge.

'Owen? Is there anything wrong?'

'No ... well, yeah ... I need to talk to you, Tom.'

'It'll be dark soon.'

Owen repeatedly glanced from Tom's face to the face of the stranger next to him. The beautiful dark-skinned woman with the striking eyes that were a brilliant blue. 'Tom. This is important.'

Tom took a deep breath. Damn it, already his plans had begun to fall apart. June had told him that she wanted to bring her mother here ... into the vampires' lair! That was just crazy. Now Owen stood there wearing an expression of total anxiety.

After taking another deep breath, Tom nodded. 'OK, Owen. But it's important you're back home before it gets dark.'

Owen nodded. Tom knew what the kid was thinking: *Tom wants to get rid of me as quickly as possible so he can be alone with this woman.*

Life was becoming more complicated, *and dangerous*, by the moment. What the next few hours would bring, only God – and maybe the devil – knew.

FORTY-FIVE

SEX.

Owen's staring at me, Tom thought, *and that's why he thinks I've brought this woman to the cottage. He's telling himself that I want him out of the house so I can rip her clothes off ... he couldn't be more mistaken, more wrong, more than one million miles off target. June's bait. We're going to use her to lure the vampires here...*

Tom had lit the fire and a golden light filled the lounge. Outside, the night was drawing closer.

Tom hurried through the introductions. 'Owen, this is June Valko. June, this is my brother, Owen.'

'Nice to meet you, Owen.' June held out her hand.

Owen had been brought up to be polite, and with impeccable politeness shook her hand. Though his expression suggested he wished the woman wasn't here.

'Tom, I'd like to freshen up,' she said, 'before we...'

Owen's eyes widened; he clearly expected her to say: *before we make love.*

June, however, completed the sentence as: 'before we have something to eat.'

179

But the damage had been done. Owen clearly expected the pair to have a raging two-person orgy the moment he left.

Tom asked, 'What did you want to tell me, Owen?'

'Right ... uh.' He glanced at June.

June picked up her shoulder bag. 'If you can just point me to the bathroom?'

'First door at the top of the stairs. The next door on the right is the spare bedroom. Put your things in there. You can ... sleep there ... my room's the one opposite.' Damn it, those words of his sounded so stilted. So bloody awkward, too; sounded like he'd read them from a card.

After she left the room Owen raised his eyebrows.

'June's a friend. She's staying over.' Tom cleared his throat. 'I don't want to rush you, but you need to get back home before it gets dark.'

'So you keep telling me.'

Tom could imagine Owen racing back to Mull-Rigg Hall where he lived. He'd scramble through the door blabbing to their mother at the top of his voice. *Tom's got a strange woman in the cottage. He almost threw me out of there. Already he'll be DOING IT with her!*

These thoughts burned inside Tom's head. Of course, it didn't matter if Tom had women to stay here. He was single – and had been for five years ever since his bride, Nicola, vanished.

'Tom? Something on your mind?'

'Uh?' Grunting, Tom turned to his brother. 'Nothing.'

'You were staring into the fire like you'd lost

your Rolex in there or something.'

'What did you want to see me about?'

'Jez. He's had an accident.'

'Oh, no. Is he hurt?'

'Bashed about a bit – his arm's broken.'

'I'm sorry to hear that. Is he at home?'

'His head smashed into the steering wheel; they're keeping him in hospital overnight for observation.'

'Steering wheel? He was driving?'

'Yeah, his dad's truck.' Owen sat down on the sofa. The worry on the kid's face was clear to see. 'It gets worse.'

Tom felt cold inside. 'How much worse?'

'Jez is sixteen. Too young to drive. He doesn't have insurance, either. Also...' Owen swallowed. 'The cops think he caused an accident yesterday. They found him near the wreck of a minibus.'

Tom whistled. 'My God. I saw news about it on television. The passengers are missing.'

'Jez's dad is convinced the police will charge him with dangerous driving and killing the people in the bus.'

'You weren't with him, were you?'

'No ... look there isn't a mark on me.'

'I'm your brother, Owen. I care about you, so you'd tell me if you were involved in the accident, wouldn't you?'

'Dad can vouch I was home when the accident happened.'

Tom couldn't hide his relief. 'Thank God for that.'

'But what about Jez? He'll go to prison, won't he?'

181

'What did Jez say?'

'What he told me was strange ... I mean *really* strange.'

'In what way?'

Owen seemed unsure how to begin. 'Heck, Tom. It's been a weird weekend. So much has happened since Friday.'

'Tell me about it.'

'Well, I met a girl. Her name's Eden Taylor. She's gorgeous.'

Tom listened as his sixteen-year-old brother explained how he'd found the metal cylinder in the forest (Tom already knew about that), and how Kit had discovered that it was an automatic camera designed to observe wildlife. On Friday evening Owen, Kit and Jez had watched the footage filmed by the camera. Tom's scalp prickled as he heard that the camera appeared to have captured images of a large animal – in fact, a HUGE animal – passing by at the dead of night.

Helsvir? Could that have been Helsvir that the camera filmed? Owen would have heard rumours about a mythical creature that supposedly roamed the valley, but he no doubt dismissed it as some laughable story. Tom began to wonder how much he should reveal to his brother regarding the vampires and Helsvir, and how much he ran the risk of appearing like an out-and-out lunatic. *Dear God, life's been getting a lot more complicated in the last twenty-four hours.*

Meanwhile, Owen spoke about visiting Jez in hospital, and how his friend's face had been so bruised that he hadn't recognized him. Owen repeated what Jez had told him about the accident, including finding the only survivor of the minibus in the road.

'Can Jez remember what caused the accident?' Tom asked.

'This is where the story gets really strange. Jez said he saw a big animal moving towards the woman ... getting ready to attack her. So Jez drove flat out and rammed the truck into this –' he shrugged – 'whatever it was.'

'Did he get a good look at it?'

'Good enough. He said it was the animal we'd seen in the video shot by the wildlife camera.' He sighed. 'Of course, it might be shock that affected his memory. Or even all those painkillers they'd given him. He was, like, gaga – completely stoned.'

'So he might have dreamt all this about driving into the monster?'

'Monster? I never used the word "monster".'

'Sounds to me like he was describing a monster.' Tom glanced at the window. Night had fallen. The world outside had vanished into sinister blackness. 'I hope the police aren't too hard on Jez.'

'But Jez has got a witness. Someone backs up his story. The woman he saved – she said the monster chased her. She told the cops that Jez deliberately crashed into the monster that attacked the others on the bus.'

June walked into the lounge, rubbing her head with a towel. 'I hope you don't mind, Tom, I used your shower. Oh? Sorry, I thought Owen

183

had gone.'

'You don't get rid of me that easily.' Owen laughed, pretending he was joking.

Tom knew that he was annoyed. The kid must have thought they both wanted him out of their love nest. Of course, that wasn't true. Owen was misunderstanding the situation.

Owen stood up. 'I'll head off now. I don't want to spoil your evening.'

Tom shook his head. 'You can't go now. It's dark.'

'I'm not scared of the dark, Tom. I'm a big boy now in case you hadn't noticed.'

Owen stood at nearly six feet tall. On the other hand, Tom knew that he wouldn't have a chance if a vampire attacked him on the way back to Mull-Rigg Hall. But was he safe there? Previously the vampires had never left the forest. Perhaps that had changed? After all, one had tried to drown Tom just a couple of nights ago.

'Owen, I really do want you to stay here.'

'No. I'm going home.'

'Owen—'

Something snapped in the sixteen-year-old. Suddenly he dashed for the door, flung it open and vanished into the dangerous night.

FORTY-SIX

'June! Shut and bolt this door, I'll be right back!'

Just a moment ago, Owen had run out of the house. He'd obviously believed that Tom had been more interested in getting all hot and intimate with the woman, rather than hearing about Jez's accident. By this time night had fallen. Owen, no doubt, intended to walk, or run, home through the forest.

Tom couldn't let him. If the vampires pounced he wouldn't stand a chance. He caught the pale flash of Owen's face as he ran. Sheer terror of what might happen to the kid made Tom's legs move with explosive power. He caught up with Owen as he raced through the trees.

'Let go of me!' Owen yelled as Tom grabbed hold.

'Come back to the house.'

'Why?'

'It's dark.'

'Why are you so worried about the dark?'

'Come back inside.'

Owen snarled. 'Why? Do you want me to watch?'

'What?'

'Watch you and your girlfriend playing wrestling tournaments on the couch.'

'Owen, it's not like that. We're—'

'Friends?'

'She's related to Nicola.'

'Oh.'

Even in the gloom Tom saw Owen's eyes widen. 'Jesus, Tom. I didn't think Nicola had any living relatives.'

'Come back inside, Owen.' He shot anxious glances into the darkness that engulfed the forest. The night had the same intensity of black that permeated a tomb. 'Please, Owen. I don't want you walking through the wood at night.'

'Why ever not? I've done it loads of times before.'

'Well, I was too stupid to warn you. It's not safe out there after dark.'

Owen paused. 'You know something? Kit Bolter told me that you killed his uncle.'

'Oh.'

'Did you? Because today was the first time I'd ever heard anything about that.' Owen sounded angry and confused. 'What made my friend say that?'

'We need to get back to the house, Owen, we really do. It isn't safe out here.'

'You're scared, aren't you?'

'Come back inside. We can get something to eat.'

'And talk?'

'And talk,' Tom agreed.

They walked back to the house. June unbolted the door and let them in. After that, Tom closed the door, turned the key in the lock, and shot the bolts across. For now they were safe.

FORTY-SEVEN

In the kitchen, Tom Westonby and June Valko put a meal together. Owen sat by the living room fire, sending texts. This could be a cosy scene of a happy family in their warm, snug cottage on a Sunday evening.

Tom knew that the situation might flip from cosy to horrific in a second. Night had fallen. June Valko was here, the last of the Bekk bloodline. The Bekks had lived in this Yorkshire valley for more than a thousand years, ever since their Viking ancestors had crossed the North Sea from Denmark.

June had consented to be bait. Their plan had more holes in it than a mesh screen, but the basic idea was that June would draw the vampires to the house, so that they might begin a dialogue with them. *That's a long shot*, Tom thought, *an insanely long shot. The vampires might not talk. They might kill instead. There are bars on the windows, the doors are locked, but there's that lift-shaft of a chimney. Damn it, the chimney flue's so wide a whole platoon of vampires could climb down there in forty seconds tops.* So this plan to draw the vampires close to the house, yet keep them outside, could be fatally flawed. Fatal for him and Owen, that is. *June has Bekk blood*

187

in her veins; she's going to be safe as houses.

June checked the oven. 'Does the orange light go out when it's hot enough?'

Tom nodded as he tipped frozen drumsticks out of a bag on to a tray. 'It'll be good to go in a minute. Would you chop those tomatoes for me? I'm going to brew coffee. We'll need plenty of caffeine.'

June whispered, 'How much does your brother know?'

'About Helsvir and the vampires? Nothing.'

'Are you going to tell him?'

'Would he believe me? Or would he think I'm insane?'

'I believe there are vampires in the forest.'

'That's because you saw them with your own eyes. Heck, you even fought one of them and saved my life.'

'So you plan to wait until the vampires come to the house, so Owen can see them?'

'We don't know for certain they'll come.'

'You said I'd be the bait to draw them.'

'That's the plan.' He lifted three mugs from a shelf. 'But whether any vampires are going to turn up tonight isn't certain. What if the vampire we suspect is your father is satisfied with seeing you? That might be enough for him. He might have gone back to haunting the forest like he's done in the past.'

'If my mother did come here, perhaps—'

'No, June, there's no way you can haul a critically sick woman through that kind of terrain out there.'

'Tom, I know it sounds insane, only I've got

this gut feeling that if somehow my mother can see my father, then...'

'A miracle will happen? She'll realize that he hadn't deliberately abandoned her after all.'

'She loved him so much, Tom. After he left that love became toxic – it poisoned her mind to the extent that she no longer wanted to live.'

He shook his head. 'Bringing your mother here will kill her. The shock of seeing those monsters out there will be enough to do that.'

With a steely expression, she said, 'The oven's hot enough.' She picked up the tray of chicken drumsticks, opened the oven and slotted them on to the shelf.

'I'm sorry, June. It's just that bringing your mother here is such a bad idea.'

'OK, Tom. OK.' Folding her arms she stared out of the window.

'I'll ... uhm ... check on Owen.'

Owen sat on the arm of the sofa. He scrolled through pages on his phone.

'Yo, bro.' Owen sounded relaxed. 'I've texted Dad to say I'm staying with you tonight.'

'What about the other thing?'

'Oh, yeah ... I told him to keep windows and doors locked.' Owen frowned. 'But I didn't see anything on the news about an escaped prisoner being on the run.'

'They think he might be making for Danby-Mask; he has family there.' *Yes, that's a humdinger of a white lie*, Tom thought. But if the vampires were getting all predatory he wanted to make sure his parents were safe. Mull-Rigg Hall had barred windows, too, and thick doors ... but, heck, nobody was safe locally from those things. Tom's anxiety had grown by the minute tonight. He realized that everyone in the valley should be warned. But what could he do to alert people to the danger? He could hardly run through the village shouting, 'LOCK YOUR DOORS! THE VAMPIRES ARE TURNING VIOLENT! SHUT YOUR WINDOWS! THERE'S A MON-STER ON THE PROWL!' *They'd pump me full of medication and call in the psychiatrists.* He could picture the local newspaper headlines: MENTALLY DISTURBED MAN RAVES ABOUT VAMPIRES.

'Tom?'

'Uh?'

'You're doing it again.'

'Doing what?'

'Staring into space and not listening to me.'

'Sorry, Owen.'

'Something's really eating you, bro. What's on your mind?'

'You can guess.'

'Nicola?'

Tom nodded. True, Nicola was always on his mind. Although tonight other worries gnawed at him. Like being cruel to June about not bringing her mother here. *Cruel to be kind ... that's what I had to be.* Also, he had the dilemma of some-how warning the local population that this had become a dangerous place. *But how do I get people to believe me?*

'Damn it, Tom, you're doing it again. You've got this look of dread on your face. Has someone told you that the world's going to blow up?'

190

'I'm just preoccupied.'

'Just haunted by ghosts more like.'

'What ghosts?'

'Figure of speech, bro.'

June walked in with a mug in each hand. When she spoke she snapped the word, 'Coffee.'

'June?' Owen began. 'How long have you known my brother?'

'Since Friday.' The woman didn't linger and returned to the kitchen.

'You've known her a couple of days?' Owen watched Tom's expression as if trying to divine what his brother was thinking. 'You only knew Nicola a few days before you married her, didn't you?'

'Owen, I don't want to talk about that tonight.'

Owen sighed. 'A text came from Jez. The police are going to question him about the accident again tomorrow.'

'Maybe it'll be a formality; you know, taking witness statements.'

'It's a pity we can't catch the monster that caused the accident. The police would believe him then.'

'The monster isn't real.' *How many white lies is that I've told Owen?*

'I wish some big, hairy bastard out there had caused the accident. Then my best friend wouldn't wind up in prison.' Owen shook his head. 'And there's another text from Eden.'

'Your girlfriend?'

'I can't call her that yet.' Owen's cheeks turned pink. 'Eden's worried about someone called Clarissa. Apparently she went missing from the village last night.'

The news interested Tom – worried him, too. 'Did she give any more details?'

'Nope. Eden's going to text me again when she finds out more.'

'You really think Eden's special, don't you?'

'Yeah, I hope this ... you know, develops into ... well.'

'A relationship?'

Owen nodded. 'That's what I'm hoping.'

'I hope so, too, Owen. Be sure to text Eden. Tell her to keep the doors and windows locked. Stress that it's important that she doesn't go out after dark.'

'Uh? This escaped prisoner?'

Another white lie slipped easily from Tom's lips. 'He's supposed to be dangerous. A real psycho.'

'And the cops say he's in this valley?'

'Somewhere close by.'

'So that's why you're all antsy about being outdoors at night?'

'I just want people I care about to be safe.' Tom's eyes strayed to the fireplace. Maybe he could fix a steel grate across the chimney flue. Make the thing vampire proof.

Meanwhile, Owen shivered.

Tom glanced at him. 'Feeling cold?'

'It's just a draught. June must have opened the back door.'

Tom slammed the mug down on the coffee table, splashing its contents. He hurtled across the room in the direction of the kitchen.

'June!' he shouted. 'June, where are you?'

FORTY-EIGHT

The door yawned open. Tom froze there in the middle of the kitchen. Outside, the forest lay smothered in darkness.

'June!'

Tom ran through the doorway into the back yard. He almost collided with the figure before he saw it. A face turned towards him, revealing a pair of blue eyes that were bright as electric sparks. When she exhaled a huge billow of white vapour poured from her mouth and went ghosting across the yard towards the trees ... it was as if that ancient forest could steal the air from her lungs.

'June? What did you see?'

A note of astonishment filled her voice. 'I didn't see anything, but I heard him. He called my name.'

'Who did?'

'My father.'

'June, you've never talked to your father, so how can you know his voice?'

She seemed dazed. 'I did hear him, Tom. He was out here, calling my name.'

Tom glanced round the yard. He couldn't see anyone. However, the line of trees started just thirty paces or so away. That forbidding mass of timber could have contained an army and he wouldn't even know it was there.

June hissed, 'Listen.'

Tom heard a faint breeze whisper through the branches. Nothing else.

'Listen, Tom. Can you hear him? He's calling my name.' She began to move away from the house. 'Wait here, I'll go and find him.'

He grabbed her wrist. 'Are you crazy? They might be trying to lure you out there.'

'Tom, let me find him.'

The light falling through the kitchen door revealed her expression of rapture. She had a sharp intake of breath; the expression of joy intensified. Perhaps she heard her father again ... or, rather, she thought she heard him, because Tom heard nothing but the breeze. The breeze blew harder. Its sheer coldness cut through his clothes, driving a chill into his skin.

'Come on, June. It's not safe out here.'

She allowed herself to be guided back to the cottage. Once inside, Tom closed and bolted the door.

Owen appeared. 'You made a right crapping mess, spilling the coffee like that. But then it's your house, Tommo.' He used the nickname jokingly. 'I got the worst up with tissues.' He held up a soggy, brown pulp. 'Have you got a cloth? I'll mop up the rest.' Suddenly, he noticed June's expression. 'What happened to her?'

'He called my name.'

Tom took one of June's hands and rubbed hard, trying to shake her out of the trance. 'Owen, there's some brandy in the booze cupboard. Will you pour a glass?'

'Are you sure she's alright?' Owen eyed her doubtfully. 'She looks like she's seen something...' he grimaced. 'Something bad.'

'Brandy, Owen.'

'Sure.' Owen collected a glass and went to the cupboard.

Guiding her into the living room, Tom stood her in front of the fire. Heat and light washed over her. Abruptly, she came out of the trance with a gasp.

'Tom?'

'You said you heard someone call your name?'

She frowned. 'Was that real? I thought I'd dropped asleep.'

'You don't remember going outside?'

'No.' She flinched back, suddenly scared. 'I went outside?'

'Someone, or something, called you.'

'Tom, we've got to be careful. Take the keys out of the doors.' Her anxiety increased. 'We've got to keep watch on one another.' She clutched his hands. 'I'm sure they got inside my head. They made me go out there.'

'I didn't put any water in the brandy. Uh ... sorry.' Owen paused in the doorway. He'd seen June holding Tom's hands. 'Here you go.' He put the glass down on the coffee table.

Damn it, Tom thought, *he'll be convinced I'm desperately in love with her.*

June released Tom's hands. 'Thank you, Owen.'

'No problem, cheers. I'll get the chicken out of the oven. It looks cooked to me. Any beer,

Tom?'

'You're sixteen, Owen.'

'Any beer, *please,* Tom?'

'Try the other fridge in the pantry. But just one bottle, OK?'

'Absolutely, my dear brother, absolutely.' He gave a gentlemanly bow. 'Dinner is served.' With that, he bowed again and vanished back into the kitchen.

June laughed. The laughter was longer and louder than what might be considered normal in the circumstances. Tom, however, suspected that she was just so relieved to be back inside the house where it was safe ... relatively safe, that is. One hint that she was still shaken by what happened was the way she picked up the glass and downed the brandy in one gulp.

'I don't know if this will keep out visitors.' He picked up long pieces of firewood that he'd sawn from hefty branches and jammed them upright in the hearth, so that they partly blocked the throat of the chimney. Flames immediately began to lick the bark. 'Hardly monster proof, but worth a try.'

June gazed at the window. 'You don't hear it, do you?'

He shook his head.

'My father's still calling my name ... but I don't think I'm hearing with my ears. Somehow he's got inside my head.'

'Don't worry, I'll stay close to you tonight.'

'I still want to try and communicate if he comes to the house.' Her voice became determined. 'I can try speaking to him from a bedroom window.'

Owen boomed from the kitchen, 'Hey, love birds. Time to eat the meat.'

Tom shook his head. 'After you, June.'

Before joining them in the kitchen, Tom cast a wistful glance in the direction of the window. The silhouettes of trees towered over the house – massive giants that seemed to be creeping closer.

Softly, he asked himself the question that had been haunting him ever since June had claimed she could hear her father calling to her. 'Nicola? Why aren't you calling my name? Have you forgotten me?'

He listened hard. All he could hear was the crackle of burning wood in the hearth. Why was his bride silent? Had she left him for ever?

'Nicola,' he murmured so the others wouldn't hear, 'please come back.'

FORTY-NINE

Kit Bolter saw the woman standing in the back yard. Light fell from the bedroom window, shining on her face. In fact, the skin that reflected the light seemed to glow brighter than the light itself. Her blond hair shone, too, as if each strand had its own internal illumination. Kit was amazed by her choice of clothes. *She's wearing a cotton dress. At night! In winter!* Kit stared in astonishment at the floaty, yellow dress that seemed no more substantial than a spider's web.

'Mother, there's someone in the yard.'

The reply his mother gave could have meant anything. A slurring sound came from the direction of her bedroom. He checked the time. Ten past nine. Damn it, her drinking had got heavier. She wanted Dad back. Dad had yelled he'd NEVER EVER come back. So a sad story, endlessly repeated the world over, of someone wanting the person they can't have and being destroyed by longing.

Kit turned his attention to the woman in the yard. Slim, pretty. Long blond hair in a Rapunzel plait. He couldn't see the colour of her eyes, even though she stared this way.

Forget her. Must be a lunatic, or a drug addict, he told himself. For some reason he found himself recalling the raging argument with Owen Westonby. What's more, he realized that their friendship had started to rot the moment that Owen had met Eden Taylor. A pretty face had sent his old friend nuts. Suddenly, Kit went a little bit nuts, too.

No, he went a lot nuts. Because he felt intense anger at the woman down in the yard. Yes, she seemed pretty. Sexy, too, in that floaty, cotton dress, with the blond plait hanging down over her full breasts. Maybe she'd be smooching round Jez before long?

Kit ran downstairs, wrenched open the door, and went out into the yard.

'Hey you!' he yelled in fury. 'This is private

property! Whoever you are! Clear off! Get away from here!' He picked up a stone and whipped his arm back like he was intending to throw a rock at an animal. 'Hey, did you hear what I said?'

She said nothing. The yellow dress rippled in the cold breeze.

Why am I doing this? This isn't like me. I never threaten anyone. I hate bullies. I hate violence. But the rage and sense of rejection by his friend made his emotions erupt. He wanted to dump that anger on the stranger.

'I said GO!'

She didn't speak; her face was hidden by shadow.

'GO!'

He lunged forward. She moved faster. Before he could even yell out she'd thrown him clean across the yard. As he lay there, she sped towards him, fast as a cat.

With a cry he scrambled away on all fours. She grabbed his foot. He felt a spike of pain in his ankle. She dragged him ... she actually dragged him across the yard. Dragged him as easily as if he weighed nothing at all.

'Leggo!'

The woman's body quivered. Anger? Excitement? He couldn't tell. All he could be sure of was that she hauled his body across the dirt. He grabbed the washing line post. When she pulled him by the foot his shoulder almost popped its joint. He squealed with pain.

Then he was free. His foot had slipped out of the shoe and she'd lost her grip.

Blindly, half out of his mind with shock, he ran. She followed with that catlike speed. *Whoosh!* Across the yard.

Kit flung himself through the doorway of the old barn. Inside, a mass of old farm equipment formed potentially lethal obstacles. A rusty plough, heaps of tyres – while shovels, pitchforks, chains, you name it, hung from roof beams like instruments of torture in a dungeon.

The stranger raced after him. She said nothing. Her feet were a light pitter-patter on the floor. CRUNCH! He ricocheted off the steel bars of a cage. Long ago, when this was a working farm, bulls were transported in the contraption. Fingers swiped at the back of his neck. He felt nails rip his skin.

He ran through the passageway formed by the bull cage. Who was this woman? Why was she trying to kill him? From Kit being the aggressor to becoming the prey had taken all of twenty seconds. He'd tried to intimidate the woman, now she terrified him. Scared and running, Kit flung himself out of the other end of the bull cage.

Stopping dead, he slammed the gate shut, crashed the bolt across. That done, he doubled back as the woman ran through the cage, not realizing the far end had been locked.

Kit shut the gate at the other end and punched the bolt across.

'Ha!' he yelled in triumph. 'I've got you. You're mine!'

FIFTY

'I've got you. You're mine!' Kit's triumphant shout rang from the walls. He'd imprisoned the stranger in the old cage that had once been used to trap and transport bulls. Now all this equipment was junk, of course. The barn itself had holes in the roof; the entire place smelt of rot. But the bull cage had worked perfectly. Built from steel bars, and measuring ten feet in length, it had an opening at each end that could be sealed shut with strong gates, designed to thwart even the angriest of beasts.

And he, Kit Bolter, had done just that. The darkness meant he could barely see the woman in the cage. *Hell, I can hear her, though*, he thought with amazement. A huge clanging hurt his ears as she threw herself at the gates that sealed her prison shut.

'Stop that,' he demanded. 'I've caught you. You have to do what I say.'

Years ago, Kit decided that madness ran in the Bolter family. Yet he thought it was the violent, drug-dealing uncles and cousins who were the crazy ones. Now he asked himself if he'd inherited the Bolter streak of lunacy, too.

A brittle clicking reached his ears in the darkness. *That sounds like TEETH! She's BITING the bars!*

He shouted, 'You were trespassing! I have every right to restrain you.' *Restrain? Dear God, I've made her my prisoner. I could go to jail for this.*

He suspected today's traumatic events had triggered his downright strange behaviour. Jez had suffered that terrible accident. Kit had been shocked to see Jez in hospital with his arm broken and face busted up. After that, the bitter argument with Owen. No wonder he was emotionally hacked up, because usually Kit could be considered an icon of sensitivity.

But this woman fascinated Kit. Her strength. Her fearlessness. Heck, her sheer strangeness. All that spoke to him in some way. What was more, from the sound of things, she was actually GNAWING at the steel bars. Now this he had to see. He clambered over a pile of plastic crates so he could reach the light switch. *CLICK!* Out of six light bulbs strung on a wire only one bulb worked. Even so, that was enough to illuminate this bizarre scene.

Here he was, Kit Bolter, with a strange woman as his prisoner. Warily, he approached the cage, his heart thumping hard. He couldn't tell if he was incredibly excited or absolutely terrified.

'Hello?' He stepped closer. 'Are you OK?'

The stranger had her back to him. She wore her blonde hair in a long, thick plait, which whipped from side to side as she attacked the steelwork with her teeth.

'You're going to hurt yourself doing that.' Resting his hands on the bars, he leaned forward

202

in order to see her better. *Bare feet? She's got bare feet. No shoes!* 'Hey, what's wrong with you?' he slapped the bars. 'It's freezing. What happened to your shoes? Hey!' This refusal even to glance in his direction annoyed him. 'Hey, listen to me.' He thumped the steelwork again.

She moved so fast she was a blur. One moment she had her back to him, the next her face blasted out of the shadows to within three inches of his.

The face at the other side of the bars belonged to a nightmare. He'd seen photographs of faces similar to this – they'd been of dead people. Kit stopped breathing; he stopped moving – he couldn't move – not so much as a finger. The sight of that nightmare face froze his muscles. The beautiful stranger stared at him. At first glance this seemed to be a girl of around his age, sixteen or so. Yet she didn't appear to be entirely human. The whiteness of that skin was uncanny. Unnatural. Her eyes? Well, they had no colour at all. They were completely white apart from the black pupils. The pupils contracted to fierce, black points. Concentrations of hatred.

That's when something incredible happened. Kit Bolter's mind broke free of the world. The breeze that made an eerie moan as it blew through the barn faded to silence. At the same instant, however, he heard things that are impossible for a human to hear. Nevertheless, those impossible sounds reached his ears.

Because Kit heard the soft sigh of dust falling through the dead air of ancient tombs. His gaze remained locked on to the stark, white face of the beautiful stranger. And yet it seemed to him

203

that he saw through her eyes, for he looked into his own face, with its dark, melancholy eyes. He saw the anxiety there for his mother's health, which forever haunted him. And he recognized the sadness over the death of his friendship with Owen Westonby.

Then he was seeing the girl again. A spectral blue appeared in her eyes. She inhaled as if she hadn't breathed in years. Gently, she took both his hands in hers. The face began to look less like a horror mask. Truly, she was beautiful.

Her lips parted. 'Help me,' she whispered.

'What do you want me to do?'

'Help me to be like you.'

'What do you mean?'

'Help me be *alive* like you.'

Anguish savagely stabbed him in the heart. He grimaced with the sheer hurt of wanting to help her but not knowing how.

'I'm sorry I locked you in there,' he said – and in a searing blast of revelation he thought: I LOVE YOU. I'LL DO ANYTHING TO HELP. ANYTHING. 'I'll open the gate and let you out.'

She didn't release his hands. In fact, the grip became tighter. Just then, he found himself believing the impossible – that they'd remain together, joined like this, for ever and ever. 'Will you help me?' she whispered. 'Do you promise?'

'Yes, of course.'

'My name is Freya. I ... I've been ill, or ... or lost...' The ghostly blue colouring began to fade from her eyes. 'Lost in the dark...'

'My name is Kit Bolter. I promise to help you.' His absolute love for her ... his impetuous, impossibly strong love meant that he would promise anything. 'Let me open the gate.'

'No, Kit ... if you let me out I'll hurt you.'

'Not now you won't: we're friends.'

She said nothing. Her eyes seemed to stare through his face into his brain.

Kit found himself making a confession. 'I know what it's like to be a prisoner of your own bad feelings. I grew up knowing that my mother drank too much. She used the bottle to damp down her misery. You see, my father had a compulsion to provoke fights with men for no other reason than his own gratification. He'd come home singing to himself – so happy with what he'd done. He'd say, "Kit, I knocked a guy clean off his feet. When I punched his face it felt soft as a baby's. Ha! By the time I'd finished he was crying like a baby, as well."' Kit felt such enormous affection for the stranger. 'At home there was always an atmosphere of violence. As I got older I felt it more and more. When my father came home I'd get pains in my stomach – it was the tension. My muscles got tighter and tighter. It felt like I was standing next to a bomb that was just about to explode.'

Freya gazed into his face. 'We can help each other. I'm sure we can.'

'I'll let you out.'

'Don't open the gate yet, Kit.'

'Why?'

'Like I said, I might hurt you. I don't want to, but I might not be able to stop myself.'

Being with this beautiful girl intoxicated him, so he didn't question such a peculiar admission

205

that she might attack him.

'But how will you get out of there?' he asked.

Freya examined the gate's locking mechanism. 'Good,' she said. 'I can't reach the bolt with my hands.'

'Why's that good?'

'Because me not being able to reach it has just saved your life.'

He smiled and felt his head spin with love for her. 'So, you like me?' OK, the question sounded needy. He needed to ask it nonetheless.

'Yes, I do, Kit.' The white eyes fixed on him. 'I can tell you're not like other boys.'

He suddenly stood taller. Those were the nicest words he'd ever heard. 'Let me open the gate.'

'No. Pass me that piece of string on the floor.'

'Why do you need string?'

'It'll take me a little while to tie a loop. Then I can sort of lasso the bolt and pull it back. That will unlock the gate, won't it?'

'Sure.' He handed her the string.

'Thanks, Kit.'

'My pleasure, Freya.'

They smiled at each other.

'Kit, go back to the house. Lock the doors. Don't come out again until its daylight. Not even if I ask you to.'

'OK.'

'Run, Kit, run!' She began to form a loop in one end of the string. 'I'll find you again soon.'

He loped back to the house, a massive grin of sheer happiness filling his face. The oddness of the situation didn't trouble him. Love is truly blind.

FIFTY-ONE

By ten o'clock on that Sunday night everyone appeared relaxed in the cottage known as Skanderberg. The living room walls reflected the golden firelight. Tom sat in an armchair, enjoying the pleasant fragrance of logs burning in the hearth. A cosy atmosphere enfolded them like a warm, fleece blanket.

Of course, the world outside was a different matter. The forest remained a cold, dark, forbidding place. As he sipped strong coffee, he glanced at the fireplace. Flames roared up the cavernous throat of the chimney. At any moment, a figure might drop down into the flames. It had happened two nights ago; that figure might make the same unorthodox entrance again.

'So you've seen our famous dragon?' Owen asked June as they sat chatting together on the sofa.

'The dragon?' She shot Tom a startled glance, clearly wondering how much Owen knew about the creatures that haunted the forest. 'What dragon?'

'This one.' Owen stood up in order to point at the carving set into the wall. 'His name's Helsvir. There are legends that Viking gods made a dragon out of corpses. Tom found this under some wood panelling when he rebuilt the cottage.'

'Oh...' June made a point of smiling. 'Your brother mentioned something about it. Isn't it the local version of the Loch Ness Monster?'

'Something like that. Viking dragons tend not to blow fire out of their mouths or fly. They're still vicious though, and prefer to live in wet, slimy places.' Owen laughed. 'You know, parents still scare their children with stories about Helsvir.'

'So you don't believe in him?'

'No way. There's lots of stuff on the Internet about Helsvir, like some people believe he's real.'

'There are rumours that something big's been seen in the valley.' Tom decided to test Owen's disbelief. After all, he knew that Jez had told him about driving the truck into some monster of an animal just twenty-four hours ago.

Owen, however, clearly preferred rational explanations. 'People see wild ponies, or stags, or even an escaped cow; everything gets exaggerated.' Owen tapped the carving with his finger. 'They say that picture of Helsvir was made over a thousand years ago. Look, you can see he's made up of dead bodies ... a kind of Frankenstein dragon. See these circles? Those are supposed to be human heads. And all these lines coming out of the body are people's legs that have somehow been grafted on. If anything, it shows that our ancestors had a wild imagination.'

June said, 'Believing in things, sometimes even in impossible things, help people live better lives.'

'You mean like angels and good luck charms?' Owen shrugged. 'Give me science any day. What do you say, Tom?'

Tom smiled. 'There's a powerful force that can't be dissected or tested in a laboratory.'

'Nuclear fusion?'

'Love.'

Owen blushed. 'If you're going to get soppy...'

'No. Think about it. People fall in love during wars. They love their children and do everything they can to make their lives better. If there's a famine or a natural disaster people strive to help their loved ones to survive. Love is the motor that drives the human race.'

'I agree, Tom.' June slapped her hands down on to her lap. 'Love keeps the human race alive.'

Owen grinned. 'Now you're both getting soppy. Uh.' His phone chirped. ''Scuse me folks.' He read the text. 'It's from Jez. He says they've given him more painkillers and he's going to ride the moon later.'

'Ride the moon?' echoed June puzzled.

'Local slang for being high or drunk,' Tom explained. He'd already told June about the accident involving a friend of Owen's called Jez Pollock.

Owen's expression became grave. 'Jez is worried about what the police will say tomorrow. He thinks they'll charge him with causing the minibus to crash.'

'I'll make some more coffee.' June headed for

the kitchen.

June must have guessed that Owen would like to speak to Tom in private, so she'd made an excuse about the coffee.

'Do you think Jez will go to prison?' asked Owen.

'He says he drove at an animal, not the bus.'

'But who'll believe that?'

'The woman from the bus backs his story up.'

'Their heads were all screwed up with shock.' Owen looked worried. 'I can't imagine Jez in prison. For God's sake, he's still at school. Prison will crap up his life, won't it? Everyone will condemn him as the kid who killed a bus full of people.'

'They haven't found the passengers yet,' Tom reminded him.

'But everyone's saying that the bus ended up where the road fords a stream, and that the bodies have been carried away.'

Tom felt for his brother. The misery on his face tugged at Tom's heart. He wished he could say something that would make him feel better. 'The accident investigators will find there's no paint from the bus on the truck. They'll have ways of knowing that Jez didn't cause the accident.'

Owen shook his head. Tom knew that his words didn't reassure him.

A chirp signalled that Owen had received another text. 'This is from Kit.' Owen frowned. 'He says he's got himself a girlfriend. Her name's Freya.'

'That's some good news.' Tom smiled.

'Is it? When guys get girls, does it always end

in them losing their best friends?'

'What makes you say that?'

'I had an argument with Kit today over Eden. In fact, it almost became a fight.'

'I'm sure you'll stay friends. After all, you both had a shock over Jez's accident. Emotions are bound to be running high.'

Owen nodded. 'I'll get the blanket and pillows for the sofa.'

'No, use my bedroom. I'll take the sofa.'

'No way. Why do you want to give up your bed?'

'You've been through a tough time. You need a good night's sleep.'

'Oh, I get it.' A smile played around his lips. ''Nuff said, bro.'

Tom planned to stay awake in the lounge in case any more visitors arrived via the chimney. Of course now Owen thought that Tom had come up with a sneaky plan. That he would stay downstairs until Owen was asleep before tip-toeing to the spare bedroom occupied by June.

At that moment, June returned with more coffee. The pair of them were determined to stay awake tonight. There was a chance the vampires would return. Both wanted to be wide awake if they did. Equally, both were determined to keep Owen oblivious of the vampires unless circumstances made it impossible.

Tom's phone did the chirping this time; a text from the local police. Tom had been requested to help find the minibus passengers. Specifically, the police wanted him to make an underwater search of part of the river nearest where the road forded the stream, and where the wrecked bus had been found. Tom knew that this meant the rescue services had given up hope of finding live survivors. This would now be an operation to recover the dead. Tom would help in the search, of course, but he didn't want to add to Owen's worries about Jez, so he said something about the text being from an old friend who had a diving school in Greece.

Owen yawned. 'I'm going to call it a day. Sleep well, you two.'

'Thank you.' June smiled. 'Good night.'

Playfully, he ruffled Tom's hair. 'Thanks for letting me use your bed, Tommo. Don't get a stiff neck on the sofa.'

'I won't. Good night, Owen. And don't worry about Jez. I'm sure everything will turn out alright.'

'Cheers, Tom.'

Tom waited until he heard the door shut upstairs. He turned to June. 'You know, he's certain that we're going to spend the night together.'

'We are, aren't we?'

Her blue eyes twinkled. She was teasing him.

He smiled. 'Yes, we are spending the night together down here. We'll be fully clothed, guzzling black coffee and pacing the floor waiting for inhuman visitors.'

She glanced at the fireplace. 'Maybe even the vampire world's answer to Santa Claus,' she said drily, referring to how the man, or the vampire rather, had arrived in the house two nights ago.

Despite the situation they both laughed. Though their laughter had a shrill quality that revealed their anxiety.

Dangerous times lie ahead, Tom told himself as the laughter surrendered to a cold feeling inside. *This is like sitting on a time bomb.*

FIFTY-TWO

Midnight in the valley. The River Lepping flowed towards the sea, just as it had done for thousands of years. Foxes barked in the forest; often that yelping bark could sound like a human cry – a lost and forlorn sound. In Skanderberg, June Valko and Tom Westonby drank coffee, and talked about how there must be a secret world that adjoins this one. A world where myth and reality, and the living and the dead, co-exist as equals. And sometimes the doorways to such a world lie open in certain places. Perhaps one of those invisible doorways had swung open nearby? Would it be only a matter of time before the lords of that realm decided to invade this world?

Upstairs, Owen Westonby lay in bed. He'd left the bedside light on and gazed up at the black beams that ran across the white ceiling. From a nail in one of the beams hung a necklace made from white cowrie shells, a souvenir from when Tom worked as a diver overseas.

What a crazy day ... what a crazy weekend. On Friday evening he'd watched video footage of what appeared to be a large animal that had been filmed by the automatic camera. He'd met Eden Taylor. He'd even taken her on the Saturday afternoon monster hunt – of course, that was a joke, just something to do. After all, Danby-Mask teenagers were in danger of dying of boredom. So anything to break the monotony, right? He thought about Eden mainly. Her face shone in his mind's eye ... those blue eyes ... the blonde hair. *Yeah, OK, and a sexy body, too. Don't forget the sexy body.* Not that there'd be any danger of forgetting about the shape of her waist, or the marvellous way her breasts enhanced her sweater. The tingles started. He licked his lips. *Eden Taylor ... I want to dream about you tonight.* Even though his thoughts were largely and hotly focused on the girl, they kept returning to Jez. His friend's face had been like one of those horror masks – all sticky wet cuts, bruises and a grotesquely swollen forehead. Worse than the injuries would be the prospect of getting into big trouble with the police.

Owen recalled the text from Kit Bolter, too. Kit had announced he'd got a girlfriend. That her name was Freya. Owen couldn't remember any local girl called Freya. Had his friend invented the girl to get even with Owen somehow? But that didn't make sense, did it? Why dream up a fake girl to get back at his friend? He shook his head, troubled. Kit had started to act so strangely over the last couple of days.

Meanwhile, five miles from Skanderberg, Kit Bolter sat cross-legged on his bed. He turned his

214

head from side to side as he examined his face in the wall mirror. Wow! Even from here he could see those scratches on his neck. *Check out that graze!* Kit touched the fiery red mark on his cheek. *She did that! Freya's amazing. She threw me across the yard like I was a doll.* Rather than feeling woeful at such rough handling from a girl he'd never met before, he felt absurdly pleased. Heck, even irrationally pleased.

'Freya's like no other girl I've met,' he murmured to himself. Then he suddenly hissed, 'Because she's a monster.' He glared into the mirror. 'No, she's not a monster. She's unique.'

Instead of thinking about those white eyes with their fierce pupils, he thought about her lovely hair, and the yellow dress. Freya had promised to come back tomorrow. Kit Bolter couldn't wait. Because he knew tomorrow night would be the most exciting night of his life.

A north wind brought flakes of snow. They came in spectral waves of white. It was as if a door had swung open to another world – one much colder than this. A woman had been waiting behind that door for five long years. Now she stepped through into this world. Her skin seemed to blaze with its own light in the darkness. The bark of the trees smouldered in her presence. Foxes fled into their burrows. Even the river seemed to shrink back when she walked along the shore.

The woman, or what had been a woman once, had known Tom Westonby. She'd loved him. She'd become his bride. Then an evil power had torn them apart.

'I'm here, Tom. We're going to be together again ... even if that means we'll be together in death.'

FIFTY-THREE

The man walked alongside the river. Snow flew out of the darkness to strike his face. The November night was brutally cold. The trees resembled black talons, stretching upwards as if hell-bent on violently clawing at the sky.

The man used a powerful flashlight to illuminate the river banks. His son had been on the minibus. Even though the rescue teams, the lazy bastards, had given up the search, he wouldn't stop until he'd found Tony. What if his son had been swept away from the bus after the crash? The current might have carried him miles downstream. He might be huddled under a bush, freezing to death. And the useless, lazy, good-for-nothing rescuers had given up, gone home, and tucked themselves up in their friggin' beds.

The Lepping surged around rocks. The breeze tugged at branches, making them groan. A sound that echoed the pain he felt. No, he wouldn't desert Tony. He'd find him. And find him alive.

The man moved faster, shining the flashlight in front of him. The river glistened blackly. Trees shivered as the breeze blew harder. The snow rushed out of the darkness. Hard flakes stung his face. His muscles scrunched up tight. He wondered if this was a sixth sense that he'd find Tony around the next bend in the river. But the sensation was so intense it sickened him. This is the kind of physical reaction someone must get when stumbling across a rotting corpse. His heart pounded. Right at that instant, he wanted to cry out. But why did he feel like this? What was happening? It was as if the world around him had become electrified – as if a huge current had been switched on.

He scrambled round a clump of bushes.

And found a woman standing there. A beautiful woman with blonde hair ... and oh, she glowed so brightly. She burned his eyes. Overwhelmed by this blistering vision, he turned away.

'Tony!'

There was his son. He recognized his face. But wait ... other faces formed a line at either side of his son. They seemed to sprout from a bulky object. All the eyes stared at him – the eyes of the dead – the eyes of the damned.

The man froze. 'Tony ... it's me.'

His son was the first to bite. The other faces bit, too, sinking their teeth into the man's skin, hurting him more than he'd ever been hurt before.

Then Helsvir set to work. The agony became unbearable. And the man's screams rang out long and loud – but unheard by human ears.

FIFTY-FOUR

June stood beside Tom in the lounge. They watched the sun rise above the treetops. Soon that blood-red disc drove away the gloom that surrounded the house.

June shook her head. 'I thought they would have come back.'

'Vampires don't obey natural laws. It's not possible to anticipate how they'll behave.'

'But on Friday night one even climbed down the chimney so he could see me.' She shivered; gooseflesh on her neck. 'I'm sure that that was my father. So why hasn't he tried to contact me?'

'He's a vampire, June. Perhaps seeing you the once was all he needed.'

'So much for our plan of using me as bait.'

'We guessed that you'd lure your father back here. We guessed wrong.'

'Damn.' She scrunched her lips together in anger. 'In my mind's eye, I could see how it would have worked. This place is built like a castle. We'd be safe in here while I talked to my father through the window.'

'Unless he pulled the chimney trick again.'

'There'd have been no need for him to do that if I stood at one of the windows.'

'Still risky,' he said.

'There are bars over the windows. He wouldn't have been able to hurt me ... not that I believe my father would harm me.'

'He might not have been able to stop himself. Vampires aren't rational beings.'

'How do you know that?'

He sighed. 'Let's say, from past observations. They don't think or act like us.'

June's eyes were hard. She didn't want to give up now. Tom knew she had some plan – admittedly a flimsy, unlikely-to-work plan – that involved somehow reuniting her father, Jacob Bekk, with her mother. Then maybe her mother would understand that Jacob hadn't left her of his own free will, and that would be enough to heal her broken heart. Tom believed the plan to be so unworkable as to be pure fantasy on June's part.

But then is my plan to find Nicola just as fantastical? I'd hoped June Valko's presence here would provoke Nicola into returning to the cottage. Am I just as deluded – and desperate – to believe my plan is any more likely to work than hers?

Five years ago, Tom Westonby had watched his bride transform into a vampire. The blush of life had fled from her face. Her veins had turned black and worm-like under her skin. Those beautiful eyes of hers had turned monstrous – the blue had faded to leave two pupils that were just so *inhuman.*

'We could try again,' June suggested. 'What if we go out into the forest after dark?'

'That could be the end of us.' He tried to sound

dismissive of the suggestion, yet secretly it excited him. If Nicola was out there he might meet her. Especially if June acted as bait again. *However, that means deliberately putting June in danger*, he thought. *Nicola might get jealous and attack June. Am I prepared to risk sacrificing an innocent woman in order to get what I want?*

His phone chirped. Another text had arrived from the police. He told June that he'd been asked to take his diving gear to where the minibus had been found and search the water for bodies.

'Have you done this kind of work before?' she asked.

'Recovering bodies?' He nodded. 'Although in this case...' He reached out and ran a fingertip over the carved dragon on the living room wall. 'I get the feeling this was involved.'

'Helsvir?'

'He might be taking more victims and merging their bones and flesh into his to make him stronger.'

'So you think the creature is intending to launch some kind of attack?'

'Could be.'

'Then we need to warn the police? We can't just—'

Tom heard footsteps on the stairs and put a finger to his lips.

Owen breezed into the lounge. 'Sorry I can't stay for breakfast. I've got to grab my stuff before I catch the school bus.'

'Nice to meet you anyway, Owen.' June held

220

out her hand.

Smiling, Owen shook it. 'Likewise. You staying around, June?'

'Maybe another day or two.'

'Good, you've brought some daylight into this place.'

'Daylight?' Tom echoed.

June smiled. 'Owen, thank you, that's flattering as well as being poetic.'

He grinned back. 'I guess it was poetic, wasn't it?'

Tom said, 'Try not to worry about Jez. I'm sure everything will be OK.'

'Cheers, Tom. I'm hoping for the same. Ciao, amigos.' With that, Owen headed out through the door. Within seconds the forest had swallowed him.

June shivered. 'I'm glad those vampires don't come out in the daylight. Even so, it's still making me anxious to see Owen out there by himself.'

'There's no guarantee they won't come out by day. There's no guarantees about anything concerning the vampires. In fact, there's no guarantee that we'll be safe here, if they decide to attack.'

June eyes became even more troubled. 'I've been thinking, Tom. I've got Bekk blood in my veins, haven't I? And the Bekks triggered the vampire curse if they ever left this place. So what happens if, by coming here, I've been infected with the curse, or vampire bug, or whatever it is?'

'I don't believe that you have.'

'Look. You've just said that there are no guarantees. What if I have the curse, too? What if I can never leave, in case I run the risk of turning into one of those things? What if I have to stay here for ever?'

FIFTY-FIVE

Owen Westonby skipped a library study period at school in order to visit Jez in hospital. Flurries of snow descended on Whitby harbour with growing ferocity. Fishermen were telling one another that a fierce storm was in its way.

Owen found Jez alone in the hospital room. The sixteen-year-old had put a bedpan (fortunately unused) on the window sill and was testing his aim by flicking paper clips at the target. His broken arm had been suspended in a sling across his chest. The fingers that emerged from the orange cast wiggled every now and again. Owen noticed that Jez now wore clothes rather than pyjamas.

'You're dressed,' Owen said.

'Your talent for observation astounds me, Sherlock.' He threw another paper clip. It bounced off the window pane into the bedpan. 'Not bad, uh? I've invented my own physical therapy.'

'I hadn't expected to see you out of bed.'

'You mean you thought I'd be dribbling and

babbling nonsense.'

'You do that anyway, so why change the habit of a lifetime?'

Jez laughed, pleased that they'd returned to their usual banter. 'I'm waiting to be discharged.'

'Don't you dare discharge yourself near me. I've only just cleaned these boots.'

Again, Jez laughed, but his face then turned serious. 'The police keep asking me questions. They want to nail me for causing the crash.'

'But you didn't though, did you?'

Jez shook his head. 'No ... the trouble is I'm not sure what happened. I remember driving the truck at a big animal. I was convinced it was going to attack the woman.'

'You're telling me there really was an animal? I thought your brains were blasted by pain-killers.'

'Sometimes I really believe that there was this big brute ... something really weird and alien, and it was the size of a whale, then...' He shrugged. 'I dunno. Maybe I dreamt it and the dream got mixed up with reality.'

'Have the police told you any more about the cause of the crash?'

'They're puzzled. You can tell by the way they look at me they're baffled.'

'If they can't prove what happened you'll be in the clear.'

'That's what I'm hoping. They've admitted that they haven't found traces of the bus's paint on my truck.' He sighed. 'But it gets stranger, Owen.'

'In what way?'

'When the cops left, I trailed them down the corridor, so I could listen to them talking about me. One of them was telling the other what a state the minibus was in, and he said that he'd seen nothing like it before. He said that the metalwork wasn't smashed inwards, like you get in a crash, but it had been ripped open and out-wards.'

'You do know that Kit and me believe you?'

'Thanks, Owen. Do you want to write something rude on my cast?'

'We did yesterday. Don't you remember?'

He shook his head. 'Not really.'

'Are you in pain at all?'

Instead of answering, he said abruptly, 'I'm going to give up school and work full-time at the farm.'

'Good idea. I might join my brother and become a pro diver.'

'Nah, you'll never do that. You've the brains to go to university. Kit will go off there, too. Of all things, he wants to get into police forensics. He'll be investigating traffic accidents.'

'I thought Kit might come along during the free period.'

'He came earlier.'

'Oh, how was he?'

'Odd, but there's madness in his family, isn't there? He might have inherited the gene.' Jez spoke as if he was joking but seemed uneasy.

'Kit told me he'd got a girlfriend.'

'Freya? He said the same thing to me, too. Apparently, she just showed up in his yard at night and they hit it off.'

'Really?'

'That's what he told me.'

'It might be because of Eden that he's acting weird.'

'Who the freaking marmalade is Eden?'

'My girlfriend.'

'Crap! Something's catching. I crash the truck into a field, and you two get girlfriends overnight.'

Later, as Owen walked back to school, he was thinking about Kit. *Here's an idea*, he thought. *Why don't we go out on a double date? Eden and me. Kit and Freya. That way we can all be friends, and Kit might stop being so cranky.* Owen grinned. He couldn't wait to suggest the idea of a double date to Kit.

PART THREE

(Regimental Testimony on the Battle of Lepping Forest as written by Colonel Fulton, Christmas Day, 1726)

I deployed fifteen cannon on the river bank. Behind the cannon stood one hundred men armed with muskets. We had been summoned by the parish priest of Danby-Mask in order to destroy a beast that had been inflicting damage upon dwelling houses, and injury and death upon the villagers.

Wisely, I had the foresight to bring a young wench from Whitby Gaol in order to bait my trap. Although the wench protested with most pitiful screams, I had her bound to a tree close by the river. More comely and voluptuous bait I have yet to see! My men laughed and readied themselves for a night of sport, for none had ever targeted their artillery cannon at a monster before. Although I candidly admit that we doubted such a creature's existence. The local peasants are such a foolish rabble. I dare say they believe in witches riding broomsticks as well as a dragon that dwells in the valley

Yet perhaps we were the foolish ones to scorn the notion of creatures born of black magic. For at midnight the river waters gave a formidable heave. The blackness yielded to a glistening of white foam. Upon my word, a leviathan burst forth. The creature heaved itself on to the shore. In the light of our lanterns I clearly saw its vile body. From beneath that vast form, which was the size of a whale, protruded human arms and legs, while studding its flanks like white pearls were dozens of human heads. They opened their mouths and emitted a serpent hiss that frightened my men. The wench screamed as the creature charged forth. Whereupon I gave the order to fire. Fifteen cannon roared. Fifteen cannon balls, I do declare, struck the beast with a sound akin to vast hands clapping together. The dragon seized the wench and tore her clear and free from where she'd been bound to the tree, before retreating into the river where it vanished.

I hereby state that the bombardment of cannon balls did no harm to the creature. Subsequent rifle fire did not even appear to scratch its monstrous flesh.

The parish priest later declared that the beast is called Helsvir. He further claimed it was constructed from cadavers by a pagan devil-god long ago.

Last night my men battled with the creature again. Many brave soldiers were taken by this monstrosity known as Helsvir. There is no sign of the missing men. I therefore conclude that they have been joined with its body in some occult manner – and now good and brave Christians have been horribly merged with pagan flesh and bone.

FIFTY-SIX

The hospital sent Jez Pollock home at four o'clock. By five o'clock Jez sat with a plate of sandwiches in the living room. His mother insisted that he take painkillers with a glass of milk, fearing that the strong medication would upset her son's stomach. His parents' faces were the essence of worry. They fussed over him, trying to reassure their boy that he was not responsible for an accident that might have cost the lives of six people.

His father's manner, however, suggested that he believed the police would soon be pounding on the front door. 'Why was a little bus like that trying to cross the stream?' His father kept repeating this mantra in bewilderment. 'Nobody uses the ford when the stream's risen over the danger mark. You'd think folk would have more sense.'

'Drink your milk, dear.' This was his mother's mantra. 'Drink your milk; it'll stop the painkillers from making you feel sick.'

'I don't feel sick,' Jez told her for the tenth time. 'If anything, milk makes me want to puke.'

'Your mother's only trying to make you feel better, lad,' his father said patiently. 'She's doing her best.'

'I'm seventeen next week.' Jez pushed the glass of milk away. 'I'm not your little boy any more.'

'How's the arm?' His father pointed at the cast.

'Itchy.' The itch had become demonic. He wanted to scream at that irritating tickle. 'You know, I've got to wear this thing for five weeks.' Picking up a fork from the table, he jabbed it inside the cast to try and kill the itch. The sudden extra pressure against the broken bone triggered an explosion of pain. *'Shit.'*

'Are you alright, son?' asked his father full of concern.

'Am I hell! A busted arm? A ripped-up face? And I'm going to prison for killing those people on the bus!'

'Your milk...'

'I'm sixteen, Mam, I'm not a kid. I'm old enough to get married. And I've got the cops breathing down my neck, because I saved that woman from...'

'From what son?' His father glanced at his mother. Boy oh boy, the quantity of worry there. The sheer anxiety. 'What did you save her from?'

A sensation of panic engulfed Jez. He'd never felt this way before. *Jesus, I feel like running away.*

Jez grunted, 'I'm going for a lie down.'

'Your milk—'

'Dump it.'

Bile rose from his stomach to burn his throat ... he could taste the evil stuff, damn it.

As he clattered upstairs his mother called up

after him, 'Try to rest, son. Call if you need anything.'

I need a one-way ticket to Peru, he told himself, feeling hot, panicky and downright scared. *The cops are going to pin the accident on me. They're determined to have some poor bastard to blame ... that poor bastard's gonna be me.*

Jez sat on the bed, his clothes all wet from sweating. Beyond the window, snowflakes sailed by. He began to pace the room; a caged animal kind of pacing. Restless ... irritable ... unable to drain away excess energy ... feeling the tension rise and rise to the point where he felt his skin would burst like an over-inflated balloon. Damn it! The cast became a God-awful weight – a great big coffin for his arm. *I want to rip the damn thing off – this is torture!* He kicked aside his slippers. A startled spider ran up the wall. *Will I be doing this in prison? Pacing my cell? Wondering if the prison psychos are going to get me in the showers?*

The walls seemed to close in. He could hardly breathe. The pain in his arm grew worse. Beneath the cast, the itch crawled over his skin. *An army of spiders in there – scurrying, crawling, biting ...* Jez longed to scream.

'I'm going to die tonight. I'm going to die!' He caught sight of his face in the mirror. The bruised oval set with glittering eyes made him flinch. He'd forgotten how beat up his face was.

A flashback put him back behind the wheel of the truck again. The darkness. The road ahead. The woman running and running and running ... stumbling ... balling up on the ground – and that

231

thing following her. No, more than following! Pursuing! Hunting! He'd driven at the monster as if the truck had become a missile. The engine roared. The monster had dozens of faces, dozens of arms, dozens of legs!

Dear God, he started to remember. He really had seen an animal. And he had saved the woman. He'd crashed the truck into its huge, slimy body...

The sound of a car sent him lurching towards the window. *The police! They're here to take me away.* Panic and sheer terror sent his heart racing. 'I haven't done anything wrong. I saved the woman...'

A car came bouncing along the lane to the farm. He expected blue lights to start flashing ... the wail of a siren. Standing there at the window, he held his breath as its headlights lit up the farmyard. *If it's the police, I'll run. No way am I going to get locked up.* The car swept up to the front door. Jez thought his heart would explode. His chest hurt, he felt pressure build in the back of his throat. Vomit getting ready to punch through his mouth.

Jez sighed. He recognized the car. The Volvo belonged to Ken Hughes. Jez's parents and Ken co-owned the milking depot just down the road. Two farms had gone into partnership to buy new equipment that would milk their herds more quickly and efficiently.

'So ... no police,' Jez whispered. 'Though I know they'll come soon. They'll fix the evidence so they can charge me with killing those people on the bus.'

Shuddering, the sixteen-year-old ripped open a carton of prescription painkillers. OK, he'd taken a dose just five minutes ago, but he needed more. His arm hurt as if it was being gnawed by rats. Felt like sharp teeth crunching at that white stick of bone in his arm. He swallowed another couple of pills. They both stuck in his throat. Milk?

'No way! Not frigging milk.'

I'm seventeen next week. I'm old enough to decide what's best for me. After a barbecue party at the farm during the summer he'd come across a bottle of vodka that still had a generous slop of spirit in the bottom. He'd hidden the voddy in a box under his bed. *Bound to come in handy one day*, he'd reasoned.

Damn it, the day had come – he *needed* some of the hard stuff. He spun the cap off, then took a massive swallow of that hellfire spirit. The painkillers slid down his throat to join their companions, which he'd swallowed five minutes ago. Good. Double bubble. A pompous voice in the back of his head warned him of 'exceeding the prescribed dose of medication'. *Shut up, I need to kill the pain.* In truth, though, he ached to dampen down this screaming anxiety. *Need something to relax me. Pills and booze. Yeah, that should do it. Drugs and alcohol.*

To his surprise he blurted with laughter. He knew that mixing strong alcohol with prescription drugs was dangerous, very dangerous ... deathly dangerous ... yet he didn't care. In the last thirty-six hours he'd gone through hell. If the next thirty-six hours were going to be hell, he wanted, absolutely wanted, pills and forty per cent proof liquor. Of course, they might kill him ... but he wasn't thinking clearly any more. Jez Pollock hadn't deliberately chosen suicide. Yet he'd embarked on a deadly route to exactly that outcome.

Snow rattled against the window pane – the sound of the soul-taker's claws. Six forty p.m. *Death approaching.*

FIFTY-SEVEN

That Monday evening, as the snow fell, Kit stared at the whisky on the pantry shelf. His mother had decided to go to the pub. She didn't usually go out at night, preferring to drink at home. Only she'd heard her ex-husband might be there. So Mrs Bolter had put on a clean dress, brushed her coat, applied lipstick and hurried to the village, praying for a miracle. Kit knew that his mother hoped to win back the man she still loved with all her heart.

Kit stared at the bottle of whisky. The amber spirit called to him now: because of what happened to Jez on Saturday night, and because of seeing Jez all bruised, his arm broken, and the threat of a police charge hanging over him. Then an argument with Owen, his other best friend, had turned violent. But worst of all: Kit had discovered a frightening darkness inside his own head. Over the years it had grown. Was it due to worrying about his mother's fondness for the whisky bottle? Or wondering if he'd follow in his father's footsteps as a violent thug? When Kit gazed into the mirror these days he saw that darkness behind his eyes. Maybe it was nothing to do with his mother's drunkenness, or his father's violent habits. He knew that a streak of madness ran in the Bolter family. *The colour of that streak is black.* Would the whisky help make the darkness inside his head vanish? At least for a while?

A mouse ran from a hole in the pantry wall, across his foot and down a crack in the floor. What a dump. Living in a place like this infested with mice, rats, and oozing with damp would make even the sanest person want to flip.

Kit opened the bottle and sniffed. Whisky fumes prickled his nose. Kit pictured himself drinking from the bottle. After that, he'd lie down on the sofa, his head lolling, his eyes glazed – just like his mother.

With a savage shake of his head, he replaced the cap, and shoved the bottle to the back of the shelf. *No ... I'm going to fight this. I'm not going to be like those other deadbeats in my family. I'm going to make something of myself. I'm going to university. I'm ... Oh, God.*

Straight away, he saw it through the kitchen window. His scalp tingled, shivers gushed down his spine, freezing his blood. There, through the glass, a pale oval framed by blonde hair. Pure white eyes gazed in at him. The black pupils:

cold drops of death.

Freya. She's come back, just like she said she would. Heart beating faster, he ran to the door and opened it. A tide of snowflakes rushed in.

There she stood. Barefooted. Frightening. Yet glorious, and beautiful, and – *somehow* – the woman he'd wanted all his teenage years. The fact that she wore no shoes in these sub-zero temperatures didn't trouble him. Freya was the miracle he'd dreamt of. Another human being who had the ability to look into his eyes and recognize the darkness that lay behind them. Instinctively, he knew she understood how he felt. Here was a human being who would be his loyal ally. A friend in adversity. Without a shadow of doubt, he knew that in Freya he would find a meeting of hearts as well as minds.

If a warning voice told him that Freya was a monster ... a vampire woman ... a creature blighted by a curse ... well, so what ... he ignored that voice. Because the harrowing events of the last twenty-four hours had caused madness to blossom in his own mind. This dead-alive creature standing barefoot in the snow ... this woman with black veins showing through her white neck and staring at him with those lovely/ nightmare eyes was his soulmate. His growing madness wouldn't permit any contradiction of that belief. *Freya is mine. I love her.*

This vision of impossible beauty moved slowly towards him. A snowflake landed between her dark eyebrows but did not melt. Skin that was colder than the snow itself wouldn't melt the flake. How could it?

'I didn't think you'd come back.' Kit's heart beat faster, sending the blood racing through his neck.

'I promised I would.' She spoke softly. 'You're the only one who can help me.'

Kit liked that feeling of exclusivity. 'Of course I'll help you.'

'Thank you.'

'What would you like me to do?'

'Promise me you'll help me tonight.'

'I promise.' He smiled. 'You can trust me.'

'I know I can.' She smiled back. The eyes gleamed as whitely as massive pearls. 'When I first saw you I realized I could trust you. You're nice. I like you.'

'I like you.' Sanity protested. However, madness beat sanity down with deranged ferocity. Nevertheless, Kit Bolter enjoyed a powerful sense of calm. OK ... the calm before the storm, he realized at a deeper, suppressed level. The storm of madness and violence would break soon. *Freya is Death in the shape of female beauty. That's poetic*, he thought. *Byronic. The beautiful and the damned belong together.*

These thoughts passed through his head as she approached. Tenderly, even lovingly, she reached out with those cold fingers and took his hands in hers.

She whispered, 'So, you promise to help me tonight?'

'Yes, I promise.'

'Good, I will hold you to that promise, Kit.'

'What do you want me to do?'

'I want you to help me to die.'

Even insanity flinched back from this incredible statement. 'You're joking,' he gasped.

'No joke, my lovely, kind-hearted boy.' Her smile was so melancholy, yet so trusting, too. 'This existence is unbearable to me. Every minute of every hour is torture. So, tonight, you will make me happy. You are going to bring this life of mine to an end.'

FIFTY-EIGHT

Tom spent the day helping the search teams. He'd donned his scuba diver's suit, the air tanks and flippers, and swam downriver. While he searched underwater, police and volunteers had walked along the banks of the Lepping. No sign of anyone from the minibus. No sign of anything. When daylight faded the police called off the search. Rescuers knew they weren't looking for survivors now, they were looking for corpses. Tom Westonby believed otherwise. What repeatedly came to mind was the image of Helsvir. The creature had taken the passengers from the bus, he was certain. Of course, he couldn't share this belief with the police. OK, they'd know of local legends about the dragon, but they didn't believe the creature actually existed. In Danby-Mask, parents used the Helsvir myth to make children do as they were told. In many a house, this kind of thing could be heard: *Jenny, if you play by the river again, Helsvir will eat you up.* Or when a parent reached the end of their tether: *Boys! If you don't behave and go straight to bed now I'll leave the back door open and Helsvir will get you!*

Perhaps the only person in the world who knew that Helsvir existed was Tom Westonby.

He glanced at his watch as he walked home through the forest. Seven p.m. In the light of the flashlight the snowflakes were dazzling flecks of white. After what happened a few days ago, when the vampire had attacked him, he knew he was pushing his luck being out here after dark, but Tom felt compelled to go home. One day his lost bride would return. The conviction that this would happen, and he'd be reunited with Nicola, was deeply rooted inside of him.

Quickly, he made his way along the path. Already snow had begun to form a thick layer on the frozen earth. A fox darted away under the bushes. Somewhere close by a bird screeched. Tom remained vigilant. Vampires might be nearby. Until Friday night they'd never even approached him before. They'd always been motionless figures out here in the wilderness. They only moved if he tried to get closer to them – and even then, they moved away from him. For the last five years they could be described as almost shy creatures. But three days ago that had changed when one had pounced and almost drowned him in the river. June Valko had been the catalyst.

Shivering, he walked faster. June would be

back at the hotel in Leppington. His plan to use the woman as bait to draw Nicola to him hadn't worked. So what next?

What did happen next shocked him so much it took his breath away.

Tom Westonby had just walked through the stone archway at the edge of his garden. Straight away, he saw a bright pool of light by the front door. In that pool of light stood two figures. The pair stared at him, their eyes glinting. Tom froze at the bizarre sight. Because there was June Valko. She gripped a flashlight in one hand, while her other hand supported a frail woman with coffee-coloured skin. A cold wind from the north drew an eerie-sounding moan from the trees in the forest.

Tom locked eyes with June as he glared at her in nothing less than fury. *How could she do this? She must be insane!*

June started speaking before he even reached her. 'Tom. This is my mother. I know you'll be angry. You told me not to bring her, but I couldn't see any other way.'

'You could have been killed.'

'I want my mother to see my father.'

'June,' he hissed, 'you know what he's become.'

'I do, but I have to give my mother at least a chance of—'

'A chance of what? Dying out here?' He glanced back. At any moment, figures could come loping out of the darkness.

'My mother deserves this chance.'

He noticed that June had dressed her mother as

warmly as possible – layer upon layer of fleeces and sweaters and a thick anorak, with its hood pulled up over the sick woman's head. But to bring a frail invalid here? Into this freezing forest at night? What was June thinking? What was more, she'd put herself and her mother in dreadful danger.

Nevertheless, Tom quickly opened the door and ushered his uninvited guests inside.

Handing June the key, he said, 'Lock and bolt the door.'

Tom lit the log fire before grabbing a thick tartan blanket from the sofa and putting it around Mrs Valko's shoulders. After she'd been warmly parcelled in the blanket, he guided her to the armchair nearest the fire.

'I'm sorry to have shouted like that, Mrs Valko,' he told her. 'I wasn't expecting you, and it worried me that you had to walk through the forest in this weather.' He knelt down by the chair so he could look up into her brown eyes. 'My name's Tom Westonby.' He held out his hand.

June finished bolting the door. 'My mother won't answer you, Tom. She doesn't talk now. Most of the time she doesn't even know what's going on around her.'

June eased the hood down from her mother's head. Tom saw how much alike mother and daughter were. They had the same coffee-coloured skin, glossy black hair and fragile build. Where June differed from her mother were her eyes. June's shone with that electric blue. Definitely those were her father's eyes. As

241

far as he knew, June was the last of the Bekk bloodline. True, there were more Bekk men and women out there in the forest. These were ones who'd been transformed by the curse. They were vampire-like creatures. Of course, they'd lost the blue colouring from their eyes. And they'd gained something in return – they'd been given a whole new biology. Tom thought of them as vampires. To all intents and purposes that's what they were. Night creatures. By day they vanished into some lair. Where that was, he didn't know. But he did know they haunted the wood by night. Although they hadn't attacked humans in the past (as far as he knew), he suspected that the vampires fed on blood taken from sheep on the high moors that flanked the valley. As a rule, they didn't kill the sheep. However, he'd heard farmers talk about their flocks suffering from inexplicable cuts.

Now he watched June helping her mother out of the anorak, all the while speaking to her in a gentle voice to reassure the sick woman. Tom realized the lady didn't look at all well. Mrs Valko's cheeks had sunk in, revealing the sharp lines of the bones in her face. The loss of weight made her eyes seem very large and round. Even though she relaxed at the sound of her daughter's voice, she didn't give any indication that she understood any of the words. Mrs Valko remained sitting there – a woman in a trance, unaware of her surroundings.

'I'll make hot drinks,' Tom said.

June followed him into the kitchen.

As he filled the kettle he hissed, 'That was a

crazy thing to do.'

'You wanted me to act as bait last night. It didn't work. We didn't see any vampires. To-night might be different.'

'So, you're using your own mother as bait? Damn it, June, even bringing her here was incredibly dangerous. It's snowing. Those paths are treacherous before you even factor in the vampires. What if she'd fallen?'

'I held on tight to her.'

'How long were you waiting for me to come home?'

'Just a few minutes.'

He flicked the kettle switch. 'And now you hope your mother's presence will bring your father to the cottage?'

'We know it worked with me being here.'

'It worked once.'

June spoke in a determined way. 'So it only has to work once again.'

'But what do you hope to achieve?'

'Achieve? I want to save my mother's life.' June took a deep breath. Her expression clearly said that she'd do everything in her power to reunite her dying mother with her father – a man who'd been transformed into a vampire over twenty years ago.

'But you haven't thought this through,' he told her. 'How do you propose to bring them to-gether? She can hardly go out there and meet him, can she?'

BANG! June slammed her fists down on to the table. 'Tom, stop being so smug, and so down-right superior.'

'June, look—'

'No, you look!' She gripped the front of his sweater, her blue eyes flashing. 'You told me that you lost your girlfriend five years ago. Yes! I believe you when you say she's become one of those vampire creatures. And I damn well know that you planned to use me as bait to draw her to the house. You gambled that my presence would be like a magic spell. That for the first time in five years you would see the woman you loved.'

'How could you know that? I never said—'

'You didn't have to tell me in words, Tom. I could see it in your eyes. You love Nicola Bekk. Yes, she's a vampire, just like my father. But, like me, you'll do whatever it takes. You want to be reunited with Nicola. Isn't that true?'

'Yes.'

'So, you were prepared to use me as bait to draw her out?'

'Yes.' Tom began to shake. Getting the truth out and clearing the air hurt, but it was a sweet kind of hurt, like drawing a deeply embedded thorn from his flesh.

'Therefore, we're both on the same side.' June released her grip on his sweater. 'We're allies. You want to find Nicola. I want my mother to see her husband with her own eyes, even if that means only looking out through a window at him.'

'But the shock? It might—'

'Kill her? Tom, she is dying of a broken heart. The doctors say her body is failing. She'll be dead in a few months. Yes, this is wildly danger-ous and utterly desperate. I even had to smuggle

244

her out of hospital when a nurse's back was turned. But what choice do I have, Tom? Besides, if you know of a miracle cure for a broken heart, why haven't you taken it yourself?'

The words he wanted to say wouldn't come out.

June spoke so tenderly, yet he sensed her steely resolve. 'Tom, you are twenty-eight. But your eyes are so unbelievably old. Terrible things happened to you in the past, so you've created this shell that makes you seem as if you're made out of stone. I know you're not like that. Under that hard armour plating there's someone who's raw and wounded.'

With the heel of his hand, he wiped his eyes. 'Made out of stone? Yes, you're right. Turning my heart to stone was the only way of surviving what happened to Nicola. That's what it felt like ... it seemed like I gradually exchanged one living cell for one cold splinter of rock. If I hadn't done that, I wouldn't have had the guts to stay here, living alone. And I'm determined to be here, because I've convinced myself that one day there'll be a knock at the door ... I'll open it and find Nicola standing there.' He shook his head grimly. 'What a stupidly impossible fantasy ... Nicola comes back; we live happily ever after? Yup, I'm living a lie, aren't I?'

'No more stupidly impossible than my dying mother meeting my vampire father.' Smiling, she kissed him on the cheek. 'Perhaps we only have to believe hard enough, and it will happen.'

'You mean, you're hoping for some kind of miracle tonight?' He smiled back, wanting to believe with all his heart that she might be right.

'Let's make it happen, Tom. After all, what have either of us got to lose?'

They made the coffee together. After that, they went back to the room where the fire blazed so brightly it seemed as if a piece of the sun occupied the fireplace. Mrs Valko sat in the armchair, perhaps daydreaming about the time she met a handsome, blue-eyed man from a faraway valley. Tom and June sat side-by-side on the sofa, where they both gazed into the fire without speaking. After a while, June reached out and held his hand. Whatever tonight would bring – good, bad, miraculous or evil – they'd face it together as friends and allies.

FIFTY-NINE

The war is coming ... the battle's getting nearer. Soon you'll have to fight for your life. The words pounded through Jez Pollock's head as he paced his bedroom that Monday evening. He didn't know exactly what form the battle would take, but an instinct for danger (perhaps bordering on paranoia) warned him that trouble was on its way. Every sound made him rush to the window. The police would come soon. They'd take him away; blame him for causing the accident. *But I didn't do it. The accident wasn't my fault.* He took another swallow of vodka. The drugs and alcohol were cooking together in his stomach. Flashes of scarlet exploded behind his eyes. His arm hurt. Why didn't the painkillers work? He picked up the packet, debating whether to take another one. A car door slammed. He scrambled to the window and wiped furiously at the condensation, not even aware that he used the arm with the cast; it clattered loudly against the glass. COPS! He angled his head to look downwards. The car pulled away from the front of the house. No ... not cops. It was the Volvo belonging to Ken Hughes who owned the neighbouring farm.

Jez sent a text to Owen. *Arm hurts so much I want to cut it off.* Quickly, he fumbled another painkiller out of the pack, swallowed it, then chased the pill down with a gulp of voddy. The sense of panic grew worse. By tomorrow, he'd be in police custody, he was certain. All the other kids would be going to school, while he, Jez Pollock, sat in a police cell. Even though he didn't realize he'd done it until he'd hit send, he'd texted Owen again. *Cops will put me in jail. Didn't crash into bus. Honest.* Straight away, he sent another text to Kit Bolter: *There's a monster out there. Smacked the truck into it.*

Footsteps sounded outside his door. He lay down on the bed, pretending to sleep.

His father stepped into the bedroom. 'Jez. Jez?'

'Uh?'

'I didn't want to wake you, but we have to go out.'

247

'Where?'

'Ken Hughes called round. There's a problem with the milking machine. Your mother and I are going to help him flush the pipes, otherwise we won't be able to milk the herds tomorrow.'

'OK.' Jez lay on his side with his back to his father, hugging the vodka bottle to his stomach so his father wouldn't see.

'We don't want to leave you alone, son. Do you want to come with us?'

'I'm fine.'

'How's the arm?'

'Hurts.'

'You could sit in the car while we clean up the milking machine?'

'No. I want to get some sleep.'

'That sounds like a good idea. Can I get you some more milk?'

'Shit, no.'

His father sighed. 'I don't blame you for swearing, son. If I were you I'd be using some real humdingers of words.'

'I love you, Dad.'

'What's that, son? I didn't catch what you said.'

'Nothing.' Jez pressed his face into the pillow.

His father told him that they'd be gone for an hour or so. Once again he told Jez that he hated leaving him alone. A little while later, Jez's mother and father drove away down the lane. The milking depot lay half a mile away. Jez accepted that farming often involved crisis management. There were always fences to fix, sick animals to treat or machinery to be repaired.

Getting the milking equipment working again by tomorrow would be vital. The cows would suffer if the milk couldn't be drawn out of their udders.

Yes, absolutely. Jez accepted the facts of a hard farming life. What he couldn't accept were the police pointing accusing fingers at innocent people – and he was definitely innocent. Jez began to pace the room again as tension began to build. Pains raced through his arm – white hot bullets of agony. His heart pounded. *The war is coming ... the battle's getting nearer. Soon you'll have to fight for your life.* But who would he fight? Who was the enemy? The enemy had to be the cops. Stood to reason. If he hadn't swallowed all those painkillers, washed down by vodka, and if his mind wasn't still ripped up by shock, he'd have used the word *paranoia* to describe his mental state right now. Paranoia: the irrational belief that you are being persecuted; the loopy conviction that people are out to get you.

Jez Pollock, however, had a gut feeling that something bad was headed this way. A vicious enemy. An enemy determined to hurt him. An enemy dedicated to making his life hell. In the midst of this mental turmoil, he identified the enemy as the police.

That was why he went downstairs to find his father's pump-action shotgun. As he climbed the stairs back to his bedroom he fed cartridges into the weapon. The cast on his arm made it difficult, but he persevered and eventually managed to load that satisfyingly heavy instrument of death.

Sweating, unsteady on his feet, he felt a delirious sense of excitement. 'OK ... Jez Pollock is ready for war. I'm waiting for you...' He grinned as he stood there swaying, with the gun pointing at the window. 'Come and get me, cops ... come and get me, if you dare.'

SIXTY

At the same moment that Jez Pollock stood aiming the gun at the window, waiting for his own personal war to start, Kit Bolter pulled on his boots, coat and fleece hat. Kit was just about to leave the warmth of the kitchen and go for a walk with his girl. OK, so it was dark out there; it was snowing; his girl was a monster; she'd begged him to help her die ... but he felt as if he'd left the real world behind. Normal rules no longer applied. Mentally, he'd crossed over a boundary to where the impossible would become possible. *No – the impossible will become inevitable!*

His phone chirped. Freya looked quizzically at the device in his hand as he checked the text that Jez had sent: *There's a monster out there. Smacked the truck into it.*

Kit knew that Jez had suffered intense psychological shock due to the accident. What's more, Kit had seen how the strong painkillers had affected his friend, sending him trippy to say the least. However, Kit wouldn't dismiss the text about the monster. Because here he stood in the kitchen with a woman in a summer dress who had skin as white as milk. Black veins wormed under the skin of her throat. Somehow she could walk through the snow barefoot, too, and not be affected by the intense cold. If this unearthly creature could be here with him, then perhaps Jez really had crashed the truck into a monster.

Freya seemed so interested in the phone that he held it out. She took the device with those uncannily white fingers. Even the nails were bluish white. She studied the text on-screen. 'It's a television,' she murmured in astonishment. 'A tiny television.'

'You can watch stuff on it like films,' he said. 'It's also a phone, and you can access the Internet, play games, take photographs, read books.'

'A phone? Where is the wire?'

'Doesn't need one.'

'There's no dial.'

'You just touch the screen.' He showed her how the phone worked as she held it; her fingers were ice cold. 'See. There's a video clip of my friends. We were at a burger place in Whitby.'

Those colourless eyes, with the fierce black pupils, scrutinized a pair of teenagers squirting ketchup all over their fries, while they laughed and joked. Kit smiled. The way she seemed so astonished by the phone pleased him. He'd impressed her, that felt good.

'Are there more of these machines?' she asked, 'Or is this your invention?'

251

'My invention?' He laughed. 'Everybody has phones like these. You can buy them from supermarkets, and from all kinds of places.'

'It must be valuable.'

'Not really. Wait ... you haven't seen one of these phones before, have you?'

'No.'

'Where have you been for the last million decades?' He spoke jokingly, forgetting for a moment that Freya wasn't like any girl he'd met ... or like any human being he'd met, come to that.

She pressed her lips together. 'I want to hurt you. Remember when I attacked you out in the yard? Well, that feeling – that urge – is still there.' The black veins in her neck began to pulsate as if her heartbeat quickened. 'I have to fight my instincts. It would be so nice to break open your skin and taste your blood.' Her respiration grew louder. 'That is why I want you to help me die. I need to be set free of this curse.' She gripped his wrist with such force he grunted in pain. 'But you won't help me die, will you?'

He shook his head. 'You know that's impossible. I'd never hurt you, Freya.'

'You wouldn't be hurting me, you'd be saving me.'

'Don't ask me to help you commit suicide.'

'You don't understand what I am.'

'I know that I like you. I've never met anyone like you before.'

She gave a grim smile. 'I hope you will never meet anyone like me again.'

'Don't say that, Freya.'

'When you look at me, what do you see?'

'You are beautiful.'

'No, Kit. Look at my eyes; they're not exactly human, are they? I come to you at night barefoot in the snow. You show me that little machine that's a television and a phone and a camera and goodness knows what else. Why do you think I've never seen one of those things before?'

'I don't know.'

'It's because I stopped being a living eighteen-year-old girl in 1965. I hated this valley so I ran away to London. Then I started to notice changes in my skin and my eyes. Gradually, I began to transform into what I am now. I'd invoked the Bekk curse. Do you understand?'

'I don't want to understand,' he growled. 'You're special. I like being with you. That's enough, isn't it?'

Just for a second, colour flooded back into her eyes. They became a bright, sparkling blue. That was when she kissed him on the cheek.

Freya gave a melancholy sigh. 'Kit, there are things you should know about me.'

'For as long as you want to talk, I'll listen.'

'You are such a lovely, kind boy.' She rested her hand on his arm. 'It will be easier for you if I show you things that you can see with your own eyes. Then you'll begin to understand.'

'Then show me.'

She hesitated, a worried expression appearing on her face. 'You will see extraordinary things. Some will frighten you.'

'I'm still coming with you, Freya.' He collected a torch from a shelf. 'Because the more I learn about you the more I'll be able to help. And that doesn't involve killing you, OK?'

Smiling, she took his hand in hers. They stepped out of the house, and then she led him by the hand through the falling snow to the forest.

She murmured, 'After you've seen what's out there, you'll change your mind. You'll understand that my death will be a blessing.'

Once again, Kit Bolter's instincts told him he'd left the natural world behind. Somehow, this realm of ancient oak and frozen earth would be a place of both wonder and terror. Whatever lay behind this mysterious veil of trees would change his life for ever. He was certain of that fact.

OK, here goes ... A moment later the darkness swallowed them. *Whatever happens now, there's no turning back.*

SIXTY-ONE

'What are you going to show me?' Kit asked Freya as they walked through the forest.

'You'll see them soon enough.'

'Them?'

She didn't answer, so Kit allowed himself to be led by the hand. Here beneath the trees the night was as black as it could get. He made out enormous oaks standing there – ancient giants that presided over this wilderness. Snow falling through branches had formed patches of white on the ground. He could see little more than that – in fact, it was so dark Freya had become a silhouette. Even though he had brought the flashlight he held off from using it. Being together in darkness brought a sense of intimacy.

What Freya had told him just a few moments ago restlessly circled his mind. She'd claimed she didn't know about modern phone technology. Furthermore, she'd claimed that something had happened to her in 1965 that had turned her into this ... this ... *No*, Kit told himself, *I can't bring myself to call Freya a creature.* Just then, moonlight broke through the cloud. There she was: a beautiful woman, with a delicately boned face, and the thick Rapunzel plait hanging forward over her shoulder. He'd put her age at no more than eighteen. So if she had been eighteen in 1965 then whatever affected her had stopped the ageing process.

Kit closed his eyes for a moment as they walked. He felt the gentle pressure of her fingers encircling his. Little more than an hour ago, he'd been preoccupied with his own state of mind. He'd worried about the streak of madness, which blighted the Bolter family, manifesting itself in him. In truth, he didn't feel any sign of mental abnormality right now, but could he be completely sane? He was accompanying a bare-footed woman through the snow. Or at least he thought he was. What if he was traipsing through the forest alone? What if this was a hallucination?

He squeezed her hand. She gave an answering squeeze. A gesture of affection? He hoped so. What's more, being able to feel her hand reassured him that this woman was real as the trees surrounding him.

Opening his eyes, he realized the moonlight had become brighter. He saw a rabbit hopping across the path in front of them. Freya's bare feet left prints in the snow. Seeing as he had his phone, he could take photos of her footprints. They'd be evidence that Freya really existed. *Come to that, would she let me film her?*

However, before he could take the phone from his pocket, she said abruptly, 'If I try to kiss you again don't let me.'

'I want you to kiss me.'

'No, Kit, promise that you'll push me away.'

'Why would I do that?'

'Because I might not kiss...'

'OK, but we can still hold hands, right?'

He studied her serious expression as she nodded. Her face formed a bone-white oval in the moonlight. The black veins snaked from under the collar of her dress, up her throat where they forked off into finer branchlets. *So what kind of blood runs through veins as black as those? And why have I fallen under her spell? Because I shouldn't be here, should I? Not alone in the wood with a ... a monster.* Kit didn't want to think of Freya in these terms. *But why doesn't she feel the cold? What happened to her eyes to make them appear like that? With no colour to them. And why doesn't vapour come from her mouth when she speaks or breathes out?* He

256

exhaled and white billowed in the moonlight.

Freya's voice dropped to a whisper. 'Hold my hand tighter. That's it. Don't let go, not even for a second.'

'Why?'

'We're here.' She fixed her eyes on his: uncanny fires seemed to dance behind them, a dancing ghost of her past life, perhaps.

Kit stared into the darkness. 'I don't see anything.'

'Keep holding my hand. Keep walking. Don't attempt to talk to them. Whatever you do, don't touch them.'

'But who am I supposed to be seeing? I can't ... oh...'

Now he did see what haunted the gloom. Moonbeams penetrated the branches catching the figures in cold, silvery rays. Kit fell silent. He even stopped breathing at the sight of these creatures. Because there, standing in a line, perhaps twenty paces apart, were men and women. They stood perfectly still. Eerie guardians of this cold wilderness. Many, like Freya, wore summer clothes. A man in a shirt and jeans. A woman in a flowered skirt and cotton blouse.

In awe, he breathed, 'They all look like you.'

'Don't talk,' she whispered. 'It might provoke them.'

Kit remained silent as he walked along the line of men and women. They had the same bone-white skin as Freya. Their blonde hair reflected styles from the last fifty years – bobbed, or permed, or long and straight, parted, or combed back – all the hairstyles were frozen in time. Just as their bodies were. Kit noted the uncanny white eyes set with fierce black pupils. When snowflakes alighted on their faces the snow did not melt: these were cold-blooded creatures.

If they turned to look at him Kit knew he would scream. However, there was one small mercy. These monstrous figures didn't appear to notice his presence. They stared ahead. They appeared to be waiting. But for what? God alone knew ... or perhaps it was a case of *Satan alone knew*. These soldiers of darkness seemed to be biding their time until the order reached them. *But what kind of order? And who from?*

Freya turned to Kit. 'Those are members of my family, the Bekk clan,' she stated in a matter-of-fact way. 'They are Blood-Eaters. Another name would be vampires.'

'Vampires?'

'For decades they've been little more than ghosts. They've haunted the forest without being seen. They haven't hurt anyone, but all that's changing. Soon they'll go down into the village and attack.'

'You're saying they're going to start killing people?'

'Not killing. Converting.' She gave a grim nod. 'They're going to transform living human beings into creatures exactly like them.'

'Why?'

'To build an army.'

'But if you're one of those—'

'Vampires? Say the word, Kit. Yes, I'm a vampire, too.'

'But if you're one of those vampires, why are

you telling me this?'

'Because when we met last night you reminded me that I was human once.'

Blood thudded in his ears as fear cascaded through him. Had he actually seen vampires? Or had he looked into the black pit of his own mind, and seen the demon that was his own madness crawling upwards, hell-bent on devouring his sanity?

Gently, she touched the side of his face. 'Over a thousand years ago, my family left Denmark, which was a pagan Viking nation back then. They crossed the sea to Britain where they tried to settle peacefully in this valley, but through no fault of their own they became enemies of the Christian population. One day, the local people launched a surprise attack on the Bekk family that lived where Skanderberg cottage now stands in the forest.'

'But that was centuries ago. What has that got to do with those *things* I've just seen?'

'My ancestors still worshipped the old Viking gods. Legends say that the gods intervened to save what remained of the Bekk family, because they remained true believers of the old pagan faith. In effect, my ancestors entered into a contract with the gods. The gods would protect them and keep the Christian enemy away as long as the Bekk family continued to worship the likes of Thor and Wodin. The problem for us Bekks is that the protection became a curse if we married outside the pagan faith, or we moved away from the valley. Those people you saw back there, my uncles, aunts and cousins, were the ones who turned their backs on the old religion. They left the valley, or married people of other faiths. Such an act triggered the curse. Like me, they transformed into vampires, and then they found themselves here in the forest. Blood-Eaters. Vampires. We feed on the blood of sheep and rabbits.'

'But that's changing?'

'Yes.'

'Surely you can stop yourself attacking the village?'

Freya regarded him with sad eyes. 'Believe me, Kit, it's taking every ounce of willpower to stop myself attacking you. I hear the blood racing through your veins. I want it, Kit. I want to feed ... believe me, your blood would taste so good. So warm ... *so full of life*.' She leaned towards him. 'Kiss me.'

Instead of pushing her away as she'd told him to, he gripped her by the shoulders. 'You said I reminded you that you were human once. Hold on to that.'

She breathed deeply. Her shoulders dropped a little as she relaxed. A flicker of blue appeared in her eyes. The black veins faded. Kit knew that just for that second she was more human than vampire.

'Why would the vampires attack the village?' he asked.

'We have no choice. We are puppets of the old gods. Even after a thousand years they want to punish people for abandoning the pagan beliefs. That's why we'll be compelled to break into the houses and ... and that's why we'll rip open the skin of innocent men and women. Once we've devoured their blood they will transform into vampires, too.'

'Is that why you want me to help you die? So you won't become part of this army?'

She nodded with such an earnest expression that he felt a tug on his heart. 'I want to help you,' he whispered, 'but not like that.'

'Go to hell, then!' Her face turned ugly with fury. 'You should leave the valley, Kit Bolter, because there's a war coming. We will win. Because we're hard to kill!'

'Freya—'

'Go away.'

She shoved him so powerfully that he crashed to the ground.

Before he could struggle to his feet he heard an explosion of sound. A huge shape came crashing through the trees, snapping branches, ripping bark from trunks.

Freya turned to face the giant creature that emerged from the darkness with the speed and fluid grace of a shark gliding through the ocean.

Freya shouted to Kit, 'I didn't get chance to tell you about Helsvir. He's the guardian of the Bekk clan. He's hate and vengeance packed into the skin of a monster.' Her eyes flashed – there was something wild, terrifying and absolutely magnificent about her. 'Run Kit, because I can't stop him. He'll tear you to pieces and make you part of him!'

Kit scrambled to his feet, though nearly all his strength had poured out of him. At that moment, he didn't think he even had the strength to scream ... *and, dear God, I want to scream right now*. Because Kit knew that he'd seen this monstrosity before. The automatic camera Owen had found: it had captured footage of the thing. And, in that instant, he knew that this was what Jez had rammed his truck into.

Kit tugged the phone from his pocket, pointed the lens at the dark shape studded with pale discs and hit play. The 'record' icon appeared on-screen – and so did the creature as it raced towards him. The monster would kill him – he knew that, but someone might find the camera. People would know what happened to him.

Freya begged, 'Run, Kit, please run. I don't want Helsvir to take you.'

He saw that Freya was scared for him.

'Get away from here, Kit!' she shouted. 'Leave the valley. Leave the country!'

The monster swept through the trees with sinuous grace. Kit sensed its sheer primordial strength. And now he began to see more closely ... heads ... human heads bristled from its body. The creature moved centipede-like on dozens of human legs. The nightmare beast would make him part of itself – he knew that was his fate.

Freya slapped his face.

'Wake up, Kit. Run for your life!'

With that, she moved towards the monster that she'd called Helsvir. She held her arms up, like someone would when attempting to stop a runaway horse.

'I won't let you take him, Helsvir. I won't!'

The creature did stop for a few seconds. Its human heads stared at Freya. A vicious hiss came from their mouths. Dozens of human eyes blazed in fury. A moment later, the creature lunged at her. She staggered backwards. The creature butted her again. Kit realized that hugely powerful beast could have swept her aside. However, for some reason it wouldn't do that, yet it continued to hiss with rage. Lunging forward again, it butted her back a couple more paces.

If it continued to do that, the monster would reach Kit in the next twenty seconds. After that, he'd be destroyed. He saw powerful arms bristling from its underside. Hands flexed, eager to seize hold of him. THIS IS DEATH. More precisely this was the engine of *his* death ... or some form of death. Kit Bolter's keen intelligence told him that this brute was the consummate recycler. It recycled the body parts of corpses into the fabric of its own body.

Kit's own head would soon adorn those flanks. He'd become the ugly, hissing organ that formed part of that monstrous flesh.

Somehow he found the strength to move. Still gripping the phone in one hand, he fled into the forest, not knowing in which direction he was headed. Then, at last, he glimpsed the farm in the distance. That was where Jez lived. It was closer than Kit's home, so he put his head down and ran. Instinct told him to make for the house of his friend.

After that, he could take his phone to the police. The phone contained footage of an extraordinary creature. And he'd also caught images of the extraordinary woman who had saved his life. When the police saw that film they'd have to believe him when he told them that Danby-Mask faced the greatest danger in the history of its existence. The vampires were coming. They would bring war and destruction.

SIXTY-TWO

In the moonlight, the farm was clearly visible across the snow-covered fields. Kit's breath erupted from his mouth in billowing explosions of white. Images spun inside his head. Of a creature the size of a truck: how it moved with shark-like grace through the trees. He also saw Freya in his mind's eye, the thick Rapunzel plait swinging as she tried to stop the creature reaching him.

Kit climbed fences, sprinted across meadows, his legs hurting from having run so far and so fast. His heart pounded. In his pocket was the phone with the precious footage. Proof that a monster existed in the valley. Somehow he had to get this to the police. What then? They'd call in the army, perhaps? Along with attack helicopters loaded with guided missiles. In any event, Helsvir wouldn't be his problem any more. By the time he reached the isolated farm he'd slowed to a plodding jog. An upstairs light burned. That was Jez's bedroom. *Thank God, he's home.*

Just as he entered the farmyard a figure darted

from the shadows. He stopped dead, his heart lurching. A moment later he smiled.

Freya smiled back. For the first time it seemed such a warm, human smile. Kit knew she didn't have to explain anything. She'd no doubt followed his prints in the snow. In any event, they were together again: that was all that mattered.

Without having to say a word they walked side-by-side, smiling at one another as they went. Kit decided that there would be a way to help Freya and make her human again. There had to be some method of driving the vampirism from her body. Then they'd be together as two human beings who cared for one another.

Kit decided to attract Jez's attention in the same way he'd done when they were boys. He picked up a piece of gravel from the yard, drew back his arm and lightly threw it up at the glass pane. Kit knew that things were looking up. *Everything's going to be OK.*

SIXTY-THREE

When Jez looked out of the window he knew that everything would be far, far from OK.

His parents had left the house a short while ago to help repair the milking equipment at the depot half a mile away. Meanwhile, the pain still raged in the snapped bone in his forearm. More vodka and more painkillers had gone down his throat.

Sweat poured out of his face, panic crackled through him. As he paced the bedroom every noise made him grab for the shotgun. So when he heard the tap of the stone against the glass he hurled himself at the gun, snatched it up and felt his drug- and booze-fuelled anxiety levels go screaming through the roof.

Because of the cast, he had to carry the shotgun in one hand as if it were an enormous pistol.

Jez flung open the window and screamed, 'Go away! Leave me alone! The accident wasn't my fault!'

A surprised voice responded with, 'Jez. It's me, Kit. What's wrong?'

In his wild paranoia, Jez Pollock believed that the police had sent Kit Bolter to trick him into opening the door. Then the cops would surge in to chain him, before dragging him away to jail for killing the people on the bus.

But this is Kit, he thought, sweating. *Kit's my friend. I can trust him with my life...*

He leaned forward through the open window. Piercingly cold air drenched his face.

Then he saw ... dear God, he saw ... A terrifying figure lurked down there. It stood just to one side of Kit, and a yard or so behind. Bright moonlight clearly revealed a pair of stark, white eyes. The phantom had been a woman once – his drug-muddled brain decided that much. A blonde plait hung down over her full breasts. But the eerie whiteness of the skin told him this individual was no longer human. What was more, the way she – it – stared at Kit suggested to Jez Pollock that she would attack.

266

'Kit! Run!' Jez rested the gun barrel over the cast on his arm. 'Kit, move out of the way! I'm going to fire!'

Kit ran forward with his hands held up. 'Jez! For Godsakes!'

Jez fired. He'd loaded the gun with bird shot. The weapon now spat a lethal cluster of pellets at hundreds of miles an hour.

'GOT HER!' Jez yelled in triumph.

The shotgun blast knocked the she-monster off her feet. She crashed to the ground. What Jez hadn't anticipated was the way the pellets would spread out as they hurtled through the air. With a cry, Kit flung his hands up to his face.

When the gun smoke cleared, he saw both the stranger and Kit lying there, motionless in the frozen yard.

SIXTY-FOUR

Jez Pollock stood at the bedroom window. His ears still hurt from the loud bang when he fired the shotgun just seconds ago. Lying there, sprawled on the cold earth, his friend Kit and the stranger. Jez stared down at the pair. The woman wasn't wearing any shoes. In sub-zero temperatures, like this? No shoes ... and only a thin orange dress. He swayed drunkenly as he told himself: *I killed them both with one shot. A murderer ... that's what I am...*

267

As if he moved through an eerie dream, he went downstairs, opened the front door and stepped out into the moonlit yard. Everything seemed so still, so silent, so wrapped up in death. First of all, he approached the stranger. She lay flat on her back. Her eyes were closed. Black veins snaked beneath her skin. The creature seemed to gleam whiter than the surrounding snow. A dozen or so marks dotted her face. This would be where the shotgun pellets had struck her.

'Where's the blood?' he asked himself, dazed. 'There should be blood.'

The prospect of touching the corpse with his bare fingers filled him with disgust, so he prodded her with the gun. Without a sound, she abruptly sat up. Her eyes opened – they were white, all white, apart from strange black pupils.

Then something even more bizarre happened. When he realized what he saw with his own eyes he thought he'd vomit. Black spots formed on her face. He saw these begin to swell, as if he watched speeded-up film of a branch coming into bud. The spots grew bigger. They bulged. Something grey and rounded emerged from the skin on her cheek.

What he initially took to be some kind of hard-shelled parasite crawling out of her face was, he realized, a lead pellet. More appeared from the cheeks, forehead and chin. The woman's flesh was actually pushing out the bullets. He watched with a stomach-churning blend of fascination and horror. The pellets emerged from the wounds before falling into her lap as she sat there.

Quickly, he chambered another round. An instinct for self-preservation demanded that he blow her head right off. He aimed the gun at her from a distance of ten inches. Her bare arm flashed in the moonlight. He felt an enormous wrench as she swept the shotgun from his hands. The gun clattered away into the shadows.

Fast as a panther, she leapt to her feet. The creature sped forward. Jez raised his arm with the heavy cast, ready to use it as a club. However, she darted towards Kit. Throwing herself down, she cradled his head in her hands. When she saw the blood on his face she arched her back, her mouth opened wide, revealing glinting teeth. For a moment, she appeared to fight some inner battle. With a sudden shriek of anger, she jumped to her feet. Before Jez had even thought of retrieving the gun she'd fled. At enormous speed, she sprinted across the field in the direction of the forest.

A groan caught his attention. Kit had raised himself on to one elbow. Blood streamed down his face, soaking his fleece. Jez felt such a surge of relief it was like an explosion in his chest.

'You'll be alright,' he panted as he tried to help his friend to his feet. When he pulled with his broken arm Jez felt such agony he screamed. Even though the pain sickened him he knew he couldn't leave his friend out here. Even if the wound didn't kill him the cold would.

Jez grabbed hold of one of Kit's wrists with his good hand. Jez had grown up moving heavy straw bales and carrying sacks of feed. Now those years of hard physical work on the farm paid off. With one hand, alone, he pulled Kit to the house and through the open front door. Once they were both inside in the warmth he locked the door, grabbed coats from the pegs and covered Kit from head to foot. For a moment, he fumbled with the first-aid kit before realizing he didn't have a hope in hell of being able to dress Kit's wounds – his fingers had all the dexterity of a fistful of frozen sausages.

Instead, he ran to the telephone, and while Kit lay groaning on the hallway floor he made the call.

'Owen!' He almost cried with relief when he heard his friend's voice. 'Owen, listen. Something terrible's happened ... Kit's been hurt. I shot him, I didn't mean to ... I've shot him in the face. You've got to help me!'

SIXTY-FIVE

The journey to Pollock's farm would take no more than five minutes. Owen Westonby sat with Eden Taylor in the back of the taxi.

'You didn't have to come with me,' Owen told her.

'They're your friends, so I'll do what I can to help.' She squeezed his hand. 'I might come across as a posh girl, but I'm not afraid to get stuck in and do what I can.'

Owen nodded his thanks. Right at that moment, he could hardly bring himself to speak. When Jez called to say that he'd shot Kit he felt as if his own breath had been blasted out of his lungs. He'd been sitting with Eden in her parents' impressively lavish kitchen, talking and laughing when – BANG – that devastating call had come. Of course, he decided to head over to Jez's straight away. Old loyalties were rock solid. If his friends were in trouble then he'd help. No questions asked. No hesitation. Of course, he'd not told the taxi driver the reason for the trip to Pollock's farm. For most of the journey he and Eden hadn't said a word. They sat there holding hands while silently wondering what bloody catastrophe awaited them.

When they arrived at the farm Owen paid the driver and, as the taxi swept away into the night, they ran to the door. Owen pounded the wood-work with his fist.

When the door swung open Owen flinched at the sight of Jez. The teenager's face had been shockingly bruised in the accident on Saturday night. Now, a wide-eyed expression of sheer horror made the discoloured face even more shocking.

'Owen ... he's through there. I-I think he's dying.' His bloodshot eyes rolled in Eden's direction.

'This is Eden,' Owen told him quickly. 'You can trust her.'

Jez grunted. 'I killed the woman. She came back to life. I shot her in the face, and she got up and walked away.'

'OK, Jez. First things first. Where's Kit?'

They followed Jez who lurched drunkenly along the hallway. Owen glanced at Eden. He guessed that, like him, she was puzzled by the bizarre statement about a woman coming back to life. However, he knew that Jez had been prescribed strong painkillers; the kid's brain must be flooded with powerful chemicals that were muddling his thoughts.

They found Kit Bolter lying on the hallway floor. His face had gone a strange, papery white. Even the texture of the skin appeared different.

Owen knelt down beside him and touched his face. 'Damn it ... he's like ice.'

Eden knelt down at the other side. 'He's going into shock.'

'Oh God.' Jez leaned against the wall. 'Have you seen the blood?'

Eden quickly checked the side of Kit's face, her sharp eyes examining the puncture wounds where the pellets had struck him. 'Ah...'

'What's wrong?' Owen's heart beat faster as fear got its teeth into him.

Briskly, Eden said, 'Owen, get me a bowl of hot water. See if you can find a roll of unopened kitchen towel, too, that'll be cleaner than the one in the holder.' She noticed the first-aid kit on the floor and began pulling dressings from the box. 'It's OK, Owen. I'm a first-aider. I know what I'm doing.'

'I'll get the water and the tissue.' He stood up. Eden's confidence reassured him. 'Jez, can you use the phone again?'

'Uh?' The sixteen-year-old appeared to have gone into shock himself.

'Use the phone to call an ambulance.'

'No!'

'Kit's hurt.'

'The police already think I've caused that bus crash. What do you think they'll do when they find out I've shot my friend?'

'We've got to report this, Jez. You can't cover up someone getting shot.'

'No, Owen ... please don't get me arrested.' Jez began to shake violently. 'Please don't make me call for an ambulance.'

'Just look at Kit. The poor kid's got bullet holes in his face!'

Choking sobs erupted from Jez's mouth.

Eden spoke calmly, but firmly. 'Owen, the water and tissue, please.'

'He needs to go to hospital.' Owen had begun to tremble, too.

'Let me clean him up first. This might not be as bad as it looks.'

'He's covered in blood.'

'I'm pretty sure the shot just nicked his skin. There don't seem to be any pellets in the wounds.'

Eden's calm air of authority worked its own magic right then. Jez still sobbed; however, he pulled up a chair and sat down so he could watch over his friend. Owen, meanwhile, went to run hot water into a bowl.

Within twenty minutes Kit sat on the sofa, propped up with cushions. Blankets covered him as far as his chin. Eden had wiped the blood from his face. In two places he had surgical dressings taped to his cheek. Another one covered his ear where the pellet had sliced away the bottommost tip of his earlobe.

Kit shook his head. 'I look like Vincent Van Gogh ... you know, after he went...' he whistled as he made slicing gestures '...you know ... with his ear.'

'How are you feeling?' Owen asked.

'Funny ... funny peculiar ... not comedy funny. Uh ... right ... it's got to be the shock, hasn't it?'

'Eden says that the pellets scratched you, rather than hitting you head on.'

'Where's Freya?'

'Freya?' Owen frowned.

'You've got Eden. I've got Freya.'

'Freya's your girlfriend?'

'Yup.' Kit rested his head against the cushion. He appeared light-headed.

'Jez is here, and Eden and me. Nobody else.' Owen glanced back as Jez and Eden entered the room. 'Jez? Have you seen a girl called Freya?'

'Someone came into the yard with Kit.' Jez shuddered as he remembered. 'That's why I fired the gun.'

Eden flinched with alarm. 'You shot Kit's girlfriend? What on earth for?'

Jez gave such a grim little chuckle. 'If you'd seen his girlfriend, you would have pulled the trigger, too.'

'You don't understand...' Kit sounded so drowsy he could barely speak. 'She's beautiful.'

'She's not human,' Jez snapped. 'How could she be? Barefoot in this. And you should have seen her eyes.'

Baffled, Owen shook his head. 'I'm sorry. Neither of you are making any sense.'

Jez said, 'I blasted her with the shotgun. She took a faceful of shot. Two minutes later she was back on her feet as if nothing had happened.'

'Thank God,' murmured Kit, smiling. 'Thank God she's alright.'

Eden asked, 'Have you known Freya long?'

'Since last night.' Kit smiled that drowsy smile again. 'Tonight I shot her...'

Owen and Eden exchanged glances. Owen knew that they were thinking the same thing: that both Kit and Jez had suddenly gone insane; they were muttering stuff about a woman being shot.

Still smiling, Kit pulled a phone from under the blanket. 'Shot Freya in a different way ... shot her with a camera ... I filmed her earlier tonight. Here ... proof...'

Eden took the phone which he held out to her.

'Play the video,' Kit told her. 'You'll see amazing things. There's Freya ... and I also filmed the monster.'

'What monster?' Eden shook her head in disbelief.

'They know which monster.' Kit pointed at Owen and Jez. 'They saw the footage from the automatic camera Owen found. The monster was on that. Last night Jez crashed his truck into it ... didn't hurt it, though. It'll take more than driving a ton of steel into the thing to hurt it.'

Owen said gently, 'You must have dreamt it.'

'OK, press play, and see for yourself ... if you dare.'

SIXTY-SIX

Tom Westonby spent most of that Monday evening moving from window to window in Skanderberg cottage. From each window he peered out into the night. The forest had become a mass of spiky, black branches. Tree trunks could have been the gigantic soldiers of some supernatural army waiting for the order to attack. Tom rubbed his forehead. He was so tired he realized that strange notions had started to haunt him. Trying to shake off the exhaustion, he walked briskly to the window in his bedroom and scanned the trees out there. So far, there was no sign of vampires. Yet an instinct for danger told him they were close.

Before Tom left the bedroom he paused to gaze at the carving of Helsvir set into the wall. These thousand-year-old carvings of the creature were part of the fabric of the house. A lucky charm? Or was it a danger sign – a potent warning to the men and women of the Bekk family, who'd once lived here, that neglecting their gods would bring about their doom?

Tom checked his phone. Owen had sent him a text. According to the information on-screen it was over an hour old. *Gone to see Jez*, it read. *He's worried and in a lot of pain.* Tom replied to his sixteen-year-old brother with what he hoped were reassuring words: *I'm sure Jez will be fine. Let me know if I can help.* Tom slipped the phone into his pocket to make sure he picked up any further messages from Owen straight away. He couldn't help but worry about both Owen and Jez. They'd been going through some heavy-duty emotions ever since Jez's accident.

Tom returned to the living room. Mrs Valko slept in the armchair by the fire. June sat on the sofa.

'Anything?' she asked as he went to the living room window.

'Nothing.' He gave a grim smile. 'Nothing but trees that is. You know, sometimes I find myself believing that the vampires can turn themselves into trees and stand there watching us. Does that sound too weird?'

'The entire forest is weird. There are weird vampires lurking out there. No wonder you have weird ideas, Tom Westonby. Coffee?'

'Thanks.'

Mrs Valko muttered in her sleep.

June's eyes held a gentle fondness as she gazed at her mother. 'The only time she does speak is when she's asleep, though I can never make out any actual words.'

He guessed what was on her mind. 'Your father might not come back. Remember, he turn-ed into one of those vampires over twenty years ago. The ones that transformed a long time ago are even less human than the more recent con-verts – if "converts" is the right word.'

'He climbed down the chimney and stood

there in the fire so he could see me. I'd be happy if he just came and knocked on that door.'

'We couldn't let him in. It would be too dangerous.'

She sighed. 'I know.'

'Do you still believe that your mother will be...' He searched for a sensitive way of finishing the sentence.

'Miraculously cured?' June's smile was a sad one. 'I don't know. All I do know is that this is my mother's last chance. The doctors can't make her heart better. What I have done, I guess, is bundle up all the bits of faith, hope and optimism I've got left, and gambled on this one slight chance. If she just catches a glimpse of her husband then that might fix something inside, and she'll get well again.'

'I hope it works. I just didn't want you to think that I'd open the door and let him in. Something tells me that inviting a vampire into the house would end in disaster, don't you agree?'

June gave him an appraising glance and knew he was being deadly serious. 'So, keep the vampires out?'

'Yes.'

'You know, as I've sat here, I've been imagining what I'd do if I saw him from the window. In my mind's eye, I see myself waking my mother. Walking her to the window then pointing him out. I can even hear myself saying, "Look, there's your husband, Jacob Bekk – he's my father, isn't he?" Of course, I then imagine my mother standing up straight, there's a big smile on her face, and suddenly she's talking happily. She's seen him with her own eyes, and that's a big enough miracle in its own right – her heart heals itself.' She tried to laugh, although it sounded more like a sob. 'Don't we humans delude ourselves? Lots of us have impossible dreams of becoming rich and famous. How many of us loyally love someone when actually they don't give a damn about us?' Her blue eyes fixed on the fire; crackling logs sent torrents of yellow sparks up the chimney. 'So maybe I am deluding myself that a man, who isn't even human any more, will appear outside the house and then my mother will see him and be cured. Tall order, huh?'

'No more than me believing Nicola will come back. She turned into a vampire five years ago, and still I expect to see her standing at that door one day.'

'Maybe that separates us from the animals?' June walked towards the kitchen. 'We humans spend half our lives expecting that impossibly wonderful things will happen to us. I'll get the coffee.'

Tom returned to his vigil at the window. Moonlight fell on to the forest, creating an ethereal, luminous glow. Heartless winds from the Arctic sent a pulse of movement through the trees, giving the impression that all those claw-like branches and gnarled trunks were shuddering into life.

June called out from the kitchen, 'I've found some cake. Hmm, lemon drizzle. Would you like me to cut you a piece?'

In the chair by the fire, Mrs Valko muttered in

her sleep. 'Jacob,' she droned. 'Jacob's coming.'

The breeze made the gargantuan oaks dance to a tune as old as time itself. That ice-cold river of air poured across the roof, drawing out a forlorn-sounding cry from this lonely house, where so many generations had lived and died.

SIXTY-SEVEN

Two miles from Skanderberg cottage lay Pollock's Farm. Inside the farmhouse, a barely suppressed violence crackled in the air. Owen Westonby and Eden Taylor stood at one end of the living room. Kit Bolter sat on the sofa at the other. One of the first-aid dressings had come free from his cheek. It swung about as he whipped his head this way and that, getting angrier and angrier. Meanwhile, Jez Pollock paced the room; he had the pent-up rage of a cornered bear.

Owen spoke loudly: 'Kit, I asked you a question: how did you fake it?'

'I didn't fake the video.' Kit touched play on the phone before holding it up, so they could see the eerie figure of the woman on-screen. Beyond her moved a massive shape that appeared studded with human faces. 'How could I fake something like that? Do I carry CGI around in my pocket? Because that's what I'd need to put a monster like this one on film!'

'Kit, you've acted so freaking weird ever

since—'

'You met *her*!' Kit jabbed a finger at Eden. 'It's like you've turned into a different person.'

Jez hugged his broken arm against his chest. The orange cast now appeared grubby and chipped. 'Owen, if you insist that animal's a fake that means you're saying that I must have smashed into the bus. You're saying I'm to blame for people dying.'

'I'm not—'

'Why won't you believe that footage with your own eyes?' Jez furiously kicked a leg of the table, making a tremendous crash that caused Eden to flinch with shock. 'That monster's my alibi!'

Owen yelled back, 'I'm just saying it takes some believing! The thing's the size of a dinosaur! How come nobody's ever noticed a dinosaur, with human heads growing out of it, tootling through the village?'

Kit was back to his old self now. He didn't even seem aware of the gunshot wounds that still oozed blood. He stood up so he could brandish the phone. The screen showed the creature pushing the woman across the ground. 'I filmed this two hours ago. The girl's Freya. She saved me from being attacked by that big ugly bastard.'

'I shot her,' Jez added. 'The pellets blasted her face and she wasn't even hurt; she just got up and ran over there to—'

'See!' shrieked Kit. 'Jez saw her!'

Eden raised her hands. 'Guys. Emotions are running high. Why don't—'

Jez and Kit both yelled at her with such ferocity she must have expected that they'd start punching her.

'Shut up, Eden!'

''S nothing to do with you!'

'You shouldn't even be here!'

'Nobody invited you!'

'Keep out of this!'

'Bitch!'

Owen's rage exploded. 'That's my girlfriend! Don't you dare talk to her like that.'

Kit finally crossed over into hysteria as he screamed, 'Bitch! Bitch! Bitch!'

Eden saw what Owen intended. 'Owen, don't!'

Owen lunged at Kit, savagely pushing him back down on to the sofa. The phone flew out of his hand to smack against the wall. Kit howled in pain.

Jez barked, 'You idiot! My alibi's on that phone!'

The sixteen-year-old lurched forward, swinging the arm with the cast. It slammed against Owen's head with a loud CLUNK. Instantly, Owen rounded on his friend, grabbing the front of his sweater. The next second, Owen and Jez fell on to Kit who was struggling to get up from the sofa. The sofa rolled backwards, leaving all three in a jumble of arms and legs on the capsized furniture. What was more, all three were yelling, swearing and threatening to spill blood.

Eden took a deep breath. With surprising calm, she said, 'Stop this. All three of you, stop it. You'll end up killing each other. Owen. Let go of Jez's arm.'

Grunting like a wounded pig, Jez scrambled free. He barged Eden aside before stomping upstairs. Kit scrambled on all fours to the end of the room to retrieve the phone.

In a small, hurt voice, he cried, 'You're a thug, Owen. If you've busted my phone...'

Owen lurched to his feet, panting. He was horrified to see the carnage he'd caused. The sofa had tipped over, in turn upending a little table on which a china figure of a milkmaid had stood. The delicate head now lay five feet from the milkmaid's body.

Eden grabbed the sofa and tried to heave it upright. Trembling, frightened by his own outburst of violence, Owen helped Eden with the sofa. He saw tears in her eyes.

Kit sat hunched against the wall as he wiped the phone with his sleeve. 'I didn't fake the video. It's real ... I filmed that animal in the forest. It's the same one that's on the wildlife camera that you found. Freya's real, too. She's a vampire.'

'You really screwed up your brain, Kit. Monsters? Vampires?' Owen gave an exaggerated performance of searching under the sofa cushions. 'Wait, I'm sure I saw a werewolf under here. Or maybe it was a goblin?'

'Screw you!' Kit jammed his middle finger up into the air. 'Screw both of you!' He scurried through into the hallway.

Owen threw his hands up and turned to Eden, ready to appeal for her take on this madness of giant creatures and vampires, only words failed him. Sighing, he flopped down on to the sofa.

With a quiet efficiency, she lifted the table back to its feet, collected the two parts of the broken figurine and studied them closely. 'A clean break,' she declared. 'Some glue should fix it.' Eden put the body and the head down on to the table.

Owen watched her straighten the cushions on the sofa. After that, she sat down beside him. For perhaps five minutes she said nothing. *Waiting for me to calm down*, he told himself. *Now she's seen the bad side of me, will she tell me we're finished?*

At last she began to talk. Eden had a talent for speaking with a calm authority, much in the way a doctor would gently explain a complicated medical condition to a patient. 'Owen, we moved around a lot when I was a child. I don't think I had a friend for longer than six months before we moved again. When you told me about Jez and Kit being your friends from when you first started school I was envious. That's a friendship to hold on to. It's something of value.'

'Eden—'

'Please, just listen to what I have to say.' When he nodded she continued: 'Owen, you told me that the three of you have been loyal friends for years. People even called you the Three Musketeers, because you went everywhere together. But what's happened in the last two days is like a bomb hitting the three of you. Jez had that awful accident. He's broken his arm. The physical pain must be terrible ... probably more terrible than we can imagine. Jez also worries that he'll find himself in court, facing a charge of causing death by dangerous driving. He might go to prison.'

Owen nodded again.

Eden rested her hand on Owen's knee as she spoke in those gentle tones. 'Tonight, for reasons we can't understand yet, he accidentally shot Kit. Luckily, Kit's not badly hurt, and I'm sure we don't have to involve doctors or the police. Both Jez and Kit are in turmoil. Their lives have exploded. They're experiencing terrible emotional stress.'

'And I ended up fighting both of them. I've been an idiot, haven't I?'

'No, not an idiot. You've experienced shocks, too. Listen, Owen. All three of you have suffered. All three of you are behaving in a way that is contrary to your natures.'

'You mean, we've gone crazy?'

'Yes, you're crazy.' She smiled. 'You're acting this way because you care about each other. But you're all in such emotional turmoil you can't deal with this explosion of events just yet. In a few hours, everything will seem different. You'll get over it.'

'You know, you are the wisest person I've ever met.'

'I don't have close friends like you do, Owen, so I spend a lot of time on the outside, watching how friends relate to one another.'

'Well,' he said, 'my ex-friends aren't going to talk to me now, are they? They'll hate me.'

'If you don't make up with them now, and you stop being friends, you'll regret it for the rest of your life.'

Owen nodded, digesting what Eden had just told him. 'OK. Here goes.' He stood up and went to find Kit.

Kit Bolter was in a back room that served as the farm office. Slowly, he moved his feet as he sat on a swivel chair, turning himself round and round. He studied the phone in his hand. Owen noticed that most of the dressings had fallen off during the ruckus. The pellet wounds in his face were red and wet.

'Kit?'

His friend didn't answer. Gently, he wiped the screen with a tissue.

'Is the phone alright, Kit?'

'It'll live.'

'How's your face?'

'It's the one I was born with ... I'm stuck with it.'

'The cuts, they're still bleeding.'

Instead of looking up, he studied the phone. 'Go on, Owen, spit it out.'

'Spit what out?'

'What I need to hear.' He didn't look up, neither did he smile.

'The video isn't fake. The monster's real. The girl is real.'

'Freya.' Still, he didn't make eye contact with Owen. 'Say her name.'

'Freya's real.'

'Excellent.'

'I'm sorry about nearly busting your phone, and I'm sorry if I hurt you.'

'Doubly excellent.'

'Do you always have to speak like Professor

Bullshit?'

Kit raised his eyes, grinning as he did so. 'Now I've successfully concluded my sulk I'll say that your apology is officially accepted.'

'I didn't mean to go crazy like that; it's just all this—'

Kit held up his hand to silence Owen. 'Pal, mate, buddy, friend. We've gone through emotional hell this weekend. Is it any wonder that we've got so cranky? Listen, I've been running complicated equations. I've calculated with complete accuracy that the friendship that you, Jez and me have has the tensile strength of nine point six billion tons.'

Owen stared at Kit as he twirled round on the swivel chair.

'Owen, you can laugh now, that's supposed to be a joke.'

Owen laughed with relief, rather than at the typically idiosyncratic Kit Bolter joke. He held out his hand for Kit to shake. Before Kit's hand made contact, Owen playfully ruffled the kook's hair.

Kit laughed, too. 'Now go and smooth things over with Jez.'

'Will do.'

'Oh ... Owen. I shouldn't have called Eden a bitch. I'm sorry.'

'You best tell her that yourself. But I'm sure everything will be OK. In the meantime, I'll ask her to put more dressings on those war wounds you've got there.'

'Eden's alright. If anything, I got frightened that you'd stop wanting to hang out with Jez and yours truly.'

'There might be plenty to be frightened of out there in the world, but never get frightened about the Three Musketeers splitting up.'

After having a quick word with Eden, Owen headed upstairs.

Jez stood at the window. His eyes were fixed on the landscape outside. The fields glittered under a blanket of snow in the moonlight. The familiar world now resembled an alien landscape.

'Jez,' began Owen.

'You don't have to apologize. I'm the one who's gone berserk this weekend. Ramming the truck. Shooting my friend. If things come in threes, you better start running now. I'll probably blow you up or something.'

'I shouldn't have yelled at you. And I shouldn't have said that Kit's video was fake.'

'Takes some swallowing though, doesn't it? How many other places in Yorkshire have dinosaurs, or whatever the hell it is?'

'We'll take the phone to the police. Let them work out what the beastie is.'

Jez held the broken arm to his chest as if nursing it. 'I do remember driving the truck at an animal. Huge it was. I rammed it, because I knew that thing was going to attack the woman lying in the road.'

'In which case, it might already have attacked the minibus passengers.'

'If it did, I'm in the clear, aren't I?'

Owen nodded. Jez sat down on the bed. All the strength had been sucked from him; he looked absolutely exhausted.

Owen asked, 'And you saw Freya, too?'

'Yup. Blasted her with the shotgun from that window. I thought she was going to pounce on Kit. Of course, my aim's crap.'

'Kit's going to be alright.'

'So we're all friends again?'

'Definitely.'

Jez held out his hand for Owen to shake. When Owen shook it Jez started to speak.

'Owen, I've been thinking. Remember in physics when we were told about when the universe was formed?'

'Sure. Big Bang and all that stuff.'

'I remember what amazed me was that after the Big Bang scientists say that there might have been thousands of universes created within a matter of seconds. For some reason, we can only see one now, and that's our universe. So where did all the others go?'

'Nobody knows.'

'What if they continue to exist? You know, like pages side-by-side in a book? What if creatures can come from those universes into ours?'

'You think that animal might have come through some kind of portal?'

'Maybe. Think about what happens in history. Every few hundred years really amazing things happen. You know, like monsters and miracles and gods that human beings see, but then these amazing things vanish again and they become myths.' Jez spoke with complete seriousness. 'What if in different parts of the world a portal or doorway opens to one of these universes and strange creatures come through? We wouldn't be able to understand what they are. I mean, they'd be inexplicable, wouldn't they? What if they're watching this world and plan to invade us?'

'I don't know, Jez. What we should do is get that phone of Kit's to the police as quickly as we can.'

'They'll have to believe that kind of evidence, won't they? They'll bring in the army and scientists and all kinds of—'

Jez didn't get any further, because a sudden concussion shook the house. This was followed by a terrifying scream. Owen knew that scream had come from Eden. She sounded as if she knew she was going to die.

SIXTY-EIGHT

Screams echoed through the farmhouse. Owen Westonby hurtled out of Jez's bedroom and down the stairs.

Kit emerged from the back room, his face white with shock. 'What's happening? Who's that screaming?'

Eden's screams of terror grew louder, more desperate.

Following the sound, Owen sped along the corridor to the kitchen at the back of the house. He burst through the door where an incredible sight met his eyes. Eden yelled as she tried to

290

shut the back door. The reason she couldn't close it was because a dozen naked arms, resembling pale tentacles, had forced themselves between the door and the door frame. A hand curled around the door from outside to grab Eden's hair.

Owen ran across the kitchen where he tried to peel back the fingers that clutched Eden's blond strands.

'Forget my hair!' she yelled. 'Just help me shut these out!'

Owen tried to push the door shut. However, the arms writhing through the five-inch gap made it impossible.

'Who are they?' Owen shouted.

'It's that animal! The one Kit filmed!'

An arm pushed through the gap, revealing bulging muscle. Fingers tried to rake Owen's face.

He flicked his head back to avoid being scratched. 'We'll have to open the door!'

'No way! We can't let it into the house!'

'Are you sure it's—'

'It's the monster, Owen! Believe me, it's the monster! And it's a lot bigger in real life than the video!'

Kit helped, too, as they tried to close the door. Just then, Jez clattered into the kitchen. He possessed real muscle and soon they managed to trap the arms between the door and the frame. The naked limbs swayed from side to side with a snake-like motion. What reinforced the serpentine effect was the hissing sound from outside.

Kit panted, 'I told you it was real.'

'OK.' Jez nodded, 'We believe you.'

'We won't be able to shut the door,' Owen told them, 'unless we can get these arms out of the way.' A hand swayed close to his face, fingers grasping blindly. All too clearly, he saw the bluish fingernails. One thumbnail had been ripped off in the struggle. Beneath the nail the raw flesh was grey and wet.

'What do you suggest?' shouted Eden. 'Because when I opened this door that thing out there rushed the house like a mad bull.'

Jez leaned sideways to pull open a drawer. 'Let me try something ... I'm starting to learn a thing or two about pain.' From a clutter of tools he pulled out a hammer.

Eden gave a grim nod. 'Do it, Jez! Give it hell!'

Jez used his good arm to deliver the punishment. The hammer struck one limb, bristling with red hairs. At the second blow the arm went into spasm, the fingers stretched out, quivering. With amazing ferocity, he beat the arms that protruded through the gap. One of the blows shattered fingers, the next cracked the bone in a forearm. The arms went frantic.

Owen called out, 'Get ready to open the door on my command. OK? We want that thing to yank its arms out – that way we can shut the door.'

'Just a couple more swipes.' Jez grinned as he aimed the hammer at a bare elbow. The impact of the steel on the elbow opened up the skin. Owen saw dirty white bone. No blood, though. Meanwhile, Eden dealt with the hand gripping those strands of hair by simply jerking her head back.

'Let it keep a souvenir!' she yelled.

The hand began a cobra-like sway with strands of blonde hair clutched in its fist.

Jez swung the hammer – the man had become a born-again warrior. The hammerhead ripped away fingernails, which pitter-pattered on to the kitchen floor, where they resembled delicate seashells.

'It's hurting,' Kit whooped. 'Jez, you hurt the bastard!'

'Alright,' Owen hissed. 'On the word *Go*. Let the door open – just by a couple more inches.'

'Not an inch more!' Eden warned.

'We don't want that sucker in here,' Kit said with feeling.

'GO!'

They allowed the door to move towards them a couple of inches. Whoever – whatever – was out there withdrew its wounded arms in a flash. Immediately, Owen and the others slammed the door shut. Eden turned the key in the lock. Owen and Kit took care of the bolts, snapping them across.

Jez wiped sweat from his eyes. 'That's a good door. It'll keep out plenty of bad guys.'

Kit raised his eyebrows. 'Will it keep out a monster? I don't think so.'

Eden darted to the window. 'I can't see it.'

'Maybe it's gone?' Jez sounded hopeful.

At that moment, they heard a loud scraping.

Owen's heart thudded as a sense of dread replaced the exhilaration he felt on successfully closing the door. 'It's climbing up the outside of the house.'

'We could run for it?' Eden suggested.

Kit shook his head. 'I've seen that thing before, remember? It moves fast. Just picture someone trying to out-swim a man-eating shark. We wouldn't stand a chance on foot.'

What Eden said next sounded so matter-of-fact, yet so profoundly shocking, that they gawped at her. 'If we can't run away from that thing, then we've got to kill it.'

Kit's eyes bulged. 'Holy Mother of God. How?'

Owen thought fast. 'Jez, where's the gun?'

'Outside.'

'Really?'

'Kit's friend knocked it clean out of my hands.' Jez grimaced. 'She didn't want shooting a second time.'

'Where is it?'

'The front yard.'

Owen nodded, knowing what he'd got to do.

Kit grabbed his arm. 'Hey, Owen, don't go out there. That thing will pounce on you in one second flat.'

'Smack pans on the kitchen walls,' Owen told them. 'Make some noise for me.'

Eden kissed him. 'Get the gun. But come back safe.'

Kit's eyes were wide – just bulging right out with horror. 'You can't. You'll be killed.' He turned to Jez. 'Your Dad's got another gun, hasn't he?'

'Sorry, guys. That's the only shooting iron

we've got.'

Owen grabbed a wok from where it hung on the wall and shoved it into Kit's hands. 'Hard as you can. Bash the walls. Keep the big guy distracted.'

Owen ran for the front door. He felt a mixture of dread and total excitement as he thought: *it's true what they say, the closer you get to death, the more you feel alive.*

Behind him, the three made an enormous clatter, striking the walls and the kitchen stove with heavy iron pans. It sounded like metal thunder. Cautiously, he opened the door on to a moonlit yard. Snow glinted. He saw drops of blood. Probably Kit's. But no gun. From the house came clanging, crashing, an immense din. Those three drummed with those pans as if his life depended on it. *Which, when it came down to it,* he admitted, *was absolutely the case.*

Owen crossed the yard, searching, hoping the creature's attention had been drawn to the hullabaloo. When he ran through deep shadow he found the shotgun by kicking it, rather than seeing it. Seizing the weapon, he ran back into the house. He closed the front door, locked it, bolted it. No sooner had he done that than there were sudden yells of panic. This time they came from the back room where, earlier, Kit had flounced away to sulk.

Eden stood at the doorway to the back parlour that served as the farm's office.

She pointed into the room. 'Look!' she cried. 'It's trying to find a way in.'

Owen ran along the corridor. 'Jez, where are

295

the shells?'

'You've got four in the magazine. I'll get more.' Jez ducked into another room where his father kept the ammo.

Owen just didn't know what to expect when he entered the back parlour. Eden followed, even though he waved his hand behind him: a stay-back gesture. He'd fired pump-action shotguns like this before, so he knew how to chamber the round. That done, he slid his finger around the trigger. The parlour extended out at the back of the house. An archway in the wall led to a conservatory made from a plastic frame and large window panes. The light in the conservatory remained off. *That's odd*, he thought, *there's moonlight ... so why is the conservatory so dark?*

'Take your time.' Eden sounded surprisingly calm. 'Think before you shoot. Choose a vulnerable spot.'

Eden Taylor was a remarkable girl. No clinging to him, no hysterics. With absolute calm, she gave him emotional support and strength with her carefully chosen words.

Warily ... slowly ... he moved towards the strangely dark conservatory. Bright moonlight should be cascading through the glass roof. *Why isn't there any moonlight? Why is it so dark in there?* Already, he found himself picturing a huge beast springing from the shadows to tear him apart.

Gripping the shotgun even tighter, he stepped through the arch into the conservatory. *So dark in here ... no light at all. It's almost as if the*

296

house has sunk underground. Total silence. Nobody spoke. The tension in his body rose, his muscles quivered. Any moment now he expected an explosion of movement as the monster attacked.

Light ... I need light. Gripping the shotgun in one hand, he used the other to flick the switch.

The light blazed. That was when he saw that the monster was closer than he expected. In fact, it was directly above him. Now he knew why it had been so dark. The creature lay on the conservatory roof, covering the glass panels, which in turn prevented moonlight from entering the room. The thing did not move ... but what kind of animal was it? Owen made out its massive bulk – a whale of a thing up there on the glass roof.

What nailed his attention were the faces. A dozen or more people gazed down. Like kids mischievously pressing their faces to window panes, these individuals forced their faces against the glass. The pressure deformed their features, pushing noses to one side and distorting mouths. All of them stared down at where he stood directly beneath them.

At first, it was like looking into the eyes of corpses – the gaze of each individual seemed out of focus and fixed; the eyes didn't move. A moment later, however, a strange, evil light appeared in their eyes. They burned with hatred. Their naked ferocity made his blood run cold.

Then the madness erupted. Kit and Jez yelled at him to run.

A clearer voice rang out over the yells. This

was Eden. 'Now's your chance, Owen.'

He raised the shotgun until it pointed directly upwards – then squeezed the trigger. Once, twice, three times. Those explosions were deafening. The pump-action weapon fired clusters of lead pellets at hundreds of miles per hour. Above him, the glass shattered.

The human heads seemed to be connected to the same nervous system. They all recoiled in the same way at the same time. They all opened their mouths and screamed together – a synchronized chorus of rage and pain.

'I recognize some of them!' Owen shouted. These were men and women from the nearby village; he'd seen them many times before as they went about their ordinary, day-to-day lives. Now they were anything but ordinary. 'Some of those people were on the bus that crashed.'

Jez seemed dazed. 'We know what got them ... it was nothing to do with me.'

Kit always reached conclusions faster than anyone else. 'Whatever that animal is, it uses people. It's recycled body parts into itself.'

The heads that Owen Westonby had blasted with the shotgun were floppy, almost boneless things now. Like the deflated udder sacks of a cow that had just been milked. Other 'live' heads hissed with fury. They glared down at their prey.

That was when the monster went to work. Human arms sprouted from the creature's flesh. They reached down through the holes that Owen had blasted in the glass, and then those dead-looking hands began to rip at the frame and what remained of the window panes.

Owen chambered another round. 'We're not going to stop it getting in!' He pointed the muzzle upwards. 'Run!' He fired the last shell, exploding a head. All that remained of the head was something like a white finger pointing down at them from the monster's body. This white 'finger' must have been what remained of the spinal column that connected the head to the creature.

'Time to go!' Owen pushed the others from the room. 'Run! Get out of the house!'

Everything happened in a blur. Soon they were running across a meadow. The moon shone down with a hard, cold brilliance. Witch fire, a light as cold as death.

'Here it comes,' Owen panted. 'It's chasing us!'

SIXTY-NINE

When Tom answered his phone in the living room at Skanderberg cottage he saw his brother's name on-screen, but a strange guttural panting filled his ear.

'Owen?'

The gasping continued.

'Owen, is that you? Are you OK?' Tom wondered if his brother was ill. 'Owen?'

'Tom! Jez was right!'

June noticed the expression on Tom's face. She

rose from the armchair.

Tom tried to make himself heard. 'Owen. I can't make out what you're saying.'

'Tom! We're heading to your house!'

'What's wrong?'

'We're being followed ... chased!'

'Who by?'

'Jez was right! He drove the truck into an animal! It was at Jez's farm. We're heading for your cottage. It's following. I don't know...'

The gasping sound filled Tom's ear. After that, the phone suddenly went dead.

'Stay here,' he told June. 'My brother's in trouble.'

'How?'

'Helsvir. He's being chased by Helsvir.'

Tom grabbed his fleece, his gloves, a flashlight, and then went to the store cupboard to find his old harpoon gun. It was the only weapon he had. Though against the monster known as Helsvir, just how effective would a spear be?

'June. Lock the door behind me. I'll be as fast as I can.'

'I can come with you,'

'Stay with your mother. Don't open the door to anyone but me.'

Seconds later, he headed away from the house, the flashlight in one hand, the harpoon gun in the other. Behind him, June Valko locked the door. Ahead, the forest lay bathed in moonlight. A wilderness of a hundred thousand trees. And somewhere out there Owen and his friends were running for their lives.

SEVENTY

At the same time that Tom headed through the forest, armed with a harpoon gun, Owen was running for his life. He still carried the pump-action shotgun which he'd used to blast the creature back at the farmhouse. With him were Eden, Jez and Kit. Their eyes were huge with shock. Sheer terror drove them to run as fast as they humanly could. Moonlight glinted on the snow-covered field. A scarecrow wearing a cowboy hat appeared to point the way, as if somehow the lone straw man understood the dreadful danger the four faced. Ahead lay the forest.

And behind them?

Behind them, a creature followed. A monster. An ugly beast that appeared to be formed from human body parts. Naked human legs by the dozen carried it across the frozen ground. Human heads bulged from its flanks. This horror moved with marvellous grace. All those legs moving with a rippling flow – a centipede way of locomotion. The creature, which was as big as a whale, glided through the moonlight. What was more, it glided fast, very fast.

Kit struggled to catch his breath; first-aid dressings hung from his face where the tape had come unstuck from the gunshot wounds. Even so, he yelled in triumph, 'See! It's real! You believe me now...'

'Keep running!' Jez shouted. 'Whatever you do, don't let it catch you!'

Jez didn't need to say any more than that. They'd all recognized faces that bulged from the monster. Somehow it had torn apart passengers from the crashed bus. Now those victims were part of the monster; their flesh had merged with that gargantuan body.

'We could split up,' Jez suggested as they reached a fence. 'It can't chase all of us.'

Eden shook her head. 'Stick together. We might have to stand and fight that thing.'

'Eden's right.' Owen helped Jez over the fence; the guy's broken arm made it difficult for him to climb. 'If we split up, it'll pick us off one by one.'

They continued towards the trees, their shoes exploding clumps of snow.

Eden panted, 'You got through to your brother? What did he say?'

'I told him we were heading for his cottage ... and that we were being chased.'

Kit groaned. 'I can't run any further.'

'You've got to.' Eden grabbed his arm. 'Focus on running. Don't think of anything else.'

The creature had reached the fence they'd climbed over just seconds ago. The monster blasted through. The violence of the impact was staggering. Pieces of timber rained down on to the field. One post even shot over their heads to crash down into the forest. This powerful example of the animal's ferocity gave Kit a boost of energy. He suddenly ran faster. No doubt in his mind's eye, he saw what would happen to his own body if the creature slammed into him.

Owen realized he was still carrying the shotgun. He almost tossed it aside; its extra weight would only tire him faster. But then he had an idea. Pausing, he aimed at the beast, squeezed the trigger and ... *click! Damn it, out of ammo. I fired the last shot back at the house.*

They were now twenty paces or so from the forest. His brother's cottage lay maybe ten minutes away ... that is, if they weren't caught. Glancing back, he saw the creature racing towards them. This thing hunted with the tenacity of a man-eating shark. Its sheer speed flung up snow and dirt, sprays of black and white. And he could hear the sound it made: those strange corpse-like faces were whispering – as if eagerly discussing how they would hurt the four young people they pursued.

'HELSVIR!' The name exploded from Owen's lips. 'Of course! I've seen that thing before.'

Even though they were running, Eden reacted with astonishment. 'Really? Why on earth didn't you tell us?'

'Yes, but not *alive* like this. There are carvings of it in my brother's cottage.'

They wove through the trees as they engaged in this gasping, breathless conversation.

Kit joined in. 'I remember seeing the pictures when we were kids. Something to do with the Vikings? A dragon?'

Owen shouted, 'Yes, and it's called Helsvir!'

Jez shouldered aside branches. 'That's not like any dragon I've seen in films.'

'Legends say that Helsvir was created from the bodies of dead warriors.' Owen's heart pounded. 'That's what we're seeing now. Those are human legs and arms, and human faces.'

A tremendous crash announced that Helsvir had reached the forest. Instead of weaving round bushes, it simply smashed through.

Kit was exhausted. 'We're never gonna outrun it. It's gonna get us.'

Eden nodded at the gun in Owen's hand. 'Ditch it. It's slowing you down.'

Jez grunted. 'Wait. I've got shells.'

Jez tugged a handful of shotgun cartridges from his pocket. Although he didn't stop running, he attempted to pass them to Owen. That was when he slipped. With a yell of agony he fell on to his broken arm. The red cartridges scattered all over the ground.

Everyone stopped to help Jez up. A hundred paces away, the monster came crunching through the forest.

Owen glanced down at the ammo.

'Leave them!' Eden's eyes brimmed with tears. She knew what he planned to do.

Owen gave a grim smile. 'You three head to my brother's place. I'll pick these up.'

'Owen, leave them.'

'Keep moving. I'll only be a second.'

'Owen ... please.' She desperately wanted him to keep running.

'We need these shells.' He raised the shotgun.

'This cannon might slow our friend down.'

'Then I'm staying with you.'

Owen nodded at his two friends. 'Kit. Jez. Take her with you, boys.'

Eden cried out, 'No! I'm staying here with you!'

Grabbing an arm each, Jez and Kit hauled her away through the trees. He could hear her shouting that she wanted to stay with him. But he knew that they couldn't outrun the monster. It was down to him to save their lives. *If I can blast its legs*, he told himself, *I might be able to slow it down.*

Quickly, he began to pick up the shells so he could load the gun. Picking them up wasn't a problem; bright moonlight revealed where they lay. The problem came when he tried to push them into the gun's magazine. His fingers were so cold that the ammo slipped from his grip. As the crunching sound grew louder (Helsvir was approaching fast) he struggled to load the gun. One shell slipped into the magazine. The next popped from his fingers and fell to the ground. He picked it up, tried again. Once more he dropped it. Then he saw the vast, dark shape glide towards him. Boy-oh-boy, this thing really did resemble a killer shark – a monstrous shark at that – one that blasted from the darkness.

Helsvir took a detour to the right, circling round as it searched for a clear line of attack.

Here it comes ... here it comes...

With his heart pounding furiously, he picked up the shells. *Don't rush*, he told himself, *you'll only screw up again.* He took a deep breath and deliberately held it.

Helsvir approached Owen Westonby – a torpedo of evil flesh blasting through the forest, ripping bark from trees, shattering branches.

Owen still held his breath. When he was certain that his lungs had warmed it up he gently blew on his fingers. They grew warmer – numbness brought on by the cold began to ease. With the warmth would come increased dexterity. *I hope so ... my God, I hope so.*

Helsvir's detour had bought him precious moments. After picking up the shotgun cartridges, he efficiently slotted them through the aperture in the underside of the gun. He gambled that the time it had taken to warm his fingers would deliver the result he needed, and that was to give Kit, Jez and Eden a chance to reach the cottage.

He murmured, 'OK, Owen. Hurt the bastard.'

Helsvir surged through the undergrowth; maybe thirty paces separated them.

Owen stood his ground, not budging an inch. Showdown. This felt like destiny.

Helsvir rushed forward. He could see the heads that budded from its flesh. The eyes blazed – and in each and every eye, a craving to hurt him. If he couldn't stop Helsvir now, he would be broken apart. He'd be incorporated into that thing; his own head would join that vile array.

When he'd fired at the creature in the house he'd aimed for the faces. He'd destroyed a good many, too. Now, however, he targeted its legs.

Carefully, he aimed the shotgun at the front legs that supported the beast. As accurately as he could he fired the first round. One of the legs took the full force of the shot. Everything beneath the knee was smashed to pulp. The injury threw the creature off balance. The mouths roared in pain. Helsvir blundered off course to smash into a tree. For a second it seemed stunned, but only for a second. It recovered enough to lunge at him again. And again he fired. The animal rolled sideways. Once more, he won a brief respite as the creature struggled to recover its balance.

Owen Westonby continued to target the legs with well-aimed shots. Each shot bought his friends time. By now, they must be approaching his brother's cottage.

He had one shell left. When he'd fired that the creature would have lost perhaps six or seven legs. Unfortunately for Owen it still possessed another twenty or so.

Owen fired the last of his ammunition. After that, he calmly turned his back on the monster and started walking. He knew he couldn't outrun the thing. However, he decided not to watch its final approach. What had been a chaotic rustling behind him turned into a rhythmic drumming sound of feet striking the dirt.

'Here it comes,' he murmured as he thought about his friends. 'I hope I gave you enough time to reach Tom's house.'

SEVENTY-ONE

The monster created from the bodies of the dead crashed through the bushes. With every second it grew closer. Owen Westonby closed his eyes.

I wish I'd saved one of the shells for myself, was Owen's last thought before he heard the shout.

'Helsvir! It's me that you're wanting, isn't it?'

Owen recognized the voice. 'Tom!'

His brother stood beside an oak tree at the edge of the clearing. His breath burst in gusts of silver in the moonlight. Straight away, Owen saw that Tom carried a diver's harpoon gun. The barbed spear glinted as Tom aimed.

Helsvir bellowed – this was savage triumph rather than rage. Instantly, it swerved away from Owen in order to hurtle towards the newcomer. Tom coolly aimed the harpoon gun until the last possible moment. When a gap of no more than a dozen yards remained between Tom and Helsvir he fired. Compressed gas, contained in a small canister attached to the gun, propelled the spear at lightning speed. What was more, that slender but lethally sharp missile was connected to the harpoon gun by a strong nylon cord. Divers used the weapons to hunt fish, and of course they didn't want to lose the spear if an injured fish swam away with it embedded in its body.

Then Owen noticed Tom's streak of genius. He'd tied the nylon cord to a tree. In a flash the harpoon penetrated Helsvir's body. Or, more accurately, the harpoon penetrated one of the human faces that poked outward from its body. The barb caught fast, resulting in the creature being fixed to the tree by the cord. Now the monster was hooked. All the faces that bristled from Helsvir screamed at the same time. Each expression was the same – rage and hurt and frustration.

Tom raced along the path to Owen. 'You're not hurt?'

'No.'

'Then run like hell. I reckon that harpoon will hold for ten seconds max.'

Owen didn't need to be told twice: he ran like hell. Or more precisely ran like the beasts of hell were just about to start pursuing him.

Owen panted, 'Tom, you've seen that thing before?'

'Five years ago. It tried to kill me back then.'

'It's Helsvir, isn't it? From the carvings at your house?'

'Yes, and he's as real as you or me.'

They bounded over a rotting log. Moonbeams penetrated the branches overhead, glittering bone-white fingers of illumination.

'That thing moves fast.' Owen sucked in a lungful of air. 'We were lucky to keep ahead of it.'

Tom shot him a grim look. 'If that thing had wanted to catch you, it would have done.'

'No, we managed to outrun it.'

Tom shook his head. 'Helsvir wasn't trying to hunt you down, he was herding you.'

'Why?'

'To keep you moving towards those.' As he ran, he nodded to where pale figures stood beneath the trees. 'Those are vampires, Owen. You would have provided them with food. And then you would have joined them – recruits for the vampire army.'

'How do you know all this?'

'There's a lot that happened five years ago that I never told anyone about ... listen to that. Big, bad old Helsvir's broken free.'

Once again, Owen heard that distinctive crashing sound as Helsvir sped through the trees towards them.

'What now?' panted Owen.

'Head for the cottage. Your friends should be there by now. See you later.'

'Wait! Tom! Where are you going?'

Tom took off along another path. 'I caused Helsvir a lot of trouble last time. He'll want to deal with me first before he comes looking for you.'

'Tom?'

'Trust me, bro. I'll meet you at the cottage as soon as I can.'

With that, Tom raced away into the gloom. Helsvir veered to the right, following the man. Owen saw that Helsvir must have snapped the cord attached to the harpoon, thus freeing itself from the tree. The harpoon itself hadn't dislodged and still remained embedded in the face

310

of a man that Owen now recognized. Tony had been a passenger on the doomed minibus. The man's head had been pinned to the side of the monster by the spear in the same way a picture might be pinned to a corkboard. Tony's eyes bulged at either side of the steel shaft. Even though the spear-point must have passed completely through his brain, he still roared with bloodlust and fury.

Owen hoped his brother was wrong about humans not being able to outrun Helsvir. Because Tom Westonby would need to move very quickly indeed, if he was going to stay out of Helsvir's many hands.

SEVENTY-TWO

The moon lit their way through the forest. At last, Kit Bolter could see the pale stonework of Tom Westonby's cottage. Owen had phoned his brother; therefore, the man would be expecting them. What he wouldn't expect was the state of Owen's friends. Kit glanced at Eden with her tousled hair. Jez Pollock lurched along, holding his arm in its now not-so-bright orange cast. Every step hurt the guy. His face bled sweat. Kit knew that he, himself, must be a shocking sight, too. Exertion had caused the pellet wounds in his face to bleed again. Blood stained his clothes. And all three were frightened and exhausted.

No wonder, he thought. *We've been hunted by a monster.*

And possibly that monster had now got hold of Owen. Mental images of Owen being mauled by the thing made Kit shake so violently he could barely keep walking. Jez was in trouble, too. The lurching grew worse; he swayed from side to side before suddenly dropping to his knees.

Kit murmured, 'It's OK, I've got you.'

What happened next went so fast he wasn't sure who had appeared to help him. A pair of hands gripped Jez's other arm, while Kit put his arm around his friend's waist.

Kit glanced up at the individual who had help-ed him. 'Freya?'

Those eerie white eyes gazed at him. She said nothing as they both gently lifted Jez to his feet. Then they walked at either side of Jez as they helped him along the path.

Just a few paces ahead, Eden watched the pair supporting the sixteen-year-old. Eden's expres-sion said it all. She'd seen so much tonight that she accepted the appearance of this unearthly creature without a word. As long as the strange woman didn't attack them, then that seemed OK by her.

During the last few yards to the cottage Owen Westonby joined them.

'I'll tell you everything later,' he said by way of explanation.

They all accepted this, too. After that, four humans and one vampire passed through the stone archway that bore the image of Helsvir, and walked up to the cottage door. Whether

312

being here would bring protection from Helsvir or not was another matter. But at least they were here. Now they would have to prepare themselves for whatever happened next.

SEVENTY-THREE

Tom Westonby wasn't usually a gambling man. Tonight, however, he was gambling with his life. He hoped he could lure Helsvir away from his brother. It was only a short while since Tom had run through the forest, drawn by the sound of gunshots. There in the moonlight, he'd watched as Owen fired at the creature's legs. Owen must have realized he couldn't kill a monster of that huge size with only a shotgun. Instead, the sixteen-year-old had attempted to slow it down by shattering its front legs.

The problem was that Helsvir moved on twenty legs or more. A problem that Tom was only too aware of as that ugly behemoth pursued him through the forest. Tom ran hard. Every breath hurt his lungs – the ice-cold air felt like shards of broken glass when he inhaled. Nevertheless, he kept running. Because if he stopped now Helsvir would pounce.

When he reached a sharp bend in the woodland path he negotiated the curve easily. A loud crash from behind suggested that Helsvir hadn't been so nimble. Glancing back, he saw what had happened. Helsvir had rolled over on to its side. Despite being the size of a very large truck, Helsvir possessed an uncanny agility. At least it had in the past. The damage inflicted by those shotgun blasts had not slowed the beast down much, but it now found it difficult to keep its balance. Tom watched Helsvir struggle to its feet. Owen's perfectly aimed shots had ripped away flesh from some of the legs that had once belonged to human beings. Other legs had been amputated beneath the knee, forcing Helsvir to run on stumps.

Although Helsvir succeeded in getting itself back on to its many feet, it took a good five or six seconds to do so. Even then it waddled uncertainly for the first few steps before picking up speed. *Good!* Tom thought. *Now I've found your weakness I'm going to use it.*

Helsvir charged after him again. Tom had to run as fast as he could. Two dozen arms still protruded from the underside of the creature like pale tentacles. If they got hold of him, they'd pluck off his limbs and his head as easily as he could pull the legs off a roast chicken. Yet he had one small advantage now. He made abrupt changes in direction as he ran. Every time he did so, Helsvir lost its balance and went crashing to the ground. This gave Tom precious seconds. The injured legs were making pursuit difficult for the creature.

Even though Tom did have that slight advantage, he knew he couldn't keep up this exhausting pace for much longer. He'd set out to lure Helsvir away from Owen. He'd succeeded in doing that. Now he had to find the fastest route back to the cottage. Although if Helsvir chose to attack, Tom was sure it would have no difficulty in tearing the place apart in order to reach its occupants.

Once again, Tom chanced his luck. Helsvir had never even touched the cottage as far as he knew. So Tom's big gamble was that the beast would leave the building alone. *How can I can be sure that it won't attack it?* Tom asked himself as he leapt over a fallen log. *Everything changed when June Valko arrived. The vampires had never attacked me before. The night she came to the cottage I nearly drowned when one pounced on me. The damn thing even climbed down the chimney.*

Helsvir slammed into the fallen log Tom had just jumped – the heavy body shattered a ton of oak into a blizzard of splinters. Tom knew that Helsvir had lost none of its strength. But he knew that Helsvir would need to repair itself soon. Owen's work with the shotgun had cost it half a dozen limbs. That meant Helsvir would need the body parts of men and women, which it could then weave into the obscene mass that formed its body.

Tom glanced back as Helsvir lost its balance at another turn in the path. With a tremendous thud it slammed into a tree. Of course, Helsvir wasn't fazed. Shaking itself, just as a dog does after coming in out of the rain, the animal started moving again. Relentlessly, tirelessly, it resumed the hunt. Tom Westonby was its prey.

All the more reason to run faster, Tom thought.

His feet pounded the frozen ground. He swerved to avoid a dead stag. Its neck had been torn open. Yet no blood had spilled from the wound. Straight away, Tom began noticing other dead animals – rabbits, badgers, foxes, wild boar – all with wounds on their throats. Yet not a drop of blood in sight – not so much as a red speck on the whitest patch of snow.

They've been drained ... And then he remembered what he'd told Owen just moments ago. That Helsvir could easily have caught Owen and his friends if it had really wanted to.

'I'm not being hunted,' he gasped in astonishment. 'I'm being herded! Helsvir's driving me into a trap!'

Tom saw figures ahead. They stood amongst the trees, white-skinned, mouths open, eyes gleaming. Tom's heart lurched with fear.

Helsvir drove him towards the vampires. They were waiting for the richest, most delicious blood of all. Human blood.

His blood.

SEVENTY-FOUR

Tom thought: *I'm in big trouble!*

Panic exploded inside his body. Exhaustion made his legs heavy as concrete. His plan had been blown to pieces. He'd intended to race back through the forest to join Owen and the others at the cottage. Only he now realized that Helsvir had been in control of the situation all along. The creature had herded him, as if he was nothing more than a stupid sheep, towards the waiting vampires. Tom saw them standing there, waiting for him amongst the trees. Tall, stick-thin figures, with white, staring eyes.

When he tried to duck along a narrow path that would take him to the cottage, he saw the way was blocked by two ancient vampires clad in corroded breast plates and chain mail. They wore expressions of savage glee as they saw Tom approach – a victim with hot blood pumping through his veins.

Tom spun round to head back the way he came. *But here comes Helsvir ...* A torpedo creature, slamming through bushes, shredding branches, exploding fallen logs.

Jolts of terror blasted through Tom. He felt nothing less than electric shocks of fear. As he saw it, he would either be claimed by Helsvir,

317

which would result in the bloody dismantling of his body, or he'd find himself in the hungry grasp of the vampires. They'd feed on his blood. Soon after that he'd find himself part of the vampire army.

'Damn you!' Tom yelled in fury.

Desperately, he headed downhill towards the river, its waters glinting in the moonlight. Liquid silver. Cold as death. Running downhill gave him extra speed, yet there was a downside, too. He was so exhausted he couldn't swerve a tree trunk. He slammed into solid timber with a heck of a thump. An agonizing blast of pain shot through his shoulder. When he bounced off the tree he went sprawling. His head struck frozen earth. The world swam dizzily round him. Trees became soft, undulating shadows. The moonlit river danced upwards into the sky – or so it seemed to him: the blow on the head had bludgeoned his thoughts into a chaotic jumble.

Tom scrambled on all fours. When he tried to climb to his feet he found his balance was so screwed he flopped back down on to his face again. He lay there panting. In close-up, he saw the gleaming white skull of a bird lying on the soil. *If I stay here ... if I let them get me ... it won't hurt that much, will it?*

Exhaustion had torn every atom of strength from him. He couldn't even lift his head. The bird skull lay there just inches from his eyes. Thirty yards beyond that were pale figures. The vampires approached. They were in no hurry. They appeared to be savouring the moment before they sank their teeth into his skin. He could almost hear the crunch of the bite – they'd munch through his throat so easily. They'd take pleasure in the human's screams and agonized convulsions.

Behind him came the heavy crunch of feet. Helsvir approached. A hand touched the back of his leg.

Where the energy came from he didn't know, but Helsvir's vile touch was enough. Tom scrambled away on all fours. The vampires moved towards him. Helsvir lunged forward, too. Tom managed to get to his feet. With a furious burst of speed, he rushed down towards the river. But he knew he was trapped. He couldn't swim far in these brutally cold temperatures. What's more, Helsvir was a formidable swimmer. The creature would easily catch Tom as he floundered through the water.

More vampires approached from every direction – there were young women – or what appeared to be young women, though they might be centuries old. There were warriors from long ago in leather tunics, or wearing rusted suits of armour. On the king's orders they'd marched into this valley to destroy the vampires. Only they'd discovered that the vampires were stronger than the knights of the Middle Ages – now the king's men were monsters, too: they hungered for blood.

Without any more of a plan than hoping to survive for a few more seconds Tom raced along the river bank. Helsvir ran so fast that it overshot the path and smacked down into the water – the force of the impact threw up an explosion of spray that, in the moonlight, seemed to blaze with an uncanny fire.

The burst of energy didn't last long. Tom began to slow; his head hung down until his chin bumped against his chest. He was dead on his feet. A figure with a flash of blonde hair leapt from the bushes.

With a last surge of strength he punched out. His fist slammed into a soft face. A pair of wide eyes stared at him. They were entirely colourless: the pupils were fierce black dots in that awful whiteness. A pair of hands grasped his elbows. Managing to wrench his arms free, he rained more blows into that once beautiful female face.

'TOM. IT'S ME.'

Everything else vanished. The vampires, the monster, the forest, the moon, the entire universe – at that instant, all of creation seemed to disappear into nothingness. Because there *she* was.

Nicola. My Nicola. He froze. The face he'd struck with his fists belonged to the woman he'd fallen in love with. Then one night five years ago she'd transformed from a beautiful woman, who'd been so alive, into a vampire. When he'd married her in that unconventional service at the village church, the ancient Viking curse had been invoked. Nicola had been damned. She'd become one of the blood-eaters. For five years he'd hoped and prayed that she'd return. Now she had.

He gazed into her face. All the fear had gone. *This is what I want,* he told himself with a great sense of surrender. *I want to be with her for ever.*

320

These thoughts went through his head in the briefest of moments. Yet it seemed as if he gazed into that lovely face for hours. Of course, those punches of his had not made so much as a mark – how could mortal blows injure a vampire? Bullets wouldn't hurt her, bombs wouldn't mark her, nor would time age her. She was immortal, indestructible, eternal.

'TOM!' Nicola shook him. 'Tom! Keep moving! Don't let them catch you!'

Her voice snapped him from his trance. Suddenly, he saw the world around him again – Helsvir rushing from the water, shaking off drops of silver. The vampires were approaching – a pack of hunters, eager to taste his blood.

'This way.' Nicola did not shout. Her voice was calm. She was determined to save the man she once loved – or did she love him still?

She gripped his hand. Together, they ran up the slope, although they were clearly surrounded by hostile vampires.

'We can't escape them,' he panted. 'I can't run any further.'

'Just a few more steps.' Her gentle voice urged him on. 'Almost there. Trust me, Tom. I can save you.'

They reached an outcrop of rock half way up the slope. Here there were streaks of snow amid black shadow. And there, directly in front of him, was an opening in the ground. Perhaps five feet wide, it resembled a gaping, hungry mouth.

Nicola turned to face him, her blond hair fluttering in the breeze. Then she spoke these astonishing words: 'Put your arms around my body ... fall with me.'

She embraced him. Meanwhile, Helsvir pounded up the slope, just seconds away from tearing Tom to pieces. The vampires loped towards him from every direction.

Nicola hugged him even tighter. Without another word, she leaned backwards, toppling them both into the chasm. Swallowed by darkness, they seemed to fall for ever.

SEVENTY-FIVE

They lay together at the bottom of the shaft. Above them, a pale ring of light revealed where the moon shone on the edges of the rock that formed the opening. Neither moved. Tom lay on his back with his head on Nicola's stomach. Only moments had passed since she'd grabbed hold of him before they both toppled into the cave. Tom thought: *she held me like that so when we hit the bottom of the shaft I'd land on her. She broke my fall. If she hadn't, I'd be dead now.*

Tom breathed deeply, catching his breath. Helsvir and the vampires had nearly caught him. *If it hadn't been for Nicola ...* His heartbeat quickened. *But Nicola's a vampire, too ... perhaps hasn't saved me at all ... perhaps she just wants what's in my veins for herself?*

He lay there in the darkness. At any moment, he anticipated the feel of her cold teeth pressing into the sensitive skin of his neck. Yet she did not move. Surely the fall wouldn't have hurt her? Outwardly, Nicola still resembled a beautiful woman; however, she had the biology of a vampire. A twenty-foot fall wouldn't injure her in the slightest.

Slowly, he raised himself on to one elbow. Enough moonlight glimmered down the shaft to reveal that they were in a cave. Sticks and dry leaves covered the floor, along with the bones of woodland animals that had tumbled down here in the past. His eyes found what he really did want to see: Nicola's face. She lay there still as death. The black veins formed their uncanny patterns on her throat. The woman gazed steadily upwards. Yes, she had the fierce black pupils and eyes that were bereft of colour, but what he noticed more was the wetness on her face. Nicola Bekk, or the creature that had once been Nicola Bekk, wept real tears.

She whispered, 'I thought if I just stayed lying here I could make this moment last for ever.'

'You came back to me.'

'It can't last ... they'll take me back soon.'

'Who will take you back?'

'You must know ... the same things that made my family into vampires. The same *evil* things that created Helsvir.'

'But you're talking to me now as if you're human again.'

'A blip ... a temporary lapse on their part, I guess. Or perhaps they're using me as bait to trap you? In any event, I'll be back there with them soon, because...' she shook her head as she tried to put into words what had befallen her. 'Because I seem to be part of *their* dream. I don't know if you can understand?'

'Who are THEY?'

'In ancient times, men and women would have called them gods. My ancestors gave them names like Wodin, Thor, Loki ... now those gods are so old their minds have started to rot. Mostly they are content to dream ... and they've made me part of their dream...' Her voice sounded so hollow, and somehow so *lost*.

Tom sat up and grasped her hand. 'I'll find a way to bring you home.'

'Something happened here in the valley to wake the gods. They were dreaming, I was part of their dream ... sometimes dying, then being alive again.' She spoke in a dreamy way herself, as if only half awake.

The realization struck Tom with the suddenness of a slap. 'June Valko. Nicola, you thought you and your mother were the last of the Bekk bloodline. But there is someone else. Her name is June Valko. Her father was a blood relative of yours. Now he's out there ... one of the vampires.'

At that moment, the light vanished, plunging them into blackness. The opening had been covered. Tom dragged the flashlight from his pocket, hit the on-button and directed the beam upwards.

'Helsvir!'

Using its huge body, the creature had sealed the opening. The flashlight revealed that its flesh had formed a wet, glistening roof at the top of the shaft. Heads that budded from the thing stared down at Tom and Nicola twenty feet below. Those dozens of eyes fed the images to Helsvir's brain. The creature's reaction of fury was voiced by those once human heads. A fierce hissing erupted from their mouths. Even the head that Tom had skewered with the harpoon stared at him, while its grey lips slid back over its teeth. A tongue that was black and wet emerged from the mouth ... a black snake of a thing sliding from its own cave of flesh.

Tom shouted, 'You can't reach us, Helsvir! We've beaten you! You'll never take us!'

The roars that burst from the mouths were a unified outburst of sound. Naked arms that emerged from the body, like tentacles, reached down towards the pair. Fingers clutched, trying to grab the mortal and the vampire.

'Not even close,' Tom thundered. 'Give up, and get back to whatever hole you crawled out of!'

The monster convulsed with rage. Dozens of hands began ripping at stones and soil at the mouth of the shaft.

Tom grabbed Nicola's hand. 'It's trying to dig its way in!' He pulled her from the bottom of the shaft as dirt rained down. Stones and boulders soon followed. Helsvir roared with fury as it tried to widen the opening so it could reach them. The entire cave shook. Falling soil turned the air brown. Meanwhile, Tom and Nicola moved deeper into the back of the cave.

Not a moment too soon, because the roar that came next dwarfed even Helsvir's bellow. The shaft imploded. The sheer violence of the creature's attempt to smash its way in had been too much for the surrounding rock. The entire section of cave roof around the opening collapsed. Tons of boulders tumbled out of the shaft. Tom hadn't heard a sound so loud before. This was like standing in the heart of a thunderstorm.

Mercifully, just seconds later, the colossal din ended. In the silence that followed, Tom played the flashlight over the mound of debris.

Tom said, 'The opening's completely blocked.'

'Then Helsvir can't reach us,' she said.

'No, it can't ... but that means we can't get out of here. We're trapped.'

SEVENTY-SIX

'This really is an extraordinary situation.'

Kit Bolter repeated these words every few minutes as they sat in the lounge at Skanderberg. When Owen put more wood on the fire he said them again.

'This really is an extraordinary situation.'

'And we need to be extraordinary people to deal with what's going to happen,' June Valko said as she entered the room, carrying a tray with coffee and cake. 'You might not feel like eating anything, but you should. What you've been through could lead to shock. So keep your blood sugar levels up.'

Owen realized that shock had started to kick in. His friends spoke in a daze.

'We've experienced extraordinary situations,' Kit said, slightly varying his stock phrase.

'I broke my arm.' Jez Pollock tapped the orange cast with his finger.

'I've been shot.' Kit pointed at the fresh surgical dressings on his face that June had applied after he'd arrived at the cottage.

Eden shivered. 'We've been chased by a monster.'

'We even picked up a vampire on the way,' Owen added matter-of-factly.

'Don't call her a vampire,' Kit protested. 'She's my—'

'Girlfriend?' Jez chuckled in a slurred, druggy way (he had just taken more painkillers). In a taunting voice he sang, 'Kit's gotta vampire girlfriend, Kit's gotta vampire girlfriend.'

June set the tray down on a table. 'Here, take a cup of coffee everyone. Try to relax.'

'Relax?' Eden looked as if she'd never be able to relax again.

'My brother should be back soon,' Owen said. 'Tom will know what to do.'

Kit picked up a slice of cake. 'Did I ever tell you that Tom Westonby killed my uncle? Five years ago he threw him from the top of a church tower.'

'That's a lie.' Owen bunched his fists. 'Take it back.'

June made a soothing gesture. 'Try and stay calm. You've been through hell tonight.'

327

Eden laughed but it sounded more like weeping. 'You don't have to tell us. We've been to hell and back, and who knows? We might find ourselves back in hell again before long.'

Owen put his arm round Eden. She gripped him so fiercely that he almost lost his balance. Gently, he embraced her.

June tried to maintain a reassuring air of normality as she handed out coffee and cake. She made small-talk, asking if everyone was warm enough. Did they want milk in their coffee? And sugar? And be sure to drink it while it's hot.

Owen stood there as Eden clung to him. Even though he didn't hear her sob (she was too proud and too strong to let anyone see her cry), her tears soaked through his shirt; he felt them against his chest. He realized June had spoken the truth. His friends were in shock. Their eyes possessed an odd, staring quality. They weren't really seeing the furniture in the lounge, or the fire in the hearth grate, they were fixating on what happened to them tonight.

Owen's blood ran cold as he recalled firing the shotgun at the thing ... the way the ammunition blasted skin and muscle from those naked human legs. The firepower of the gun had been awesome ... horrific, too. Then Tom had saved him by drawing the monster away into the forest. *Was Tom alright? Had the creature caught him? What if ...* His heart started to beat faster. Panic tore through him; he realized he was clenching his fists as he hugged Eden. And, as he pictured Tom being ripped apart, his gaze locked on the carving of Helsvir that was set in the living room wall. There it was – the teardrop shape, the legs bristling from the bottom, the line of heads. Right then, he wanted to scream.

What changed the atmosphere was the bizarre sight of a lady gliding through the doorway from the staircase into the room. For a moment, Owen thought that this was a phantom coming to claim their souls.

June explained. 'This is my mother.' She quickly went to the woman and guided her to the sofa where she sat her down. 'My mother's not well,' June added. 'She doesn't speak, so she'll just sit here quietly.' June gave them a gentle smile. 'Can I ask you all to speak in quiet voices, and not to do anything to upset her?'

That seemed to do the trick. Everyone nodded, and the tension appeared to ease: an automatic response to being in the presence of an ill person – to be calm and softly spoken for their sake.

For a while, nobody spoke. At last, however, Eden inhaled deeply as she took comfort in having Owen's arms around her. 'That girl ... the one who joined us as we walked to the cottage...'

Kit murmured, 'That was Freya.'

'Is she really a vampire?'

Kit sighed. 'To be truthful, I guess she is.'

'And is she still out there?'

Jez looked out of the window. 'Yup. Standing right outside the front door.'

'Then I'm not dreaming all this?' asked Eden, as if hoping she was.

'No, you're not.'

This understated exchange hadn't disturbed

the peace of the room. The fire crackled, its golden light glowing against the stone walls.

Eden nodded, digesting the information. 'Then she won't come into the house?'

Owen gave her a reassuring hug. 'No, the door's locked.'

Kit went to the window. 'But she will stay out there to guard us.'

'But who will guard us from her?' Eden gave a nervous laugh. 'Sorry, it's just that ... heck, I admit it: I'm scared.'

Kit's expression was serious. 'Freya's scared as well. She's trying so hard to be human. The trouble is she has to fight her vampire instincts. Freya has this urge to attack us – in fact, she did warn me that she might bite me, but she's managed to stop herself.' He began to sound hopeful. 'So there's a chance she might become human again, isn't there?'

June nodded. 'I hope so, because my father's out there. He's one of those things.'

Jez suddenly leaned closer to the glass as he stared out. 'Is that your father?'

June rushed to the window. Owen joined her.

Outside the front door stood Freya; the blonde Rapunzel plait hung down her back. She remained completely immobile – a statue formed from uncannily white flesh. The moonlight revealed bushes, trees and the old stone arch that marked the boundary between garden and forest. The figure of a man stood beneath the archway.

'Is that your father?' Owen asked.

'No.'

Kit pointed at another figure. 'What about

330

him?'

'No; besides, he seems to be wearing a suit of armour.'

Jez pointed at a man emerging from the shadows. 'Is that him?'

'No ... none of them are.'

'None of them are?' Owen's heart gave a lurch. 'Just how many of those things are out there?'

Kit said, 'I've counted six.'

'I make it seven.' Eden moved closer to the window. 'No, make that eight.'

That sense of panic returned. Owen's heart pounded. 'I'll be right back.'

Quickly, he made his way upstairs where he looked out of every window. Moments later he was back.

'I've got some bad news,' he said. 'Those things have surrounded the house.'

Eden's eyes widened. 'Will they attack us?'

Kit spoke with plenty of force. 'You can bet every penny of your life savings they will.'

Owen agreed. 'Tom said that they plan on turning us into creatures like them. Vampires.' He gazed out of the window at the pale figures. 'We're under siege. Whatever happens, we can't let them get into the house. If we do, we'd be better off dead.'

SEVENTY-SEVEN

TRAPPED. That simple word radiated a formidable power. Tom Westonby shone the light on to the boulders which blocked one end of the cave. This was the area where the shaft entered through the roof. The opening was gone. No doubt the vertical shaft itself had been filled with debris during the rock fall. Helsvir hadn't succeeded in digging Tom and Nicola out of the cave – what the creature had done instead was seal them into their tomb.

Up there on the surface was the forest. The vampires would probably still be surrounding the entrance of the shaft, although they were now denied the opportunity of feasting on Tom's lifeblood. No doubt Helsvir still circled the opening, roaring with frustration. Both Nicola and Tom were beyond its reach.

Nicola stood there beside Tom. She didn't move; those strange eyes remained fixed on his face.

'We're definitely trapped,' he told her. 'There's no way out that I can see.'

Even so, he continued to examine the cave. The torch revealed that they were in a space no larger than the average domestic garage. Brown rock formed the walls and ceiling. Littering the floor were leaves, twigs and the white bones of animals. He realized that most people finding themselves trapped underground would start screaming in panic. Yet complete calm filled him. In fact, he'd have described his state of mind as serene. *Because I've dreamt of this moment, haven't I?* He chuckled. *No, not falling down a hole into a cave. I've dreamt of being reunited with Nicola Bekk. And here she is. We're together again. Yes, we're trapped. We can't escape. The air will soon start to run out and I won't be able to breathe, but, get this, I'm not scared. I'm not one little bit frightened.* He chuckled again.

'What's so funny?' she asked.

'For the last five years, ever since you went away, I've imagined what it would be like when we found each other again. I never imagined it would be in a place like this.' He slapped his hand against the brown rock. 'But I don't care. We're together again – that's all that matters.'

She stared at him in surprise. 'Tom, you do understand what I've become? I'm a vampire. I might attack you ... bite you.'

'You won't.'

'Oh, Tom, this isn't easy for me. Don't you understand? I do want to taste your blood. I want your blood in my mouth and running down my throat. I'm hurting inside, I want that so much.'

'But you're resisting the urge, aren't you?'

'Only just, Tom, only just.' She gave a shake of her blonde head. 'Being here with you reminds me what it's like to be human ... you must understand, though, I'm hanging on to that tiny scrap of humanity by my fingernails.'

'What if we sit here side-by-side and keep talking? If I remind you about the time we met, and how much we liked one another?'

'Tom, you are in danger from me. I might not be able to stop myself hurting you.'

Sitting down on a boulder, he patted the space beside him. 'Sit down. We'll talk about when we met.'

For a moment, she stared at him – the fierce black pupils were intense points of darkness. At last she nodded before sitting beside him on the boulder.

He rested his hand on her hand. 'Do you remember when we first met?'

'Ah...' A sigh fell from her lips, as if there was pain in remembering, yet happiness, too. 'The freshwater pool in your parents' garden.'

'You were doing such a crazy thing.' He smiled. 'Imagine – standing in a pond at midnight?'

'I remember how the water felt ... cool, silky, sensuous ... after a hot summer's day that pool was so refreshing.'

'When you were a little girl you used to walk all the way from your cottage in the woods to paddle in the water.'

'Did I?'

'That's what you told me.'

'*Ah...*' That sigh again. Happiness and sorrow. 'I remember now ... the lady who owned the house before your parents invited my mother and me there.'

'That was my aunt. She died, and our family

moved into the house until her son was old enough to inherit it.'

'Her son? Yes...' Nicola's voice rose. 'I remember him, a little boy with blonde hair.'

'He's sixteen now.'

'Is he?'

'He says that he'd like to be a professional diver like me.'

'I'm sure I'll remember his name...' She rested her fingertips against her smooth forehead. 'I should be able to remember ... I must.'

'My parents adopted him. I think of him as my brother now.'

She closed her eyes. 'Please let me remember his name.'

Something cold squirmed inside Tom's stomach. He realized that Nicola had lost more than her humanity when she became a vampire. The curse had erased many of her memories, too – all part of the dehumanizing transformation.

'I want to remember his name,' she murmured as she sat there with her eyes closed. 'Please let me remember.'

Tom didn't reveal the name of his brother. He realized that this was a vital part of the battle Nicola was fighting to regain her humanity. What if she remembered more? Was there a chance it might break the curse? If she could remember her past life in greater detail, would that be enough to resurrect the beautiful, mortal woman that he'd fallen in love with?

Her hand suddenly tightened around his with awesome strength. 'Owen. Yes, I remember. That's the boy's name: *Owen*.' Nicola opened

335

her eyes again.

Her eyes were blue. That beautiful, clear blue that he remembered so well. Blue as the sky. Yet they were blue for only a moment. Quickly, the colour bleached out of them. Once more, they possessed the glistening whiteness of boiled eggs. The pupils resumed their intense blackness. *But for an instant those eyes had been mortal again.* They were just as he remembered them when he'd seen Nicola for the first time: when she had dipped her bare feet in the fresh-water pond. After that had come a turbulent, sometimes violent time. They fell in love, and he discovered the existence of Helsvir. The monster acted as protector of the girl and her family. The downside was that Helsvir saw Tom Westonby as a threat. The monster had tried to destroy him. Then came the night of the flood, which engulfed the village. What followed led to the horrific moment when he'd triggered an ancient Viking curse. This resulted in Nicola transforming into the creature that she was now. For the want of a more accurate description she was a vampire. A blood-eater. A thing of the night. More than anything in the world, he longed with all his heart to reverse the process. Once again, he wondered if the cure would be to encourage Nicola to relive her past. The more she remembered of her upbringing as a human, the more the vampire elements of her nature might fade away.

For a while, they reminisced about happy times together. Those precious summer days half a decade ago were magical. Sometimes they found themselves laughing over a funny incident from the past. At that moment, it didn't even seem they were trapped in a cave. The place didn't smell bad, it felt warm, there was no noise from outside. Helsvir and the vampires were safely on the other side of tons of rock.

Nicola laughed pleasantly. 'Do you remember when you set out all those chairs in the garden?'

She is remembering, he thought. *The past is coming back to her.* Once again, flashes of blue returned to her eyes. What was more, the black veins in her throat had faded. *It's working. She's becoming human.* Even though his heart surged, and he wanted to jump up and shout and dance happily around the cave, he remained calm. *Don't rush this. Nice and easy does it. Keep encouraging her to remember. Memory is the magic spell. It's turning her from a vampire into a human being. Whatever you do, don't blow this chance.*

They talked about the chairs in the garden. It all stemmed from the time she'd revealed a happy memory of when she was a little girl. His aunt would hold garden parties at the house not far from where she lived. Later, when everyone else had gone home, Nicola would play amongst the chairs on the lawn, pretending to be members of the audience at a fancy music recital.

A flicker of blue in her eyes. A blush of pink in her cheeks.

I'm winning, he told himself. *I'm bringing Nicola back into the world of the truly alive.*

The cave felt warmer, almost cosily warm. That brown rock, which had seemed so dull and earthy, had acquired a pleasantly golden hue. The colour of deliciously toasted bread. They were safe down here. Nothing could hurt them. He squeezed her hand and she squeezed his back. Here they were: two lovers reunited.

Why the truth had taken so long to strike Tom he didn't know. But as the batteries in the torch started to expire, and its light drew dim, he realized they must have been trapped in the cave for two or three hours. He checked his watch. *Five hours? We've been down in this little hole for five hours!* That was when an alarm inside his head shrieked its warning. *Five hours trapped in a confined space. No access to the outside world. No ventilation.* He rested his fingers against the side of his neck. His pulse raced there – a frantic little motor behind the skin.

Lurching to his feet, he gasped. 'Don't you feel it?'

'Feel what?' she smiled.

'I'm breathing faster ... like I've been running. My heart's racing, too.'

'You ran from Helsvir, remember?'

'That was five hours ago.' He tried to take a deep breath; it felt as if a leather belt had been tightly buckled around his chest. 'There's no ventilation down here. We're running out of oxygen.'

She stood up. 'I never noticed anything wrong.'

'That's because you don't need oxygen. You don't have to breathe. You're a vampire.' Purple spots bloomed in front of his eyes. 'That means you're immortal.'

'Tom?'

'The irony, huh? We've found each other again ... but now I'm going to suffocate.'

'There must be a way out of here.'

'Through those tons of rock? Not a chance.'

The tightness in his chest became a vicious pain. His heart thundered as it laboured to drive what little oxygen remained in his bloodstream through his body. A hopeless exercise, because carbon dioxide levels would be building up in this confined space. Tom knew that once the oxygen dipped below a certain level he would effectively drown, even though this was dry land.

'What a place to die,' he panted. 'In a ready-made grave.'

'Stop pacing. Conserve the air.'

'What's the point? I'd only postpone my death by a few minutes. Dear God ... this feels like an elephant's standing on my chest.' He leaned against the rock wall. 'There's no ... no goodness in the air. It's gone bad.' Shadows streamed through his eyes into his brain, shutting everything down, switching off vital organs.

'Tom, sit down.' She put her arm round his shoulders.

'I know what'll save me. Make me into a vampire, too!'

'I can't.'

'All it takes is for you to bite here.' He pulled his collar away from his neck. 'Do it.'

'No.'

'Don't you see? Once I'm a vampire I won't need to breathe. You'll stop me from suffocating down here.'

'No!'

'Nicola, it's the perfect way to save me.'

'Tom—'

'Listen. We'll be together. What does it matter if we're trapped down here for a hundred years? We won't age. We can't die. This is perfect!' He cupped his hand behind her head and pulled her face towards his neck. 'Do it! We'll be the same. Not even death will keep us apart.'

'Tom, stop it.' She broke away from his grip. 'Listen to me, Tom, being a vampire is like being an animal. Your memories vanish. You act according to vile instincts. You don't control your life. Are you listening to me?'

He lurched across the cave. Oxygen starvation was killing him. 'I've got no options, have I? I'm dying.'

'Being a vampire is worse than death.'

'Nicola, we'll be together!' He dropped to his knees. A choking sound began in his throat. 'Make ... make me into what you are.'

'Never!'

'Nicola,' he panted, 'after you left me, don't you think I woke up night after night, wishing you'd transform me into a vampire? We would be together. We'd never have to part.'

'Not like that. Not by becoming a vampire.'

'I love you.'

'But we wouldn't be in love any more. How can a monster like me love anyone? Or be loved?'

'For five years I've dreamt of being with you again.'

'I saw you, Tom. You became a recluse. You turned your back on the world.'

'I WAS WAITING FOR YOU!' The cry robbed him of the last of his strength. He slumped forward, gasping.

She knelt beside him and gently eased his head on to her lap. 'You can't die.'

'No air...'

'You won't die, because you've got to save lives.'

'I can't even save my own.'

'Listen to me, Tom Westonby. I remember you kissing me for the first time. I remember when we first made love.' The blue returned to her eyes. The vampire heart inside of her had just become a few degrees more human. 'You came to this valley and I started to live like a human being.' A flush of pink reached her cheeks. 'Now I remember what it's like to be human. It might not last for long ... but you made it happen.'

'Thank you.' He smiled. 'Then maybe this is our destiny. Me, dying here. You being almost human again. Perhaps that's all we can ask for.'

'No, don't you see? You've got to get out of here.'

'I can't.'

'Tom, you must kill Helsvir.'

He shook his head. 'Can't...'

'You saw that he's injured. He's going to need to replace those parts of himself that are damaged. He'll need human victims to do that.'

'That's not fair, Nicola. Helsvir can't be my problem any more. Don't you see what's happening to me? In a few minutes I'll be dead.'

'Tom, before I found you I saw a group of young people go into the cottage. Now where do you think Helsvir will go first for victims? His legs have been damaged, so he'll find people that are close by. Those people in your cottage will be taken first. He'll rip them apart and embed the limbs and heads into his body. Remember, he's like a Frankenstein. He uses body parts to rebuild himself.'

Tom stirred. 'My brother's in the cottage. I sent him there.'

'You mean Owen?'

He nodded, groggy.

She pulled him to his feet. 'Wake up!'

'Can't.'

'You will wake up. And you will kill Helsvir.'

'Kill him? How?'

'I don't know, but *I know you*, Tom. You'll find a way.'

His legs gave way under him. 'Still trapped down here ... no way out.'

Her savage glare scanned the cave walls. Though the flashlight had almost died, he could still make out the brown walls of his tomb. With a sudden movement she pointed at water dribbling through a fissure.

'If water's coming in here, there must be a way out.'

Even though Tom had almost lost consciousness, he still flinched with surprise when Nicola attacked the wall. The power of her arms was uncanny. She ripped away an entire slab of rock with her bare hands. As it fell, a surge of water entered the cave.

'There's an opening here,' she shouted.

'But does it lead to the outside?'

'You're going to find out.' She caught hold of him and half-carried him to the void in the rock. 'Then you will find a way to kill Helsvir. I know you can do it.'

He leaned into the opening. Cool air washed his face. So there must be a route to the surface after all. He breathed deeply. The numbness in his body seemed to vanish in seconds. His chest hurt, his head ached like fury, but he realized he had life-giving oxygen again.

'Kill Helsvir?' he asked. 'I didn't just imagine you saying that?'

'You've got to kill him, because he needs new victims, and he'll know the cottage is the nearest place to find them.'

'Then that's what I'll do, Nicola. I'll kill the monster.'

Tom didn't think twice about the potentially fatal consequences of dead-end tunnels or flooded caverns. He crawled into the narrow passageway that the underground stream had eroded from solid bedrock. The way was dark, slimy and wet. This felt like wriggling through the moist gut of a gigantic animal. Not that it would stop him, Tom Westonby. Nicola was right. He had to reach the cottage before Helsvir. The lives of his brother and his brother's friends depended on him now. *So: no hesitation; no turning back.*

SEVENTY-EIGHT

At the very same moment that Tom Westonby struggled through the narrow cave beneath the forest, Kit Bolter stared out of the window in horror. A cold, hard moon illuminated the scene. Kit watched as Freya tried to prevent the vampires approaching the front door of the cottage. When the creatures found their way blocked, they reacted with shocking ferocity.

Kit screamed when he saw a male vampire punch Freya so hard in the face that the blonde plait whipped back. She crashed to the ground. *This is vampire on vampire violence.*

'No!' Kit ran to the door. Watching Freya take that violent beating was unbearable. He'd stand by her, fight with her – to the last breath of his life, if need be.

As he grasped the key, ready to unlock the door, Owen pounced, dragging Kit back.

Owen shouted, 'We mustn't open the door.'

'Freya's out there! Did you see how that bastard attacked her?'

'Kit, she's not human. She doesn't feel pain.'

'Not human?' Tears streamed down Kit's face. 'Not human. Jesus Christ, Owen! She's human enough to take a beating in order to save us.'

Owen shouted across to Jez who stood by the

window, 'What's happening now?'

Jez shrugged, puzzled. 'It's weird ... it's hard to explain.'

'Damn it, Jez, try.'

'That big bastard punched Freya half way across the garden.'

Kit gasped. 'Is she OK?'

'She's standing on the path again.' The cast on his arm clicked against the glass as he leaned against it to take a closer look. 'The guy that attacked her is ... well...'

Kit struggled to break out of Owen's grip. *'What's that thing doing to her?'*

'It's weird ... he's doing nothing. A second ago, he punched her – *whack!* – right in the face. Now he's just stood there like a statue.'

Everyone fell silent in the cottage, digesting what Jez had just told them. Jez remained by the window. Kit felt Owen's grip on his arms, preventing him from opening the door. Eden's hand covered her face in a frozen pose of horror. June Valko sat on the sofa with her arm protectively around her mother. Mrs Valko, alone, appeared unfazed by the extraordinary drama being played out both inside and outside the cottage. But then, according to June, the woman didn't speak. In fact, she seemed disconnected from reality. Mrs Valko was mentally adrift in her own world.

At last, June broke the silence. 'I don't understand. Why are vampires fighting vampires?'

Kit at last managed to shrug himself free of Owen's grip. 'Don't you see? Most of the vampires can't think for themselves. They're puppets

... something else controls them. Freya's managed to break the control. I don't know how she's managing it, but she's almost human.' He took a step towards the window. 'It's OK, Owen, I won't try and open the door again. I just lost it for a moment back there.'

Jez grunted. 'Be sure that you don't. There must be twenty vampires out there. The second that door opens they'll rush in here, and then our blood will be their blood – do you follow?'

Kit nodded. 'Listen, I've been thinking. The vampires are like remote-controlled robots. Something, whether it's an evil spirit, or the devil, or something we don't even know the name of, wants them to attack us.'

'Tom said that they'll try and recruit us into the vampire army. Though when he says "recruit" he means...' Owen pretended that his fingers were jaws biting his throat to get the message across.

Kit lightly ran his fingertips across the pellet wounds on his face. They still stung, but not enough to distract him from using his keen intelligence to process what he'd seen and heard in the last few hours. 'Freya is strong enough to overcome whatever's controlling her.'

'For now,' Eden pointed out. 'It might only be temporary.'

'If it's temporary that means there's the potential to make it permanent,' Kit said. 'I believe that because she's interacted with us, talked to us, and is now trying to protect us from harm, that's causing her to become more and more human.'

June shivered. 'What if she does transform

back into a human being? That means she's in danger out there. I mean, vampires are almost indestructible, aren't they? But if she becomes mortal she could be killed by those things.'

'Let her into the house,' Kit pleaded. 'Let her in where she'll be safe.'

'Hardly safe,' Owen pointed out. 'We're under siege here. The vampires have surrounded the place.'

Eden went to the window and shuddered. 'You know what those vampires remind me of? Chess pieces ... see? They're like chess pieces on a board, waiting for someone to decide what move to make next.'

June sounded scared. 'In that case, they might make a move we don't expect.'

Owen checked the door. 'Everything's bolted. There are bars over the windows.'

'You might want to find a way of barricading the fireplace.' June's eyes fixed on the opening to the chimney. 'There are other ways in here.'

Jez Pollock groaned. 'Guys, I've got bad news.'

The tone Jez used put ice into Kit's veins – his entire body shivered.

'I'm sorry...' Jez continued in that grim voice. 'I can see Helsvir coming this way. The monster's found us.'

SEVENTY-NINE

Tom struggled along the passageway. Dark, claustrophobic, narrow – the rock walls pressed against his back and chest so fiercely that at times he couldn't even breathe properly. He'd left the main cave almost ten minutes ago. Meanwhile, the luminous hands of his watch told him the time approached midnight.

What drove him was what Nicola had said. Helsvir had been damaged. It would need to rebuild itself using human body parts – arms, legs, heads. The nearest people were in his cottage. They included June Valko, her sick mother, and Owen and his friends. *I'm responsible for them*, Tom told himself as he kicked his way through water and dirt in that narrow tunnel. *I told them to go to the cottage.* He remembered what else Nicola had told him: he must kill Helsvir, otherwise the creature would continue its rampage into the nearby village of Danby-Mask. Innocent men, women and children would be asleep in their beds. Their lives were in his hands.

Despite the cold, the exhaustion and the thudding headache caused by nearly suffocating in the cave, Tom forced himself onwards. Behind him, worming her way in the dark, was

348

Nicola. Every so often, when the gap between the rock walls became crushingly tight, he'd feel her hand push him through.

Blindly, he kept squirming forward. Then at last: he felt springy tendrils scratching his face. Were these roots? He couldn't tell in that all-encompassing darkness. All he could do was grit his teeth and keep pushing ahead. Almost immediately, he felt a cold rush of air against his face. He shoved his hand into a mass of springy stuff in front of him. His hand broke through. Moonlight pierced the vegetation, and he realized that these must be bushes that grew around the hole where the underground stream flowed out into the river. Yes ... he could hear the flow of water.

Tom scrambled out on to the river bank. He stood there in the moonlight gratefully sucking in lungful after lungful of fresh, forest air. The sheer physical effort of escaping from the cave had worked up so much of a sweat that his body gave off white steam. A moment later, he helped Nicola from the hole in the ground. Strangely, her skin remained that luminous white, despite crawling through the tunnel. In fact, it appeared as if her body repelled dirt and water. Natural things couldn't abide contact with her unnatural flesh, or so it seemed.

'You must get to the cottage as fast as you can,' she hissed. 'Helsvir might be there already.'

Those words were enough. Immediately, he loped in the direction of home. Fortunately, the vampires had vanished from this part of the wood. Had they been drawn to the cottage, too? After all, they were allies of Helsvir. Both Helsvir and those undead creatures had been created by the Viking gods for their own evil schemes. Helsvir needed human beings to repair its body. The vampires wanted blood. They'd find plenty of both in Skanderberg.

A bright moon lit the way. Nicola ran alongside him. He noticed she was barefoot, and she still wore the same clothes that she'd worn when he last saw her five years ago. That had been the night the vampire curse had been triggered, and she had transformed into the creature he now saw beside him.

When she suddenly stopped running, and stood there as if in a trance, staring into space, he remembered that she'd warned him that the pull of being a vampire was a strong one. Nicola had said she wouldn't be able to retain her self-control for long. Was her vampire nature reasserting itself? What if she attacked him? Despite knowing that he had to get back to the cottage, he couldn't bring himself to leave Nicola here. Not now that they were finally together again.

'Nicola?' he panted. 'It's me, Tom. Try and hold on. Remember who you are.'

'Tom?'

He tried to smile. 'You haven't forgotten me already?'

It seemed to him that somewhere behind those eyes she fought to retain control of her body. Yet something else was hungrily trying to seize control of her.

Resting his hands on her shoulders, he looked

into those stark, white eyes. 'I'm Tom Westonby. Five years ago we were married. OK, it was the strangest wedding ceremony in the history of matrimony, but we made a declaration in front of others that we wanted to be together for the rest of our lives.'

'Tom...' The faintest of colours ghosted through her eyes: the palest of blues. Her human nature struggled against her vampire instinct. 'Tom ... yes ... I remember.' She took a deep breath – when she exhaled, it didn't mist the air like his breath did, from warm, living lungs. Her internal organs must be terrifyingly different from his.

'Hold on to being Nicola Bekk.' He smiled as he corrected himself: 'No. Hold on to being Nicola *Westonby*.'

'Tom ... about Helsvir...'

'I know what you're going to say. You told me to kill him, remember?'

'It's more important than that. Listen, I don't know how much longer I can hold on to being me. I'm afraid of losing control and hurting you. But I must tell you something vitally important about Helsvir.'

'Go on.'

'He's the key to this. The gods channel their power through him ... he's like ... like a power cable. Helsvir conducts the gods' power to the vampires. Do you understand?'

'How do you know this?'

'I've seen it happen.' Her voice became distant, as if she spoke in her sleep. 'The old gods are shadows now ... they're corrupted ... rotted ...

351

their minds are so ancient that they're fading ... like a picture on a wall exposed to strong sunlight ... its colours grow faint. The gods' minds have faded, too. Their ability to think is almost gone. All that's left is hate. And as their hatred grows stronger something like dementia takes over. They're angry with the human race – that's all they can understand now.'

'These gods ... are they the old Viking gods? Thor? Wodin?'

'They've been known by different names all over the world. Perhaps they were good once ... now they are evil ... they've got to be stopped from hurting any more human beings. They'll kill everyone if they get the chance. That's all they exist for now; they want the human race to suffer.'

She exhaled, and he felt her breath on his face. The air from her lungs was colder than the surrounding air. It could have come from some Arctic wilderness.

He hugged her. 'Hang on, Nicola. Be human! Stay human! Do you understand?'

A blast of cold vapour poured from her lips into his ear. 'Helsvir ... he is the power line. He transmits the power of the gods. Through him they control us. Tom ... kill Helsvir, then everything will be alright again ... everything will be wonderful.'

'You'll come with me to the cottage?'

'Yes, but we must be quick. The human qualities you see in me now are only temporary.' She gave a sad smile. 'Soon, *they* will take control of me again. Then...' the smile faded. 'I will do terrible things, Tom. I will hurt you.'

They started to run. Tom Westonby's heart pounded. This wasn't purely exertion – this was the dread of knowing that he might already be too late. The cottage might lie in ruins. Already, Helsvir could have begun its gruesome harvest of body parts.

EIGHTY

Tom Westonby saw what surrounded his cottage. He groaned in despair. The vampires that had congregated at the cave had made their way here. Worse ... far, far worse ... Helsvir had arrived, too. Even though Owen had blasted away several of its legs with the shotgun, many of its limbs remained intact.

The monster glided in vast circles around Skanderberg. This menacing action made Tom picture a killer shark circling a lifeboat full of defenceless shipwreck survivors. Round and round the cottage went the beast. Its huge bulk smashed garden fences. It ripped away branches as it scraped against trees. Helsvir steadily picked up speed. No doubt when the creature had decided it was moving fast enough it would simply crash through the house walls. Its victims inside wouldn't stand a chance.

Nicola wasn't breathless – but then how could she be? Her respiratory system was no longer mortal. She never seemed to tire. He, on the other hand, panted hard. His breath came in billowing white clouds.

'Tom, kill Helsvir.' She spoke calmly. 'Remember, he's the key. Without him the gods can't control *them*.' She nodded at the vampires surrounding the house.

'How can I destroy that thing?' he panted. 'Dynamite wouldn't kill Helsvir.'

'You must find a way. Otherwise he'll start attacking people. The ones in Skanderberg will be his first victims tonight.'

'I'll have to get inside the cottage. That'll give me time to come up with a plan.'

'You won't have long. Soon Helsvir will attack.'

Helsvir continued to circle the building, moving faster and faster. Now even tree trunks shattered when the beast struck them.

Tom raced towards the front door. Before he was even half way there, a bulky figure emerged from the bushes. The white eyes revealed that this was one of the vampires – and it wouldn't be friendly. With its mouth open wide, it lunged towards him. Nicola moved even faster. She flung herself on to the creature, and both she and the male vampire slammed to the ground.

'Run!' she yelled. 'Get to the house!'

Tom ran. The problem now came from Helsvir. The creature sped towards him, fast as a torpedo. In ten seconds flat, Helsvir would slam his body to jelly.

A pale shape flashed in the corner of his eye. *Nicola? No, this isn't Nicola. But why is another vampire helping me?* He didn't know why, but the woman appeared to be on his side. He glimpsed her long, Rapunzel-style blonde plait as she put herself between Tom and his attacker. This she-vampire didn't attempt to fight Helsvir ... no, it was too formidable for that. Even a vampire wouldn't have the strength to defeat it. Instead, she hurled herself *under* the creature. Her body formed a hard enough obstacle to cause those legs of Helsvir's to trip, and the creature slammed down, throwing up a spray of dirt and snow.

Tom didn't hesitate. He sprinted for the door, shouting as he ran, 'Owen! June! It's me!'

Silhouettes of heads appeared at the windows. The door flew open. In a heartbeat, he'd hurled himself through the entrance. The door crashed shut behind him.

Owen turned the key in the lock, yelling, 'Am I relieved to see you, bro!'

Tom tried to catch his breath. Here in the lounge he saw June standing by her mother. Mrs Valko sat in a daze on the sofa. Jez Pollock stared in shock at Tom dripping mud, sweat and water.

Kit Bolter spun away from the window. 'Freya just saved your life!'

'Freya?'

'She's a vampire. But I know she's trying really hard to become human again.'

Tom nodded: *yes, Nicola's striving to do likewise.*

Kit gave a sob. 'She made that monster fall to save your life ... but she's lying out there now.

355

She's not moving. That thing hurt her...' Abruptly, he sat down in a chair with his hands over his face.

A teenage girl that Tom vaguely recognized from the village went to comfort him. Tom realized that this must be Owen's girlfriend ... Eden? Yes, that was her name: Eden Taylor.

Meanwhile, Owen turned to Tom. 'What do we do now?'

'We can't escape,' Jez said. 'Those things have got us surrounded.'

Owen seemed so vulnerable as he asked, 'Tom? How are we going to get out of here in one piece?'

'I'm going to kill Helsvir.'

'How?'

'I haven't a clue.'

'You best think of something soon,' Jez said, peering out of the window. 'That thing's getting ready to charge.'

And charge it did. Stone walls convulsed as that ugly beast struck. Ceiling lights danced. A flood of black soot, dislodged by the impact, whooshed down the chimney to kill the fire.

'It's trying to smash down the walls!' shouted the girl.

'No, it's not.' Tom listened to loud scraping sounds coming from the stonework outside. 'Helsvir's climbing on to the roof. It's going to rip its way through the tiles – *that's the way it's going to get us.*'

They stood there in the lounge, faces upraised, staring at the ceiling. Already, debris cascaded down on to the ground outside. Helsvir had harvested plenty of human arms in the past. Now many hands set to work, ripping away roof tiles. Beneath those tiles, the attic. Separating the attic from the bedrooms were flimsy boards. Once it had burrowed into the bedrooms that only left the timbers above their heads. The creature would soon smash through those to reach its defenceless victims.

'We could run for it?' Jez suggested.

Owen snapped, 'There are vampires waiting out there for us to do exactly that. We wouldn't stand a chance.'

June's eyes flashed with fear. 'Is there a basement we could hide in?'

Tom shook his head. By now, he had to shout over the thunder of demolition, 'The only way we're going to survive is by killing Helsvir.'

'How?'

Again he could only repeat the painful admission: 'I just don't know.'

Kit stared out of the window at a pale figure lying on the ground. 'She's not moving,' he moaned. 'That bastard killed her.'

'Kit,' Tom crossed the room to him, 'she's not alive.'

'She is. Freya liked me.'

'Freya's not alive in a way we understand. She was a kind of robot. Evil forces controlled her body.'

'Liar!'

Tom knew he didn't have long, but at that moment he decided to tell the truth. They had to know what was happening here. 'Listen ...

everyone listen.' Even though the creature fero-
ciously tore at the roof, they did listen to what he
told them. 'Over a thousand years ago the
Vikings believed that their lives and destinies
were controlled by a whole family of gods headed by a deity called Wodin. I can't even begin to
understand how it happened, but the gods still
have some residual power. Their sole reason to
exist is to get their revenge on human beings,
because people stopped worshipping them.'

Tom saw that they believed him – perhaps they
felt they had no choice. Because it might be that
just one splinter of this information would be
vital for their survival. Helsvir abruptly paused
its demolition work. Tom couldn't help but wonder if the monster was eavesdropping on what he
had to say.

Regardless of the monstrous eavesdropper
Tom continued, 'In my mind's eye, I see them,
those old gods of the Vikings: they're no longer
worshipped, they're bitter, resentful. They hate
human beings. They want to make us suffer. So
how do they manage to hurt people? Well, those
pathetic creatures that were once gods still
control Helsvir and the vampires out there.
They're like a bitter man who's no longer re-
spected and who has no authority over others, so
what does this bitter failure do in order to feel
big and powerful? Imagine he owns a vicious
dog. Whenever he sees a neighbour's cat in his
garden he opens the door and orders the dog to
kill his neighbour's pet. There's nothing to
actually gain from killing the cat. The crime
doesn't bring him respect again, or make people

like him. In fact, his neighbours hate him all the more. And the more he's hated, the more isolated and bitter he becomes, and the more he'll use his dog to carry out his sadistic work.'

June put her arm round her mother's shoulders. 'So these gods have no special reason for attacking us?'

'They might get the pleasure a sadist experiences from hurting people. That's all. There's no grand master plan other than inflicting misery and pain on human beings.'

Kit yelled, 'What the hell are you waiting for? Kill the monster! That's what you promised, isn't it?'

Eden's eyes were trusting. 'Try something. Please.'

Owen bunched his fists. 'I'll go with you. I'm not afraid.'

'Thanks, Owen, but we need to find its weak spot; its Achilles' heel. Ordinary weapons, even if we had them, wouldn't destroy it.'

With a tremendous crash the chimney stack fell on to the path outside.

Tom thought hard. *What did Nicola tell me? She said that Helsvir acts as the power line of the gods. They feed power through Helsvir in some way. That in turn controls the vampires. So Helsvir is the key. Destroy him and you kill the power.*

Dust swirled down the staircase, followed by splinters of woodwork. Helsvir must be breaking through the boards in the attic. Soon he'd lower that ugly body of his into the bedrooms. After that, probably the weight of all that flesh alone would be enough to cause the bedroom floor to collapse. *That's when he rips us apart. We're helpless as chickens in a cage.*

Nobody moved. They stared at Tom in mute hope.

It's all down to you, Tom, he thought. *Their lives depend on you getting smart.*

The sounds of destruction intensified. Wood splintered. Dust poured through gaps in the ceiling boards.

Tom began to speak his thoughts aloud: 'Helsvir is strong enough to simply bust through the walls. So why has it chosen to come down through the roof?'

Eden nodded at the carving. 'Probably doesn't want to damage his ugly portrait.'

Tom's backbone tingled. 'You might have something there. Yes! He's being careful not to damage images of himself.'

Jez shrugged. 'They're just old carvings.'

'Not just old,' Tom pointed out. 'Ancient. Very ancient. Over a thousand years old. In fact, they're supposed to be as old as Helsvir.'

'So, they are important?' Eden's eyes flashed with hope.

'Wait, let's think this through.'

A ceiling board crashed down on to the floor beside him.

'Think it through fast, Tom,' June warned. 'That thing's going to come through the ceiling any minute now.'

'We're only going to get one chance at this.' Tom ran his fingers through his hair, trying to speed up the flow of thought. 'Think, think!

Ancient buildings, churches, temples have sacred components to them.'

'Architecture?' Jez shook his head. 'You really want to spout about architecture at a time like this? We're all going to end up being part of that ugly bastard!'

Tom studied the wall carving. 'Ancient buildings often had specific parts that were sacred – altars, shrines, sacred chambers. In the past, even domestic homes would have good luck symbols, or rooms that were dedicated to gods or ancestral spirits. So why is this so special?' He slammed his hand against the carving of Helsvir. When he did so, the creature upstairs suddenly halted its destruction. The thing seemed to hesitate, because it sensed a threat nearby. Tom said, 'These carvings are dotted throughout the house. They're not here for decoration – THEY'RE HERE FOR A PURPOSE!'

Eden nodded. 'Ancient Egyptian tombs had magic bricks. They were supposed to keep grave robbers and evil spirits away.'

Owen gripped her hand. 'Listen to Eden, Tom, she knows what she's talking about. She's got brains.'

'Magic bricks. Magic carvings. These are the key!' Tom slapped the carving again, and Helsvir grunted loud enough to shatter a light bulb. Tom ran towards the kitchen. He was fired up, ready for action.

Owen shouted, 'What are you going to do?'

Exhilaration blasted through Tom. 'These carvings aren't just pictures of Helsvir. SOME-HOW THEY'RE PART OF HIM.' He gave a wild grin that might just have been the wrong side of crazy. 'It's time to start some demolition work of my own!'

EIGHTY-ONE

Tom grabbed a large hammer from the store-room that led off from the kitchen. When he returned to the lounge the others stared as if he'd gone insane.

'It's the carvings!' he shouted. Meanwhile, Helsvir continued to rip its way through the roof. 'Somehow, these are part of the circuit! Nicola told me that Helsvir acts as a power cable for the gods. Gods – vampires – Helsvir – these carvings! They're all connected!'

Owen, June, Eden, Kit and Jez gawped in amazement (they even seemed scared of him). Tom approached the carving of Helsvir that had been made over a thousand years ago. Gripping the wooden shaft in both hands, he raised the hammer above his head. More plasterwork cascaded down; clouds of dust misted the air. Helsvir undertook the demolition work with a vengeance. Soon he'd smash his way in. *After that ... well ...* Tom shuddered. *Best not imagine what comes after. Because that's when Helsvir starts demolishing us.*

With a fierce yell, Tom Westonby swung the hammer. Sparks flew from its massive steel head when it struck. The carving of Helsvir split in two, right through the centre of its body.

Suddenly, the beast stopped its destruction. In fact, it stopped making any noise whatsoever. Tom sensed its utter shock, as if it had felt a stab of pain.

Eden gasped. 'It worked. You broke the stone, and it stopped!'

Helsvir did pause. But only for a moment. With renewed fury, the monster began its attack on the building again. Woodwork screamed as planks were torn apart.

Owen shouted: 'You've got to smash them all!'

Quickly, he broke the carving in the back of the fireplace – this had been hidden under a thick coating of soot for years. Did he imagine it, or did Helsvir pause yet again, if only for a second? Tom ran into the kitchen. There, another slab portraying the brute had been embedded in the stonework. Tom rained down hammer blows. With each *SMACK* of the hammer he heard the creature upstairs give a grunt of pain. On the tenth blow the carving exploded. Shards of rock hit Tom in the face. In the reflection of the kitchen window, he saw blood pour from a cut in his cheek. Yet he felt no pain; instead, there was exhilaration. Because Helsvir stopped dead again. The monster seemed to be hurting, but couldn't understand what inflicted the pain.

Tom had smashed the carvings downstairs. *Now for the two upstairs.* When he ran through the living room to the staircase Owen joined him.

Tom thundered, 'No! Stay here!'

'I want to help.'

'It's too dangerous.'

'I'm not frightened.'

'Owen, if you follow me up those stairs I'll throw you back down them. Stay here!'

A massive thump shook the walls. One of the ceiling boards fell to the floor. Helsvir would be in the living room in no time at all. With a glare at Owen to stay put Tom ran up the staircase.

Chaos dominated the upper floor. Dust covered everything. Furniture had been upended by the tremors caused by Helsvir's powerful assault. There were huge holes in the ceiling. Red roof tiles littered the carpet. Ceiling lights swung wildly. Tom's shadow lurched along the walls. The sheer noise of the roof's destruction deafened him. It sounded like a series of explosions. Ceiling boards, planks, sections of water pipe, electric cables – they all hung from the ceiling.

There were two carvings of Helsvir upstairs: one in his bedroom, one in the spare bedroom. Shouldering the door to his room, he plunged through the doorway.

BIG MISTAKE.

Helsvir's gargantuan form bulged down through a gash in the ceiling. Only the black oak beams, which were as strong as steel girders, prevented the creature from slithering into the bedroom. However, as soon as it accomplished that manoeuvre, its bulk would fill the entire room. No doubt the weight of the thing would be enough to collapse the floor beneath it, enabling this vicious predator to enter the living room below. Then it would claim its next victims.

The carving had been fixed into the wall by his bed, meaning he had to cross the room directly beneath the monster. Up there in the attic crawl space it seemed as if a whale had been dropped through the roof. Of course, this was a 'whale' with human arms, legs and heads.

The instant Tom charged into the room the heads twisted to look at him. Eyes blazed with fury. Naked arms reached down. Fingers raked his head; he felt a burning pain as hanks of hair were ripped from his scalp. *Smash the stone! Then get the hell out!* He lunged deeper into the room. A hiss of fury came from that ugly array of heads. Helsvir knew what Tom intended.

Just five more feet – he could smash that engraving. Another part of the circuit would be broken. Helsvir would be a step closer to destruction.

CRASH! Following that explosion of sound the light went out. Blackness engulfed the room. Tom couldn't see – as simple as that. He'd been rendered sightless. When he raised the hammer, hoping to strike the carving blindly, he felt hands grip his wrist. Helsvir was fighting back.

Tom struggled to break free. But more hands grabbed him. A moment later, he felt himself lifted clear of the floor. Damn it! He'd be the first of Helsvir's victims tonight. He'd be torn to pieces. His limbs and head would be married to the monster's flesh. Fingers dug into his throat – blazing spikes of agony – he screamed.

He could see nothing. Helsvir would dismantle

365

him in the darkness. He'd feel everything, though. This wouldn't be a delicate, pain-free dissection. Tom could do nothing but wait for the tidal wave of agony as his joints gave way under the pressure.

Suddenly a brilliant light filled the room.

'TOM!'

Tom blinked. His brother was there, carrying a lantern above his head. The hammer fell from Tom's hand, and in a flash Owen grabbed it. With the lantern in one hand, he swung the hammer up at the monster's pale limbs.

Tom managed to croak, 'No ... the slab ... break the slab.'

Owen set the lamp down. After that, he gripped the hammer shaft in both hands and took a massive swing at the carving. The first blow cracked it wide open from top to bottom, bisecting the monstrous teardrop shape.

Helsvir convulsed with pain. The hands lost their strength, fingers uncurled – a second later, Tom slammed to the floor. Straight away, he was on his feet.

Owen threw him the hammer. He caught it one-handed.

Tom could breathe again. 'There's one last carving inside the cottage ... it's in the spare room. Quick! Before it recovers!'

Owen snatched up the lamp and they ran under the vast bulk of Helsvir; its arms and legs had been hanging limply; now they twitched as it regained its senses.

They made it to the spare room. Ceiling boards had been torn away, as if they were no more substantial than tissue paper. Helsvir quickly repositioned itself in the attic, so it could stretch its arms down between the ceiling timbers to grab the pair. Tom didn't hesitate. Once again he swung the hammer. The carving in the wall exploded with such force that both men were blown back off their feet. Clearly these slabs contained a potent energy. With all his heart, Tom hoped that energy had now been released harmlessly.

Every face above them that budded from Helsvir twisted in expressions of agony. Eyes scrunched shut. Groans erupted from pale lips. The monster was hurting. Tom had been right about the carvings being vital to Helsvir's existence.

Owen whooped. 'You did it! The circuit's broken!'

Flashes of light filled the room. Searing burst of blue. Lightning in miniature. The air smelt like burnt toast. Tom realized that the odour of burning was, in fact, the atoms of the air being scorched. That lightning seared the atmosphere in the attic. Up there in the crawl space, the whale-like Helsvir began convulsing.

'The walls!' Owen shouted.

Now every building block in the wall began to split in two. A sound like a gunshot accompanied every crack in the wall.

As the brittle snapping grew louder, Tom shouted, 'Get downstairs.'

Tom noticed that gloops of black stuff were dropping from Helsvir – the creature had begun to melt. Its many heads started to lose shape.

Faces grew soft – they slid from their skulls as smoothly as an omelette slipping from a pan.

Tom followed Owen downstairs. Even as they entered the room they heard screams from outside.

Eden stared through a window. 'They're dying,' she breathed. 'The vampires are dying.'

'Nicola!' Tom's heart plunged. 'Nicola!' Unlocking the door, he flung it open. There, an extraordinary sight met his eyes. So extraordinary that he stopped dead in order to witness what happened next.

EIGHTY-TWO

The moon shone down on to the forest that surrounded the cottage: the trees formed a silent, black ocean.

Eden was right. The vampires were dying.

Male and female vampires could barely stand. Their legs gave way, dropping them into a kneeling position. They cried in pain. And at the top of the ruined cottage, in the wreckage of the roof, Helsvir cried out, too – or rather the heads that budded from its body screamed in pain. What struck Tom so forcibly was that exactly the same cry came from different mouths.

The vampires' flesh began to dissolve. Faces slid off in one piece – soft masks of wet flesh.

Beneath the faces were naked skulls. Helsvir was dying. The vampires were dying. Breaking the stone carvings had worked.

Two more slabs remained outside. Perhaps enough damage had already been done to the mechanism which fed the occult power to the creatures. Maybe Tom didn't need to smash the last two carvings. Yet he knew it would be foolish to leave them intact. There could still be a chance that the creatures might regenerate in some way. He quickly took the hammer to the engraving embedded in the house above its front door. With two swift blows he shattered it.

Immediately, a man began to shout in a loud voice – angry, bitter words. Tom sensed that – yet he didn't understand the words themselves. A gut instinct told him that what he heard was the dead language of the Vikings. The angry, shouting voice brought Owen, Kit, Jez and Eden from the cottage. They walked along the path, completely unafraid now, as they watched the end of the vampires.

The deep male voice thundered from the mouths of the dying creatures. The same words poured from all those different mouths at the same time – a perfect lip sync.

Eden marvelled at what she saw. 'They are puppets, aren't they? Nothing more than ventriloquists' dolls? Something's speaking through them. They never did have minds to think for themselves. This is remote control.'

Kit ran forward. 'Freya ... Freya... .'

He caught her as she sank to the ground. For some reason she didn't speak with that guttural voice. Instead, she resembled a young woman who'd been overcome by exhaustion.

'Kit...' she smiled. 'Everything's alright now. I'm happy you're safe...'

Seconds later, she trickled away through his fingers as her body instantly liquefied.

'Freya.' Grief-stricken, he gazed down at the stain on the grass. Moonlight glinted on the thick plait of blonde hair, yet even that vanished before his eyes. It was like watching hot water being poured on to sugar. One moment the plait was there, the next it wasn't. 'Freya...' Silently, he began to weep.

Jez tried to console his friend.

Kit savagely pushed him. 'Keep away! You don't understand ... none of you do ... I loved her!' He lowered his head to sob into his hands.

Owen glanced at Tom. 'There's one last carving.'

Tom nodded. 'The one in the archway. I'll deal with it.'

The angry voice that boomed from the mouths of the vampires in that harsh language which none of them understood faded to a whisper. Glancing back, Tom saw that Helsvir had all but melted away. What was left of the creature dripped down the outer walls of the cottage like gallon upon gallon of black treacle – thick, sticky, glistening. But dead. Definitely dead.

Tom approached the archway at the entrance of the garden. In the stonework that formed the span was the last surviving engraved image. The weather had eroded it, yet he made out the teardrop shape of the body, the many legs and the line of circles that depicted its host of heads. Tom swung the hammer. The slab shattered into a hundred pieces.

This time a yell of such power erupted from the mouths of the dying vampires that he staggered, dropping the hammer. Everyone in the garden slammed their hands over their ears. Blue lightning flickered from what remained of Helsvir.

The angry voice returned. The vampires moved their mouths as the same words roared from their lips. This time in English:

'NEXT TIME, TOM WESTONBY ... NEXT TIME, WE WIN!'

Tom thundered back: 'GO TO HELL!'

The voice abruptly fell silent. All the remaining vampires slumped to the ground. Whatever had given them the strength to move, talk and fight had gone. Those creatures melted, leaving nothing but dark smears in the dirt.

Tom checked on everyone there in the garden. 'Are you all OK?'

Owen had taken Eden by the hand; they nodded. Jez stood with one hand resting on Kit's shoulder – a gesture of compassion and friendship. Kit still knelt there, staring at the ground where Freya had dissolved into the earth.

June and her mother. Tom ran back into the cottage. June stood in the living room, gazing at the sofa where her mother sat as if asleep.

June turned to him, tears filling her eyes, and yet she was smiling. 'He came back to us, Tom. After you went into the garden my father walked into this room. He was human again. He sat

371

beside my mother, took her hand and said her name. She recognized him, Tom. She smiled and said, "Hello, Jacob" – said "Hello", just like he'd only been away for a few minutes, not twenty-nine years. Then they sat smiling at one another. They were so happy ... And then...' a tear rolled down June's face '...my mother closed her eyes ... she'd waited for him for so long, even though her heart was giving out. But he came back, and they were together again. That's when she knew she could go. There wasn't any pain ... she just slipped away.'

'And your father?'

'He smiled at me. I'm sure he recognized me as his daughter ... I don't know what happened next, other than he just melted away. Thank you, Tom.'

'I didn't do anything,' he said gently.

'You let me stay here with my mother. We went through a terrible time tonight, but everything turned out good in the end, didn't it? Just for a moment before she died, my mother was the happiest she'd been for years. And I'm happy for her.'

Owen called through the door. 'Tom. Not all of them are dead.'

Tom went outside. A young girl stood on the lawn. She seemed baffled, as if she'd just woken up from a deep sleep.

'That's Clarissa,' Eden said in astonishment. 'She went missing two days ago. Those things must have made her into a vampire. What if the ones that have been transformed recently have come back to life? Real life, I mean. Warm blooded. Breathing.' Eden took hold of Clarissa's hands; gently she began to reassure her.

Tom's heart leapt as he searched for Nicola, but he dreaded what he might find. She'd transformed five years ago. Was that too long ago for the evil spell to be lifted? Or had she melted away, too?

Tom ran through the archway and across the rubble of the last carving of Helsvir. He entered the forest where shafts of moonlight pierced the branches. His breath shot through his lips in dazzling white clouds. His heart thudded. For a while, he seemed to be running at random ... that is, until he realized some sixth sense was guiding him towards a clearing.

There, a figure stood in clear moonlight. Blonde hair fell around her shoulders. Slowly, he approached her, his breath still bursting from his lips in explosions of white. Nicola watched him. The blue colour had returned to her eyes. But that had happened before; it didn't mean she was human, did it? Perhaps she still had the heart of a vampire? He recalled how she'd whispered to him earlier tonight. The air from her lungs had been ice cold. That inhuman body hadn't warmed her breath. There had been no flash of vapour from her lips. That was evidence of her not being human.

Without warning, the colour might vanish from her eyes. If it did, would she continue to exist as one of those unearthly creatures? A taker of blood? A vampire? Or would she melt to nothing, like the others?

'Nicola?'

She seemed dazed.

'Nicola, speak to me.'

She said one word: 'Tom.' And that was enough to fill him with happiness.

It wasn't so much that she spoke his name. What mattered most ... what was so incredibly important ... was that he saw white vapour flow from her beautiful lips. Living, human lungs had warmed the air.

'That's the breath of life,' he told her gently.

'So this is real,' she whispered – he felt her hot breath on his face. 'I'm no longer a vampire?'

'This is real. And you've finally come home to me.'

'Helsvir?'

'Dead.'

'You know something?' She managed a trembling smile. 'For the first time in years I feel the cold.'

'You're starting to shiver. Here.' Slipping off his jacket, he eased it around her shoulders.

Tom Westonby knew she'd feel more than the cold now. Time would start to flow again for Nicola, his bride of five years ago. She would age. One day she'd be old, and suffer the aches and illnesses that come with living life. *But that proves she's mortal.* His heart filled with joy. *If she's mortal, then she can be loved and she can give love. We can grow old together.*

They walked back through the trees. The silver eye of the moon seemed to close drowsily as a bank of cloud drifted across. And even before they'd reached the old archway, snowflakes began to fall. Tomorrow, the valley would be covered with clean, white snow – it would be like a fresh page, waiting for the story of the rest of their lives to be written upon it.

EPILOGUE

Ten weeks later.

They are an ordinary young couple staying in the hotel. Tom Westonby knew that was what the other hotel guests thought when they saw Tom and Nicola strolling through the lobby to the restaurant. *They'd never be able to guess the horrific events we experienced such a short time ago.*

Tom sat down at a table facing Nicola. She smiled at him, her blue eyes twinkling happily. They were together again after five long years of a living death (for her: actual; for him, that's what the solitude felt like). They ordered the meal and drinks, and Tom relished the normality of it all: dining out with the woman he loved.

After the drinks arrived, Tom poured Nicola a glass of red wine.

She held up the glass in a toast. 'To us.' Her smile grew even warmer.

'To us.' He smiled back as they clinked glasses.

Helsvir's dead. The vampires are destroyed. The Viking gods are defeated. Life is good.

Yet, at that moment, Tom heard a clicking on the window pane.

Nicola laughed. 'I think he wants feeding, too.'

A large black crow squatted on the window ledge. It pecked at the glass in the restaurant window. Its eyes were bright as black gemstones – they had a glittering, cruel quality. The bird stared in through the window at them, and Tom felt a trickle of absolute cold run down his spine. He knew that according to a number of legends the Viking gods had the power to see through the eyes of the crow species. That in turn made him wonder if the destruction of the vampires and of Helsvir had been too easy ... too neat ... too final.

What if those vengeful gods had abandoned their old weapons, namely Helsvir and the vampires? What if those ancient deities had adopted new strategies? What if their new weapon against humanity was a beautiful young woman? Specifically, the one who sat with him at this very table? A Trojan horse? A human virus? A covert assassin?

Tom looked into her eyes. Yet he did not see evil there. Then again, how many times does a man or woman look into the eyes of a lover and never guess what secret thoughts and hidden dreams are concealed within their heart? Perhaps Nicola really was mortal again? Maybe her dreams revolved around a life with him and having his children? After all she'd gone through, what would she be like as a mother?

'Our friend the crow's seen enough,' Nicola said.

Tom watched the bird fly away. The creature soared towards the west and the setting sun – a direction traditionally associated with the land of the dead, the realm of ghosts.

And Tom wondered if this really was the end of the vampires, and of Helsvir, and the cruel and vengeful gods of the Vikings.